THE KRISHNA KEY

Ashwin Sanghi ranks among India's highest-selling authors of English fiction. He has written several bestsellers (*The Rozabal Line, Chanakya's Chant, The Krishna Key*) and a *New York Times* crime thriller called *Private India* together with James Patterson. Sanghi has also penned a non-fiction title, *13 Steps to Bloody Good Luck*.

He was included by *Forbes India* in its Celebrity 100 and is a winner of the Crossword Popular Choice award. He was educated at Cathedral and John Connon School, Mumbai, and St Xavier's College, Mumbai. He holds a Master's degree in business management from Yale University. Ashwin Sanghi lives in Mumbai with his wife, Anushika, and his son, Raghuvir.

You can connect with Sanghi via the following channels:

Website www.sanghi.in
Facebook www.facebook.com/shawnhaigins
Twitter www.twitter.com/ashwinsanghi
YouTube http://www.youtube.com/user/ashwinsanghi
Instagram http://instagram.com/ashwin.sanghi
LinkedIn http://www.linkedin.com/in/ashwinsanghi

ASHWIN SANGHI

THE KRISHNA KEY

First published by Westland Ltd in 2012
Reprinted by Westland Publications Private Limited in 2018
61, 2nd Floor, Silverline Building, Alapakkam Main Road, Maduravoyal,
Chennai 600095

Westland and the Westland logo are the trademarks of Westland Publications
Private Limited, or its affiliates.

Copyright © Ashwin Sanghi, 2012

ISBN: 9789381626689

25 24 23 22 21 20

Typeset by Art Works, Chennai

Printed at HT Media Ltd, Gr. Noida

Author's Note

I am obliged to my wife Anushika and my son Raghuvir, who ungrudgingly tolerated my persistent absence from their lives while I was writing this book. They are my inspiration, my life and my very breath.

I am beholden to my parents, Mahendra and Manju, who supported me in all my endeavours, including my writing. Also, many thanks to my brother and sister, Vaibhav and Vidhi, who picked up the slack, at work, and at home, while I was working on this project.

My aunt, Aparna Gupta, is my eternal friend and guide, but has never hesitated to critique my work. I am thankful to her for playing the role of sounding-board while this novel was a work in progress.

I am grateful to my editor, Prita Maitra, and my publisher, Gautam Padmanabhan, without whom none of my novels, including this one, would have emerged from their manuscripts. In addition, I am thankful to Paul Vinay Kumar, Renuka Chatterjee, Anushree Banerjee and Satish Sundaram at Westland who have always supported me wholeheartedly.

Gunjan Ahlawat and Kunal Kundu deserve special mention for the beautiful cover design as also Vipin Vijay for putting it all together. My thanks to Rupesh Talaskar for the illustrations inside the pages of this novel. My gratitude, also, to Vishwajeet Sapan for the key Sanskrit translations.

A big thank you to Ameya Naik and Kushal Gopalka who helped create the audio track of the central shloka of this novel. Finally, a special thanks to Hemal Mathija, Shalini Iyer and Saurabh Sharma from the 'Think Why Not' team who helped create the video trailer.

I am thankful to various authors and producers of original or derived works. A separate acknowledge-ments section at the end of the narrative lists these in detail.

I am fortunate to be the grandson of the late Shri Ram Prasad Gupta and grandnephew of his brother, the late Shri Ram

Gopal Gupta. Their blessings move the fingers that hold my pen.

Finally, I am deeply aware of the fact that when I sit down to write, the words that flow from mind to matter are merely through me, not from me. How do I convey my thanks to the real writer—the formless, shapeless and endless Almighty—for his blessings?

Perhaps this book will answer that question.

Warning

This book uses several images to explain details within the story. Flipping to the back of the book prematurely may result in your inadvertently viewing some images that could act as plot-spoilers, hence this is not advised.

Disclaimer

This is a work of fiction set in a background of history. Public personages, both living and dead, may appear in the story under their given names. Scenes and dialogue involving them are invented. Any other usage of real people's names is coincidental. Any resemblance of the fictional characters to actual persons, living or dead, is entirely coincidental. No claim regarding historical accuracy is either made or implied. Historical, religious or mythological characters, events or places, are always used fictitiously.

MAP OF KINGDOMS DURING
THE MAHABHARATA ERA

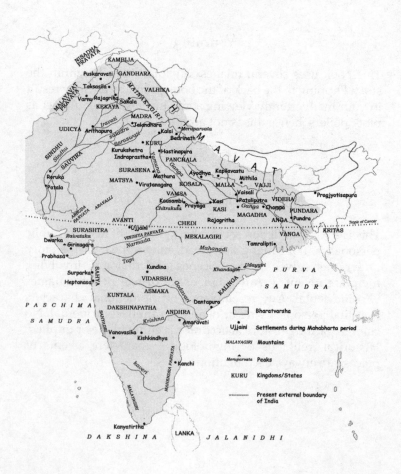

Who really knows, and who can swear,
How creation came, when or where!
Even gods came after creation's day,
Who really knows, who can truly say
When and how did creation start?
Did He will it? Or did He not?
Only He, up there, knows, maybe;
Or perhaps, not even He.

—Rig Veda 10:129

Let me start at the very beginning... even before I was born. One of my ancestors was King Yayati. He was cursed by the sage Shukracharya for having been unfaithful to his wife, Devayani, who was Shukracharya's daughter. The curse was that Yayati would grow old prematurely and thus be unable to enjoy the pleasures of his youth and potency. Later, Shukracharya relented and softened the blow: Yayati would be spared if one of his sons, Yadu or Puru, accepted the consequences of the curse. The older son, Yadu, refused, but the younger, Puru, agreed to take it on himself. As a reward, Yayati chose Puru to succeed him as king, in place of Yadu. The enraged Yayati enlarged upon the punishment to his elder son. 'Neither you nor your descendants will ever occupy a throne!' he prophesied, in a fury. The unlucky Yadu left his home and settled down in Mathura where his lineage flourished. Yadu's descendants were the Yadavas, of which I was one. Yadavas, since then, have been king-makers, but never kings. Puru went on to become the patriarch of the kingdom of Hastinapur—into which the families of the Kauravas and Pandavas were born.

Anil Varshney did not know that he had less than twelve minutes left to live. His modest house in the Hanumangarh district of Rajasthan was deathly quiet at this hour except for the humming of the desert cooler. Varshney loved the silence. It allowed him to immerse himself entirely in the strange letterings and symbols that lay before him.

Work was meditation and prayer for India's youngest linguist and symbolist who had shot to instant fame when he succeeded in deciphering several ancient hieroglyphs from the Indus Valley civilisation. Fluent in over fifteen languages, Varshney had ten publications to his credit including the most widely used multilingual dictionary of Indian languages. He was to ancient writing systems what Bill Gates was to operating systems.

His living space was fashionably disorganised, reflective of the eclectic genius that inhabited it. The bedroom was rarely used because most of Varshney's life was spent at archaeological sites, particularly Kalibangan, the most important Indus Valley site in Rajasthan. His living room had no furniture except for a desk and a patterned-fabric couch that had seen better days. The bare floor was littered with stacks of books, bundles of research papers, as well as cardboard boxes filled with the objects of Varshney's study—seals, pottery fragments, scrolls and parchments.

On the desk before him lay a small rectangular seal, around 20 x 20 mm, apparently made of conch shell. The seal had a square peg in the back. Strangely, the peg had no hole for inserting a ring into, as was usual with seals of this type. Three ancient animal motifs of a bull, unicorn and goat were engraved in an anticlockwise direction on the face of the seal. And it was this frozen tableau that seemed to be the focus of Varshney's attention.

His desk was strewn with papers on which he had made sketches and scribbles. A notebook computer stood open on a corner of the desk, its screen-saver having been triggered an hour earlier. A brushed-steel desk lamp shone a single, wide beam of fluorescent white light on the seal and the papers surrounding it. Varshney, oblivious to everything else around him, was closely examining the images on the seal with a Carl Zeiss 20X magnifying glass.

Varshney's outward appearance was that of a geek: ill-fitting clothes, uncombed hair, and shirt pockets stuffed with a variety of Rotring Isograph pens. His face was blemished with mild eruptions of acne and his personal hygiene left a lot to be desired. But grooming, bathing and dressing were completely inconsequential in his world. Varshney had spent several years at various Indus Valley sites—including the recent one at Kalibangan—painstakingly creating a database of eight thousand semantic clusters from his lexicon of thirty Indian languages. For the first time since the excavations at Harappa in 1921, Varshney now seemed to have found a way to explain the strange hieroglyphs on over five thousand seals discovered at such locations.

Varshney was oblivious to his surroundings and did not observe the shaft of light falling on the floor that gradually widened as the main entrance door to his house was quietly opened, the lock having been expertly picked. He did not notice the beam of light disappearing as the door was gently closed. He did not hear the quiet footsteps of light rubber soles on the ceramic-tiled floor, nor did he feel the breath of the stranger on his neck. He only screamed when he saw the intruder's face reflected on his computer screen but by then it was too late. No sound emerged from Varshney's throat because the visitor had tightly clamped a chloroform-soaked handkerchief over his nose and mouth.

Paralysed with fear, Varshney struggled to lash out with his hands. The desk lamp fell crashing to the ground and suddenly his house went completely black. Varshney found his right arm being viciously twisted behind his back while the handkerchief retained its vice-like grip on his face.

A searing pain shot up his arm, bringing tears to his eyes and momentarily stunning him. He could feel himself passing out as the chloroform slowly worked its way into his system. Soon, there was complete stillness—and silence.

The intruder effortlessly lifted the unconscious Varshney from his chair with his latex-gloved hands and placed him on the floor with his back upright against a wall and his legs stretched out before him. He unzipped the belt pack around his waist and took out a roll of duct tape with which he efficiently gagged his prisoner. He then proceeded to bind his captive's hands behind his back with some more tape. With almost choreographed movements, the assailant delved into his waist bag and took out a little self-inking rubber stamp. He placed the rubber end of the stamp on Varshney's forehead. The resultant image on his victim's forehead was of a small, crimson, wheel enclosed within a circle.

With Varshney still unconscious, the attacker quickly surveyed his victim's inventory of ancient artefacts. He ignored everything except the three-headed animal seal that had been Varshney's object of attention prior to the attack. He took out a small plastic specimen bag, placed the seal in it and then placed the object back into his waist bag. Where were the other three?

Knowing that the seal was one of a set of four, he searched the living space meticulously for the remaining ones, along with the base plate that he knew was meant to hold the four seals together. Each card-board box was minutely examined, desk drawers were opened, and even the sofa cushions were ripped open. Coming up empty-handed, the assailant muttered a curse under his breath. 'Damn!'

Resigned to an only partial victory and having surveyed his handiwork, he took out a Swann-Morton scalpel that had been custom-engraved with the initials 'R M' from his belt bag, bent down over Varshney's comatose body and with surgical precision thrust the scalpel into the sole of Varshney's left foot, leaving it embedded in the flesh. It gashed through an artery. Blood spurted out while Varshney—still unconscious—began his long and agonising march towards death.

The killer next took out a paintbrush from his belt pack. He gently dipped it into the puddle of blood that had formed around Varshney's left foot and began to write, with the air of a calligrapher, on the wall above Varshney's head:

> *Mleccha-nivaha-nidhane kalayasi karavalam*
> *dhumaketum iva kim api karalam*
> *kesava dhrita-kalki-sarira jaya jagadisa hare.*

*Now let me tell you a little bit about my parents.
Ugrasena was the benevolent chieftain of Mathura,
but his son Kansa—who was my maternal uncle—
was a rogue. The only being Kansa seemed to care
about was his sister Devaki, my mother. Devaki had
just married my father Vasudeva, a prince from a
neighbouring kingdom and the son of Shurasena,
a descendant of Yadu. The newlyweds were about to
leave Mathura and Kansa was heartbroken to see his
sister leave. On impulse, he decided to play charioteer
so that he could spend more time with her. They had
barely travelled a few miles when a booming voice from
the heavens mocked Kansa. 'You fool! Devaki's eighth
son is destined to kill you and you shed crocodile tears
over her departure?'*

Ravi Mohan Saini surveyed the classroom and smiled at his
doctoral student, Priya Ratnani, seated in the last row, before
dimming the lights. The nineteen other students besides
Priya were part of the master's programme in ancient
Indian history. The students allowed themselves to relax.
A presentation usually meant that Saini would not have
time to single out any of them to answer tricky questions.

Just a couple of months over forty-five, Ravi Mohan Saini
was one of the stars at St Stephen's College in New Delhi.

He taught that most interesting course in the university, the History of Mythology. Besides the fact that he had a BA from Oxford and a PhD from the University of Memphis, what made him one of the most popular professors was his easy-going nature and dashing good looks. Just a little under six feet tall, Saini had been blessed with godlike physical charms—swarthy features, well-proportioned limbs, toned muscles, an unblemished complexion and wavy hair. He rarely paid any attention to his grooming but his two-day stubble only seemed to enhance his sex appeal to the starry-eyed young women who hogged the front row at his lectures. He was the exact opposite of the geeky Anil Varshney—his closest friend in school. It had never ceased to amaze their teachers that the two of them were such close friends.

The first PowerPoint slide came up. Wordlessly, it simply showed a night sky filled with an assortment of stars. 'Confused?' asked Saini. 'Don't worry. You're not in Astronomy-101. What you see before you is merely a conjunction of Saturn with Aldebaran.'

Before any questions could be asked, he quickly clicked his remote presentation pointer and advanced to the next slide, which was equally mysterious.

'What we have here is another important planetary formation—retrograde Mars before reaching Antares,' continued Saini, amused by the bewildered expressions on his students' faces that were dimly visible from the light reflected off the presentation screen.

Happy to string his students on a little further, he quickly advanced to the third and final slide. 'A lunar eclipse near Pleiades—or the Seven Sisters,' he announced perfunctorily, before switching off the projection system, and brightening the classroom lights. The reprieve had been short-lived.

'There are many who believe that the *Mahabharata* is a myth. Indeed, many of you view the epic as a collection of stories based upon wisdom of the ages but you do not see it as an actual historical event. Well, we're going to change your assumptions today,' announced Saini.

Sitting in the last row, Priya chuckled at the collective surprise this generated. She was completing her doctoral dissertation on the historicity of the *Mahabharata* under Saini's tutelage and had been through the material beforehand.

Saini continued. 'In the *Mahabharata*, it is said that Sage Vyasa, its author, met Dhritarashtra, the father of the one hundred Kaurava princes, on the eve of the great war and warned him of the terrible planetary omens that he had seen. One of the omens was a conjunction of Saturn with Aldebaran; another was retrograde Mars before reaching Antares; and yet a third was a lunar eclipse near Pleiades. The very three conjunctions that I just showed you,' said Saini. There was a stunned silence as his students digested this information.

Seeing an arm shoot up, he paused and nodded at the student. 'So what were the slides you showed us?' asked the sceptical young man. 'Simulations of ancient night skies or photographs of modern equivalents?'

Saini smiled. 'Very good question. The slides you saw were computer simulations using a software that recreates the skies as they would have been observed from Kurukshetra — the scene of the epic battle — on any given day of any given year in history. We need to thank Professor Narhari Achar from my alma mater, the University of Memphis, for his path-breaking research into this topic. Professor Achar searched for all the years in which there was a conjunction of Saturn with Aldebaran and found one hundred and thirty-seven such conjunctions in history. He then searched for those dates on which Mars was retrograde before reaching Antares. This resulted in just seventeen overlapping dates. Finally, he searched for those dates on which there was a lunar eclipse near Pleiades and was left with just a single date on which all three astronomical events happened simultaneously.'

Saini paused. He loved taking little breaks at the very moments when his students wanted him to proceed further. 'From the exercise conducted by Professor Achar, it is evident that the Mahabharata war must have occurred in 3067 BCE—around five thousand years ago,' said Saini finally.

Everyone in the classroom seemed too surprised to ask any follow-up questions. The only amused face was that of Priya, who continued to smile silently. She knew that the good professor was bang on target.

I'm told that Kansa was furious when he heard the voice from the heavens. Grabbing Devaki by her hair, he pulled out his sword to chop off her head just as my father Vasudeva fell at Kansa's feet. 'If the prophecy is true then you need not fear Devaki. It's her eighth son that constitutes a risk to your life. Both Devaki and I are willing to be your prisoners and I shall personally deliver her eighth child to you, Kansa. Please spare Devaki. She is innocent,' he pleaded. Duly pacified, Kansa ordered his guards to take my father and mother back to Mathura and to securely lock them in prison. It is said that upon reaching Mathura, Kansa's furious father Ugrasena roared, 'What utter nonsense is this Kansa? Release Devaki and Vasudeva immediately for they are innocent. If you disobey me, I shall have you locked up!' Kansa laughed demonically. 'It is you who shall be in prison, old man. You've outlived your utility and your entire army is now personally loyal to me. Guards, arrest my useless father!' commanded Kansa. The guards seized the old and frail ruler and carted him off to prison to join my father and mother in the dungeons.

'You were wrong, Prof! It was two possible years—3067 BCE and 2183 BCE—that remained as viable alternatives for the Mahabharata war according to Achar's research,' said Priya as they sat in Saini's office sipping sugary milk tea.

Priya was just shy of forty and her athletic lifestyle was evident from the perfect figure that she managed to maintain in spite of the occasional indulgences in sugary milk tea. Daughter of a famous lawyer, Priya had disappointed her father when she elected history over law as her metier. Educated at St Xavier's College, Mumbai, she had proceeded to King's College, London, for an MA in history. Returning to India, she had begun teaching before she tracked down Saini and persuaded him to accept her as a doctoral student so that she could develop a thesis on the historicity of Krishna and the events of the *Mahabharata*. Quick-witted, beautiful, energetic and intelligent, Priya was precisely the sort of distraction that Saini did *not* need.

Saini's life was his work. He had loved someone once. He had even married her during his days at the University of Memphis. Five years later, they had drifted apart when they realised that the only exciting part of their lives had been the novelty and freshness of the relationship. Marriage seemed to have ruined it all. The divorce had been quick and painless but it had forced Saini to reengineer his life and move back to India.

'You are right Priya,' said Saini, 'but when one superimposes the information that Bhishma, the grand-uncle of both the Pandavas and the Kauravas, died in the month of *Magha*— which occurs after the winter solstice—the only remaining date is 3067 BCE. This emerges as a unique date for the Mahabharata war.'

'But simply arriving at a possible date for the Mahabharata war does not prove that it happened,' countered Priya. Priya had the habit of playing devil's advocate in order to analyse a point, even if she was in agreement with the hypothesis.

Saini was quick to rise to the challenge. 'Hence we must look outside the *Mahabharata* to see if any other sources can corroborate this date. Let's not rely on Indian sources and instead turn to Greek references, shall we? Megasthenes, the Greek ambassador in the court of Chandragupta Maurya, made the first written reference to Krishna. In his account, Krishna is called *Heracles*. The Greeks renamed many Indian deities after their own, and the Greek usage of the name Heracles was influenced by the term *Hari*, the common expression used for Krishna. Now what does Megasthenes tell us about Heracles? He writes that the *Sourasenoi* held Heracles in high esteem. Who are these Sourasenoi?'

'If I'm not mistaken, the Sourasenoi were actually the *Shurasenas*—the Yadava descendants of Vasudeva's father, Shurasena. Krishna was a Yadava himself,' said Priya.

'Full marks to the backbencher,' joked Saini. He continued, 'Megasthenes goes on to describe their main city, *Methora*. Any guesses where Methora was?'

'*Mathura*!' exclaimed Priya.

'Precisely!' said Saini. 'Krishna is recorded by the Greeks as having lived a hundred and thirty-eight generations before the times of Alexander and Chandragupta Maurya. We may take the midpoint of Chandragupta's reign as 307 BCE. Now, assuming twenty years per generation—which is a fairly good average where ancient Indian dynasties are involved—Krishna should have lived 2,760 years before 307 BCE. Do the arithmetic! You'll end up with 3067 BCE, the very same date arrived at by Achar's astronomical observations!'

Priya had a twinkle in her eyes. 'You're preaching to the choir, Professor. I was just testing you,' she said smiling.

Not quite convinced of her sincerity, Saini emphatically drove his point further. 'Just for some fun, let's also look at a third source, shall we?' he asked. 'The *Surya Siddhantha* is an ancient work on astronomy that provides the foundation for all Hindu and Buddhist calendars. This particular treatise tells us that at precisely midnight on 18 February in 3102 BCE, *Kaliyuga* began. As you know, Kaliyuga is the last of the four stages that the world goes through as part of the cycle of Yugas described in the Indian scriptures, the three previous ages being *Satyayuga, Tretayuga* and *Dvaparayuga*. Hindus believe that human civilisation degenerates spiritually during the Kaliyuga—almost a Dark Age—because people get distanced from God.'

'How does the beginning of Kaliyuga tell us anything about the date of the Mahabharata war?' asked Priya mischievously, half-aware of the answer.

Saini considered the question carefully before choosing his words. 'According to Hindu philosophy, the very first event to distance us from God was the death of Krishna. Krishna was an avatar of Vishnu and his passing away symbolically marked the dawn of Kaliyuga. If we believe the *Surya Siddhanta*, the Mahabharata war took place around 3067 BCE, not 2183 BCE.'

Priya nodded as she digested Saini's words and asked, 'Achar examined verses from various parts of the epic. One of his conclusions was that when Saturn is at Aldebaran it brings great bad tidings. Do you believe it?'

'Do you know the only other time in contemporary history when Saturn has been in Aldebaran?' asked Saini.

'No. When?'

'The last occurrence of Saturn in Aldebaran was on 11 September 2001—a date that we now remember as 9/11. Still have doubts?' asked Saini with a wry grin.

'If the Mahabharata war took place on a definite date and at a definite place, why is it that we have been unable to find any evidence of the existence of Krishna, the protagonist of the epic?' asked Priya, putting aside her sugary brew in disgust.

Saini shrugged. 'Lack of evidence does not imply lack of existence. In 1610 there was no evidence of the sun being at the centre of the solar system. Five years later, the Roman Inquisition tried Galileo for proposing such a preposterous theory. Did it mean that the solar system, as we know it today, did not exist? A few hundred years is all that it takes to accept new evidence. In the search for a historical Krishna, we are exactly where Galileo was in 1610—on the brink of a major discovery that the rest of the world has not yet accepted.'

Saini paused and then leaned forward and asked conspiratorially, 'What if I were to tell you that the Galileo moment has arrived?'

4

Kansa's reign of terror intensified after his self-elevation. Even the powerful sages were not spared. They prostrated themselves before the Devas who rushed to meet me at my home in Vaikuntha. 'Save the world from Kansa's pillage, O Lord Vishnu!' they pleaded before me. I opened my eyes and calmly said 'Have no fear! When righteousness is in peril, I incarnate on earth to protect the downtrodden. I shall soon take birth as Devaki's eighth son and shall slay the evil Kansa.' Duly appeased, the Devas thanked me and went back to their abode, awaiting my arrival on earth.

The white BMW X3 sped along the old Mumbai-Pune highway. In the driver's seat was a satisfied young man, content at having completed his task as per plan. On the seat next to him was a zipped-up belt bag that contained the tools of his trade. His eyes remained glued to the road before him but they seemed almost lifeless and robot-like. He was just a little over five feet and seven inches tall, but his upper torso was like that of a bodybuilder, the evidence of many workouts on a multi gym. His hair was jet-black and cropped to a military crew-cut.

Taarak Vakil's flight from Jaipur to Mumbai had been delayed and by the time that he had picked up his car from the extended-stay parking lot at the airport, it was past midnight. There was no traffic at this hour. He pressed the power button of his car's audio system to activate the music and the vehicle's air-conditioned interiors were soon drowned in a Sanskrit chant. It was the same verse that he had painted on Anil Varshney's wall. '*Mleccha-nivaha-nidhane kalayasi karavalam; dhumaketum iva kim api karalam; kesava dhrita-kalki-sarira jaya jagadisa hare!*'

Midway between Mumbai and Pune, he turned off into a private road. The sign outside simply bore the name of the business—Sambhala Stud Farm. His father, Dr V. Y. Sharma, had started the business of breeding horses with five mares and a stallion after completing veterinary training in the Sixties. It had been an uphill struggle that had eventually paid off. Sambhala now bred the finest derby winners in the country and was among the top two hundred listed companies on the Bombay Stock Exchange.

Taarak drove down the winding road and passed the equine viewing gallery, the automated horse-walkers, exercising turf tracks, veterinary clinic, and stables. Sambhala had grown from a couple of acres to India's largest integrated horse-breeding infrastructure, spread out over an area of just under a hundred acres. The BMW X3 sped past the gentle incline of the road until it reached the parking space designated for it just outside the sprawling country home.

He turned off the engine, took the belt bag off the seat, got out of the vehicle and ran directly to a side-entrance that led to his suite of rooms. It allowed him to come and go as he pleased without having to use the main entrance used by his parents. His mother had not been too happy with this arrangement but his father had stood up for his son's right to privacy. 'Let the lad be, Sumati. If you love your children, you must let them sprout wings and fly,' Dr Sharma had said to his wife.

'Have you seen the strange tattoos on his chest?' the worried mother had asked. 'He's spinning out of control. He no longer uses the name that we gave him at birth—Sampat Sharma—and instead goes by the ridiculous name of Taarak Vakil. I never know when he comes or goes. Sometimes I don't see him for weeks at a stretch, and you want me to give him wings?'

'Relax. He's still at the very top of his law class, isn't he? Our son is a gifted and exceptionally intelligent young man. We should be cautious of cramping his style,' Dr Sharma had advised his wife.

Taarak walked into his room, entered his bathroom and locked the door. He peeled off all his clothes, including his underwear, and placed them in a front-loading washer-dryer built in to one of the tiled walls. His upper torso was a veritable maze of tattoos—his muscular chest having turned blue from the intricate symbols that could not be individually discerned. However, at the centre of the various other images, was a large blazing sun.

He stepped into the shower cubicle where he allowed pressurised jets of steaming hot water, helped by generous quantities of antiseptic soap, to remove any traces of his nocturnal activities.

Emerging from the shower with a towel around his waist, Taarak headed directly to a walk-in closet within which was an electronic safe. Punching in a sequence of ten digits, he opened the vault, and noticed the brown leather tray inside that contained several identical gleaming Swann-Morton surgical scalpels—each bearing the initials 'R.M.' He had used one of these the previous day to surgically bleed Varshney. *No need to worry. There's enough stock for the future.*

From his belt bag, he carefully took out the plastic specimen bag that contained the seal that he had stolen from Varshney's residence. He placed the belt and the plastic specimen bag separately inside the safe and then locked it. He would examine the seal later.

Still wrapped in his towel, he made his way to the living area of his suite. In one corner was located a contemporary brushed-steel oversized birdcage that had only one occupant—his pet parrot, Shuka.

'Morning Shuka,' he said solemnly to the parrot. 'Good morning, Master,' came the parrot's squawky trained reply. Pleased, his master changed the water and the birdseed inside the cage.

Putting on a pair of jeans and a white cotton tee shirt, he locked the door to his suite and walked over to the stables. The gate marked 'Deedee' was the one that he was headed for. He loved horses, having grown up on a stud farm. His father had presented him with Deedee when he was just fifteen. He would spend hours exercising, grooming, and feeding the horse. The stud farm's eight-times champion had sired Deedee. The champion had produced over two hundred winners and over a thousand wins, earning stakes in excess of several millions at the derbies.

'How are we today, Deedee?' he asked the horse, patting him affectionately. Ensuring that the stirrups had been run up the leathers before starting, he placed his saddle so that the pommel was over the horse's withers. Walking around to the other side, he attached the girth and, reaching under Deedee's belly, he tightened it just enough to be snug. Having bridled the horse, he swiftly mounted him, caressed his mane lovingly and said 'Let's go, Deedee!'

As they trotted out into the meadows, Taarak took out his iPhone from the back pocket of his jeans and pressed a speed-dial key. The husky female voice that answered simply asked 'Yes?'

'Namaskar, Mataji,' said Taarak respectfully.

'Namaskar. Has the first one fallen?' asked the mysterious voice.

'Yes. He's dead,' replied Taarak.

'Good. Do you have them?' asked the husky voice.

'Only one. He should have had four—from Dwarka, Kalibangan, Kurukshetra and Mathura. Unfortunately, I only found one seal inside his house,' gulped Taarak. There was a pause at the other end. Taarak was nervous.

'Don't worry. Those shall also be ours. Did you find the base plate?' asked the voice.

'No, it wasn't there, Mataji,' replied Taarak nervously.

'All in good time,' said the voice. 'Let us pray. Repeat after me, *Om Shri Prithvi Raskshakaaya Namah…*'

'*Om Shri Prithvi Rakshakaaya Namah,*' repeated Taarak.

'*Om Shri Maangalya Daayakaaya Namah,*' recited Mataji.

'*Om Shri Maangalya Daayakaaya Namah,*' echoed Taarak.

'*Om Shri Mooladhar Chakra Poojakaaya Namah,*' chanted Mataji.

'*Om Shri Mooladhar Chakra Poojakaaya Namah,*' parroted Taarak.

The phone conversation continued until all one hundred and eight names of the Almighty had been duly recited.

5

My parents, Vasudeva and Devaki, were dumped in a squalid dungeon with damp walls. Even though the prison was duly fortified, they were bound with chains to the walls under Kansa's orders. Some months later, my mother gave birth to her first son. Kansa knew that he had nothing to fear from the first seven children but the mischief-making Sage Narada paid him a visit and confused him. 'Kansa, which is the eighth child?' he asked meaningfully. 'Doesn't it depend upon the direction in which one counts? If one counts backwards, the eighth could very well be the first... or the first could be the eighth!' Kansa rushed to the prison cell, yanked the new born out of my mother's arms and smashed the innocent baby against the prison walls. Blood and gore spattered my parents as they looked on in shock and despair.

Blood and gore spattered the walls and floor. Inspector Radhika Singh looked at the corpse without any hint of emotion though. She had seen too many dead bodies over the years in her job. Her eyes mechanically scanned the lifeless form lying in a puddle of blood. She noticed the little wheel-like symbol on the victim's head as well as the Sanskrit shloka written on the wall above him. She stared at the Swann-Morton scalpel custom-engraved with the initials 'R M'. There was very little that escaped Singh's attention.

Radhika Singh had begun her career as a teacher of history, geography and civics at the Mayo College. Born in small-town Ajmer, she had been heart-broken when her husband, a commandant in the Border Security Force, had been shot dead by two Jaish-e-Mohammed terrorists. Not only had Radhika courageously attempted to defend her husband, she had also succeeded in stabbing one of the assailants, thus leading to his capture. Widowed at the age of just thirty, Singh had been seething with anger at the blows life had dealt her. Her anger had coincided beautifully with an experiment to open the country's first All Women Police Station—or AWPS. Awarded the Kirti Chakra for her bravery by the President of India, Singh chucked her lecturer's job at Mayo and joined the Indian Police Service, one of the first few women to do so. Soon, Singh had found herself absorbed into a fifteen-member team that was focused on preventing and solving crimes against women.

A year later, Singh, along with around fifty women from various divisions of the IPS, signed up to undergo commando training. Thirty of them were shortlisted and went through a harrowing twelve-week training course. Besides basic physical training, firefighting and martial arts, the women commando trainees had also been taught off-road driving, horse-back riding, sand running, swimming, parasailing, unarmed combat, wall-scaling, rowing, and rock-climbing. They had also been given training in handling AK-47s and light machine guns. Other elements of the training programme had included bomb detection and disposal, and hijack and hostage handling. Back on the job three months later, Singh had won the gold medal in the state police shooting championship, beating policemen and male commandos in the process.

Now a veteran in the police force, Singh was usually referred to as 'Sniffer Singh' among her colleagues for her beagle-like ability to follow a scent to its source. Not only was she extremely bright, she also had the doggedness of a mule and the strength of an ox. She could persevere on a search for days on end while young men who were half her age would give up out of sheer exhaustion.

Forty-three years old, Radhika Singh had the body of a Rajput warrior queen but the analytical mind of a Tamil engineer. Her staple diet consisted of almonds, whole milk and cigarettes. At the oddest of times she would reach into her pockets and pull out a handful of almonds to chew slowly and thoughtfully. The smoking was a habit from her combat training days but she genuinely seemed to believe that the almonds and milk were adequate detox agents for the nicotine. Judging by her appearance, the almonds and milk seemed to be doing their purported job. Radhika had a perfectly trim figure that belied her age. Her complexion was as smooth as the ivory on the handle of her personal Smith & Wesson.

Singh's early marriage had been an arranged one but she had eventually fallen in love with her husband, unlike in most arranged marriages where love was optional. Her world had shattered into millions of tiny shards on the day that he died. From that day on, she had chosen to take on a new spouse—her work. It was almost as though the pursuit of criminals was her way of paying tribute to her husband's departed soul. Her aloof behaviour attracted disparaging remarks from male colleagues but Singh was beyond caring. Her only care seemed to be to aggressively pursue criminals and to bring them to justice. In moments of melancholy or despair, she would count prayer beads and meditate to the chant of *Hari*. In a police force known only for its apathy, incompetence and corruption, cases assigned to Radhika Singh rarely remained unsolved for long.

'I want photos of the victim's head, and get the photo of that symbol on his forehead enlarged,' she barked to Rathore, her sub-inspector. 'Take blood samples from the victim as well as from the puddle of blood around him. Also check to see if the shloka on the wall is written with the same blood.'

Rathore meticulously made note of her instructions and relayed her orders to subordinates. 'Do we know who the victim is?' asked Singh.

'Ma'am, the victim seems to be one Mr Anil Varshney. His body was identified by the servant who reported to work at his usual time at eight in the morning,' replied Rathore to his boss.

'Has the medical examiner seen the body yet? Do we have a time of death?' asked Singh.

'Not yet, ma'am. Varshney was a symbolist who was working on a project at the archaeological dig at Kalibangan. According to the servant, Varshney had a visitor over for dinner. The servant was told that he could leave after washing up the dishes.'

'At what time did the servant leave?'

'Around nine at night.'

'And had the visitor left by then?'

'The visitor was supposed to drive to Delhi via Jaipur at night but he was still with Varshney when the servant left.'

'Check the servant's background and verify his movements,' said Singh absentmindedly, counting the prayer beads in her pocket while her subconscious recited the name of

Hari. 'Get the entire house fingerprinted, especially that scalpel in the victim's foot. Ah, and yes, find out for me what that shloka on the wall means. In the meantime, find out who this visitor was. It seems that he was the last person to see Varshney alive. He could well be a psychopath for all we know and I have no intention of letting him get away so easily.'

The years passed and five more sons were born to my parents in prison. Upon the arrival of each child, Kansa would visit the dungeons and instantly murder the newborn. Devaki was mentally and physically worn out. To see six sons murdered in quick succession was like a nightmare without end. In the meantime Lord Sheshnag—who had incarnated as my younger brother Lakshmana in a previous era when I had been born as Rama—entered Devaki's womb so that he could take birth as my elder brother Balarama, Devaki's seventh child. Through divine inter-vention, the foetus was transferred to the womb of Rohini, Vasudeva's first wife, who was living in Gokul, and the result was an apparent miscarriage of the seventh child for Devaki.

Ravi Mohan was in the classroom, reading the note that his friend Varshney had handed over to him during their visit to Kalibangan. He had tried reading and rereading it several times but still could not make any sense of what his friend was trying to say. *Damn the linguist in you, Varshney, for making everything so complicated,* thought Saini.

D'etale r'aknahs! Edise-Breta-Weulb DNA. Rats anispiter. Axis Red Nerrus ajar! Sitih saliak roh salak. XNI dialer, dial, devil. Pitta pott Felnox. Strap lamina on stats. Peek slipup desserts. Tub trams. A kit saw slarem. Un warder!

Fed up with Varshney's gobbledygook, Ravi Mohan Saini put away the note in his pocket and began reviewing the previous day's material with his students, when his class had unexpected visitors. Inspector Radhika Singh and Sub-Inspector Rathore marched into his classroom accompanied by their New Delhi counterpart.

'I'm arresting you—Ravi Mohan Saini—on suspicion of the murder of Anil Varshney,' said Rathore in a monotonous voice. 'Article twenty paragraph three of the Constitution of India provides you with the right against self-incrimination. You may also consider engaging legal counsel if you wish. Please come with us.' The last sentence was courteously delivered but was an order, not a request.

The shocked students began excitedly whispering among themselves. Impossible! Saini epitomised the refined and gentle academic. It was ridiculous for anyone to imagine that he was capable of murder.

'Murder? Anil is dead?' asked Saini incredulously. 'I met him just two days ago. He was alive and well. There has to be some mistake!'

'There's no mistake, Mr Saini,' said Inspector Radhika Singh calmly. 'The body of Anil Varshney was discovered at his house the morning after you had dinner with him. You were the last person to see him alive, which also means that you are our chief suspect. I think that it's better that we carry on this conversation in custody.'

Saini nodded dumbly, almost as if he had not registered anything that had been said. Digesting the news of his best friend having been murdered was bad enough; he was now being accused of murder, and dragged to prison in front of an entire class of students. Could things possibly get any worse? Priya, seated as usual in the last row, stood up. She walked up to Radhika Singh and asked, 'Do you have a warrant for his arrest?'

Singh nodded to Rathore who pulled out the warrant from his shirt pocket, unfolded it and passed it to Saini. Saini was too dazed to read it and blindly handed it over to Priya who scanned it carefully.

'Can Professor Saini apply for bail?' she asked.

'Yes but given that the murder took place in Rajasthan, Mr Saini's arrest is at the hands of the Rajasthan State Police, not the New Delhi Police. Mr Saini shall have to come with us to Jaipur where he shall be placed in custody and interrogated at Central Jail. His lawyer may apply for bail before the Chief Judicial Magistrate within twenty-four hours of his arrest,' explained Rathore.

Priya nodded. Turning to Saini, she said, 'Don't worry, Prof! As you know, my father—Sanjay Ratnani —is a leading criminal lawyer. I'll ask him to represent you. I'm sure that he'll be able to clear up this mess. For the moment, though, I don't think you have any alternative but to go with them.'

'We have a police vehicle waiting outside. We do not believe that you're a flight risk and as a matter of courtesy we're not cuffing you,' explained Rathore as he gently led Ravi Mohan Saini—leading academic turned accused murderer—to the police vehicle that waited outside. Saini already seemed mentally and physically worn out. His nightmare without end was just beginning.

Ravi's mind struggled with the events that were happening around him as he tried to recall his last meeting with Varshney in Kalibangan.

It was finally time for me to arrive on earth and I appeared before Devaki and Vasudeva in their prison cell. Seeing me in my omnipotent form, Devaki and Vasudeva fell at my feet. I told them that it was time for me to take birth as their eighth son. I also told them that I would make them forget my visit so that they would get to experience the normal joys and pains of parenthood. In the meantime, Yashoda—the wife of my father's cousin Nanda—would deliver a baby girl in Gokul. My father was commanded by a voice to swap the babies as soon as Devaki gave birth to me.

The temperatures had reached forty-nine degrees on the Celsius scale that day. The archaeological site at Kalibangan was a frying pan. One could crack open a raw egg on a rock and watch it cook instantly.

Surrounded by miles of sand dunes and occasional thorny babul bushes, the road from Hanumangarh railway station on the Delhi-Bikaner line to the largest prehistoric excavation site in Rajasthan was pock-marked with craters and potholes. The Mahindra Xylo off-roader vehicle struggled to cope with portions where the road had entirely disappeared.

Inside the vehicle along with Anil Varshney was Ravi Mohan Saini—Varshney's closest school buddy. Both men were sitting in the rear of the vehicle while the harried driver attempted to navigate the treacherous peaks and troughs. Varshney was playing host to his friend who was on a visit to Rajasthan to attend a seminar. It had not required too much persuasion to entice him to visit Kalibangan, the oven-like temperatures notwithstanding.

'Why on earth would any sensible human being have established an urban settlement here in the middle of this arid desert?' asked Saini, his last few words almost entirely garbled due to an unanticipated plunge of the vehicle.

Varshney laughed. 'It's time for you to start re-writing your history texts, Ravi! The evidence from remote earth-sensing satellite pictures is clinching. More than five thousand years ago, a mighty river—commonly referred to in the Vedas as the *Sarasvati*—flowed through this arid desert and into the Arabian Sea. The nothingness that you see around you was lush vegetation and pastureland five thousand years ago! Kalibangan was part of this great Sarasvati civilisation.'

'So the Sarasvati was not a mythical river, as claimed by some eminent historians?' asked Saini playfully, knowing that the question would get Varshney's goat.

'The idea of the Sarasvati being a mythical river is just as ridiculous as the Aryan invasion theory which held that the Indus Valley civilisation was destroyed by hordes of attacking westerners pumped up by hallucinogenic *somaras*!' said Varshney indignantly as he splashed some mineral water from a bottle on his face. Settling back into the seat of the vehicle, Varshney rummaged through the papers in his leather satchel. After a couple of minutes he was finally able to find what he was looking for. He pulled out a map and opened it out clumsily for Saini's benefit.

'See this?' he asked, emphatically stabbing with his finger on the image. 'This map has been created by stitching

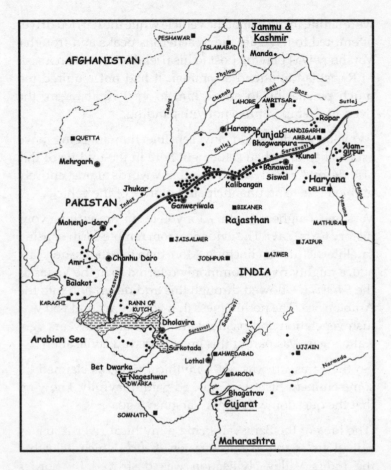

together images taken by satellites of ISRO—the Indian Space Research Organisation. Archaeological excavations and geological findings corroborate these pictures. The Indus Valley civilisation was only called by that name because the first few sites discovered were on the banks of the Indus. It's now a proven fact that over two thousand of the two thousand six hundred sites were actually along the once-mighty River Sarasvati. Wouldn't you say it's time the Indus Valley civilisation was renamed the Sarasvati civilisation?'

Saini looked down at the map that Varshney was holding. The dried-up riverbed of the Sarasvati was clearly visible. Five thousand years ago, the Sarasvati would have been India's mightiest river with the Yamuna and the Sutlej as mere tributaries. Tectonic movements of the Indian subcontinent had resulted in the Sarasvati migrating west-northwest. The effect was that its two tributaries, the Yamuna and Sutlej, migrated in opposite directions, the former joining the Ganga and the latter joining the Indus.

'I'm pretty certain that you haven't brought me here to the middle of the desert to discuss rechristen-ing an urban civilisation,' quipped Saini. 'Come on, out with it!'

Varshney laughed nervously. There was no point hiding anything from Saini. Their childhood friendship meant that Saini could read Varshney like an open book. Varshney folded the map, put it back in his satchel and withdrew from his bag a small cardboard box. He handed it to Saini wordlessly. Saini opened the lid.

Inside the box was a felt-lined casing on which lay a single rectangular seal measuring just 20 x 20 mm. At the back, the seal had a square peg without the customary hole, which was usually provided for a ring band or string. Saini drew in his breath and felt his heart racing as he looked at it.

I was born on the eighth night of the waning moon in the month of Shraavan during an auspicious Rohini Nakshatra. As per my instructions, Vasudeva walked out of prison carrying me in a basket. In order to facilitate this, I ensured that all the prison guards remained in deep slumber while my father's chains simply snapped open. I also caused the gates of the prison to swing open, allowing him free passage. It turned out to be a night of torrential rain, and getting from Mathura to Gokul involved crossing the River Yamuna, which was in full spate. With not a single boatman in sight, my father decided to hold the basket containing me over his head and cross the ferocious river unaided. When Yamuna realised it was I in the basket, she miraculously abated so as to allow my father to cross easily.

'Where did you find this?' asked Saini excitedly, as he held the seal in his hand.

'A very dear friend, Dr Nikhil Bhojaraj, has been carrying out deep-sea diving expeditions off the coast of Gujarat. His team discovered it and sent it to me. They figured that I was probably just the person to make sense of the symbols,' explained Varshney.

'Symbols? These look like animals,' began Saini.

'Exactly. These are motifs of a bull, unicorn and goat that have been engraved in an anticlockwise direction on the face of this seal. You do realise the significance, don't you?' asked Varshney.

Saini nodded his head in amazement. 'The most common image on the seals of the Indus Valley civilisation—excuse me, Sarasvati civilisation—is that of the unicorn. It's a purely symbolic animal but is of immense importance. There are references to a very prominent unicorn in the *Mahabharata* called *Ekashringa*, literally the one-horned, which appears as a prime symbol of Vishnu-Krishna and the Vedic knowledge he taught. The unicorn is connected to the *Varaha Avatara*, or boar incarnation, of Lord Vishnu...' he began excitedly.

'Yes, yes,' interrupted Varshney impatiently, 'but here's another more important hint for you, my friend. *Mudra-yaasah gacchantu rajno ye gantumipsavah; Na chamudra praveshtavyo dwaarpaalasya pashyatah...*' he began in Sanskrit.

Saini laughed. 'Absolutely! What you've just recited is the exact passage from the *Harivamsa*—an appendix to the *Mahabharata*—that contains a reference which says that every citizen of Dwarka should carry a three-headed mudra—or seal—as a mark of identification. The sentence that you've just quoted goes on to say that it is the duty of the guards to see that every citizen carries the seal and that none without a seal is allowed to enter. But what does this have to do with your excavations at Kalibangan?' asked Saini.

'Many similar seals have been discovered at various sites with these specific motifs. For years we've been fed the notion that Krishna was merely a mythological figure, a product of our collective imagination down the ages. We've also been told that Sarasvati sites predated the age of the Mahabharata by several thousand years. That's utter nonsense, my friend. The Sarasvati civilisation was not a pre-Vedic settlement. It was the greatest Vedic community on earth and it was the inhabitants of this great development who wrote the *Vedas* and the *Upanishads*. That's why Kalibangan and Mohenjodaro are so important. We've discovered fire altars in Kalibangan, thus proving the fact that this indeed was a Vedic settlement. In Mohenjodaro we discovered the Great Bath used for ritual bathing, another hallmark of Vedic worship. We've also discovered hundreds of seals containing images of the swastika, a symbol of Vedic origin, in addition to seals depicting yogic meditation. The Sarasvati was the living river on the banks of which Duryodhona and Bhima fought their last grim duel of the Mahabharata war. What you are holding in your hand is a relic of Krishna's ancient passport system for his kingdom of Dwarka that is described in the *Harivamsa*!' exclaimed Varshney, his face flushed with excitement.

'So how do I fit into your plans?' asked Saini, intrigued and excited.

Varshney looked at Saini. 'You are not just my best friend, Ravi, you are almost my brother. One day you will realise that this statement is not a burst of sudden emotion but is based on logic. I know your genetic makeup, my friend! What I've just shown you is the seal that was discovered off the coast of Dwarka. This seal shall be returned to Dr Nikhil Bhojaraj, the one who discovered it. What I'm about to give you for safekeeping is an almost identical seal that I discovered in Kalibangan. A third seal was discovered in Kurukshetra and I have handed it over to yet another friend, Professor Rajaram Kurkude who has his research laboratories in Jodhpur. I shall tell you about his cutting-edge nuclear research over dinner tonight,' said Varshney, lowering his voice in a vain attempt to evade the hearing of the driver who was occupied with keeping the vehicle from rolling over. 'The fourth seal was found in Mathura and is presently in the safe custody of our friend Devendra Chhedi.'

'Devendra Chhedi—the genetics expert? The one who rigged the school principal's WC to explode as his rear touched down?' asked Saini with a broad smile.

'Precisely. He's still a rascal, but now gets paid for his scientific experiments!' joked Varshney. 'These seals are part of a set of four.'

'Why are you leaving these seals with Bhojaraj, Kurkude, Chhedi and me?' asked Saini, accepting a small brown paper sachet containing the similar Kalibangan seal held out by Varshney.

Varshney looked into his friend's eyes and whispered, 'Because the four of you are the only people that I can trust. I cannot afford to have all four seals kept together. The risk of losing them together is far too great. There's greater safety in numbers. I believe that these four seals together point us in the direction of Krishna's most prized possession.'

Varshney paused and took a deep breath. 'These four seals also have a base plate—a ceramic plate that can hold them together,' said Varshney. 'The plate came up for auction in Sotheby's recently and I was able to convince my employers—VSKBC Heritage Ltd—to bid for it. We succeeded in buying it for a rather large sum of money.'

'Where is it?' asked Saini.

'It's in a safe deposit box. The instructions to the vault management are that if anything should happen to me, they are to contact you and apprise you of the contents,' said Varshney.

'Anything specific that I should know about this particular base plate?' asked Saini curiously.

'Just that it was handed down through generations even though the seals were lost in antiquity,' replied Varshney. 'The base plate eventually reached the hands of Raja Man Singh who was a great Krishna devotee in the sixteenth century. Raja Man Singh had a Sanskrit inscription engraved into the plate and installed it in a Krishna temple that he built in Vrindavan.'

Saini nodded.

'Guard this seal with your life, Ravi. I am sending to you by email photographs of all four seals. If something should happen to me, do everything within your power to bring these four seals and the base plate together. Together, they constitute what can be called *The Krishna Key* — they can unlock the truth to the historical Krishna for future generations.'

Varshney then handed a note to Saini. 'It's specially written for you. Use it when you feel the need.' The eyes of the vehicle driver remained pinned to the hazardous road. The two men sitting at the back did not notice that the driver seemed to be the owner of a rather expensive mobile phone and that that the voice memo-recorder of the phone was active and blinking.

When my father reached Gokul, he hurriedly looked inside the basket and saw that I was completely dry. Unknown to my father, Lord Sheshnag had been behind us throughout the Yamuna crossing and had spread his protective serpentine hood over my basket against the pouring rain. My simple father realised that this was a night of unending miracles. He quickly made his way to Nanda's house, placed me in Yashoda's bed and picked up Yashoda's daughter. He then made his way back to the prison in Mathura where he placed the baby girl next to Devaki. I made the chains snap back on his wrists; I made the gates lock shut and I made the guards wake up to the sounds of a crying infant.

The driver of the Mahindra Xylo that had ferried Anil Varshney and Ravi Mohan Saini to Kalibangan stood in front of his employer nervously. The expensive mobile phone was in his hand and was playing back the conversation that had been recorded at the phone's maximum permissible volume. As the conversation ended, he clicked off the phone and grinned sheepishly at her.

'You have done well,' said Mataji, swinging her legs out of the car and standing up in the desolate wooded area that served as their rendezvous point. She placed her hands on her lower back and allowed herself to arch backwards until she heard the familiar crick. Having stretched herself, she straightened up and tossed him a sealed bundle of crisp thousand rupee notes. 'I am pleased with your effort.'

Encouraged by her appreciation, the operative plucked up his courage. 'It's not my place to ask, Mataji, but why is the Krishna Key so important to you?'

Mataji smiled as her right hand continued to clutch and rotate a hundred and eight beads on a string, each bead an opportunity to recite the name of the Lord. *Om Shri Prithvi Raskshakaaya Namah,* she mentally recited as she counted the first bead. *One who is protector of the earth.*

'Are you sure you want to know?' she asked. 'Too much knowledge can be a curse at times, son.' *Om Shri Maangalya Daayakaaya Namah,* thought Mataji as she counted her second bead. *One who bestows purity.*

The driver lowered his eyes to avert her gaze. 'Only if you think it's appropriate, Mataji. I'm your humble servant and shall obey your orders without question. It's just curiosity on my part.'

Mataji was already on her fifth bead. *Om Shri Kartum Shakti Dhaarnaaya Namah. One who bears the power of performance.*

'Then listen,' said Mataji. 'Krishna was the eighth avatar of Vishnu—a manifestation of a form of energy that we shall call *Vish*. The exact opposite energy of *Vish* is *Shiv*. While Vish, creates and preserves, Shiv destroys.'

'And how does this relate to the Sarasvati civili-sation seals that Varshney and Saini discussed while seated in my car?' asked Mataji's obedient operative.

'So far, most historians have believed that the inhabitants of the Sarasvati civilisation were Shiv-worshippers. Do you know what the symbol of Shiv looks like?' Not waiting for an answer, Mataji pulled out a printed image from a manila folder lying on the front seat of her car.

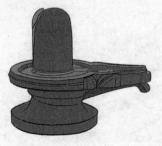

'See this?' she asked, pointing at the picture. 'We Hindus are taught that this symbol is a Shiv *lingam*. A phallic representation of Lord Shiv, right?' she continued.

The operative was confused. Why was Mataji giving him a crash course in Hinduism? He nodded vigorously in order to humour her. 'Yes. That is indeed what we've been taught,' he said.

Mataji nodded appreciatively. 'Good. Now let us examine the salient features of a Shiv lingam, shall we? It's made up of two parts. The first is a cylindrical structure made of polished stone. The second is the surrounding coils or grooves ending in a spout. In Shiv temples, a pot of water hangs over the cylindrical structure, allowing water to continuously drip on it at regular intervals. This water then empties itself out through the spout,' she explained, pointing to each of the constituent elements as she described them.

The dutiful driver looked at the image, his confusion only heightening with every passing minute. Mataji pulled out a second picture from the same manila folder. 'Now see this,' she said, holding up the second picture next to the first. 'This is an aerial view of the Bhabha Atomic Research Centre—BARC—on the outskirts of Mumbai. Notice the parallels between the two pictures?'

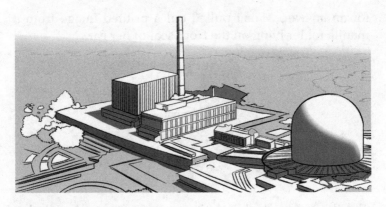

The operative gasped. The similarities were strikingly obvious! Mataji laughed as she saw his reaction. She let him hold both illustrations so that he could scrutinise them closely. She had already counted her way to the fiftieth bead. *Om Shri Munistutaaya Namah—the One who is praised by sages and seers.*

'We often forget to observe what is in plain sight! The cylindrical structure that you see in the picture of BARC is the core nuclear reactor. Its shape is identical to the cylindrical structure of the lingam,' said Mataji. 'Like the cylinder of the Shiv lingam, the nuclear reactor too needs a regular supply of water to cool it down as it heats up during the process of generating energy. Notice the coils around the main reactor? Those are the structures built to dispose of the water—just like the coils around the lingam!'

She continued, 'Think about it. It's only in a Shiv temple that the water flowing from the lingam is not consumed as holy water. Why? The water from a Shiv lingam is not drunk for precisely the same reason as the water from a nuclear reactor is not potable—it is charged water. Why are most Shiv temples always found near a source of water, say a river or lake? That's because Shiv lingams—just like modern-day reactors—need water for cooling the core. Do you know that no one is allowed to cross the spout of a Shiv lingam during *pradakshina*—the circumambulation of the lingam during worship? People have to turn back as soon as they approach the spout because the spout represents irradiated water.'

'So BARC was designed along the lines of a Shiv lingam?' asked the dazed driver.

'On the contrary, my son. What I'm trying to tell you is that the Shiv lingam is *not* a representation of some god called Shiv. It's an ancient symbol to represent a supreme force, an energy that our ancestors chose to call *Shiv*. This energy was the exact opposite of another energy form called *Vish*. The people of the Sarasvati civilisation knew these forms of energy. Modern man prides himself on having discovered nuclear power. Little does he realise that far greater powers were available to society and civili-sations during the Vedic age and the Mahabharata!' said Mataji triumphantly as she stepped closer to her operative, her right hand mechanically counting her prayer beads. She was on her hundredth one. *Om Shri Mukta Sanchaarakaaya Namah. One who wanders freely from place to place.*

'And the Krishna Key leads us to this energy?' asked the operative.

Mataji stood with her face inches away from that of the operative. He could feel her warm breath on his face. Looking directly into his eyes, Mataji said, 'Oppenheimer, the father of the atom bomb, is said to have quoted the *Bhagwad Gita* after witnessing the first successful test of the bomb in 1945. His words? *I am become death, the destroyer of the worlds.* Oppenheimer had learned Sanskrit specifically with the intention of being able to understand the Gita. The passage in the Gita that says what Oppenheimer was quoting is: *I am become time to end the world, set on my course to destroy the universe.* The clues to an ancient nuclear age are right before us in the ancient Hindu scriptures, my son!' she exclaimed as she used her left hand to plunge the knife that was hidden in the folds of her sleeve into her operative's stomach.

As his body crumpled to the ground, she knelt down beside him and whispered into his ear, 'There was a reason why I asked you if you wanted to know more. Too much knowledge is always a curse, son.'

She realised that she had reached the hundred and eighth bead—the last one. *Om Shri Yoga Poornatva Daayakaaya Namah*. She silently mouthed the words. *One who bestows completeness to Yoga.*

She rambled on incoherently as she twisted the knife into his abdomen while gazing into his terror-stricken eyes until his final breath escaped him.

Kansa rushed to Devaki's prison cell as soon as he was informed that the eighth child had been delivered. My mother protested. 'Dear brother, it's not a boy! It's a poor helpless girl. The prophecy spoke about an eighth son, not a daughter. Please don't kill her, I beseech you!' Kansa instinctively knew that he had been deceived. 'I don't know how you have managed to trick me but I shall kill her anyway—just to be sure!' he shouted and grabbed hold of Yashoda's daughter. As he threw her against the wall, she miraculously rose up in the air as Mother Shakti and mocked him. 'Fool! Your slayer is already born and lives safely in a place where you shall be unable to harm him! Get ready to die, O evil one!'

Jaipur's infamous Central Jail had been built by the British in 1855 and was located in a densely populated area of the city called Ghat Gate. Central Jail was famous for all the wrong reasons, though.

In a sensational case, conmen had duped a city jeweller of ornaments worth millions. Lodged at Central Jail, the crooks had been assisted in their escape by the junior warden, who had not only ensured that the cells were conveniently left unlocked but had also thoughtfully arranged for a taxi to remain on standby for the fleeing culprits. The golden rule of Central Jail was that those who had the gold made the rules.

Data from the Rajasthan prison system showed that the number of deaths of inmates due to lack of medical services was ever burgeoning. One prisoner died every fourth day because of the unsanitary conditions. Prisoners were usually stacked up in cells like sardines, with eight inmates sharing a single blanket, the healthy ones often sharing breathing space with tuberculosis-infected inmates. The toilets overflowed, forcing many prisoners to defaecate directly into open drains.

Inter-gang rivalry, prisoner suicides, torture of under-trials by prison authorities, and extortion were common occurrences. It was in this hotbed of grime and crime that Ravi Mohan Saini was inventoried, fingerprinted, photographed and placed.

Seated in one of the interrogation cells that stank of urine, he awaited the arrival of the cops who had arrested him. He could feel the sweat trickling down his back as he sat in the hot, humid and squalid cell, nervously drumming his fingers on the table in front of him. Next to him sat his lawyer, Sanjay Ratnani—Priya's father. Ratnani had already indicated to Saini that he would stay quiet throughout the interrogation. 'The interrogation has no meaning—we can always claim that it was written up under coercion. No, it's more important to see what she has on us… I'll let her talk!' he said.

Momentarily, the cell door opened and Inspector Radhika Singh walked in holding a file that had Saini's name on it.

She sat opposite him and opened the file on the table. 'The case against you is watertight,' she said. 'Your fingerprints are on the entrance door. We had our colleagues in Delhi search your apartment and they found this ancient seal.'

She placed the plastic specimen bag containing the seal that Varshney had given to Saini on the table. She continued, 'We know that it belongs to Anil Varshney because it is documented in his collection of photographs and bears his fingerprints too. You stole it!'

Saini looked at it. It was the Kalibangan seal that Varshney had entrusted him with, identical in almost every detail to the Dwarka seal that Varshney had shown him in the car. Saini gulped nervously. His throat felt parched, but he was reluctant to take a sip of water from a glass that seemed to hold half an inch of muddy sediment at the bottom. 'Anil was my friend. He invited me to Kalibangan to show me the fascinating work that he was doing. Yes, I was at his house. I even had dinner with him. Quite obviously, you are going to find my fingerprints everywhere in his house! But that does not mean that I killed him!' he pleaded.

Singh scrutinised Saini's expression, almost as though she were hoping that his guilt would be reflected within his eyes. The only expression that Saini provided was that of extreme discomfort—from the heat, humidity and stench. Measuring her words carefully, she asked, 'And the seal. How do you explain that, eh? It was obviously something very valuable considering the fact that you were willing to kill a childhood friend over it!'

'I did not kill Anil Varshney! He gave me the seal for safekeeping. He said that he would explain the details later. I can assure you that when I left Anil's house he was alive and well. Why don't you focus your efforts on finding the real killer rather than stitching me up for a crime that I did not commit!' demanded Saini indignantly.

Singh pulled out a photograph from her file. It was a 6 x 4 glossy close-up of the scalpel that had been used to bleed Anil Varshney to death. Clearly visible on the handle of the scalpel were the initials 'R.M.'

'Then maybe you would like to explain to me who else's name has these initials, Professor Ravi Mohan?' hissed Radhika Singh. The blood drained from Saini's face and he felt an overwhelming need to throw up.

Singh knew she had the upper hand. She quickly flung another photograph towards Saini. It was a graphic still of Anil Varshney's lifeless body lying in a puddle of blood. Plunged into his left foot was the scalpel; on his forehead was the wheel-like symbol, and above his head on the wall was the shloka written in blood.

Saini recoiled in horror. It was the first time that he was seeing the manner in which his friend had been brutally slayed. Ignoring the sediment in the glass, he took a gulp of water and regretted his decision as soon as his nostrils picked up the fetid stench emanating from it. 'Welcome to Central Jail, Professor Saini,' mocked Radhika Singh. 'We have our own special brand of water for the inmates here. It's called Eau de Sewage!'

The vomit that had been building up inside Saini erupted like a fountain from his mouth, splattering Singh's uniform and the file papers. 'Bastard!' she yelled, as she attempted to salvage her file and papers. 'You did that on purpose!'

At that moment Radhika Singh realised that her prime suspect had passed out from shock, dehydration and exhaustion. What she did not realise was that in the confusion that followed, his lawyer had picked up the specimen bag containing the seal and had concealed it in his jacket with the speed and dexterity of an experienced pickpocket.

A furious Kansa summoned his ministers. 'It seems that I have been deceived and that my prophesised slayer is alive and well. What should I do?' he asked. 'O lord, let us send out armed groups in all directions. We should kill all infants that are less than two months old. This will take care of the problem and will mitigate the risk that you face,' suggested one of them. Kansa smiled. The mayhem started and thousands of infants were snatched from their mothers' arms or murdered in their cribs in a ruthless drive across the land, their parents weeping hysterically as the mass infanticide proceeded. Little did the parents know that all the children killed were simply souls that needed to spend only a few days on earth to complete their karmic debts. Luckily, I remained safe, tucked away in idyllic Gokul, in the care of my foster-parents—Nanda and Yashoda.

'Myocardial infarction!' yelled the prison doctor as Saini's heart went into overdrive. 'Code Blue!'

A couple of nurses ran in. One quickly started oxygen therapy in order to ensure that the heart had to work as little as possible when delivering oxygen to the rest of the body. The other nurse began monitoring Saini's heart rate and pressure and connected him to the electrocardiogram unit to measure his heart rhythm.

'We have no time!' shouted the prison doctor. 'We have to shift him to a specialty heart hospital immediately. Nurse, call for the ambulance immediately and phone ahead to Fortis Escorts to tell them that I'm on my way with this patient.'

The Code Blue alert regarding Saini's cardiac arrest had sounded and Priya came running to his bedside. She noticed that the doctor had commenced CPR while his assistant had taken out the defibrillator and was hurriedly issuing instructions to the nurse. 'Nurse, charge unit to 200 joules!'

'Yes doctor,' she replied, as the assistant applied the gel pads, one on Saini's upper chest, below the right clavicle and the second below his left nipple. He pressed the paddles firmly onto the gel pads, applying twenty-five pounds of pressure. 'All clear!' he shouted as he depressed the shock button on the paddles. Saini's body jerked with the jolt of the current as the doctors stared at the monitor apparently looking for a stable rhythm.

As the monitor bleeped, Saini's bed was rolled out— surrounded by medical personnel—towards the waiting ambulance with Priya and the prison doctor running alongside. She waited for the emergency personnel to load him into the ambulance and then got into the vehicle along with the doctor. The sirens were switched on and the familiar red and blue lights on the roof of the ambulance were activated as they sped towards their destination.

Built on a sprawling six-acre plot, Fortis Escorts was Rajasthan's first super-speciality hospital, located in Malviya Nagar in the heart of Jaipur. If one headed south of the hospital along Jawaharlal Nehru Road and went around the Jawahar Circle Garden, one could be at Jaipur airport in less than ten minutes from Fortis Escorts.

Suddenly, the prison doctor tapped on the screen separating the driver from the rear of the ambulance. The ambulance driver manually slid the glass screen open on the assumption that the doctor had some instructions for him. Before the driver could observe who had knocked, a punch hit him on the lower left side of his face. It was a powerful uppercut that knocked his head violently towards the windscreen. The ambulance spun out of control as the driver's foot accidentally hit the accelerator. The ambulance lunged forward clumsily and crashed headlong into the rear service gate of the Clark's Amer Hotel, located a stone's throw away from the airport.

'Quick! Punch me hard on my face!' yelled the doctor to Priya.

'Why?' asked Priya before realising that the doctor needed an insurance policy to protect him from the inquiry that would inevitably follow. Understanding that there wasn't a moment to lose, she swung her right fist at the doctor's mouth and drew blood. She recoiled instinctively only to see the doctor holding out a plastic bag stuffed with clothes.

'Run inside the hotel and go quickly to room number 322. Inside the bag are dark glasses, new clothes and two photo ID cards issued under aliases for you and Ravi Mohan. A private taxi—a Toyota Innova—is waiting at the main entrance of the hotel. Get into it. The driver will take you to a private charter aircraft belonging to Titan Aviation. The pilot won't ask you any questions,' explained the doctor breathlessly.

'But where are we going?' asked Saini weakly.

'Jamnagar—Gujarat,' replied the huffing doctor. 'It's the closest airport to Dwarka.'

My foster parents—Nanda and Yashoda—were forced to perform all the religious ceremonies relating to my birth and naming in secret. They were terrified that Kansa would find me. The family astrologer, Gargmuni, told them, 'Krishna is a manifestation of God. Stop worrying. He shall protect you and all the citizens of the land from Kansa's wicked deeds. Raise him carefully, though, because many demons will try to kill him on the orders of Kansa.' My foster parents didn't know that Kansa's spies had followed Gargmuni and that Kansa now knew where I was.

Ravi Mohan Saini tried recalling the events leading up to his escape as he ran towards Room 322 of the Clark's Amer Hotel.

He had been having a nightmare. Saini had felt a little monster sucking on a straw that was lodged deep inside his left foot, and with each gulp of Saini's blood, the parasitic monster became bigger and Saini smaller. 'Leave me alone!' he shouted as he thrashed his arms wildly, but the monster had pinned down his arms and was busy plunging a needle into the veins of his wrist.

'Nurse! Hold the patient down, he's delirious,' shouted the prison doctor as Saini had flailed his arms, ripping off the bandage that held the glucose drip in place on his wrist. A minute later, Saini had been wide awake and aware that the monster had been a figment of his imagination, probably stirred into overdrive by the photographs of his childhood friend having been bled to death from his foot.

As the blurred images became sharper, Saini had become aware that he was lying on a metal-frame bed in the prison infirmary and was surrounded by several people— the prison doctor, a nurse, the prison warden, Priya and her father.

Priya's father, Sanjay Ratnani, was India's highest paid criminal lawyer although he liked to joke that his earnings the previous year had been a measly one thousand nine hundred rupees. The figure was accurate, except for the fact that it had accrued each minute of the year, irrespective of whether he had been awake or asleep, in court or attending a page-three event, in India or abroad, eating breakfast or brushing his teeth.

Ratnani had served in various posts including as Chairman of the New Delhi Bar Association. A maverick to the core, the rebel in Ratnani forced him to take up cases that were lost causes, high-profile crimes, or simply controversial. Ratnani had been brought up in a family of extremely modest means and through sheer grit and determination had succeeded in obtaining his matriculation degree at thirteen. He went on to bag an LLB at the tender age of seventeen. As per the university rules, the minimum age for qualifying as a lawyer was twenty-one but a special resolution passed by the authorities had allowed him to start practising at eighteen. The principle that Ratnani lived by was that good lawyers knew the law but great lawyers knew the judge.

'She has it in for you, my boy,' said the gruff Ratnani. 'Inspector Radhika Singh is out to get you, and trust me, when she decides to go after someone she usually succeeds. They call her Sniffer Singh in the police force. So why don't you tell me the real story, huh?'

'I promise you that I did not kill Anil Varshney,' said Saini weakly. 'I just happened to be in the wrong place at the wrong time.'

'Talk freely son,' advised Ratnani. 'You're among friends,' he said, winking at the prison warden, who smiled at the legal veteran. The prison doctor and infirmary nurse quietly left the cordoned-off bed, leaving the patient alone with his lawyer, his student and the warden.

'Varshney was my buddy. I would willingly have laid down my life for him. All I know is that he was on the verge of a major historical discovery and that he was very worried that enemies would possibly try to wrest it from him. My instinct tells me that his murder was related to his research,' Saini struggled to say, running out of breath by the end of the sentence.

'Our problem is that the seal given to you by Anil Varshney was found in your possession. Your fingerprints were present at the murder site. You were the last person seen at the victim's house. Worst of all is that damn scalpel that has your initials on it. Sniffer Singh has more than enough circumstantial evidence to hold you indefinitely without bail,' said Ratnani cautiously.

'You spoke of four seals,' said Priya. 'One was given to you —and was discovered by the police at your house. What did Varshney do with the other three?'

'Anil had three other close friends besides me. The first, Dr Nikhil Bhojaraj, lives aboard an exploration ship that is anchored off the coast of Gujarat. Another friend, Rajaram Kurkude, is a nuclear scientist based in Jodhpur. Finally, there's Devendra Chhedi, a life sciences researcher in Chandigarh,' whispered Saini. 'I know that Anil meant to leave one seal with each of us. Apparently, he spoke with Bhojaraj and shared his plan with him.'

'Listen to me carefully, Ravi,' said Priya's father. 'It's critical that you meet Bhojaraj and get him to back up your story. His testimony would dramatically alter the case against you.'

'But I'm in custody!' protested Saini.

'Not for long,' explained the seasoned lawyer. 'The glass of water with the dirty sediment that caused you to puke? It was put there by my good friend, the prison warden. It had been spiked with Ipecac syrup to induce vomiting. It gave us the perfect excuse to bring you to the infirmary. Now that you're here, we're ready to put the second part of our plan in motion.'

'Second part? What's that?' asked a confused Saini.

'You shall have a minor heart attack later today. As abundant precaution, the prison warden will sign off papers to shift you by ambulance to Fortis Escorts Hospital in Jaipur,' explained Ratnani as Saini's eyes widened in incredulity.

'Heart attack? I'm absolutely fit, except for the effects of that putrid water that I drank inside that stinking cell!' said Saini in protest.

'Relax, son,' said the warden, 'you won't have a real heart attack. We simply need the cooperative infirmary doctor who is waiting outside to certify that you had palpitations. It's important that the drama is enacted realistically and that the medical printouts back it up, though. That would be more than enough reason to shift you.'

'But I'm innocent!' argued Saini. 'Why are we resorting to extra-legal means to secure my release?'

'My daughter respects you immensely, Professor,' explained Ratnani. 'She's brought me into the picture to ensure that you don't spend the rest of your life in a lockup. Now, will you let me get on with the job of saving your ass?'

Saini looked at Ratnani and then at Priya. He saw her eyes pleading with him to accept her father's instructions. He sighed. 'Very well, I'll go along with whatever you say.'

Ratnani smiled as he spoke to Saini. 'You know the proverb that good lawyers know the law and that great lawyers know the judge?'

Saini nodded.

'What they didn't tell you was that the very best lawyer in the land doesn't need to know the judge because he usually dines with the prison warden!' guffawed Ratnani as he slapped the warden's back jovially.

The prison doctor stood quietly outside the curtain to the cubicle, listening to the conversation, clutching a small syringe that was ready and waiting to be used on the patient inside. He knew what he had to do.

No sooner had the cubicle emptied out, the prison doctor moved in. Saini had nodded off, possibly courting his demons once again. The doctor held up the syringe to the light and checked the quantity of fluid inside it. He pressed the plunger to bring a few drops of the liquid to the tip of the needle before stabbing the needle into Saini's thigh. Epinephrine was a commonly used drug for handling emergency allergies. More commonly known as adrenaline, it was also capable of accelerating one's heart rate. It could be fatal if administered in the wrong dose. But this was just the perfect dose—sufficient to cause the symptoms of a heart attack without actually causing one.

*'He's alive. I felt it in my gut and now I know for sure,'
said Kansa to the demon Putana. 'Go trace him to
Gokul and finish him off once and for all,' he instructed.
The demonic witch, Putana, transformed herself into
a beautiful woman and reached my foster-parents'
home. She told my mother Yashoda that she was the
wife of a pious Brahmin and wished to breastfeed me
in order to bestow longevity upon me. My innocent
foster-mother placed me in Putana's lap blissfully
unaware that the milk being fed to me was poisoned.
But I—an incarnation of Vishnu—know everything. I
bit Putana hard and sucked out her praana from her
breast, causing her to die instantly. Upon her death she
switched back into her original demon's form while I
continued playing carelessly in her lap.*

The private turboprop aircraft to Jamnagar made Saini
and Priya feel like they were travelling in a bullock cart
on a potholed road even though the distance from Jaipur
to Jamnagar was just a little under four hundred nautical
miles.

The Beechcraft King Air C90 was a four-seater that
shuddered as it took off, its PT6A-20A engines struggling
to lift four thousand kilos of weight. The pilot gave their
ID cards a cursory once-over and then left them alone.

'Let's hope that Bhojaraj is willing to back up your story. One can only hope that Varshney also shared your name with Bhojaraj when he spoke with him,' said Priya to Saini, as the aircraft reached cruising altitude.

'I see no reason why Bhojaraj shouldn't help. His archaeological undersea expeditions off the Dwarka coast are all about proving that the great city described in the *Mahabharata* did exist. It is his hypothesis that if Dwarka existed, Krishna must also have existed. Varshney's discovery of identical seals at Kalibangan, Kurukshetra and Mathura take the hypothesis one step further—that both Krishna and his beloved golden city of Dwarka would have been part of an evolved settlement, the Sarasvati civilisation,' explained Saini, the professor in him emerging once again.

'But is our final destination of modern Dwarka the same one as the mythical city built by Krishna?' asked Priya.

'Oh no! Modern Dwarka is simply a municipality of Jamnagar district in Gujarat. Krishna's city was called by the Sanskrit name of *Dwarawati—the city of many doors.* It's possible that the legendary city of Krishna may exist close by but it's certainly not visible in modern Dwarka, which is like any Indian city, helplessly attempting to cope with the usual problems of overcrowding, pollution and traffic. The common belief among local residents is that Krishna's city was submerged six times and rebuilt on each occasion, hence modern Dwarka is supposedly the seventh incarnation of the original,' explained Saini.

'But Krishna was born in Mathura—a city that lies over a thousand kilometres north-east of Dwarka. Why did Krishna travel this incredible distance to establish a city?' asked Priya, pointing out the two cities on an airline route map that she had found in the seat pocket.

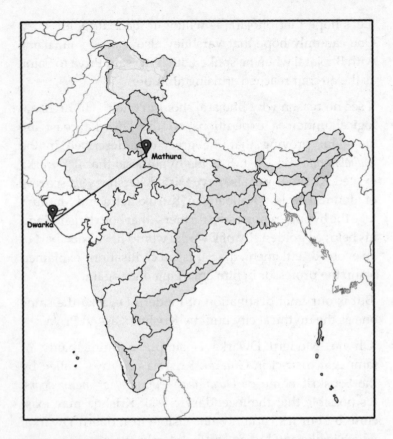

Saini thought for a moment about how he should frame his reply. 'Well, as you know, the *Mahabharata* recounts the fact that Krishna killed his maternal uncle and the evil ruler of Mathura—Kansa. He then installed Kansa's father—Ugrasena—as chief of Mathura. Krishna was a Yadava and his clan was quite possibly the first democratic society ever. They were a federation of eighteen tribes and each tribe had their own chieftain—like Ugrasena of Mathura—but all of them jointly elected one single Yadava leader as their supreme governor. Krishna was the elected governor of his time and was thus the de facto ruler of all eighteen clans—without the title of king,' he said.

'Precisely. So why shift a thousand kilometres?' asked Priya.

'Jarasandha—Kansa's father-in-law who was the powerful ruler of Magadha—tried to avenge Kansa's slaying and attacked Mathura eighteen times. He failed to capture it, owing to the defensive tactics employed by Krishna and his brother Balarama, but on the final occasion Krishna realised that he would have to make a strategic withdrawal if the Yadava tribes were to make any material progress at all. Their lives and material resources were being entirely expended on defending Mathura,' said Saini. 'It was a conscious decision to shift his capital to Dwarka, which was over a thousand kilometres south-west of Mathura and thus out of reach of Jarasandha's army. It was a decision that would result in Krishna being branded *Ranchor*—the one who leaves the battlefield—forever. Even today, people in Gujarat refer to Krishna as Ranchor.'

Priya noticed that Saini was scribbling notes as he spoke. Curious, she looked at the yellow notepad that Saini was writing on.

Krishna's departure—Revati—26 Sep, 3067 BC

Krishna's arrival in Hastinapur—Bharani—28 Sep, 3067 BCE

Solar eclipse—Jyeshtha Amavasya—14 Oct 3067 BCE

Full moon lunar eclipse—Krittika—29 Sep, 3067 BCE

Mahabharata starts—Saturn in Rohini, Jupiter in Revati—22 Nov 3067 BCE

Winter solstice—13 Jan 3066 BCE

Bhishma's death—Magha shukla ashtami—17 Jan 3066 BCE

Balarama pilgrimage on Sarasvati begins—Pushya day—1 Nov 3067 BCE

Balarama returns from pilgrimage—Sravana day—12 Dec 3067 BCE

Ghatotkacha is killed—Moon Rise at 2 am—8 Dec 3067 BCE

'What in heaven's name are these dates?' she asked.

Saini smiled. These are dates derived from the planetary calculations that I was presenting to the class the other day. I would like to give these to Dr Bhojaraj and see whether his archaeological finds are in sync with them.

Below them was a vast expanse of water. They were crossing the Gulf of Kutch. A few moments later they saw an extra-long jetty protruding into the waters. The pilot's voice crackled over the PA system: 'What you see down below is the Reliance Jamnagar Marine Terminal. The ship moorings are located fifteen kilometres away from the coast. The moorings are for importing crude oil and also for exporting diesel and gasoline. Hold on, you'll be able to see the world's largest oil refinery in Jamnagar as we begin our descent…'

The pilot continued intoning as their aircraft crossed the Gulf of Kutch, flew over Reliance's mammoth refinery and began its descent into Jamnagar airport just as the sun was also setting.

With Putana dead, Kansa's counsellors presented him with another option. The typhoon demon, Trinavarta, was despatched to Gokul to kill me. Seeing me playing alone in the courtyard, Trinavarta lifted me off the ground and soared high into the clouds. Nanda and Yashoda ran after me, aghast at the sight of their beloved child being carried away by a typhoon. A struggle ensued in which I was able to strangle the wind out of Trinavarta. Depleted of all his energy, Trinavarta was compelled to drop me back on earth and into the waiting arms of my adoptive parents.

Dr Nikhil Bhojaraj's assistant was waiting. A young Tamil man in his thirties, he received them at Jamnagar airport with a cheery 'Welcome to Gujarat.' Vigorously shaking Saini's hand, he said, 'Dr Bhojaraj has asked me to take you to Dwarka where you are to spend the night at a hotel. Tomorrow morning, a launch will take you to our team's exploration ship which is anchored around nine kilometres off the coast.' Their car headed directly for Dwarka, a distance of over a hundred and thirty-seven kilometres from Jamnagar. Once inside the car, Priya noticed that Saini was attempting to keep his excitement in check. He kept referring to his notes and also jotted down further remarks at the margins.

Saini was convinced. All his evidence pointed to the great war having taken place five thousand years ago. He knew it in his gut. Even though he was a hunted man who was on the run consequent to a prison break, the history professor in him was excited that he would soon meet Dr Bhojaraj and see the ancient objects that his team had discovered off the coast of modern Dwarka city. While he prayed that Bhojaraj's story would get him off the hook with Inspector Radhika Singh, he was also hoping that Bhojaraj's finds would corroborate his own theories about the Mahabharata war and the historicity of Krishna.

Priya looked out of her car window only to see the usual mess that greeted visitors to most growing Indian cities—potholed roads, bullock carts jostling for space with smoke-spewing trucks, beggars, tea vendors, stray dogs, and hapless policemen who could not possibly control any of the chaos surrounding them.

Priya spoke up. 'I was told that Krishna had asked the most famous architect of his times—Vishwakarma —to build Dwarka for him. Judging by what I see outside, Vishwakarma didn't do a very good job!'

The young Tamil man smiled. 'That's a funny thought, ma'am. Yes, it's true that Vishwakarma built the city on the submerged remains of a previous empire, *Kushthasthali*. Massive expanses of land were reclaimed from the sea in order to achieve this. The fabulously beautiful city of Dwarka that emerged in Gujarat was a city of palaces, gardens, lakes, temples, sculptures, and unimaginable wealth.'

'So you believe that Krishna's Dwarka does exist?' asked Saini.

'Oh, absolutely! Until quite recently, most historians had viewed the legendary Dwarka of Krishna as a mythical city but for many explorers like Dr Bhojaraj, Dwarka has always existed. Dr Bhojaraj had been part of the famous archaeologist S R Rao's expedition team in the Eighties when they began diving off the coast of Gujarat to search for the legendary Dwarka. The team soon discovered underwater stone walls and six layers of ruins—proof of what was written in the ancient texts that the city had been built upon previous cities. They located an ancient harbour, seals with animal motifs, Vishnu idols and even massive triangular stone anchors—indicative of the flourishing maritime trade of Dwarka,' recounted the enthusiastic assistant.

'Where exactly were the explorations carried out?' asked Saini, his adrenaline pumping as they approached Dwarka. Bhojaraj's assistant took out his iPad and pulled up a map of Dwarka on the screen and pointing to it said, 'The Archaeological Survey of India and the National Institute of Oceanography initially discovered a submerged ruin just off the present-day city of Dwarka at a depth of fifteen to twenty metres below sea-level. They thought that they had discovered Krishna's Dwarka.'

'So what was the problem?' asked Saini.

'The problem was that the dates of our finds did not match yours. Our team consisted of expert underwater explorers, trained diver-photographers and archaeologists. We combined geophysical surveys with echo-sounders, mud-penetrators, sub-bottom profilers and underwater metal detectors and carried out twelve marine archaeological expeditions. The antiquities recovered were sent to the Physical Research Laboratory for dating. Using thermo-luminescence and carbon dating, we found that the artefacts belonged to a period around three thousand seven hundred years ago.'

'But that's impossible! The astronomical data from the *Mahabharata* tells us that the war must have happened around five thousand years ago. This is validated by the Greek accounts too!' exclaimed Saini.

'Precisely. So the underwater find just off the coast of the modern-day town of Dwarka could not be Krishna's Dwarka because the articles discovered are around thirteen hundred years too late. But Dr Bhojaraj has now proposed an incredibly simple theory that should help pinpoint the real Dwarka,' said the assistant.

'And what is that?' asked Saini.

'It has much to do with climate change—in this case the creation and destruction of the ice age,' said the assistant, drawing Saini's attention to a new set of maps that he had brought up on his iPad. On it were two outlines of the Indian peninsular coastline. The first one showed what the landmass of the Indian subcontinent would have looked like several thousand years previously, whereas the second showed the same landmass in the present day.

Indian peninsula: 21,000 years ago

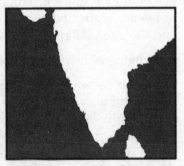

Indian peninsula: Present day

'Consider what happens during an ice age,' began Bhojaraj's assistant. 'The temperature of the earth's surface and atmosphere decline substantially. This drop results in accumulation of glacial ice. The most recent ice age in our history began around a hundred and ten thousand years ago, peaked twenty thousand years ago, and concluded around ten thousand years ago. Thereafter glaciers began to melt and released massive quantities of water into the oceans. Obviously, sea levels began to rise. The rise in the world's average sea level has been around one hundred and thirty meters over the last eighteen thousand years. The effect was the inundation of almost a quarter of a million square kilometres of land along the west coast of India!'

Saini digested the information and hesitantly asked, 'So the real Dwarka was not the submerged city that you discovered off the western coast of India?'

The young Tamil assistant looked at Saini squarely and confidently answered, 'Well, yes, it was, but it was a Dwarka of a later age. The coast of India was several miles further out into the sea during Krishna's times. If we continue our explorations outwards along the ocean floor we will find older remains. Dwarka is a continuum—a city that was built and rebuilt seven times. The most recent reconstruction is modern-day Dwarka city but the oldest is out in the ocean, where rising sea levels have inundated it. We've estimated that it is nine kilometres along the seabed of the Gulf of Kutch at a depth of between twenty-five and forty metres!'

Lord Shiv was eager to see me in my human mani-
festation. He transformed himself into a sadhu and
came to Yashoda's house begging for alms. Mother
Yashoda took some food and money outside for him,
but he refused to accept any of it. He simply wanted
to see me. Worried about my safety after the recent
spate of events, my mother agreed to bring me outside
on the condition that the sadhu would promise to only
look, not touch. He agreed. She brought me out and
the sadhu fell to his knees when he saw me. He had
tears in his eyes as he beheld me in my human
manifestation. Shiv and Vishnu after all, are only two
sides of the same coin.

'And what proof do you have that the city that lies underwater is the same Dwarka that is described in the *Mahabharata*?' asked Saini.

'A cursory reading of the *Harivamsa* tells us that that land was reclaimed from the ocean in order to construct Dwarka,' said Bhojaraj's assistant. 'If you want I can show you a translation of the relevant *Harivamsa* passages on my iPad.'

Saini accepted the offer and the assistant pulled up a page that had the original Sanskrit text along with English translations underneath. The text described how Dwarka was conceived and constructed:

Kalpiteyam maya bhoomih pashyadhvam devasadmavat namachasyahkritampuryaahkhyaatimyadupayaasyati. Krishna said, 'Look at this land selected by me. It is almost like heaven. I have also decided a name for this city by which it will become famous.'

Iyam dvaravati nama prithivyam nirmita maya bhavishyati puri ramya shakrasyev amaravati. 'This city made by me on earth, named Dwaravati, will be splendid like the Indra's city of Amaravati.'

Tasminneva tatah kaale shilpaachaaryo mahaa-matiha vishvakarma surashreshthaha krishnasya pramukhe sthitaha. At that very instant, the preceptor of architects, Vishwakarma, the best among the devas with great intellect, stood before Krishna.

Vishvakarmovaacha shakrena preshitah kshipram tava vishno dhriitavrata ki nkarah samanupraaptaha shaadhi maam kim karomite. Vishvakarma said, 'O Vishnu, the One who is firmly resolute! Sent here urgently by Indra, I have come here as your servant. Tell me, what do you want me to do?'

Tadiyam puh prakashaartham niveshya mayi suvrata matprabhaavanuru paishcha grihai-shcheyam saman-tatah. Krishna said, 'Construct a city for me, suitable to my splendour, along with houses showing your incredible skill.'

Mama sthaanamidam kaaryam yathaa vai tridive tathaa martyah pashyantu me lakshmim puryaa yadukulasya cha. 'Make my palace as though it were in heaven. Let men see my city as the seat of prosperity of the Yadava people.'

Sarvametatkarishyami yattvayabhihitam prabho puri tviyam janasyasya na paryaapta bhavishyati. Vishwakarma said, 'O Lord, I will do all that you wish but the area that you have marked will be insufficient as a city for your people.'

Yadichchetsaagaraha kimchidutkrashtumapi toyarat tatah svaayatalakshanya puri syatpurush-ottama. 'If the king of the oceans yields some space, O the best among men, then the city will be adequate and proper with all good signs.'

Evamuktastatah krishnah praageva kritanish-chayaha saagaram saritaam nathamuvacha vadatam varaha. Hearing what was said, Krishna, the best among speakers, who had already made up his mind, spoke to the ocean—the lord of rivers.

Samudra dasha cha dve cha yojanaani jalaashaye pratisamhriyatamaatma yadyasti mayi manyata. 'O Ocean! Please leave an area of ten and two yojanas within you, if you respect me.'

Avakaashe tvaya datte puriyam mamakam balam paryaaptavishaya ramya samagram visahishyati. 'With the area that would be yielded by you, this city will be sufficiently large to support my entire army.'

Tatah krishnasya vachanam shrutva nadanadipatih sa marutena yogena utsasarja jalashayam. Hearing Krishna's words, the ocean, along with the help of wind, left the area hitherto occupied by water.

Saini reached the end of the extract and looked up at the assistant who was smiling. 'In ancient texts, even science was conveyed in magical terms. A complex task of engineering—land reclamation—has been described as praying to the ocean to yield twelve yojanas of land,' he said.

'I am familiar with the *Harivamsa*,' said Saini. 'But how does this passage prove that the city that you are exploring under water is the same Dwarka that is described in it?'

'All the structures discovered by us thus far have shown that the foundations are not in the ground, they are on a bed of specially placed boulders,' said the assistant.

'So? What does that prove?' asked Priya.

'As far as I know, the traditional method of land reclamation involves throwing massive quantities of boulders into the sea. As the waters withdraw, one is then free to construct on the bed of rock that has thus been created. We now have scientific evidence that land reclamation was undertaken in ancient times!' exclaimed the assistant excitedly as Saini stared at him, dumbfounded.

A short while later, Bhojaraj's assistant dropped off Saini and Priya at their hotel, promising to take them to the exploration vessel the following morning. Thirty minutes later he noticed that an SMS had just come in on his mobile phone. It simply said, 'Will proceed with plan tomorrow.'

With Putana and Trinavarta dead, Kansa had exhausted his options, until he heard a voice one day which seemed to come from an invisible speaker. 'Who are you?' asked Kansa. 'I am Shakatasura,' replied the voice. 'I was very proud of my physical beauty and ended up being cursed into invisibility by a jealous sage, but I can be of service to you, O Lord.' Whereupon Shakatsura came to Gokul, and on finding me, pushed a cart with great force towards me. Unconcerned, I kicked the cart with such force that it flew up high into the air and shattered into thousands of tiny pieces.

The news of the ambulance crash had reached Rathore within fifteen minutes of the event. He had been on his way to play a game of squash at the Police Gymkhana when his phone rang. After listening to the report from his junior, he had pulled up alongside the pavement to get his thoughts in order.

He expected that all hell would break loose when he conveyed the information to Radhika Singh. He took a deep breath and pressed the speed dial on his mobile phone.

'Yes Rathore?' asked Singh, picking up the phone within the second ring.

'I have some bad news. They were shifting Saini to Fortis Escorts when the ambulance driver was ambushed. He's suffered concussion and has not regained consciousness yet. The prison doctor claims that he was overpowered by Saini and Priya—he has a bleeding nose and cut lip to prove it,' said Rathore.

'Where did the accident occur?' asked Singh. There was no hint of annoyance or irritation in her voice.

'Near the Clark's Amer Hotel,' replied Rathore.

'It's only a few minutes from Clark's to the airport. Check all flight manifests of aircraft out of Jaipur. Interrogate the general manager of the hotel. Get that rodent of a prison doctor to meet me immediately. This episode is far too conveniently contrived,' barked Singh, taking a few small pauses for her nicotine fix.

'I'll get on it immediately,' replied Rathore.

'And Rathore…' began Singh.

'Yes?'

'Have Saini's name included as a wanted fugitive on our website as well as that of the CBI. He's a famous academic—crank up the PR machine. Get the word out to a few news channels,' said Singh.

'I shall get on it immediately.'

'And one final thought Rathore…' said Singh.

'Yes?'

'Make sure that Sanjay Ratnani's movements are monitored. Track the cell phones of both him and his daughter—Priya. No point trying to track Saini's mobile because it is still with the custodial sergeant. The seal that was lying along with other evidence in the interrogation room has disappeared.

I instinctively know that Ratnani is behind all of this. Make sure that we know where he goes, whom he meets and what he does,' said Singh, stubbing out her cigarette and reaching for her prayer beads so that she could recite the name of Hari.

Now let me tell you a little about the birth of my true love, Radha. Chief Vrishabhanu was returning from his bath in the Yamuna when he saw a pond. In its centre was a stunning golden lotus containing a beautiful baby girl. A voice from the heavens said to him, 'She is Radha, destined to be the consort of the eighth incarnation of Vishnu. Take her home, O Lord.' Vrishabhanu and his wife were delighted to have Radha because they were childless. But Radha did not open her eyes for the first five years and her parents assumed that she was blind. In reality, she was simply awaiting my arrival. When I was born, Vrishabhanu invited my foster family to his home for lunch. The five-year-old Radha—who had kept her eyes closed till then—opened her eyes and the first image captured by her eyes was that of my face!

Ravi Mohan Saini climbed up the short ladder on the starboard side of Bhojaraj's research vessel, *R/V Radha*. Priya, who had climbed up first, offered her hand in mock chivalrous fashion to assist him. He gallantly declined.

The young Tamil assistant of Dr Nikhil Bhojaraj was still in the launch. 'Please proceed down the corridor to Dr Bhojaraj's lab. He's expecting you. I'll just settle the launch owner's bill and be right with you,' he shouted above the din of the boat's outboard motor. Saini nodded his assent and walked towards the laboratory, with Priya a couple of steps behind him. Luckily, direction signs marked all significant areas of the vessel. *Radha* had been built by Hyundai Heavy Industries—the largest shipbuilding yard in the world and the direction signs were typical of Korean attention to detail.

'Isn't it strange that there seems to be no one managing the boat?' asked Saini. 'I would have imagined that this vessel would have been buzzing with activity given that it is the focal point of Bhojaraj's undersea exploration.'

'It's possible that they're in a team meeting of some kind,' ventured Priya, as they reached the door to Bhojaraj's laboratory. Saini paused outside the door and knocked. It seemed the polite thing to do before entering someone's workspace.

There was no answer. Saini looked at Priya quizzically and knocked once more. When there was only silence, Saini caught hold of the door handle, pulled it downwards and swung open the door easily. The sight that greeted him made him want to jump off the boat and into the deep blue waters without a life jacket. He would have done so, had he known that the Tamil assistant was busy informing the authorities of a murder on board *Radha*.

'God almighty!' muttered Saini as he attempted to overcome his fear and revulsion. He tiptoed gingerly to the far wall on which a Sanskrit shloka had been written in blood. Just underneath the shloka lay the slumped body of Dr Nikhil Bhojaraj, his legs at right angles to his torso, surrounded by a pool of blood that had begun to coagulate. Stabbed into the sole of his left foot was a scalpel that bore the initials 'R.M.' On his forehead was the rubber-stamp imprint of a lotus flower. Almost identical in every respect to the murder scene photograph shown by Inspector Radhika

Singh to him in Jaipur. No, but the emblem on Varshney's forehead had been a wheel-like symbol, whereas this one was the image of a lotus.

'Do you know how to check a pulse?' asked Saini.

'I don't know how to do it on the neck,' said Priya. 'I can only check for it on his wrist. You will need to cut the duct tape away.''

Noticing a pair of specimen scissors on one of the lab counters, Saini grabbed it and quickly cut through the layers of tape, leaving yet more of his fingerprints by way of vital evidence for the police.

Priya knelt and took Bhojaraj's arm. She felt around his wrist until she found a vein just underneath his thumb. After a minute, she looked up at Saini who was standing over her and shook her head. 'No pulse. He's gone. Let me call someone for help,' said Priya, standing up and walking out of the laboratory.

'Anyone home?' she shouted within earshot of Saini. There was no response. The only sound was the steady hum of the power generator and the gentle lapping of waves against the hull of *Radha*. She tried the door to the utility room but it was jammed shut. She tried another door but it led to a storage closet. The next door led her to the common room where she immediately noticed seven members of Bhojaraj's team lying comatose in assorted positions—some seated on their chairs and a few having fallen to the ground. One of them had fallen asleep while eating his breakfast and the right side of his face lay in a plate of scrambled eggs.

She returned to Saini who seemed to be absorbed by the shloka on the wall. 'Do you have your mobile phone with you? I need to take a few pics,' he said.

'What? We need to get out of here. You've been set up! Bhojaraj's entire team has been sedated. If the police get here, they're bound to pin this on you!' she said.

'Do you have your mobile phone or not?' repeated Saini impatiently, continuing to stare at the shloka that had been written in blood on the wall. Priya wordlessly reached into the pocket of her Levis, pulled out her Samsung Galaxy Xcover and handed it over to Saini who had acquired an almost robotic demeanour. He pointed the phone at the wall and took a few photographs of the shloka and returned the phone to her.

'Are you done playing detective?' she asked acridly. 'I don't think you understand the seriousness of the situation you're in. Bhojaraj has been killed in exactly the same manner as Varshney was. In both instances, you were at the scene of the crime. None of the crew was awake, so there's no one to vouch for the fact that you reached here *after* he was killed. Even the assistant who brought us here on the schooner has disappeared, so we have no way of getting to shore except by manoeuvring this massive ship towards the coast, which seems impossible, given our limited expertise.'

Saini seemed oblivious to her comments. He was staring at a silver bracelet that lay on the floor. Bending down to examine it more closely he noticed that it bore someone's name. He screwed up his eyes to discern each letter. *Taarak Vakil. Could it be the killer's name?*

Saini seemed lost in thought. He carefully picked up the bracelet and placed it in his trouser pocket. Looking like he was engaged in Zen meditation, he began scanning the maps that had apparently been the object of Bhojaraj's attention earlier. 'Incredible! Hindu scriptures talk of the universe consisting of the *saptadweep*—seven islands— but all seven islands were right here in Dwarka itself... Dwarka was the world! This is pathbreaking research!' he exclaimed. He paused for a moment before he spoke again. 'Could you email yourself those photos I just took?' he asked Priya.

'Sure. The data network seems to be working fine,' she replied. She quickly attached and emailed the photos to her personal account. 'Why?' she asked, putting the phone away.

'Because the phone may be unusable once we jump into the sea,' said Saini.

No one called me Krishna in Gokul. I was lovingly called Kanhaiya or Kanha—the adolescent—by the village folk. My pranks and naughtiness were a frequent topic of discussion. My insatiable appetite for butter earned me the title of 'Maakhan Chor' in the village. I would creep into milkmaids' homes along with my friends, break open the butter pots and have a feast. When the women would run complaining to Yashoda, I would put on my most innocent face, shed a few tears, and claim that I was innocent. Invariably, Yashoda's heart would melt and she would be unable to scold me. Instead, she would pick me up and shower even more of her maternal love upon me.

The fisherman aboard the small fishing boat floating a short distance from the *Radha* was almost done for the day. His vessel was a rather basic and primitive craft but was ideally suited to the one function that its owner needed it to perform—fishing. This particular type of boat could not be sunk despite any number of tumbles. The boat was small, but due to the independently sealed buoyancy chambers beneath, the sea could safely wash over the deck without swamping it. A polyurethane-insulated compartment below his deck had been provided to protect his daily catch from the hot sun, preserving some of its freshness till reaching shore. In the event of an emergency, the fisherman could simply hold his catch in the fishing net, tie it to the craft and use the lightweight boat as a floatation device.

The fisherman who owned the boat—Iqbal Patel—had started his day at dawn and was rather pleased with his catch. He was humming a Bollywood tune as he headed for the shore—when he was shocked out of his reverie by two human heads bobbing in the water, followed by two pairs of hands reaching out to grasp the edge of his boat.

Having convinced himself that the two heads and four hands were not parts of a mutated sea monster, Iqbal cleared his throat and spoke. *'Tamme kaun chho?'* he asked in Gujarati, a tad nervous that the individuals asking for help could very well be Pakistani spies. Neither Saini nor Priya spoke his native tongue, so they explained to him in Hindi that they needed his help as their own boat had developed a technical snag some distance out to sea. Iqbal suspiciously helped them into his tiny craft. As Saini and Priya sat down in exhaustion, Iqbal, scrutinised them suspiciously.

Fishing off the coast of Gujarat was an inherently risky enterprise. Both Indian and Pakistani naval vessels operated in these waters and it was not uncommon for innocent fishermen to be arrested by opposite sides for having strayed across international boundaries. Iqbal was a Koli—a member of a fishing tribe. The word *koli* meant *spider* or alternatively, one who could weave a web-like fishing net. Most Kolis were Hindus but several of them had been converted to Islam during the Mughal period. Many of them had retained their old Hindu surnames even after conversion—hence the Patel in Iqbal's name.

There was an uncomfortable silence between Iqbal and his uninvited guests. Countless questions were racing through his mind. *Who were these two? What had really happened to their boat? Would he be questioned by the local police for assisting them? Were they Indian or Pakistani nationals? What had they been doing so far out at sea? Was he obliged to report them when they reached land?*

Perceiving that their host was not entirely convinced by their explanation, Saini tried thinking of how they could make an ally out of Iqbal. 'Is your mobile phone still in the pocket of your jeans?' he asked Priya.

'Yes,' she replied. 'I don't know whether it's working, though. I vaguely remember being told that this model was waterproof—let's see…'

'If it's working, I want you to gift it to our host,' said Saini.

'It's our only means of communication…' began Priya.

'Buy another basic phone with a prepaid SIM card when we reach the city. GPS satellites and the network providers are probably tracking your phone on the instructions of the cops. Every step that we take is being followed by Radhika Singh and Rathore —besides the others who want to set us up,' warned Saini.

Priya nodded in understanding. She quickly punched in a sequence of letters, numbers and characters into her phone. 'What are you doing?' asked Saini.

'Punching in the code for a factory reset. I don't want any of my past messages to be accessible to others. Should I chuck the SIM card and give him just the phone?' she asked.

'No. Give it to him with the SIM card intact,' said Saini emphatically.

'Why?' asked Priya.

'Let Radhika Singh and Rathore keep looking for us in the Arabian Sea for a few days,' said Saini with a broad grin on his face, as Priya offered her phone as a keepsake to the grateful Koli fisherman, who was also now smiling.

Sometimes my elder brother Balarama and I would go into the cowshed and catch a calf by its tail. The little animal would end up dragging us around in the mud and we would soon be covered in it. Yashoda never attempted to spank us for such naughtiness. Once, when I had stolen butter for the umpteenth time, Yashoda tried tying me to a huge grinding mortar. I kept using my powers to shorten the rope thus making it impossible for her to tie me. I relented when I saw tears of helplessness in her eyes. Taking pity on her, I allowed the rope to elongate so that she could successfully tie me up. I then continued walking with the mortar tied to my back. As I passed between two Arjuna trees, the mortar got wedged between the trunks, and the two mighty trees fell—and turned into demigods. I thus liberated them from Sage Narada's curse that they would have to spend a hundred years as trees due to their arrogance.

The message from the Special Crimes Division of the Central Bureau of Investigation—or the CBI—was simple. A murder had occurred in Gujarat. The modus operandi was strikingly similar to the one being investigated by the Rajasthan Police. It was time to tackle the crime centrally, given the fact that the perpetrator—or perpetrators—had conceivably crossed state borders.

Radhika Singh read the message a second time slowly, chewing the last of her almonds as she went through it. This was not a good development. Controlled by the Department of Personnel and Training in the Ministry of Personnel, the CBI usually took directions from its political masters and the result was a plethora of unsolved cases, allegations of partisanship and insinuations of corruption. Even though the CBI was the official Interpol unit for India, it was hardly an exemplary division in the world of policing.

Radhika read through the details that had been shared by the Indian Coast Guard. Bhojaraj's research ship, *Radha*, had been discovered floating more than thirteen nautical miles off the Dwarka shoreline by a Chetak helicopter belonging to the Indian Coast Guard Air Station at Daman. It had been sent there after an anonymous tip-off from a man with a mild Tamil accent. The tip-off had corroborated a call received by the police control room in response to the television bulletins. The chopper had alerted the *ICGS Vishwast*, a Coast Guard vessel patrolling the Gujarat coast, and armed personnel from the *Vishwast* had boarded *Radha* after repeated attempts to establish radio contact had failed.

The comatose crew had been shifted to the naval hospital. Taking into fact that the ship had also been the scene of a ghastly crime, and given that the ship had been outside the territorial waters of India, the Coast Guard had informed the CBI instead of the Gujarat Police. The matter had been brought to the attention of one of the Special Directors of the CBI—Sunil Garg—who had noticed the glaring similarities between the two cases.

Radhika preferred that the case remain entirely with her. Taking a deep breath, she picked up her desk phone and called Sunil Garg. She would need to play her cards carefully—very carefully indeed. She smiled as she waited for him to pick up the phone, her free hand rotating her prayer beads. When Radhika Singh smiled, which was a rare occurrence, it usually meant that she had already won the game.

One day my cowherd friends and I were playing when my friends chanced upon what they thought was a mountain cave. But the cave was actually the mouth of the demon Aghasura—an eight-mile-long snake. I was very worried when my friends rushed in because I knew that it was no cave. I followed them inside in order to save their lives as also to finish off Aghasura once and for all. The serpent swallowed me whole, but once I was inside Aghasura's body, I allowed myself to grow to mammoth proportions until I ended up choking the snake demon to death.

The research vessel bore the name *R/V Radha* for a specific reason. The chief scientist on board, Dr Nikhil Bhojaraj, had decided that it was only appropriate and befitting that *Radha* should be the floating vessel designated to search for Krishna's fabled city! She was much more than a floating vessel, though. She was a technologically advanced mobile research station capable of transporting scientists, divers, archaeologists, mariners, their submersibles and their equipment with a high degree of safety and comfort. She had been customised to carry state-of-the art electronics, analytical computers, and navigational and communications systems to collect and decipher information that was gathered from the exploration missions that the team undertook. Seventy feet in length, weighing in at seventy-seven tons and boasting a cruising speed of sixteen knots, *Radha* was constructed almost entirely from fiberglass. The vessel had berthing for eight scientists and two crew members.

Radha had a well-designed deck plan. The deck aft of the ship included a substantial work area, a steering station to manoeuvre the vessel, and a dive platform at water level to provide divers and sub-mersibles easy and safe access to the water. Hydraulic connections, an A-frame, a winch and a mixing station for Nitrox—a special gas mixture used in technical diving—provided additional capabilities for scientific research projects. To assess latitude and longitude, the standard navigational charts of the *Radha* were augmented by a DGPS or Digital Geographic Positioning System.

Radha also contained a substantial research laboratory on board. The main laboratory was a large, open-space, general-purpose lab directly accessible from the main deck whereas the bio-analytical lab was isolated from the rest of the area to allow for sensitive equipment and temperature control. Deeper inside was a wet lab that allowed scientists to collect and analyse seawater samples in an uncontaminated, watertight environment.

Inside the laboratory of *Radha*, Nikhil Bhojaraj had been looking at the printouts while awaiting his visitors—Saini and Priya. He smiled to himself. It was a smile of quiet satisfaction from the realisation that his goal was near. The laboratory was devoid of human activity excepting his own. Most of his team members were in the common room having breakfast. The hum of the vessel's air-conditioning system provided a comforting background score to the whirring of his brain. He looked at the computer-generated map in front of him.

The present-day satellite map of modern Dwarka city was on the printout. If one saw this particular printout, it seemed as though most of Dwarka city was part of the mainland with the exception of Bet Dwarka island. However, when one saw the territory via high-resolution terrain data capture using Light Detection and Ranging—LiDAR technology—it became evident that Dwarka would have been a cluster of islands rather than a single homogenous land mass connected to the mainland. It would have been a city-state extending up to the island of *Shankhodhara* in the north and *Okhamadhi* in the south.

It also explained the hundreds of stone anchors that had been discovered by the team. It was evident that the people of Dwarka would have been seafarers and that vast ships would have docked here. The island layout of the city-state of Dwarka had disappeared in modern times but the ancient layout would have justified the Sanskrit name of Dwarawati—the city of many doors. *Krishna and his people were not referring to the doors of houses and palaces when they gave their city a name. They were alluding to the vast number of sea openings by which ships could enter Dwarka!*

The *Mahabharata* recounted that flags were to be seen fluttering along the walls of Dwarka. Bhojaraj had even discovered the heavy stone bases of flag posts along the perimeter walls. Of course, his crowning moment had been the discovery of the seal bearing the motif of a three-headed animal representing the bull, unicorn and goat which he had proudly shared with Varshney.

He was expecting his visitors soon. Anil Varshney had mentioned Ravi Mohan Saini's name to him when they had last met and Bhojaraj knew that Varshney and Saini had been school chums. He was puzzled to have received a call from a woman calling herself Priya Ratnani requesting for an appointment as well as an airport pick-up from

Jamnagar. Damn academics! Always had airs of superiority and couldn't do anything by themselves.

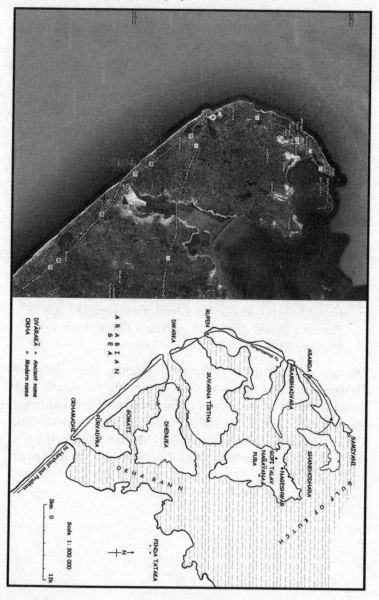

He heard the sound of a motorboat approaching. It would be Saini and Priya being brought over by his assistant. He stood up and stretched himself. A few feet away was a wall upon which a forty-two inch LCD was tuned into NDTV news on mute. Bhojaraj glanced at the screen for barely a second when he saw the photo along with a text box next to it. The photo was a mug shot taken of Ravi Mohan Saini when he was checked in at Jaipur Central Jail. Bhojaraj would never have identified the man in the photo by name had it not been for the running ticker underneath that kept scrolling the words 'Murder suspect Ravi Mohan Saini escapes from Jaipur jail. Contact 0141-2612589 if you have any information.' Next to Saini's photo was a text panel that contained information about Saini so that the public could identify him:

Name: Ravi Mohan Saini. Aliases: None. Case number: 1883767. Sex: Male. Nationality: Indian. Community: Punjabi. Age: 45 years 4 months. Height: 5' 11" . Weight: 78 kgs. Eyes: Blackish- brown. Hair: Black. Distinguishing marks: Black birthmark on right ankle. Warrant issued: Jaipur Magistrate's Office. Warrant number: RJ/S/12/34176. Charge: Murder.

The man who wanted to see him that morning was a fugitive! Bhojaraj quickly accessed Google on his notebook and typed in 'Ravi Mohan Saini'. The first entry that came up was a news item from the *Hindustan Times*, New Delhi. The brief story explained that Ravi Mohan Saini had been charged for the murder of Anil Varshney and that he was on the run having broken out from Jaipur's Central Jail. *Anil Varshney was dead!*

All forms of life in the Yamuna had begun to die because a ten-hooded ocean serpent called Kalia had been releasing venom into the waters. With the intention of putting an end to the Kalia menace, I jumped into the Yamuna on the pretext of bringing out a ball that had fallen in. After a struggle with Kalia, I emerged from the depths of the water dancing upon the hood of Kalia. 'Please spare him, O Lord,' pleaded Kalia's wives, and in an act of divine magnanimity, I spared Kalia's life but asked him to leave the Yamuna immediately so that life in the river could prosper once again.

Bhojaraj stood frozen to the floor for a moment. He felt numb—almost paralysed by shock and fear. His friend, Varshney, was dead and the very person accused of murdering him was on his way over to meet him. What was the purpose of such a visit? To kill him too? Having deliberated the issue for a couple of minutes, he walked over to the phone that hung by the entrance door of the lab, picked it up and dialled the telephone number that was scrolling on the screen.

The phone was answered by Rathore's team within three rings. 'Hello? Is that the police control room? Yes? My name is Nikhil Bhojaraj and I am about to be paid a visit by Ravi Mohan Saini...'

The door was suddenly flung open and the punch that caught him on his nose and mouth was delivered with the force of a sledgehammer, cutting off his sentence midway. He fell backwards on the floor, and passed out. The frogman stepped into the laboratory, quickly locked the door behind him and hung up the phone that was dangling from its cord. At the other end he had heard the police operator saying, 'Hello? Sir, could you please give us your exact...'

He was wearing a scuba suit, swimming fins, and a facemask. He had scuba tanks strapped to his back and around his waist was a watertight rubber bag. Taarak Vakil pulled off his facemask and unzipped his rubber bag.

He took out the duct tape from his bag, efficiently bound Bhojaraj's hands behind his back and then proceeded to gag him with a chloroform-soaked wad of gauze and some more of the duct tape. Dragging him to the wall furthest from the door, he propped up Bhojaraj so that his legs were stretched out on the lab's floor but his back remained upright against the wall.

He swiftly took off Bhojaraj's left shoe and within the blink of an eye had plunged another one of his Swann-Morton scalpels with the custom-engraved initials into his victim's foot. As blood began to flow, he dipped his paintbrush into the pool of red and carefully reproduced the shloka behind Bhojaraj's head.

Mleccha-nivaha-nidhane kalayasi karavalam
dhumaketum iva kim api karalam
kesava dhrita-kalki-sarira jaya jagadisa hare.

Taarak hurriedly reached into his waist bag, took out another little self-inking rubber stamp and positioned it on Bhojaraj's forehead. The image that resulted was a small, red lotus blossom enclosed within a circle.

He knew that it was a matter of minutes before Saini arrived. In his haste, he did not notice that the silver bracelet that he usually wore on his right wrist had slipped out of his waist bag—into which it had been placed for his underwater sojourn—and now lay on the floor, the chain lying in a serpentine coil.

The first seal had been discovered by him at Varshney's home. The second seal had been discovered by the police at Saini's residence. He efficiently scanned the laboratory for the third and fourth seals that were unaccounted for. All that he could find were printouts, charts and maps. Taarak was uninterested in the hundreds of specimens that Bhojaraj's team had discovered under the coastal waters of Dwarka. All that he wanted was the two very specific seals that remained unaccounted for.

Concluding that the seals were not on board, he tiptoed to the lab entrance and placed his ears to the door in order to determine whether anyone was outside. Satisfied that there was no one in the passage, he unlocked the door, opened it and gingerly stepped out. He crossed a short corridor, reached the open deck and turned right in the direction of the crew's common room where they all seemed to be having breakfast. He looked around to see where the utilities room was located. He figured that it would probably be close to the common room, based on the technical drawings that he had reviewed the previous day. He was right. Having located the utilities room from where power, air-conditioning, and filtered water were supplied to the rest of the vessel, Taarak began unstrapping the second cylinder from his back.

Taarak's scuba-diving equipment included the usual two cylinders on his back. In ordinary scuba gear, a manifold valve was normally used to connect the two cylinders, thus providing a greater amount of air to breathe for longer dive times. Oddly enough, in Taarak's rig, only one of the cylinders on his back was connected to his breathing hose.

He quickly took off the second unconnected cylinder from his back and coupled it with the air intake valve of the air-conditioning plant. The cylinder contained trimethyl phentanylum, an extremely powerful opioid, significantly more potent than morphine. Within sixty seconds, everyone on board would be fast asleep.

Heading over to the deck again, towards the starboard, Taarak could see a diesel fume-spewing launch—probably carrying Saini and Priya—making its way towards the *Radha*. He crouched low and headed to the port side of the vessel. He put on his facemask and took the primary mouthpiece of the remaining cylinder's breathing hose into his mouth. Positioning himself at the edge of the vessel, he stepped off the *Radha* with a large stride, holding his hand over the mask and his arms over the loose diving gear. Taarak Vakil had been on board for less than six minutes.

His planning, though, had commenced a couple of days earlier. Just as Saini and Priya's private charter flight had been descending into Jamnagar, a small speck could be observed in the Gulf of Kutch. It was a boat—a small but powerful Stingray 225SX that had started its journey from the Gateway of India in Mumbai and was floating a few hundred metres away from the Dwarka shoreline. On board, in splendid isolation, was a lone occupant who was listening to his favourite shloka while polishing a scalpel.

Taarak Vakil's iPhone had started ringing a couple of hours later. His ringtone was a snappy rendition of the chant that he scribbled on walls and heard in his car. He waited for the shloka to be rendered in its entirety before taking the call. One could not allow a sacred chant to be cut off midway. It was disrespectful.

'Namaskar, Mataji,' said Taarak in a hushed voice.

'Namaskar. Saini has reached Dwarka. He is scheduled to meet Bhojaraj tomorrow morning,' said the mysterious voice. 'You took one seal from Varshney's home while another was discovered by the police in Saini's home. The third and fourth could be with any of Varshney's three friends—Bhojaraj, Kurkude or Chhedi.'

'I see. What are my instructions?' asked Taarak.

'You already have an insider in Bhojaraj's crew. He will do as you ask. Message him that you are moving ahead with the plan. He will send you the technical drawings of the exploration ship.'

'Your word is my command,' said Taarak putting down the book that he had been reading. He revved up the engine of his Stingray 225SX. He needed to get his scuba gear ready.

He had been reading Homer's *Iliad*. He placed his bookmark at the point where the wise old Nestor had been telling the warrior Diomed, 'Life and death are balanced as it were on the edge of a razor. Go then, for you are younger than I...'

Tired of the perennial threats to my life, my foster-father—Nanda—decided that it was safer for the family to leave Gokul. The village elders pleaded with their chief, but he was determined. 'The east of the Yamuna is unsafe for Krishna. I shall shift my family to Vrindavan. If you so wish, you may come with me,' he said to his people. The next day, Nanda loaded up his bullock carts and, along with Yashoda, Rohini, Balarama and me, began the trek towards Vrindavan. It was only then that he noticed that the entire village of Gokul was also moving along with him. Apparently, the villagers couldn't bear the thought of being without me! It was a world of intense friendships and my closest friend was Sudama who later studied with me at the gurukul.

'We need to rethink our strategy,' said Saini, sipping the hot chai gratefully. They were holed up inside a small room of a run-down hotel in Porbandar—the birthplace of Mahtama Gandhi. It was coincidental that Porbandar had also been the final home of Krishna's childhood friend—Sudama.

Having successfully jumped ship and taken a free boat trip back to Dwarka with the Koli fisherman, Saini had decided that it was too risky for them to go back to the Dwarka hotel in which they had spent the previous night. In fact, it was only a matter of time before every law enforcement agency in the country would be on the lookout for a psychotic serial-killing professor assisted by his slavishly obedient doctoral student.

They had hitched a ride on a truck headed to Porbandar— around ninety kilometres from Dwarka. Prior to boarding the truck, Saini had tried to use his ATM card to withdraw cash in Dwarka, knowing full well that his usage would be tracked. They didn't have an alternative, though. They needed cash to survive the next few days. Unfortunately, the longish soak in the Arabian Sea had made the ATM card as well as their credit cards unusable.

Saini had counted the wet currency that remained between the two of them. It was barely five thousand rupees. 'My father has solicitor friends in Ahmedabad and Baroda. I'm sure that if I were to talk to him, he could get someone to deliver cash to us in Porbandar,' suggested Priya. They then went to a garments shop from where they purchased some dry clothes and simple walking shoes. After that they headed to the closest convenience store from where they purchased the cheapest Nokia mobile phone with a prepaid SIM using the aliases provided by the Jaipur doctor.

Back at the hotel, Priya had phoned Sanjay Ratnani. 'Dad? I need some help… ' she began. In a small control room in New Delhi, a flashing icon on a computer terminal indicated to the monitoring agent that a conversation worth listening to was in progress. Sanjay Ratnani was receiving a call on his mobile from a prepaid number that was unknown. The conversation was silently recorded on the hard disk of the computer while triangulation of locations began.

While Priya was talking to her father, Saini took out the silver bracelet that he had stolen from the murder scene and looked at it in the palm of his hand. He scanned each letter and satisfied himself. Yes, it did spell the name

Taarak Vakil. But who was Taarak Vakil? And if he were the killer of both Anil Varshney and Nikhil Bhojaraj, what was he after? He absent-mindedly wrote down the name on a piece of paper and began to jumble the letters. Playing word games was an old habit picked up from Varshney, the linguist. Saini's face turned white with fear when he saw the letters rearranged.

When jumbled up, the letters contained in the name Taarak Vakil now spelt out a name that every theologian in India would be familiar with. *Kalki avatar*—the tenth incarnation of Vishnu.

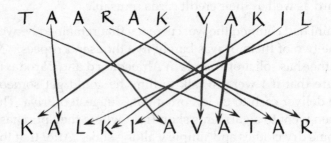

He gestured to Priya to end the conversation with her father quickly. As she hung up, he showed her the word jumble. Priya's face, too, drained of colour as soon as she saw it.

'But what is the connection between our murderer and the Kalki avatar?' asked Priya.

'Isn't it obvious? Our killer is someone who believes that *he* is the Kalki avatar! The murders are somehow connected to that belief!' declared Saini as Priya continued to silently wonder about possible next steps, given the circumstances.

Each year the residents of Vrindavan would pray to Lord Indra for rain. Upon our arrival in Vrindavan, I suggested to Nanda that we should worship Govardhan Hill, which provided us with nature's bounty, instead of praying to Indra. As soon as the villagers started performing rituals to appease Govardhan, Indra became jealous and sent a massive storm to uproot the houses and trees in Vrindavan. Everyone came running to me for protection. I immediately lifted Govardhan Hill so that everyone could take shelter underneath it. Duly humbled, Indra realised his error and was contrite.

'The Kalki avatar is supposed to be the tenth incarnation of Vishnu, isn't he?' asked Priya, pouring some more tea from the kettle into her glass. The Porbandar hotel may have been a dump but they served good tea.

'Yes, according to Hindu mythology, Vishnu had nine earlier avatars. The first was as *Matsya*—the fish. The second was *Kurma*—the tortoise. The third incarnation was as a boar—*Varaha*. Fourth, he was incarnated as *Narasimha*—the half-man, half-lion form. These were the incarnations that happened during Satyayuga,' explained Saini.

'Satyayuga was the first of the four yugas, right?' asked Priya even though this was material that was familiar to her. It was almost as though she wanted Saini to revisit the material step by step.

'Yes. There are supposed to be four stages that the world goes through as part of the cycle of yugas described in the Indian scriptures, the three previous ages being Satyayuga, Tretayuga and Dvaparayuga. We are currently in the fourth and final stage—Kaliyuga,' Saini reminded her obligingly.

'So, which incarnations of Vishnu appeared after Satyayuga?' asked Priya.

'Satyayuga was followed by Tretayuga. The fifth incarnation of Vishnu, *Vamana*—the dwarf, appeared during this Satyayuga. He was followed by a sixth avatar—that of *Parashurama*.'

'And when did the most famous incarnations—*Rama* and *Krishna*—appear?' persisted Priya.

'Rama, the king of Ayodhya, appeared as the seventh incarnation during Tretayuga,' continued Saini, patiently. 'The eighth avatar appeared during the third phase of the world—Dvaparyuga. Vishnu appeared as Krishna to teach the world about dharma. The ninth avatar of Vishnu was none other than the great Gautama Buddha,' concluded Saini.

'What happens during the fourth stage, Kaliyuga, the Dark Age of humanity?' asked Priya.

'*Kalki*—which literally means the destroyer of evil —is expected to appear towards the end of Kaliyuga, the age in which we live. He shall be the tenth avatar of Vishnu, and shall be sent to destroy evil and to purify the earth once more,' said Saini, feeling a chill travel up his own spine as he spoke those words.

'How would one recognise the Kalki avatar?' asked Priya.

'According to the *Kalki Purana*, the Kalki avatar will be born in a village called Sambhala...' began Saini.

Midway between Mumbai and Pune, Taarak turned off into a private road. The sign outside simply bore the name of the business 'Sambhala Stud Farm'.

'The Kalki avatar is the apocalyptic horseman. He is depicted as seated on his white stallion Deva Datta...' continued Saini.

His father had presented Taarak with Deedee when he was just fifteen. He would spend hours exercising, grooming, and feeding the horse. Deedee — DD — or Deva Datta.

'It is predicted that Vishnu will take birth as the Kalki avatar and become the son of Vishnuyasa... and his wife, Sumati.'

His father — Dr V Y Sharma — had started the business of breeding horses... 'Let the lad be, Sumati. If you love your children, you must let them sprout wings and fly,' Dr Sharma had said to his wife.

'The *Kalki Purana* says that the Kalki avatar has obtained the blessings of Lord Shiv and that Lord Shiv has presented him with a parrot — Shuka...'

'Morning Shuka,' he said solemnly to the parrot. 'Good morning, Master,' came the parrot's squawky trained reply. Pleased, his master changed the water and the birdseed inside the cage.

'... and a dazzling bright sword — Ratna Maru...'

Punching in a sequence of ten digits, he opened the vault, and noticed the brown leather tray inside that contained several identical gleaming Swann-Morton surgical scalpels — each bearing the initials 'R.M.' for Ratna Maru.

'Kalki is described as wearing golden armour with a large emblem of the sun in the centre of his chest plate...'

His upper torso was a veritable maze of tattoos—his muscular chest having turned blue from the intricate symbols that could not be individually discerned. However, at the centre of the various other images was a large blazing sun.

'The *Srimad Bhagavatam* says *atha tesham bhavishyanti manamsi vishadani vai, vasudevanga-ragati-punya-gandhanila-sprisham, paura-janapadanam vai hatesv akhila-dasyushu* Translated into English, this passage says that *displaying His unequalled effulgence and riding with great speed, He will kill, by the millions, imposters who have dared dress as kings,'* concluded Saini.

He looked at Priya. She was absolutely quiet. Saini thought that he had stunned her into silence.

'Did you take a printout of the photographs that I asked you to email to yourself from the ship?' asked Saini.

Priya nodded. 'Yes. There was an internet café not far from the hotel and I was able to access my email from there. Here they are,' she said, pushing some A4 size printouts on the coffee table towards him. Saini looked at the printout. He scrutinised the shloka written on the wall behind Bhojaraj's body. It was an ancient Sanskrit shloka:

> *Mleccha-nivaha-nidhane kalayasi karavalam*
> *dhumaketum iva kim api karalam*
> *kesava dhrita-kalki-sarira jaya jagadisa hare.*

He had read it before. It was the tenth verse of the *Sri Dasavatarastotra*, a passage that described the ten avatars of Vishnu. Translated into English, it read:

O Kesava! O Lord of the universe! O Lord Hari, who has assumed the form of Kalki avatar! All glory to You! You appear like a comet and carry a terrifying sword to bring about the annihilation of the wicked barbarian men at the end of the Kaliyuga!

'When I looked at the body of Bhojaraj, I noticed that the killer had left a symbol on his forehead—a lotus, I think.

And in the photos that Inspector Radhika Singh showed me of Anil Varshney's body, I think that the symbol stamped on his head was a chakra—a discus. Don't you see that all these symbols point to the same thing?' asked Saini rhetorically.

'What?' asked the still quiet Priya.

Saini got up from his chair and walked over to the peeling wall on which hung a calendar. It was the sort of calendar that bore images of Hindu gods and goddesses and was mass-produced for a few rupees each Diwali by every shopkeeper in town. He flipped through the calendar until he came across the month in which Vishnu had been featured. 'See this picture of Vishnu?' he asked, pointing to the image.

He pointed out the four arms of Vishnu and then said, 'Vishnu is always depicted as carrying four symbols in his four hands. The *Upanishads* describe Vishnu as saying:

In one hand, which represents the cohesive tendency, I hold the discus, shining like an infant sun, symbol of the mind.

In another hand, which represents the tendency towards liberation, I hold the lotus, symbol of the causal power of illusion, from which the universe rises.

In yet another hand, which represents the creative tendency, I hold the conch, symbol of the five basic elements.

In my last hand, which represents the notion of individual existence, is the mace, symbol of primeval knowledge.'

'So the murderer is leaving behind symbols of Vishnu at the scene of each murder?' asked Priya.

'Two murders and two symbols. We know that there are four symbols of Vishnu. It means that two more killings are yet to happen,' said Saini grimly.

Downstairs in the lobby of the Porbandar hotel, a sub-inspector from the Gujarat Police was showing photographs of Saini and Priya to the receptionist. The photograph had been sent by his colleague in Rajasthan—Sub-Inspector Rathore—based upon the tapping and triangulation of a cell phone conversation.

One day, Radha and her friends went to bathe in the river. They undressed, placed their clothes on the riverbank and began frolicking in the water. They did not observe me collecting their clothing and scampering up a tree. When the gopis came out of the river, they could not find their garments —until they heard me mocking them from above and telling them that I had their things in my possession. They begged and pleaded with me to return them but I did not oblige the ladies. I was having too much fun! As a last resort, Radha plunged into the water in anger. I immediately threw down the gopis' apparel and dived in after her only to realise that her anger had been contrived in order to get me to return the gopis' clothing and to join her in the water.

'Two more killings? Who will be killed?' asked Priya.

'Think about it. Anil Varshney had one of the seals—the one that he planned to return to Nikhil Bhojaraj. He was murdered and the seal stolen. The second seal was with me and I too would have been killed had it not been for the fact that I was arrested and the seal in my possession taken over as evidence by the police. The killer thought that Nikhil Bhojaraj had the third seal. He too was killed. I know that Anil was planning to send the third and fourth seals to Professor Rajaram Kurkude who has his research laboratories in Jodhpur and Devendra Chhedi—a life sciences researcher,' said Saini.

He paused. 'What this means is that the killer knows that there are four seals and he plans to go after the people who have them,' he blurted out.

'But what is so special about these seals?' asked Priya. 'What could be so significant that it causes someone to consider taking four lives?'

'I believe that the answer lies in Dwarka—or possibly in Somnath,' said Saini.

'Somnath?' asked Priya.

'Let's revisit what the *Mahabharata* tells us, shall we? According to the *Mahabharata*, the war of Kurukshetra ended with the destruction of the Kauravas—all one hundred sons of Dhritarashtra and Gandhari were killed. It is said that on the night before the passing away of Duryodhana, Krishna paid a condolence visit to Gandhari. Gandhari was grieving for her sons and in her grief she cursed Krishna for causing the utter destruction of the entire Kaurava lineage. She predicted that Krishna's own lineage would cease to exist after thirty-six years. As per legend, thirty-six years later, there was a massive flood and the seawater rushed in to claim the city of Dwarka. Krishna took his Yadava tribes by boat to higher ground—to a place called *Prabhas Patan*—around two hundred kilometres away. Do you know what Prabhas Patan is today known as?'

Priya nodded. 'Prabhas was the ancient name for Somnath,' she replied.

'Precisely. Once Krishna's Yadava clans—the Haihayas, Chedis, Vidarbhas, Satvatas, Andhakas, Kukuras, Bhojas, Vrishnis, Shainyas, Dasarhas, Madhus, Arbudas and others

—had reached the higher altitudes of Prabhas, they began celebrating and became intoxicated. This led to a brawl in which they killed one another. Krishna and his brother Balarama had to flee for their own lives into the jungles of Prabhas. Balarama gave up his life through yoga while Krishna sat under a tree in meditation. A hunter—Jara— saw Krishna's left foot moving, mistook it for the twitching ear of a deer and shot an arrow in its direction, wounding him fatally,' explained Saini.

He paused. 'You do see the connection, don't you?' he asked.

'You mean the fact that both the murders have been contrived by stabbing the victim in the left foot, almost like a re-enactment of Krishna's death?' asked Priya.

'Exactly!' exclaimed Saini. 'Whatever the murderer is after is possibly at Prabhas Patan—modern Somnath. But before we do anything else, we need to meet these two other scientists and warn them of the danger that lurks. We also need to find a way to get all the four seals together so that we may decipher them.'

'How? I do not have any contact information for either Professor Rajaram Kurkude or Devendra Chhedi,' said Priya.

'You haven't been keeping yourself updated on matters of science, dear Priya,' mocked Saini. 'Professor Rajaram Kurkude has been in the news for a major discovery.'

'What discovery?' asked Priya, mystified.

'A layer of radioactive ash was discovered by Professor Kurkude over a three-square-mile area, ten miles west of Jodhpur,' elaborated Saini. 'An incredibly high rate of birth defects and an even higher rate of cancer among the inhabitants had prompted the research project. The radiation levels were so strong that the local administration and the state and central governments jointly took the decision to cordon off the region. Kurkude's team has apparently unearthed an ancient city where they have found adequate proof of an atomic blast dating back thousands of years—anywhere between five thousand to twelve thousand years ago.'

Saini got up from his chair and paced the room. 'We must catch a train to Jodhpur so that we can get to Rajaram Kurkude,' he began.

Both Saini and Priya were stunned as their room door came crashing in and a group of armed policemen rushed in. Their guns were pointed at Saini and Priya. Their commanding officer shouted 'Raise your hands above your heads so that I can see them. Do as I say and no one gets hurt!'

25

Kansa kept up his efforts to have me killed for fifteen years but was unsuccessful. Finally, he sent his servant Akroora to invite me to a Dhanush Yajna—the ceremony held to worship the great bow of Shiv. Akroora was one of my loyal devotees and secretly divulged the nefarious intentions of Kansa to my foster-father. Balarama and I sat in Akroor's chariot but our way was blocked by the gopis who refused to let the chariot move. I got down and saw Radha standing in a corner looking forlorn. I told her, 'Don't worry, Radha. I shall soon return and make you my queen.' Radha looked at me and smiled with tears in her eyes. 'I know that will not be possible, Kanha,' she said to me. 'It was different when you were living the life of a cowherd. I am a simple country girl and would die in the confines of a palace. But promise me two things,' she said. 'Ask and they're yours,' I replied. 'You must always reside in my heart,' said Radha. 'And what is the second promise?' I asked. 'Let people know that the way to reach you is through me. Let our names be used together in perpetuity,' she said.

Both Saini and Priya had their hands locked in cuffs. They were unceremoniously loaded into a blue police van, which shuddered as the engine was cranked to life. Two policemen sat opposite the two fugitives on a long bench that mirrored the one that Saini and Priya were seated on.

A few minutes later, the door of the van opened once more and Saini gasped involuntarily. Inspector Radhika Singh, accompanied by Sub-Inspector Rathore, got inside the van. 'Get out!' barked Radhika Singh at the two constables who were seated opposite Saini and Priya. The hapless paan-chewing cops were happy to oblige. Radhika Singh's reputation for relentless discipline preceded her—even in Gujarat. Radhika Singh and Rathore sat down where the constables had been seated.

Radhika Singh appeared remarkably fresh, but Rathore looked bleary-eyed from the stress that he must have been subjected to after Saini's and Priya's escape. Ignoring the 'No Smoking' sign inside the van, Radhika pulled out her cigarettes, placed one between her lips and lit it. She was in no hurry. Having taken a deep drag, she began to talk as the van lurched forward clumsily.

'As you can see, you are extremely important people. Inspector Radhika Singh and Sub-Inspector Rathore do not usually take the extra precaution of accompanying fugitives back to base, but in your case we've made an exception. After two high-profile murders, I cannot afford to lose you once again,' began Radhika Singh, as she released a puff of acrid smoke into the interiors of the ramshackle van. Her other hand was inside her trouser pocket absentmindedly counting her prayer beads, chanting the name of *Hari* in her mind.

Saini knew that it was pointless trying to talk his way out of the situation. Radhika Singh had already made up her mind that he was guilty and she was determined to see that she made him hang for it. He kept his mouth shut.

'Stand up, both of you,' commanded Radhika. Both prisoners followed her instructions obediently. She quickly patted down Priya while Rathore did the same to Saini. 'With the two of you, I can't afford to take any chances,' she explained as she sat down once again. Saini maintained his silence. He knew that Radhika was attempting to provoke him.

'Cat got your tongue, professor?' asked Radhika Singh mockingly. 'You were a fool to pull the prison break stunt on me, but were even more foolish to proceed to Nikhil Bhojaraj's boat and kill him. You—along with your femme fatale accomplice—are now my prime suspect for two murders, not one.'

The dusty and noisy police van made its way towards Porbandar railway station. It was hot and humid inside the interiors and Saini's brow was covered with sweat. His throat was parched and his lips were dry. He licked his lips nervously, wondering how he was going to get out of the mess that he was in when his ears were suddenly deafened by a massive explosion.

The police van swerved sharply to the right in order to avoid the crude IED that had been placed in their route. The suddenness of the swerve resulted in Saini and Priya being tossed backwards against their bench but it had exactly the reverse effect on Radhika Singh and Rathore. Both police officers fell forward and found themselves on the floor of the police van. The van driver slammed the brakes as hard as he could to bring the aging junk heap to a screeching halt.

Before either of the cops could get up, Saini indicated to Priya that this was a make-or-break moment. Radhika Singh lifted herself from the floor but went crashing down once again as her chin made contact with Saini's foot. Rathore too received a stunning uppercut from Priya's sandals. Saini looked grimly at Priya. Time was running out and they had won only a minute's reprieve.

Just as they were wondering how to get the van door open, a tricky operation given that their hands were cuffed, they heard another smaller explosion from the rear. Plastic explosives were being used to blast open the lock of the rear door of the van. The doors swung open and Saini and Priya were greeted by a black-masked commando carrying a semi-automatic in one hand and metal cutters in the other. 'Quick! Get out of the van! We have very little time—police reinforcements will be here soon,' he yelled at them as he efficiently snapped off their cuffs with the cutter. He helped Priya off the van by extending his arm out to her for support and when she was down he quickly pressed an envelope into her hand. 'Take it,' he urged. He then pointed to the motorcycle that he had arrived on, signalling to Saini that he should make a quick exit on it. Having tumbled out of the van, Saini jumped onto the motorcycle and motioned to Priya to get behind him.

'Drive it at maximum speed along this road. Up ahead is a small grocery shop—it's called Shreeji General Stores. Ditch the bike there. The railway station is a two-minute sprint from there. I'm coming after you,' instructed the commando frantically as he slammed shut and bolted the rear doors of the police van with Radhika Singh and Rathore still inside. He then ran around to the front of the van where he pointed his weapon at the driver and informed him that he would not hesitate to kill him if he did not get out of the vehicle. The terrified driver abdicated his seat within seconds.

Saini mounted the motorbike—a Yamaha with a 150cc engine. With Priya seated behind him they raced down SVP Road, the arterial road leading to the railway station, avoiding meandering cows and diesel-spewing auto rickshaws as they made their second escape from the police in seventy-two hours.

26

In Mathura, Kansa arranged for us to stay in a palace designated for visiting kings and princes. He planned to have us killed in the night. One of his aides advised against this. 'The two boys have already been welcomed as heroes in town. If they are found dead in the state guest house, you shall be blamed, O Lord. No, let Kuvalayapida execute this deed.' Kuvalayapida was a massive elephant that had been fed intoxicants all night so that he would trample me in his inebriated state the next day. As our chariot was passing through the streets Kuvalayapida came charging at me. I got down from the chariot, caught hold of the elephant's trunk and swung him into the heavens. The pachyderm fell dead to the ground some distance away. 'Glory to Krishna,' shouted the spectators in the street.

Within a couple of minutes he saw the shop—Shreeji General Stores. It actually bordered the train yard. Saini and Priya quickly dumped the motorcycle and sprinted across the open tracks to the platform, which was buzzing with life. Tea vendors were calling out their ware while young boys selling cheap plastic toys and samosas harangued visitors who were trying to figure out how to get through the surging crowds.

'The Delhi Sabli Express is the train that we need,' decided Saini. 'Jodhpur is not on the main line. We must go to Falna and from there we will drive to Jodhpur. Let's see if we can get reserved berths—it's a sixteen-hour journey.' They ran up to the ticket window and asked for two berths on the Delhi Sabli Express. Seats on Second-AC were unavailable but sleeper berths on First-AC were. Saini discovered he couldn't afford the fare given their strained cash reserves. Priya handed over the envelope that the black-hooded commando had given her. Looking inside, Saini found it contained twenty-five crisp one-thousand rupee notes.

'Where is he?' asked Saini as he paid for the tickets. 'I've no clue,' said Priya. 'He had said that he would come after us but there's no way that we would recognise him, given his mask.'

'Any idea who he is?' enquired Saini, as he took the tickets from the reservations clerk and placed them in his wallet. 'Possibly someone sent by your father to assist us?'

'Impossible to tell,' said Priya who seemed to be deep in thought. They began to walk towards the platform when they noticed swarms of khaki-clad policemen taking up positions in different parts of the station—near the entrance, the platform, the toilets, the booking counters, and the vending stalls. Saini had bought their tickets just in the nick of time.

'The railway station is under surveillance. They're looking for us. We need to figure out how to get through this. C'mon, quick—I have an idea!' exclaimed Saini as they popped inside a garments shop—Badrudin Ansari & Sons. It was a small ten-by-ten space that looked as though the heaps of garments stacked ceiling-high would come tumbling down in the event of a single miscalculated step. They quickly bought two black all-enveloping *burqas*. The owner, a kindly octogenarian with no teeth but a long flowing white beard attempted to wrap the garments in brown paper but every movement of his was slow and laboured.

Saini fidgeted. They didn't need the damn wrapping, but taking the garments from the vendor in a hurry would attract even more suspicion than the fact that two Westernised tourists who spoke no Gujarati had suddenly chosen to buy burqas. After a wait that seemed like an eternity, the shopkeeper handed over a neatly wrapped parcel duly tied with string. They walked out and headed in the direction of a garbage dump that seemed to be the only place where the police did not have a presence. Unwrapping their burqas, they quickly wore them over their clothes, their disguise hiding their heads and faces.

With greater confidence in their step, they headed over to the platform to await the arrival of the Delhi Sabli Express. The platform TC glanced at their tickets and waved them through disinterestedly. The constables on duty at the platform were looking for an urbane history professor accompanied by a jeans-clad doctoral student. They ignored the two burqa-clad Muslim women on the platform.

On the outskirts of Porbandar, the police van had been ditched in an alley with Radhika Singh and Rathore still locked inside. A small piece of plastic explosive with a ten-minute timer had been stuck to the lock. It would give him enough time to make his getaway before setting the cops inside free. The black-hooded commando peeled off his mask and walked briskly to the main road to hitch a ride. A jovial sardar truck-driver stopped and offered him a lift.

'My name is Jaspreet Singh, *puttar*. What's yours?' asked the driver genially.

'Taarak,' replied the young man. 'Taarak Vakil.'

While I was battling wild elephants, my uncle Kansa was busy organising the Dhanush Yajna. Before him lay the divine bow that had been gifted by Parshurama to Kansa's ancestors. 'O Mighty Lord, please ensure that the bow is not broken before tomorrow. It is prophesised that if anyone breaks the bow before the Dhanush Yajna, the breaker would bring about the annihilation of the owner of the bow—in this case, you,' implored Kansa's head priest. Kansa had the bow kept on a pedestal in a heavily guarded hall. When Balarama and I were walking through the streets of Mathura with Akroor, I expressed a desire to see the bow. When we reached the pedestal, I asked the guard if I could lift the bow. He started laughing. 'It took twenty men just to bring it here and you think you can lift it. Be my guest,' he mocked. I picked up the bow with one hand and broke it into two pieces. Wordlessly, I walked over to the statue of Shiv and placed both pieces before him in obeisance. Shiv had paid his respects to Vish, it was now time for Vish to pay his respects to Shiv.

Professor Rajaram Kurkude's laboratory in Jodhpur was like the setting of a science fiction movie. A pre-existing concrete-framed building had been transformed into a modern state-of-the-art laboratory for his research. The ten-thousand-square-foot lab was located within a multi-building research enclave. The original structure had been reused, retaining the floors, columns and roof. However, a new exterior skin built of channel glass, metal panels, and perforated metal screens had been cleverly used to transform the building while bathing the interiors with sunlight. Row upon rows of gleaming laboratory tables and equipment stretched into the blazing sunlight that burst down from the generous skylights. Located within Kurkude's laboratory was also a web-based data warehouse for radioactive information and readings. All data derived from his studies was automatically stored at a centralised depot.

In stark contrast to the ultramodern architecture were the objects that were on display on the walls, the waiting rooms, the conference room and the passages. Esoteric art, mystical geometric designs, ancient artefacts and mysterious scrolls punctuated the white space. Kurkude was not only a nuclear scientist but also a history buff. He knew more about Mesopotamia and the Indus Valley than many of the historians who published papers about them.

Kurkude was describing his findings with his team via a PowerPoint presentation. It was a weekly tradition among his team to jointly discuss everything that had been discovered or analysed during the preceding seven days in order to establish a plan of action for the week that followed.

The team had discovered a layer of radioactive ash over a three-square mile area, ten miles west of Jodhpur. Kurkude had been called in when the local administration had noticed a very high rate of birth defects and incidence of cancer in the area. Kurkude had been stunned. The levels of radiation had registered so high on his Geiger counter that he had recommended cordoning off the region entirely.

An earlier visit to the region by an English archaeologist, Francis Taylor, had led to the discovery of etchings in some nearby Hindu temples. Duly translated, the etchings were a prayer to be spared from the 'great light' that was coming to lay ruin to the city. Inhabitants had been quick to jump to the conclusion that the radiation was the result of ancient nuclear material. Kurkude, however, was a scientist. It was his job to prevent hasty and ill-conceived conclusions.

'Are we really dealing with an ancient nuclear explosion or is this simply radiation caused by some other event?' asked Kurkude during the team inter-action. He loved asking such questions because it forced everyone to rethink their assumptions.

'There are sufficient clues from all around India to indicate that nuclear warfare could have happened in ancient times,' said his immediate deputy, a young nuclear physicist from IIT.

'Please do elaborate,' suggested Kurkude to the IIT man.

'Well sir, a scientific paper by two researchers—David W. Davenport and Ettore Vincenti—recorded the scholars' belief that an archaeological site they investigated in Mohenjodaro was destroyed in ancient times by a nuclear blast,' explained the IIT man. 'When archaeologists reached street-levels during excavations of Harappa and Mohenjodaro, quite often, skeletons were found lying or seated in positions indicating that an event had instantaneously wiped out civilisation there. Human beings were found unburied and often appeared as though they had been in the midst of routine daily activity. Forty-four skeletons were found in positions that indicated that they had met instant deaths. The skeletons in question were thousands of years old and are among the most radioactive ever found—almost equal to those left behind at Hiroshima and Nagasaki. In fact, Russian researchers found a skeleton that had a radioactive level that was fifty times greater than normal. Why are we so suspicious of the possibility that nuclear technology may have been available to our ancestors? Doesn't the *Mahabharata* speak of it? I'm referring to the line quoted by Robert Oppenheimer that you have all read about.'

The next day, there was no Dhanush Yajna because there was no bow! Kansa was furious with me when I reached the wrestling arena. 'Which one of my wrestlers will you fight?' he demanded agitatedly. 'Whichever one you choose,' I replied. Kansa sent his most ferocious wrestlers one by one, but I prostrated them all. Eventually, only the two greatest wrestlers of Mathura were left—Chanur and Musthika. Chanur attacked me while Musthika attacked Balarama. I dodged Chanur as I would a wild bull, allowing him to charge and charge me again and again, swerving at the last calculated second, until I saw my opportunity. I leapt unexpectedly on Chanur, pinned him down and rained blow after blow on him until he stopped breathing. Balarama, on his part, caught hold of Musthika's arms and twisted them behind his back until they snapped.

Kurkude smiled. He liked the young man's passion. To egg him on a little, Kurkude threw a spanner in the works. 'Yes, indeed we have measured the abnormally high levels of radioactivity at this particular site. But the reason for such radioactivity could be completely different to the hypothesis of an ancient nuclear war. After all, Rajasthan has been used as a nuclear testing site by the Indian government. It is also a state that has nuclear power facilities. And how do we ignore the possibility of radioactive contamination—as encountered in Narora?' asked Kurkude.

Kurkude's IIT deputy was ready to take up the challenge. One of their team members had been visiting a project in the neighbouring town of Narora. The Geiger counter in his bag had gone crazy as soon as he had reached the canteen for a tea break. Upon further study, it was discovered that the radioactivity emanated from the firewood used to brew the tea. Extensive investigation into the issue had led to the revelation that the firewood had originally been used as scaffolding inside a nuclear power plant. This firewood had been contaminated and should have been stored as low-level waste but had instead been sold to an unscrupulous contractor who had then sold it back to the canteen for a profit.

'The fact that there was contamination at one site does not explain the exceedingly high radiation levels at another!' argued the IIT man. 'There are other cities in northern India that also show indications of explosions of great ferocity. One such city—between the Ganges and the mountains of Rajmahal—was subjected to very intense heat. Massive walls and foundations of the ancient city are lying fused together—vitrified! There is clearly no evidence of a volcanic eruption at Mohenjodaro or at any other Indus Valley cities. The intense heat required to melt clay vessels or fuse foundations can only be explained by a massive nuclear reaction.'

Kurkude nodded. He was in overall agreement with the assessment. It was indeed impossible to explain the incredibly high radiation levels in the area in the absence of the hypothesis of ancient nuclear activity. Western scientists brought to the Rajasthan site had found strata of clay and green glass. It was a well-known fact that the exceedingly high temperatures of a nuclear explosion usually melted clay and sand, hardening them into glass immediately after. Similar strata of green glass were also left behind in the Nevada desert after the Americans had carried out atomic tests there.

Kurkude spoke once again. 'The creator of the modern atomic bomb—Oppenheimer—was apparently asked after the first test explosion how he felt after having exploded the first atomic bomb on earth. Oppenheimer had replied that it probably wasn't the first atomic bomb, *but the first atomic bomb in modern times*. Was Oppenheimer giving us a clue that the technology for atomic energy could already have existed? Should we take the *Mahabharata* seriously or should we dismiss it as science fiction of an earlier era?'

One of the older members of the team—the engineer who had discovered contamination of the canteen firewood— gestured that he wished to speak. Kurkude nodded.

'Oppenheimer is said to have quoted the *Gita* after witnessing the first successful test of the bomb in 1945. Apparently he said, *"I am become death, the destroyer of the worlds."* This is remarkably similar to the line in the *Gita* which actually says *"I am become Time to end the world, set on my course to destroy the universe."* But let us not only focus on that single line, sir. The *Mausala Parva* of the *Mahabharata* describes the destruction of a terrible weapon. The passage within the *Mahabharata* that I am referring to says:

> *The unknown weapon is radiant lightning, a devastating messenger of death, which turned all to ashes—a single projectile charged with all the power of the Universe. An incandescent column of smoke and flame as bright as a thousand suns rose in all its splendour, a perpendicular explosion with its billowing smoke clouds; the cloud of smoke rising after its first explosion formed into expanding round circles like the opening of giant parasols. The corpses were so burned as to be unrecognisable. Hair and nails fell out, pottery*

broke without apparent cause, and birds turned white. In a very short time, food became poisonous. The lightning subsided and turned into fine ash.

If this isn't the description of a nuclear blast, then I don't know what is!' exclaimed the greying engineer.

'What is the view regarding the Kurukshetra finds?' asked Kurkude.

'We cannot disregard the findings of Professor A A Gorbovsky from the former Soviet Union,' said the IIT man. Several years prior to the discovery of radioactivity in Rajasthan, this archaeologist had discovered a human skull in the fields of Kurukshetra —the scene of the epic battle between the Kauravas and Pandavas. Modern Kurukshetra lay just a few miles north of New Delhi. Gorbovsky had taken the skull back to his own laboratory in the former Soviet Union and carbon-dated it. His findings revealed that the skull had belonged to someone who had died around five thousand years ago. Incredibly, the skull continued to emit radiation!

'So when the *Mahabharata* spoke of a *Brahmastra*—the deadliest weapon known to mankind in those days, was it talking about an atomic bomb?' asked the senior engineer.

Kurkude thought about the question and then spoke. 'An even more relevant question, dear team members, is this: did the Brahmastra cease to exist after the time when the Mahabharata war took place? Or does it still exist, hidden away from plain sight?'

Seeing that his two prized wrestlers were dead, Kansa jumped into the ring himself. I calmly told him, 'I am Vishnu. I shall forgive you if you take refuge in me.' But the arrogant Kansa, blinded by rage, was unwilling to see reason. As he ran towards me, I caught hold of his arms and tossed him up into the air. As soon as he landed on the ground, I caught hold of his limbs and broke them systematically. Finally, I caught hold of his neck and twisted it until his head snapped. Kansa was dead. The arena was filled with cheers as joyous crowds cheered Balarama and me for ridding them of their evil ruler.

The Delhi Sabli Express chugged its way through the rocky border terrain of Gujarat and Rajasthan, heading towards Falna—the station at which Saini and Priya would have to disembark for Jodhpur. Luckily, they had a sleeper coupé cabin to themselves so they could lock the door and take off their burqas. They had stocked up on mineral water, fruit and biscuits so that they would not need to depend upon the pesky and inquisitive attendant.

'Do you really believe that the ancients had scientific powers to cause nuclear explosions?' asked Priya, biting into an apple.

Saini thought about the question for a moment and then replied, 'Their understanding of energy and matter was far greater than ours, Priya. Let's take a simple example, shall we? Any student of physics is made to carry out an experiment in which white light is passed through a triangular prism.' He quickly sketched a prism and the effect that it had on white light on a napkin and showed it to her.

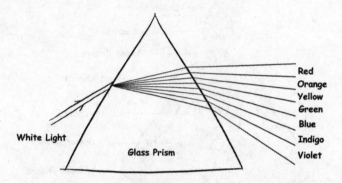

'What's your point, Prof? I've done the experiment myself during my school days. How does this explain anything?' asked Priya impatiently.

'The ancients not only knew that one could split white light into seven constituent colours but also that one could take seven constituent colours and *combine* them to produce dazzling white light. But their knowledge went far beyond that, and I'll hopefully be able to convince you after I explain this next bit to you. Hear me out patiently,' he said.

Priya waited expectantly.

'You recall that ancient seers in India believed that there were sacred *chakras* in your body?' asked Saini.

Priya nodded. 'The concept of chakras originates in Hindu texts and is featured in tantric and yogic traditions of

Hinduism. The name is derived from the Sanskrit word for wheel,' she replied confidently. 'Indian *yogis* believed that chakras existed in the subtle body of living beings. Chakras are whorls of energy—rotating vortices of subtle matter that are considered the focal points for the reception and transmission of energies.' Priya took her own napkin and sketched the locations of the chakras for Saini's benefit.

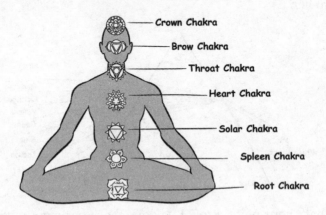

Saini laughed. 'I had no idea that you knew so much about chakras,' he said in amazement.

Priya smiled. 'I spent several years learning medi-tation and yoga in school. It's a part of my life that I usually do not discuss,' she said dismissively. There was an uncomfortable silence for a few seconds.

Saini cleared his throat and resumed. 'Ah! Er... well, if you know that there are seven chakras, you would also know that Indian classical music as described in the *Upanishads* has seven notes of melody—*Sa, Re, Ga, Mu, Pa, Dha,* and *Ni.* These seven notes roughly correspond to the western *Do, Re, Mi, Fa, Sol, La,* and *Ti.* It is my hypothesis that the seven notes correspond to each of the seven chakras within us. The chakra is activated when the frequency of the note matches the frequency of the given chakra.'

'Yes, that could be possible. But we were never taught to meditate using Sa, Re, Ga, Ma, Pa, Dha, and Ni. We always meditated to the sound of *Om*,' said Priya.

'Think about it Priya,' said Saini excitedly, 'seven colours combine to form one universal light—white light. If you combine the seven frequencies of melody what sound will you get? *Om*—the universal sound! You did not realise it while meditating, but the reason that you were reciting the universal sound is because it includes the frequencies of the seven notes that are needed to activate the seven main chakras!'

'But what does this have to do with nuclear energy?' asked Priya.

'Everything! Modern scientists now believe that there are *seven* broad forms of energy—mechanical, heat, chemical, radiant, electrical, sound, and nuclear. It is my reasoned guess that the ancient yogis knew this. They also knew that each of these could be broken into seven constituent elements! It's impossible to understand *how* they knew this, but they *did*. Even their most important and exalted river—the Sarasvati —was part of the Saptasindhu, *the seven rivers*. Vedic knowledge was derived from the Saptarishi—*the seven sages*. Even Dwarka was the embodiment of Saptadweep—*the seven islands*. The Vedic calendar was based on the *seven*-day phase of the moon!' exclaimed Saini.

'Point taken, but it still brings me back to the nuclear question,' argued Priya determinedly.

'Priya, what if the ancient seers had found a way to combine multiple sources of energy into a single one? What if the meditation that they practised on the banks of the Sarasvati was simply an ancient technique to concentrate multiple energy forms into one?' asked Saini.

Priya looked thoughtful. Saini continued, 'If an opera singer can shatter a wine glass, why do you think it is impossible that sound energy could move the massive stones required for constructing Stonehenge or the Great Pyramids of Giza? And if it is possible that ancient Indian sages had the ability to use sound energy to move massive objects then why is it impossible that they had the ability to create massive explosions?'

Saini ran his fingers through his hair and took a deep breath. 'We have forgotten the vast repository of knowledge that existed in Vedic times,' he continued. 'For example, children in school are taught that the sun is ninety-three million miles from the earth and that the speed of light is a hundred and eighty-six thousand miles per second. Would it surprise you to note that Sayana, a fourteenth-century Indian scholar, in his commentary on a hymn in the *Rig Veda* says, *"with deep respect, I bow to the sun who travels 2,202 yojanas in half a nimesha"*. For your information, a *yojana* is about nine American miles and a *nimesha* is 16/75th of a second. Do the conversion, Priya! Sayana is simply stating the obvious—that sunlight travels at a hundred and eighty-six thousand miles per second!'

'And the ancient rishis knew this in the absence of any scientific instruments? Fascinating!' murmured Priya.

Immediately upon killing Kansa, Balarama and I rushed to the prison where our parents—Vasudeva and Devaki—were locked up. We touched their feet, sought their blessings and set them free. We then headed to the cell in which the old chieftain, Ugrasena, was being held captive. He was overjoyed to see us and we sought his blessings too before leading him to his rightful place in the state assembly hall. I was now acknowledged as a Yadava and a Kshatriya. I was sent for training to Sage Sandipani and was then accepted into the ruling Yadava council that had been reconstituted after the slaying of Kansa. Unfortunately, another Yadava, Prasenajit, was killed whilst out hunting, and a fabulously famous stone called the Syamantaka was found missing from his person. My reputation as a butter thief preceded me and I ended up being the one accused of the theft!

The truck sped along NH15, the arterial route linking Gujarat to Rajasthan. The jovial truck-driver, Sardar Jaspreet Singh, kept up a steady stream of conver-sation even though the young man had little to contribute.

Taarak Vakil found himself looking out at the monotonous stretches of road surrounded by vast tracts of unending scrubland. All he wanted was to reach Abu Road Station— the railway junction prior to Falna—quickly. The rhythmic drone of the truck engine and the unending uniformity of the landscape were making him drowsy. His thoughts drifted back to his childhood. He ignored the truck driver — who seemed to be oblivious to Taarak's unresponsiveness —and allowed his mind to drift.

'Have all of you completed your homework assignments?' asked Mr Kapoor, their disciplinarian mathematics professor. 'I shall quickly call out your names; please confirm that you have handed them in.'

'Sachin Mishra?' asked Mr Kapoor.

'Yes, sir. I've handed it in.'

'Usman Sheikh?'

'Yes, sir. Done.'

'Venkat Iyer?'

'Yes, sir—handed in.'

'Sampat Sharma?'

There was an uncomfortable silence in the classroom.

'Sampat Sharma?' repeated Mr Kapoor.

A feeble voice from the back of the class said, 'I'm here, sir.'

'I'm not taking attendance. Have you handed in your home-work assignment or not?' asked Mr Kapoor brusquely.

'No, sir. I had done it, but I seem to have left it at home by mistake,' explained the visibly nervous boy.

'Wait for me outside the classroom,' said Mr Kapoor sternly. The boy got up from his desk, walked out of class, and stood obediently outside the door to the classroom. Mr Kapoor continued with his homework roll-call. After he had finished, he picked up a frightening-looking eighteen-inch ruler, bound with brass at both ends and substantially thicker than the usual foot rule. Outside the classroom, he faced his young student. 'Hold out your left hand,' he said.

The little boy trembled as he held out his hand and closed his eyes in fear of the pain that was yet to come. Mr Kapoor tapped the ruler on the boy's palm just to be sure of his aim and—Whack! Sampat yelped in pain and sucked in his breath from the anguish. He could already see a reddish welt developing along his palm.

'I'm not done yet. You will never forget to bring your homework ever again, after I'm done with you today,' said Mr Kapoor, loud enough for the class to hear him inside. 'Hold out your hand again and keep it held out until I tell you that you can put it down, is that clear?'

Tears were rolling down Sampat's cheeks as he nodded at his teacher and held out his left hand once again. Whack! Whack! Whack! The last one was delivered with the brass edge. The boy was sobbing in pain as he crumpled to the floor to nurse his bleeding hand.

'Get up, you scoundrel. Turn around so that I may now attend to the backs of your thighs!' ordered Mr Kapoor, unmoved by the pitiful sight of the crying and helpless child.

Sampat got himself up off the floor, stood up and turned around to face the wall. He tightened his thigh muscles while continuing to whimper softly. He gasped as the first blow hit his thighs with the force of a whip.

'Stop that this instant,' came the voice from behind Mr Kapoor. He spun around to determine who had the temerity to interrupt him while he was disciplining one of his students. Before he could say anything, he received a swift hard slap across his face.

'You call that discipline? You're nothing but a coward —a poor pathetic weak little man who probably will never pick a fight with someone his own size!' she spat at him. She was a new trainee teacher, having joined school just a week earlier. Mr Kapoor stood frozen to his spot. He was too dazed to react. Never in his twenty years of teaching had something like this happened to him. The young woman grabbed the ruler from the professor's hand and hissed into his ear, 'I know that I'll be fired from this job because of you. I don't give a damn! But if I get to know that you have touched a hair on the body of this boy, trust me, I shall personally inflict the most horrifying pain on you. Is *that* clear?'

It was Mr Kapoor's turn to nod like a meek little schoolboy, holding a cheek that had turned bright pink from the resounding slap.

The young—and rather beautiful—teacher bent down to Sampat and held out her handkerchief. 'Wipe your tears,' she said gently.

Sampat gratefully took the hankie and wiped his eyes. He was about to hand it back to her when she held his hand and quickly dabbed at his palm with it. 'Keep it,' she said. 'It will absorb the blood. Go to the infirmary and have the wound cleaned and bandaged. Meet me after school's out. I shall wait for you outside the gate.'

'Thank you, ma'am,' whispered Sampat, relieved as well as confused by this turn of events.

'Henceforth, you shall never allow anyone to get the better of you. I shall help you become a man—respected and feared by all.'

'I don't even know your name, ma'am.'

'It doesn't matter. I am the equivalent of a mother, sent here to protect you. You may call me Mataji.'

Satrajit, a Yadava chief, had worshipped the sun god, Surya, devotedly. When Surya appeared before him and granted him a wish, Satrajit asked for the precious Syamantaka stone, which Surya generously bestowed upon him. Satrajit presented the stone to his brother Prasenajit. Unfortunately Prasenajit was attacked by a lion. Having killed Prasenajit, the lion made off with the stone but was himself attacked by Jambavan, the king of bears, who carried it away. With my reputation as a butter thief, the needle of suspicion pointed to me. I had to prove my innocence so I set out to track down the bear's cave and retrieve the stone. Mercifully, I was successful in my endeavour.

The police van had remained locked for ten minutes until the explosive attached to the lock went off. By that time, the truck had been spotted by a police patrol. Tired and irritated, Inspector Radhika Singh climbed down and sat in the police jeep along with Sub-Inspector Rathore. The silence was deafening. Not a word was spoken while she lit up a cigarette. After taking a deep puff, she used one hand to start plucking at her prayer beads while the other was used to quickly dial the number of Sunil Garg, Special Director of the CBI.

'Hello? This is Radhika Singh,' she said, speaking in a calm and relaxed manner. 'We've had a small setback, but nothing that is insurmountable. Our suspect and his accomplice are on a train to Falna, which is the last station on the route. They will disembark there and will probably find road transport to get to Jodhpur from there. Could you get your plainclothes team to survey Falna station? I'll speak to my chief in Jaipur and get him to organise an armed contingent in Jodhpur to stand by in reserve. It's just that our suspect is rather clever and I'm afraid that he may slip through our fingers if he sees too many men in khaki.'

The conversation was short, and lasted for less than a couple of minutes. Rathore wondered why Radhika had failed to mention to the CBI Special Director that Saini and Priya seemed to have an accomplice who had held up a police van at gunpoint, but he knew better than to second-guess his tempera-mental boss.

Taking another puff of her cigarette, she looked at her GPS-enabled smartphone. On the screen she pulled up a map that showed the contours of Gujarat and Rajasthan. Visible was a flashing blue dot that was travelling along the railway line from Porbandar to Falna. The signal was being transmitted by a small adhesive microchip that had been placed by her somewhere in the recesses of Priya's clothing.

'Stand up, both of you,' Radhika had commanded them inside the police van. Both prisoners had followed her instructions obediently. She had quickly patted down Priya while Rathore had done the same to Saini. 'With the two of you, I can't afford to take any chances,' she had explained as she sat down once again, having surreptitiously stuck a small adhesive microchip—the size of a baby's thumbnail—on Priya's clothing.

She continued observing the blue dot that indicated that her quarry was indeed on the Delhi Sabli express. She had seen it travel from Porbandar to Wansjaliya, Bhaunra, Lalpur, Jamnagar, Hapa, Rajkot, Wankaner, Surendranagar, Viramgam, and on to Ahmedabad.

It was now matter of just a few short hours. The train would next touch Sabarmati, Mahesana, Palanpur and Abu Road before reaching Falna—the transit point where Saini and Priya would have to disembark to reach Jodhpur.

Her anticipation and excitement levels kept increasing with every station that the train covered. Finally, Falna! She gripped her phone tightly, hoping for some good news from the CBI, but her face soon turned red with anger. She saw that the blue dot was not stopping at Falna but seemed to be proceeding to Beawar and Ajmer on its way to Delhi. How could that be? Why had they changed their plans?

While Radhika Singh continued to fret and fume, Saini and Priya were ensconced inside an air-conditioned Tata Safari that they had hired from Abu Road Station, the junction prior to Falna. It was two hundred and fifty kilometres from Abu Road to Jodhpur but given the empty stretches of desert road, the journey would take less than four hours.

Inside the toilet of the Delhi Sabli Express, the small microchip had been gently inserted into a narrow gap between train window and compartment wall. It continued to transmit a signal to the GPS satellites up above in the heavens.

Having found the stone, I was well within my rights to keep the Syamantaka for myself but I gallantly returned it to Satrajit. He was penitent for having wrongly accused me and, as recompense, he offered his daughter Satyabhama's hand in marriage to me, along with the Syamantaka itself. I accepted the hand of Satyabhama but refused to accept the stone. Some time later, I was on a journey away from Dwarka when a plot was hatched to kill Satrajit. A Yadava called Satadhanwa killed Satrajit, took the Syamantaka and left it with Akroora—the same person who had helped Balarama and me by warning us of Kansa's intentions. When I heard of this, I tracked down Satadhanwa and killed him. I then called Akroora and forced him to confess. Akroora told me the truth about the conspiracy. As reward for his confession I allowed Akroora to remain the custodian of the stone on one condition. The stone was to always remain in in my city.

The Delhi Sabli Express had arrived at Abu Road Station at 5:28 am. Saini and Priya had quickly made their way to the taxi stand from where they had been able to negotiate for a vehicle that would take them to Jodhpur. A young driver had offered them a discount of twenty per cent and that had clinched the deal.

Saini was quiet. He knew that the odds were stacked against him. Yes, they had succeeded in giving the cops the slip three times—in Jaipur, Porbandar and Falna, but that did not take away from the mess that he was in. He also felt guilty for having dragged Priya into it all.

He looked at her as she slept in the backseat of the Tata Safari. Her hair was tousled after the trip and there were dark circles under her eyes—but the almost-forty woman still looked beautiful. After many years, Saini found himself being drawn towards this caring person who had thrown in her lot with him even though she had no good reason to. For the first time since his divorce, Saini experienced the longing for physical and emotional intimacy. He forced himself to look away and concentrate on the notepad that lay on his lap.

How and why had Krishna made the long and arduous trek of over a thousand kilometres from Mathura to Dwarka? The answer came to Saini like a flash. Mathura lay along the banks of the River Yamuna—a tributary of the once mighty Sarasvati. If Krishna had simply followed the route of the Yamuna to the point where it met the Sarasvati and then followed the Sarasvati to the point where it drained out into the sea, he would have reached the Rann of Kutch—a metaphoric stone's throw away from Dwarka. Mathura and Dwarka were simply the starting and ending points of a river route provided by the bountiful Sarasvati!

Looking around him at the dusty desert road, Saini found it difficult to believe that most of Rajasthan would have been fertile land watered and nurtured by the flowing waters of the Sarasvati. He recalled Varshney telling him about the radiocarbon-dating project of ancient waters below the desert. Varshney had requested nuclear physicists to visit the sites that he was excavating in Rajasthan. Until then, physicists had usually carried out radiocarbon-dating of carbon-based matter—wood, cloth, and bone—by studying the carbon-14 isotope. Unfortunately, this process was of little use when it came to studying ancient waters. Upon Varshney's request, two scientists from the Bhabha Atomic Research Centre had drawn samples from wells in various parts of Rajasthan. They had found palaeochannels in which the water continued to flow subterraneously. They had found that this groundwater was enriched in stable isotope content and minimal tritium content, thus indicating an absence of modern recharge. Calibrating the dates, they had found that very little recharge had occurred after 3200 BCE—this was roughly when the Sarasvati had started drying up. Just around the time of Krishna and the Mahabharata!

They had been travelling for over a hundred kilometres along NH14. Then, they took a slight left and started driving along NH65. This was the final stretch that would take them into Jodhpur city. Saini and Priya had decided that it was better not to inform Rajaram Kurkude of their intended visit. What if he tipped off the police? No, it would be safer to drop in unannounced—even though that would be somewhat impolite.

He saw Priya stir from her nap. As she opened her eyes, she saw him smiling at her. 'Good morning,' he said to her, 'we're almost there. You want to get a bite to eat before we try meeting Kurkude?'

She nodded. 'I'm starving. I also need to make a phone call.'

'To whom?' asked Saini.

'Dad. He must be worried sick about me by now,' she replied.

They instructed the driver to stop at a nondescript restaurant, one among thousands that dotted the arterial highways of India—and quickly ordered some breakfast, which was surprisingly good—aloo parathas with curd and pickles, washed down with masala chai. Priya then took a short walk and made her phone call, while Saini attempted to wash his face and brush his teeth with toiletries acquired from the convenience store attached to the restaurant.

Thirty minutes later their car drove up to the gate of Kurkude's research facility. The gate was locked and there was no security guard on duty. However, an electronic panel with a speaker asked them to identify themselves.

'My name is Ravi Mohan Saini, and I'm here to see Professor Rajaram Kurkude,' said Saini into the microphone. He noticed that the built-in camera light was flashing, indicating that the person at the other end was probably scanning his image.

'Do you have an appointment?' asked the voice.

'No. Please tell him that I was asked by Anil Varshney to meet him. Tell him that it concerns an artefact that has been left by Anil Varshney with him,' explained Saini, growing increasingly uncomfortable with the extended explanations.

'Just a moment please. I shall check with the professor,' said the voice. A beep indicated that the two- way communication system had been temporarily shut off.

After what seemed like an eternity, there was another beep and the voice came back online. 'The professor will see you. The gate will open shortly. Please drive straight through to the reception block. The professor's secretary— Miss Gonsalves—shall be waiting for you there.'

The beep indicated that the voice did not want an acknowledgement or thanks from Saini.

33

I was the son of Vasudeva. Vasudeva's sister was Kunti.
Kunti was married to Pandu — the king of Hastinapur —
and a descendant of Puru. Kunti had received a boon
from a sage, Rishi Durvasa, that she would bear five
sons sired by whichever gods she chose. She had tested
the boon in haste and the sun god — Surya — had given
her a firstborn, Karana. Shamed by the fact that she
was unwed, Kunti had set the infant Karana afloat on a
river in a basket. Luckily, he was found by a charioteer
and was brought up by him. After her marriage to
Pandu, Kunti used the boon to produce three more
sons — Yudhistira, by Dharma; Bhima, by Vaayu; and
Arjuna, by Indra. Kunti gifted the remainder of the
boon to Pandu's second wife — Madri — who produced
twins, Nakula and Sahadev from the Ashwin twins.
The five recognized children of Kunti and Madri were
the Pandavas — my first cousins. Pandu soon died
and my aunt moved back into the Hastinapur palace
of the blind King Dhritarashtra — Pandu's brother.
Dhritarashtra and his wife Gandhari were the parents
of one hundred sons known as the Kauravas, the eldest
of whom was Duryodhana. Also in the palace lived
Bhishma, the king's uncle, who had renounced the
throne and had taken a vow of celibacy so that his father,

Shantanu, could marry a fisherwoman Satyavati who had insisted that she wanted the throne for her own children by him.

The gate rolled open slowly and they drove through the long driveway that was surrounded by dense groves of *neem* trees—the only variety that seemed to grow in the arid desert climate of Rajasthan. Once they reached the main reception block, they were received by a short, plump woman—Miss Gonsalves. She instructed the driver on how he could reach the visitor's parking lot and handed over two ID tags to Saini and Priya to wear around their necks. 'Please follow me,' she instructed as they headed towards the research block where Kurkude's office was located.

As they were ushered in to Kurkude's spacious office, Saini felt a tightening of his stomach. Would Kurkude simply hand him over to the authorities as a murder suspect?

Kurkude got up from his desk and walked over to Saini and Priya and stuck out his hand. The hand-shake was firm and professional—not overly friendly. Dressed in a starched white lab coat, Kurkude was a man in his fifties, with two large bushy tufts of white hair on either side of his head. The centre of his head was entirely bald. On the bridge of his nose sat a pair of Gandhi-style spectacles. Eccentric genius, thought Saini to himself, as a primary character assessment.

Miss Gonsalves closed the door and retreated to the outer office, while Kurkude led Saini and Priya to the corner sofa of his office. 'So, what may I do for you, Mr Saini?' asked Kurkude. If he knew that Saini was a murder suspect, he was doing an excellent job of not showing it.

'Thank you for seeing us without an appointment, sir,' began Saini. 'Both you and I shared a common friend— Anil Varshney, who was murdered a few days ago. Before someone else tells you, it's better that I let you know that, according to the Rajasthan Police, I am the prime suspect for his murder.'

Saini allowed the words to sink in. He soon understood that Kurkude had nothing to offer by way of expression or words, so he continued. 'The truth is, I was called by Anil Varshney to his archaeological dig at Kalibangan so that he could share with me one out of four seals that he had in his possession. He told me that he would be leaving one with me, one with you, and the other two with Dr Nikhil Bhojaraj and Devendra Chhedi.'

Kurkude nodded. 'Yes, it's true. Varshney did leave one of those seals with me for safekeeping. It's still in my custody.'

'Sir, I did not kill Anil. He was my best friend. We grew up together! After his murder, the police searched my residence and found the seal that he had given me for safekeeping. They assumed that I had killed him in order to steal it. This is Priya Ratnani—my doctoral student. We both had to flee Jaipur. Our first point of call was Dwarka, so that we could meet Dr Nikhil Bhojaraj. Unfortunately, he had been killed before we could talk to him. We were very concerned that the killer could come after you—and hence our effort to warn you by coming here,' explained Saini.

'Well, as you can see, I'm alive and well,' said Kurkude. 'I do not believe that you are a killer, Mr Saini. I may be old and verging on senility but I'm a rather good judge of character. Tell me how I can be of help to you.'

'Well, sir, while I do not have the seal that Varshney had given me, I do have a photograph of the seal stored on my data cloud. If I could compare the seal that you have with the photographs, it may point me in an appropriate direction,' said Saini.

'That's easy enough. Anything else?'

'I would be grateful if you could pick up the phone and speak with Inspector Radhika Singh and tell her that you have met me and that the four seals were indeed given by Varshney to his friends for safe-keeping. It would help corroborate the statement that I made to her,' said Saini.

'I shall do that immediately after our meeting. Now, shall we have a look at the seal?' asked Kurkude, getting up from the sofa and walking over to his desk. He took out a small key from his lab coat and opened a drawer. Inside the drawer was a built-in safe. He punched in a few numbers and waited as the door swung open gently, with a slight whirring noise. He put his hand inside and pulled out a small brown paper envelope. Opening it, he gently pulled out the seal and placed it flat on piece of white blotting paper on his desk. 'Would you care to come over here so that you can have a look?' he asked Saini and Priya.

They both got up from the sitting area and went over to the desk. They gasped as they saw the third seal, which was virtually identical to the two previous ones. Saini could feel his heart beating faster as he picked up the seal to have a closer look.

34

It was soon time for the children to be educated in the duties of kingship. Their granduncle, Bhishma, enrolled the Pandava and Kaurava princes to be trained in archery under the most renowned guru of the age, Drona. My cousin, Arjuna, turned out to be Drona's very best student. As his fees, Drona asked the boys to capture an enemy king—Drupada—for him. While the Kauravas failed, the Pandavas under Arjuna succeeded. The incident sowed the seeds of jealousy and enmity between the two groups. On graduation day, a competition was organised by Drona to showcase the prowess of his students. Arjuna excelled in all the tests but, unexpectedly, another warrior by the name of Karana appeared and outshone Arjuna. It was soon discovered that he was the son of a charioteer. My cousins, the Pandavas, argued that Karana could not compete with them given that he was not a Kshatriya. The fools did not realise that Karana was actually their brother! Ironically, it was Duryodhana who came to Karana's rescue. 'Karana is a Kshatriya by merit even if not by birth. I'm making him the king of Anga!' declared Duryodhana. Karana swore permanent allegiance to Duryodhana on that day.

Saini picked up the seal and examined it more closely. Like the others, this one too was a small rectangular seal—

probably around the same size of 20 x 20 mm—made of conch shell. The seal had a square peg at the back and, as usual, the traditional hole in the peg for inserting a ring was missing. The same three ancient animal motifs—bull, unicorn and goat—were engraved in an anticlockwise direction on the face of the seal.

Saini put the seal down on the blotting paper and looked up at Kurkude. 'Do you have any theories regarding this seal?' he asked.

Kurkude smiled. 'I'm a simple nuclear physicist, my boy. I deal with things that can be explained, not the divine!' he exclaimed.

'Interesting,' murmured Saini.

'What?' asked Kurkude.

'Interesting that you should view the divine as unexplainable,' said Saini.

'But that's true, isn't it? The ancient Egyptians saw the sun rise in the east and set in the west. They didn't know what it was, so they called him *Ra*—the sun god—who travels across the skies in his chariot. Given that the rising and setting sun couldn't be explained, it became divine. The sun lost its divine status when man learned that it was a giant ball of energy around which the other planets revolved. *The divine is simply that which cannot be explained at that given moment in history,*' concluded Kurkude.

'In your world, God will cease to exist as science advances,' joked Saini.

'What you say isn't untrue. With every advance in our understanding of the world, we leave less that cannot be explained. As that happens, there's less room for God,' said Kurkude, smiling.

'Can I take a photo of the seal, please?' asked Saini.

'Of course, be my guest,' said Kurkude, genially.

'I don't have a phone,' Saini went on, 'and the one with Priya is a very basic unit without a camera. Could you take the photo on your phone and mail it to this email address? I know that Varshney had already sent me photographs but I would like to compare his photos against the ones taken here.'

Saini quickly jotted down his email address on the blotting paper on Kurkude's desk. Kurkude used his Blackberry to take a picture and email it to Saini. He then placed the seal back in the envelope and returned it to the safe.

'I'm given to understand that your team is researching the possibility of an ancient nuclear blast in an area of Rajasthan. Do you personally believe that the Brahmastra referred to in the *Mahabharata* could have been an atomic bomb?' asked Saini.

Kurkude laughed. 'The source of *all* knowledge is to be found right here along the banks of the Sarasvati, my boy. Why not nuclear energy? Have you ever been to Egypt?' he suddenly asked.

'Yes. Many years ago during a university-sponsored trip,' replied Saini.

'Did you see the pyramids?'

'Of course!'

'More specifically, did you see the stepped pyramid —the great flat-topped *Mastaba of Djoser*—a precursor to later pyramids?' asked Kurkude.

'Yes. It's like a series of platforms, with each higher platform smaller than the base below it,' replied Saini.

'How would you react if I told you that the Mastaba of Djoser is described perfectly in the *Baudhayana Sulbasutra* —a manual of ancient Vedic geometry?' asked Kurkude.

'With some disbelief,' admitted Saini. 'I've read translations of the *Baudhayana Sulbasutra* but cannot recall any reference to the Mastaba of Djoser.'

'That's because the manual describes in precise detail the building of a *Smashaanachitha*—a funeral altar. The Mastaba of Djoser, built around 2700 BCE, is an inverted Vedic funeral altar down to the very last detail,' said Kurkude triumphantly.

'But how did that happen?' asked Saini.

'All construction needed geometry and it was the *Vedas* that gave the world geometry,' explained Kurkude. 'The present English word, *geometry*, is derived from a Greek root which itself was derived from a Sanskrit word— *Jyamiti*. In Sanskrit, *jya* means an arc or a curve and *miti* means the correct perception or measurement. The prayer in the *Egyptian Book of the Dead* is more or less identical to the *Taittiriya Samhita*, which prescribes the invocations to be used at a funeral altar. It says *"May we gain prosperity in the world of our fathers."* Uncanny, wouldn't you say? The world deludes itself into believing that it was Pythagoras who gave us the famous theorem regarding the hypotenuse of a right-angled triangle but the *Baudhayana Sulbasutra*, which was written five hundred years before Pythagoras, states that a rope stretched along the length of a diagonal line produces an area which the vertical and horizontal sides make together. So who invented the Pythagoras theorem— Pythagoras or Baudhayana?'

'You mean that Pythagoras got it from the *Vedas*?' asked Saini.

'Don't take my word for it. The French philosopher Voltaire was the one who vehemently declared, "Pythagoras went to the Ganges to learn geometry." Indeed, Abraham Seidenberg, the author of the *History of Mathematics*, sees the *Sulbasutra* as having been the common origin for all ancient mathematics—be they in Babylonia, Egypt or Greece. The Vedic seers conceptualised not only the Pythagorean theorem but also the decimal system, the concept of zero, and infinity. Even the binary system—so very common in modern computers now—was originally developed via Vedic verse meters!' declared Kurkude.

'So the seals that Varshney gave us could be pointing to something that is outside of India? Like Mesopotamia, Egypt or Sumeria?'

'What is this Sumeria that you historians keep talking about?' asked Kurkude crossly. 'In the *Vedas*, we refer to Mount Kailash as *Meru*—the abode of the gods. In Sanskrit, if one wants to describe something as *holy*, one simply adds the prefix *su* before the given word. So *Meru* becomes *Sumeru*, and it is from this Sanskrit word *Sumeru* that the name for the *Sumerian* civilisation was born!'

'So you subscribe to the view that the ancient civilisation of Sumeria had Vedic roots and was developed using Vedic knowledge?' asked Saini.

'Oh, absolutely!' declared Kurkude, with complete conviction. 'It was the westward movement of the Vedic people towards Sumeria that caused the rift between *Asuras* and *Devas*!'

'That's interesting,' said Saini. 'In early Vedic literature, the term *asura*, was actually a nomenclature indicating respect. It translated to *almighty*. It was later applied to people who moved westwards. We know that the Sarasvati river started drying up around 3200 BCE. The result was a splitting up of the Sarasvati civilisation, which had flourished along its banks. Some people moved eastwards towards the Ganges and some moved westwards—in the direction of Sumeria. This resulted in the westerners being called Asuras and those who remained within Vedic territories being called Devas. A simple enmity caused by climatic change!'

'And that would explain why later Zoroastrians viewed Asuras—or *Ahuras*—as good people and Devas as the villains. The exact opposite of Vedic culture,' said Priya.

'Precisely,' replied Saini. 'Those who reached the Tigris-Euphrates valley continued to remain moon-worshippers. The founder of Judaism, Abraham, also came from that region, and his family, too, were devotees of the moon. We should not forget the fact that the names Abraham and Brahama are only separated by the placement of a single letter—A. Abraham's wife was Sara and Brahama's consort was Saraswati—too many similarities to be passed off as mere coincidences. The subsequent language of the region—*Avestan*—was virtually identical to Sanskrit. The region's future religion—Zoroastrianism —produced religious books called the *Gathas* that contained passages that were identical to verses from the *Rig Veda*.'

Kurkude was nodding profoundly as he said, 'I recall reading somewhere that *Yahvah*, the name given to God in the Judaic faith, is to be found as an epithet for *Agni* in the *Rig Veda* a total of twenty-one times, sometimes as *Yahva, Yahvah, Yahvam* and *Yahvasya*.'

'So if I had to take Varshney's search to its logical conclusion, in your opinion, where should I look?' asked Saini.

'Within yourself, Mr Saini. Within yourself,' said the Einsteinian thinker, as he led them out of his office to the outer reception area where the plump Miss Gonsalves usually sat.

Indeed, Miss Gonsalves was seated at her desk, but her head was tilted backward and her throat bore a vicious gash from which blood had poured out onto the desk, drenching her clothes and papers in claret-red.

35

Dhritarashtra now decided that Yudhistira, my aunt Kunti's eldest son, would be named heir-apparent to the clan's leadership. Dhritarashtra's decision sparked outrage among the Kauravas, particularly in Duryodhana, who believed that he was the rightful claimant. Duryodhana thereupon hatched a plan to murder the Pandavas. He built a beautiful house for my aunt and cousins, but from inflammable lac. The house was set ablaze when the Pandavas were inside it. The Kauravas assumed that they had finished off their rivals, but unknown to them, the Pandavas had escaped into the forest via an underground tunnel. Whilst in the forest, my cousin Bhima was able to slay a monster called Hidamba in a violent encounter. The duel was observed by Hidamba's sister, Hidimbi, and she fell in love with Bhima. Hidimbi was able to charm my aunt Kunti into accepting her as a daughter-in-law. Bhima and Hidimbi had a son called Ghatotkacha, but soon it was time for the Pandavas to move on. When Bhima was leaving, the young Ghatotkacha came up to his father and tenderly said, 'I shall always be there for you whenever you need my help, dear father. Just think of me and I will come to your side.' Ghatotkacha would be needed many years later—at Kurukshetra.

Professor Kurkude let out an anguished scream as he beheld the sight of his murdered secretary. There was no one around, and the outer office only had a single exit, so it was obvious that the assailant had left the room.

'Should I call an ambulance?' asked Kurkude.

'No point. She's already gone,' said Priya, checking for a pulse.

'Who could have done this?' asked Kurkude, befuddled and grieving simultaneously.

'My gut tells me that it's the same person who killed Varshney and Bhojaraj. He probably wanted to kill you but learnt that we were already inside with you. It was simply a question of bad timing,' said Saini.

'Should we call the police?' asked Kurkude.

'My worry right now is for your personal safety. It's highly likely that the murderer is somewhere on these premises. We cannot afford to have you murdered too, Professor! This person is extremely intelligent and seems to know everything that we are doing. I wouldn't be surprised if this person even has accomplices in your team. No, I suggest that you come with us. You'll be safer with us,' explained Priya.

'But I can't simply leave my office, my staff and my work! This is my life!' exclaimed the old grey-haired scientist.

'We're not asking you to leave it forever. Just for a few days. By then we may have a clearer idea of who is behind these killings,' Saini said persuasively.

'Where are you headed now?' asked Kurkude.

'Chandigarh. We have to meet Devendra Chhedi and see the seal that was sent to him. It's the only logical thing to do,' said Saini. The professor shrugged his shoulders helplessly. He knew that the options before him were pretty limited.

'Is there any way to reach the parking lot without going through the reception block?' asked Saini. 'It may look very suspicious to your staff to see you exiting the building in a hurry along with the two of us.'

'From my outer office, there's a passage that leads to our data warehouse. There's an exit from the data warehouse to a garden pathway that winds its way to the parking lot. We could take that route,' suggested Kurkude.

'Fine. In the meantime, I suggest that you go back to your desk and take out the seal that is lying locked in your safe. With you gone, it is virtually certain that the safe will be broken into. It's safer with you than in your drawer,' said Priya as Saini busied himself pondering their exit route from the building.

Fifteen minutes later they were in the car park. The driver was dozing peacefully inside the car when Saini, Priya and Kurkude reached the vehicle. Saini quickly put his hand through the rolled-down car window and nudged him awake. 'Where to?' asked the driver sleepily.

'Get ready for another long trip,' said Saini. 'You need to get us to Chandigarh. How far is it by road from Jodhpur?'

'A little over seven hundred kilometres. If we're lucky, we can make it in about twelve hours,' said the driver.

'Why don't we take a flight to New Delhi from Jodhpur? We could get a flight into Chandigarh from there,' suggested Kurkude, as they stood outside the car.

Saini whispered to Kurkude, 'After this murder, Radhika Singh will think that I've killed your secretary and kidnapped you. There will be a police lookout at all railway stations and airports. No, driving is the safest way of getting there. Now come, we don't have much time!'

Saini got into the front seat of the car, leaving the two rear passenger seats for Priya and Kurkude. 'Let's go,' he said to the driver hurriedly.

'Yes, sir. We'll need to top up the fuel on the way though,' said Taarak Vakil as he revved up the engine of the car casually, smiling to himself at the happy turn of events.

36

My cousins soon heard about a grand Svayamwara that was being held for the hand of Draupadi, the princess of Panchali and daughter of King Drupada—the very same Drupada who had been captured by the Pandava princes as dakshina for Drona. The Pandavas attended the competition in disguise. The contest involved stringing a heavy bow and shooting five arrows directly into the eye of a single metal fish that rotated on a wheel overhead with only its reflection in a pot of oil to guide the archer. Princes from several kingdoms attempted to achieve the task but the only one who succeeded was Arjuna. Karana had also been sent to participate by Duryodhana, but as he rose to take his shot, Draupadi said 'I cannot allow the offspring of a mere charioteer to try his luck for my hand in marriage.' Humiliated, Karana withdrew, but he would not forget Draupadi's stinging words.

'You are indeed fortunate to have parents whose names are Vishnuyasa and Sumati, child. Do you know who else has parents by that name?' asked Mataji.

'No, Mataji, I don't,' said little Sampat.

'Have you heard of Rama and Krishna?'

'The heroes of the *Ramayana* and the *Mahabharata*?' asked Sampat.

'Yes. Both were avatars of Vishnu. Vishnu is reborn on earth whenever there is evil to be vanquished. The world that we live in has turned wicked once again, my son. It's time for Vishnu to appear once again. This time he shall appear as the tenth and final avatar —also known as the Kalki avatar,' she explained.

'Kalki avatar? So the Kalki avatar's parents are supposed to be Vishnuyasa and Sumati?' asked Sampat.

'Yes. I am blessed to have met you. You are the Kalki avatar and shall banish wickedness from this world. But to do that, you need to be physically, emotionally, mentally and intellectually strong. I shall train you for this purpose. No one will ever be able to pick on you again,' she said.

'What will I have to do?' asked Sampat.

'First. The secret that you are the Kalki avatar must remain only between us. Not even your parents should know that I have told you this. Is that understood?'

'Yes, Mataji.'

'Second. You shall come to school every day—but classes end at three o'clock, right? You shall meet me at the school gate each day at that time. I have rented a house that is a few minutes away. You shall be with me for four hours each day. I shall bring in appropriate instructors to teach you Sanskrit, the scriptures, Vedic mathematics, martial arts and meditation. You cannot miss a single day of this training. Are you ready for that?'

'Yes, Mataji.'

'Third. There shall be no compromise on your schoolwork. You must do your homework and I want you to be at the top of your class. Out of the four hours that you spend at my house, one hour shall be set aside for schoolwork. I do not want your parents or your teachers to get suspicious. Are we agreed?'

'Yes, Mataji.'

'Fourth. You shall continue to be known by your old name, Sampat Sharma, in school and at home, but when you are with me, you shall be known by your spiritual name.'

'What name is that, Mataji?'

'Taarak Vakil is the name that you shall be known by. I shall explain the significance of it to you later in life. Wear this silver bracelet with your new name on it. It's a gift from me to you and signifies that I am now your guru. Let me assure you that eventually the world shall fear, respect and tremble before your name and presence. Are we in agreement, Taarak?'

'Yes, Mataji,' said Taarak, allowing Mataji to clasp the silver bracelet around his wrist.

'Good. Our very first lesson shall be in memorising the 108 names of Vishnu.'

'Why are there 108 names, Mataji?' asked Taarak.

'Good question. It relates to ancient Vedic know-ledge. See my prayer beads? How many beads does my rosary have?'

Taarak quickly counted the beads. 'A hundred and eight,' he replied.

'Why 108, Taarak? Why not one hundred? What's so special about 108?' prompted Mataji.

Taarak shrugged. 'I've no idea, Mataji.'

'The rosary represents the ecliptic—the path of the sun and moon across the sky. Yogis divide the ecliptic into twenty-seven equal sections called *nakshatras*, and each of these into four equal *padas*—or steps—marking the 108 steps that the sun and moon take through the skies,' explained Mataji. 'But do you know what's even more remarkable about the number 108?'

Taarak waited expectantly, and was rewarded.

'What's truly amazing is the fact that the distance between the earth and the sun is exactly 108 times the sun's diameter. More incredible is the fact that the distance between the earth and the moon is 108 times the moon's diameter. Finally, do you know that the diameter of the sun is 108 times the earth's diameter? The ancient yogis knew this! That's why 108 is such a sacred number.'

'So is 108 a representation of God?' asked Taarak.

'Yes. Can you add up the individual digits of 108 and tell me what you get?'

'That's easy. The answer is 9.'

'Nine is a very special number, Taarak. The number 9 represents wholeness. What's particularly magical is that if you multiply 9 by anything, the answer is always 9 when you add the digits together. Try it! What's 2 x 9?'

'Eighteen,' answered Taarak confidently.

'Now add the digits of 18 together and tell me what do you get?'

'Nine!' exclaimed Taarak.

'Very good. Let's try another one. Slightly more difficult. What's 15 x 9?'

'A hundred and thirty-five,' answered Taarak, after doing the multiplication in his head.

'And 135 is made up of three digits—1, 3 and 5. Add them together. What do you get?'

'Nine!' squealed Taarak, excited to see this magic in action.

'That's why 9 represents God. That's why we have 9 nights of *Navratri*; that's also why we worship the *Navagraha*—the 9 planets. God multiplied by anything is always God, since God is all there is!'

I was present in Drupada's court the day Draupadi's Swayamvara was held. I was also there when Arjuna returned to his mother and told her that he had won a grand prize and asked for her advice on what he should do with it. 'Whatever it is, you must share it equally with your brothers,' Kunti commanded. Hence, Draupadi ended up wedded to all five brothers in an instance of polyandry. I felt that this was the appropriate time to introduce myself to my aunt. I fell at Kunti's feet and said, 'I am your nephew, Krishna. I am your brother Vasudeva's son, and your sons are my cousins. It shall be my duty to protect them and Draupadi!'

The road from Jodhpur to Chandigarh was an almost perfect south-north route that would take them via Jhajjar, Rohtak, Panipat and Ambala to Chandigarh. Having stopped at a gas station for a quick top-up of the fuel tank, they headed out to State Highway 22 that would eventually bring them to National Highway 71.

A short distance from where the State Highway started, they saw a police check post blocking traffic. All vehicles were being stopped and checked. 'Stop the car,' hissed Saini to the driver. Even though Taarak knew why he was being asked to stop, he feigned ignorance. 'Why should we stop, sir? This is the correct route to Chandigarh,' he said.

'Find a way to avoid the police checkpost,' said Saini reluctantly, unaware of the fact that Taarak wanted to avoid the cops just as much. The owner of the Tata Safari at Abu Road Station was lying dead in a ditch. Taarak had quickly donned the dead taxi driver's clothes and had assumed his new role, offering a twenty percent discount to Saini in order to ensure that he was hired.

'Yes sir,' retorted Taarak smartly as he took a sharp left at a chemist's shop in order to avoid the check post.

'I'm not too familiar with Jodhpur roads so I will need to get down and ask for directions,' said Taarak as he parked the car on the side of the road and got out. He had a short chat with a taxi driver in the distance and re-joined them. 'He said that we should go first to Mandawar. From there, a road will take us via Laxmangarh to the National Highway. It will help us avoid the police check post,' he said as he turned the ignition. Saini nodded while Priya and Kurkude, seated in the back of the car, remained absolutely quiet.

Within ten minutes they were out of Jodhpur and on their way to Mandawar. As the hustle and bustle of the city gave way to sand dunes and unending vistas of the Thar desert, Taarak settled back in the driver's seat and allowed himself to relax. His mind wandered for a while before focusing on his childhood once again.

'Taarak, this is Pushpendraji. He shall be teaching you *Sastravidya*,' said Mataji.

'What is Sastravidya?' asked Taarak.

'Our Indian scriptures—particularly the *Ramayana* and *Muhabharata*—contain descriptions of the ways in which combat was conducted in ancient India. This included both armed and barehanded strategies. The *Mahabharata* provides detailed descriptions of the intense battle between Arjuna and Karana, in which bows, swords, trees, rocks and even bare fists were used. An encounter in the *Ramayana* shows how two fighters used boxing manoeuvres with clenched fists whilst simultaneously incorporating kicks, head butts, finger strikes, and knee strikes. The result was the development of sixteen key principles of Indian martial arts. These are the only sixteen principles that you shall need to learn. Having learnt these, you shall be a master of Sastravidya and it will be impossible for the uninitiated to fight you,' explained Pushpendraji.

'Does Mataji also know Sastravidya?' asked Taarak.

'Absolutely. She was trained by me in her school. Why don't you show dear Taarak your skills, Mataji?' said Pushpendraji.

Before Taarak knew what was happening, a slim Ninja spike flew from Mataji's left hand—it had been carefully concealed in her sleeve. It twirled in the air momentarily before it hit the wall just above Taarak's head. 'See what training can achieve, Taarak?' asked Mataji, smiling. Taarak nodded seriously.

'Here is some vermillion paste. Put a tilak on my head and then touch my feet,' instructed Pushpendraji. Taarak did as he was told. Pushpendraji then said, 'Now hold out your right hand please.' As Taarak did so, Pushpendraji took a bundle of *moli*—red and yellow thread used by Hindu priests while performing religious ceremonies—and wove it around Taarak's wrist. 'You are now officially my disciple. Each day we shall practice Sastravidya for an hour. In a few years you shall be as strong as a bull, powerful as a tiger, fast as a cheetah and clever as a fox! *Om Namah Shivaya!*'

'Guruji, why do we use the word "Om" in all our prayers?' asked Taarak innocently.

'Let me answer that for you,' said Mataji. 'The word "Om" is not only used by us, Taarak. It is to be found everywhere. Even in the English language.'

'Really? In what form?' asked Taarak.

'Think carefully. The word "omniscience" means infinite knowledge. It starts with the sound of Om—or Aum. The word "omnipotent", which means a person who has infinite powers also starts with Om. The word "omnivorous", which implies the ability to absorb everything also has Om as the starting point. The word "omen", implying a predictive sign of a future event, also has Om in it. A trusted intermediary between parties, with the authority to award a verdict, is called an "ombudsman"—once again we have Om. Om is an expression of divinity and authority and that's the reason why *Aum* is to be found even in the Christian *Amen* and the Islamic *Amin*,' explained Mataji. Taarak digested the information offered, realising that the education that he was receiving from Mataji was priceless.

Taarak snapped back to the present and forced himself to focus on the road. A few hours later, he stopped the car at a roadside restaurant. 'We still have a long way to go. It's better that we get a meal,' he said as he got out. Saini tipped him so that he could buy his meal, which Taarak accepted in chauffeurly fashion.

Upon a signal from Saini, Priya and Kurkude remained seated in the car. 'I'll call for our food right here,' said Saini. 'It's important for us to get some time to talk without the driver present. We should discuss our plan of action upon getting to Chandigarh.'

'I would imagine that our first priority would be to meet Devendra Chhedi and see if he has one of the seals in his possession,' said Priya.

'True, but what after that? As of now, I'm probably wanted by Radhika Singh for three murders and a kidnapping. How do I prove my innocence?' asked Saini taking a bite from the sandwich that a waiter from the restaurant handed him through the car window. The waiter had also brought three cups of coffee. Priya stretched out her arm and gratefully accepted the coffee that was on offer, passing on a cup each to Kurkude and Saini.

'It's rather simple, dear boy,' said Kurkude, taking a sip of his coffee. 'You were with me in my office for around an hour. My secretary, Miss Gonsalves, was alive when we started the meeting—in fact, she was the one who showed you into my office. Thereafter she closed the door and sat down at her workstation in the outer office. By the time that we ended our meeting, she had been murdered. It's quite obvious that neither you nor Priya could have killed her. I'm your alibi for the third murder. I'm sure my testimony will help get you off the hook with Radhika Singh,' he said, as he opened the car door to get out and use the restroom.

I had not imagined that slaying Kansa would result in the creation of yet another powerful enemy—Jarasandha, the king of Magadha. Jarasandha was furious that I had killed his son-in-law, Kansa, and that I was wielding political power in Mathura. He attacked Mathura and the old chief Ugrasena helplessly suggested that we surrender owing to the overwhelming odds against us. Balarama and I decided to take the battle into Jarasandha's camp and, even though we had much smaller forces, we succeeded in defeating Jarasandha. The defeat only made Jarasandha even more determined to teach me a lesson. He attacked Mathura seventeen times and on each occasion, Balarama and I were able to repel his forces. The eighteenth time would be different though.

Sitting inside the cafeteria sipping tea and eating a samosa, Taarak recalled the events at Kurkude's research laboratory. He had left Saini and Priya at the reception block along with Miss Gonsalves. She had offered him directions regarding how to get to the parking lot but he had ignored those. He had left the car just outside the reception block and had quickly stepped back inside in order to follow the clicking high heels worn by Miss Gonsalves.

Once she had shown Saini and Priya into Kurkude's office, she had settled down in her own chair and had pressed a key to activate her desktop computer. She had felt the cold steel of a scalpel against her throat within a few seconds but had been unable to cry out because Taarak had clamped his hand over her mouth.

'Listen to me very carefully,' he had hissed into her ear. 'I shall slit your throat if you do not cooperate. I want access to the data warehouse records and will need your password. Log in to the records from here so that I may access them. If you do as I say, you shall live to tell this story to your grandchildren.'

Terrified by the sharp metal pressing against her throat, Miss Gonsalves had quickly entered her user name and password into the login box on her screen. Taarak relaxed a little. This had turned out to be easier than he had expected. He loosened his grip over her mouth for just a moment and she let out a muffled cry. Luckily for him, the thick doors of the office prevented the noise from carrying into Kurkude's inner office. 'Damn you, woman,' he muttered. 'You have forced me to kill you.' The slitting of her throat was swift and clean, given the efficiency of the Swann-Morton scalpel. He placed the used scalpel in a handkerchief, which he then put into his pocket.

Taarak quickly inserted his USB flash drive into the desktop and began downloading the files that he wanted. He counted the seconds while the download happened— he was concerned that he would be caught with the corpse of Miss Gonsalves by a chance visitor to Kurkude's office. It was also possible that Kurkude or Saini would emerge at any moment from the inner office.

He was relieved when the download ended and he was able to pull out the flash drive and head back to his car. Secure inside his pocket was the flash drive. It contained the radiation readings from all the sites that had been surveyed by Kurkude's team. Retrieving the car, he had slowly driven to the visitors' parking lot, as originally recommended by Miss Gonsalves. Once there, he had resumed his role as a chauffeur—snatching forty winks while waiting for his masters. He was content.

Taking another bite of his samosa, Taarak looked at the cafeteria around him. He noticed Kurkude in the distance. It was evident that the old man had stepped outside the car to take a leak. Taarak got up from his chair and turned his gaze towards the parked car. Saini and Priya were still inside and seemed to be having a discussion while eating.

He realised that a golden opportunity had presented itself to him.

Having decided that he needed a different strategy if he wanted victory over me, Jarasandha approached my cousin, Shishupala, who hated me. Shishupala suggested to Jarasandha that they form an alliance with Kal Yavan, a neighbouring king, who had a blessing from Shiv that he could not be killed by any weapon, God or demon. Soon, Jarasandha laid siege to Mathura once again, this time in tandem with Kal Yavan. I knew that the situation was grim, so I decided to walk out of the city gates—unarmed. I challenged Kal Yavan to unarmed combat. The moment Kal Yavan agreed, I began running. Kal Yavan ran after me, calling me a coward. What he did not know was that I was leading him into the cave of Muchukunda. Muchukunda had received a blessing from Indra that if anyone disturbed his sleep, they would turn into ashes. I quickly draped my shawl on Muchukunda. The furious Kal Yavan came rushing in, saw my shawl, assumed that it was me on the floor and kicked the sleeping figure. Muchukunda opened his eyes and instantly turned Kal Yavan into ashes.

Saini and Priya were inside the car, finishing their sandwiches and coffee. In between mouthfuls, Priya decided to play the devil's advocate. 'Is there any proof that Krishna actually existed? Isn't it possible that Krishna was just a character in a fictional story, a product of a great writer's imagination?' she asked,

Saini scoffed. 'Let's forget the *Mahabharata* for a moment. The earliest reference to Krishna is found in the *Chandogya Upanishad*. The passage that refers to Krishna says: *Ghora of the Angirasas spoke to Krishna, the son of Devaki. My thirst has been quenched, he said. And till the very end of his life he upheld the three key principles: Krishna is aksita—indestructible; Krishna is acyuta—eternal; God is praana samhita—the very flow and essence of life!* Priya, you may hold the view that the *Mahabharata* is just a story, but how do you explain Krishna's name appearing in the *Upanishads*, works of the highest spiritual magnitude? Krishna is even mentioned in the *Rigveda* as the seer of Vedic hymn. He is once again mentioned in the *Atharvaveda* as the slayer of the Keshi demon. No, it would be impossible for Krishna to figure in these ancient works if a historical personality by that name did not exist,' said Saini indignantly.

'But the Krishna of the *Vedas* is a scholar, not a playful cowherd,' argued Priya. 'It seems almost impossible to reconcile the two characters. The Krishna of the Mahabharata war was almost ruthless whereas Krishna the cowherd was a combination of innocence and fun.'

'Again, Priya, the answer is to be found in the River Sarasvati. We know that the river was still flowing during the time of the Mahabharata. We are specifically told that Krishna's brother, Balarama, refused to participate in the war and decided to leave for a pilgrimage to various sacred spots along the river for the duration of the battle,' explained Saini. 'When the Sarasvati dried up, it resulted in the great river civilization decaying. The inhabitants were forced to move away towards new sources of water—either east towards the Ganges basin or west towards the Indus basin or even further towards the Tigris-Euphrates valley. The drying of the Sarasvati would have erased pasturelands entirely. Cattle populations would have dwindled, with entire herds getting wiped out.'

'What does cattle depletion have to do with the distinction between Krishna the cowherd and Krishna the statesman?' asked Priya.

'Everything!' exclaimed Saini. 'When the easterners reached the Ganges basin, they needed to revive their cattle populations. The easiest way of doing this was to make their icon—Krishna—into a cowherd. What was the name they gave Krishna? *Gopala*. The word emerges from *gow*—meaning cow—and *pala*—meaning the preserver or protector. It will surprise you to note that the same tradition carried into the west too. The Egyptians sacrificed most animals with the exception of the cow. The cow was considered sacred to Goddess Hathor. *Hesat*—the divine cow—was an earthly manifestation of Hathor!'

'So Krishna was given the status of a cowherd to preserve cattle numbers?' asked Priya.

'Not just cattle but the entire agricultural way of life,' said Saini. 'The name *Krishna* is derived from *Krishi*—the Sanskrit word for agriculture. The new migrants to the Ganges basin needed milk, ghee, and butter. They also relied on cow dung for fertiliser and fuel. By making Krishna into a cowherd, they ensured that their way of life could be preserved and their depleted cattle counts could be revived. But the cow eventually transformed all parts of society. Even today, when a Hindu performs prayers, the Brahmin will usually ask him for his *gothra*—his lineage. But the word *gothra* actually means a herd—or line—of cows! Why, even the founder of Buddhism, Gautama Buddha had a name that had a link to Krishna's cows!'

'How?' asked Priya.

'The name Gautama is derived from two words *gau*—or cow—and *uttama*—or greatest. Combined, the two words mean the greatest cow or the ultimate cow. The word "gau" also referred to the white colour of cows, and hence Gautama was also the ultimate white light,' said Saini smiling. Even the most sacred spot of the Buddhists is Bodh Gaya. *Gaya* is simply another word for *cow*. Gaya is mentioned in the *Ramayana*. In the epic, Rama, along with Sita and Lakshmana, visited a place called Gayapuri to make offerings to the spirit of their father, Dasharath. This Gayapuri is modern-day Bodh Gaya. Now do you see why Hindus consider Buddha as the ninth avatar of Vishnu?'

Priya was quiet as she digested the information. Saini continued breathlessly, 'Virtually all of Krishna's abundant names revolve around the cow—*Gopala, Godharin, Gomateshwar, Gopa, Govardhana, Govinda, Gosvami*. You'll be even more surprised when I tell you that your last vacation spot had a name derived from Krishna's cows!'

Priya screwed her eyes. 'My last vacation? You mean the trip that I took along with my father to Goa?' she asked incredulously.

Saini laughed. 'The *Mahabharata* refers to the region that you now call Goa as *Govarashtra*—literally meaning *a nation of cowherds*. It is from this word Govarashtra that one derives the modern name of Goa,' he explained, his eyes twinkling. 'Everything has a connection to the cow. The ancient Greeks worshipped a primordial earth-goddess. Do you know what her name was? *Gaia*—or as we would say, Gaya!'

'And speaking of the ancient Greeks, where is our ancient nuclear physicist? He has been gone for over thirty minutes,' wondered Saini, looking at the digital clock on the dashboard of the car.

Having defeated Kal Yavan on the eighteenth attack, I could have chosen to stay on in Mathura but it was turning out to be a costly proposition in terms of human life. Thousands of soldiers and citizens would die each time Jarasandha attacked. I called Vishwakarma, the divine architect, and asked him to build me a magnificent city in the middle of the sea. He bowed down before me and accepted the assignment. I then called the Sea God and asked him to give me some land in the ocean. The Sea God spat out some water from the ocean and created an island for me. This would be my new city for the Yadavas—the city of Dwaravati. Filled with palaces, temples, gardens and lakes, it would be the most magnificent city ever built. Surrounded by water on all sides, it would be impossible for Jarasandha to attack it. This single instance of retreat on my part earned me the title of Ranchordas—one who deserts the battlefield.

Taarak had carefully watched the old scientist enter the gents' restroom. He left some cash on the table for the waiter to settle his bill and briskly walked to the restroom, being careful to remain out of Saini's line of sight. Once inside, he looked around. There was only one person using a urinal on the left side of the toilets. On the right was a row of doors leading to the WC cubicles. Taarak walked over to the washbasin and began washing his hands even though he didn't really need to. He was simply waiting for the man using the urinal to leave.

After a minute's wait, the bathroom emptied out and Taarak walked over to the row of doors leading to the WC cubicles. Of the four doors, two were open and the other two were locked. Taarak bent down to look under the two closed cubicle doors, which ended almost a foot above the ground. Below one of the doors he could discern a bucket and mop. He realised that it was probably the maintenance crew cleaning up inside.

Under the second door, he saw a pair of shoes with undone trousers lying bunched up over them. Evidently the old scientist was relieving himself. Taarak thought on his feet. This was a perfect opportunity to obtain the seal that was probably on Kurkude's person and to finish him off once and for all. He felt inside his trouser pockets. The rubber stamp, paintbrush and scalpel were with him.

He looked around. No one was in sight. He stepped a few paces away from the cubicle door so that he would have the advantage of momentum when knocking it down. Just as he was gearing up to propel himself into the locked door, he heard a familiar voice.

'Ah, I see that you're here. I hope we can move on now?' asked Saini cheerfully.

'Yes, sir, of course,' said Taarak, resuming the tone and demeanour of the ever-dutiful driver.

'Any idea where Professor Kurkude is?' asked Saini.

'I'm not sure, sir,' said Taarak. 'It could be him inside that cubicle.'

'Let's check,' said Saini as he walked up to the cubicle door and knocked gently. 'Is that you inside, Professor

Kurkude?' he asked. There was no response from the occupant inside.

'Professor, can you hear me?' asked Saini, his voice significantly louder as he knocked firmly on the door. He was greeted by more silence.

'That's it, we're knocking down this door,' said Saini. Taarak could not believe the turn of events. He had been on the verge of knocking down the door to kill the old man inside, when he had been interrupted by Saini. Now Saini was in the process of knocking down the very same door.

As the door's bolt gave way, the picture that emerged was of a slumped-over professor sitting on the commode, with the seat cover down and his underpants still around his waist. His trousers lay crumpled over his shoes and his limp body showed no visible signs of life.

Saini went into panic mode. He grabbed Kurkude's head by his hair and looked into his eyes. They looked like the lifeless eyes of a corpse. He rushed outside and called Priya in. She ran inside, ignoring the sign that read 'Gentlemen'.

'Check his pulse!' yelled Saini. Priya bent down and placed two fingers under the angle of Kurkude's jaw to check the carotid pulse. 'See how I do it,' urged Priya. 'You never know when you will need to do it yourself!' Saini observed Priya as she went about checking Kurkude's pulse. 'He's alive,' she said at length.

'Then why is he looking dead?' asked Saini. 'Has he had a stroke or heart attack? What should we do?'

Taarak stepped in. He opened the professor's mouth and sniffed. He smiled. It was alky-breath usually caused by chloral hydrate being metabolised through the lungs instead of the liver. 'He's been drugged,' said Taarak, omitting to mention the nature of the drug that had been used. 'If we help him outside and get him into the car he should be fine in a few minutes.'

Saini breathed a sigh of relief. He had been wondering how he would ever extricate himself from the situation that he had found himself in. He had just been delivered a lifeline. 'How do you know so much about medicine?' asked Saini, amazed and a little curious.

'My father worked with horses, sir,' explained Taarak. 'I got to know a bit about sedatives from him.'

'Well, you have my sincere thanks,' said Saini. 'Without you, I would have been forced to call for an ambulance for the professor—quite unnecessarily, I might add. C'mon, let's get his trousers up and then let's help him to the car.'

Saini did not notice that a small brown paper envelope that was inside Kurkude's pocket had been skilfully extracted by the eager-to-please driver and that the envelope with the seal inside it was now in the chauffeur's possession.

After Satyabhama, I went on to marry Rukmini — the sister of Rukmi, the ruler of Vidarbha. Rukmi had arranged for Rukmini to marry my cousin Shishupala, the ruler of Chedi and an ally of Jarasandha. I abducted Rukmini and married her, thus making an enemy of Shishupala. I went on to marry many princesses — from Kosala, Madra, Avanti and Kekaya. I eventually had 16,108 wives! These marriages were arranged in order to consolidate my power. They were political alliances more than anything else. As a Yadava, I was not a king and could never be one. My retreat from Mathura meant that I needed more allies — including the Pandavas. My aunt, Kunti, who was very happy to see me, was also wondering what had brought me to meet her. I smiled and told her, 'You can now return to Hastinapur. The Kauravas will not dare to harm you given the fact that your daughter-in-law has the powerful Drupada for a father.' Upon my advice, the Pandavas returned to Hastinapur. I spoke to Vidura, Dhritarashtra's half-brother. 'The only way to ensure that there is peace is by dividing the kingdom in half. Convince Dhritarashtra that it is necessary,' I explained to Vidura. In open court, Dhritarashtra gifted the region of Khandavaprastha to the Pandavas to establish their own kingdom as per the sage advice of Vidura.

Radhika Singh fidgeted as the airplane touched down. Seated next to her was Rathore, looking haggard and dishevelled. Radhika's right hand was in her pocket, counting beads, while her mind was busy reciting the name of *Hari*.

Deducing that Saini had managed to evade the police checkpoints in Jodhpur, Radhika and Rathore had considered placing a call to Sunil Garg, the Special Director of the CBI. The obvious destination that Saini was headed for was Chandigarh, the city in which Devendra Chhedi lived.

'Why don't we get our men to put up inspection barriers at Rohtak, Panipat and Ambala? Those are transit points that they will have to cross on the way to Chandigarh,' said Rathore.

'No. We can't take a chance. They have Professor Kurkude with them. Let's not do anything that causes them to panic. We don't know what they might end up doing to the old man in a situation where they feel cornered,' said Radhika.

'So we simply allow them unhindered passage to Chandigarh?' asked Rathore incredulously.

'Well, yes,' said Radhika Singh smiling. 'But this time we shall reach their destination before them. We shall fly to Chandigarh and meet Chhedi beforehand. We shall be waiting for them when they walk into Chhedi's office.'

'There's the other matter of the secretary's murder,' began Rathore.

'Yes?' asked Radhika.

'The cut on the neck that killed her was neat and precise. I spoke to the medical examiner. He says that the cut was definitely made using a scalpel. I sent him a photograph of the two scalpels that we had found at the murder scenes of Varshney and Bhojaraj. The examiner says that he can say with some certainty that the slashing of the secretary's neck was done with something similar,' said Rathore.

'But why kill the secretary at all?' asked Radhika. 'It doesn't fit the pattern! For starters, the scene wasn't staged at all. No scalpel, no symbol, no mantra, no bleeding left foot. This was a random act of violence, not part of the originally planned series of murders.

'Did you speak to the information technology department of Kurkude's lab?' resumed Radhika.

'What was I supposed to check with them?' asked Rathore, expecting a reprimand any moment for a lapse.

'When the secretary was killed, her computer terminal was in front of her—switched on. Did anyone access any information from the terminal and, if so, what was accessed?' asked Radhika.

42

The Pandavas cleared the forest of Khandavaprastha by burning it down. The god of fire—Agni—was pleased with the offering and presented me with a discus called the Sudarshan Chakra. He also presented Arjuna with a powerful bow called the Gandiva. Nothing survived the forest fire except for a single demon called Maya. Maya asked that his life be spared and that in return he would build the Pandavas a magnificent city as their capital. This came to be known as Indraprastha. It soon became the most prosperous city in the land and Yudhistira ruled it wisely, applying the principles of dharma to his administration. I also suggested that my five cousins establish ground rules in respect of their personal lives, particularly in respect of their marriage to Draupadi. Each brother would have access to Draupadi's bed chamber for one year at a time. This was to prevent disharmony among the five. All the brothers were also allowed to marry other women so that they would have companionship for the four years when Draupadi was inaccessible to them.

Professor Kurkude opened his eyes and squinted a little. The harsh sunlight hurt his eyes. He had been made to lie down on the rear seat of the car with the car doors wide open. 'What happened to me?' he asked, looking up into the faces of Saini and Priya. Taarak stood respectfully a few feet away.

'You were poisoned, sir,' said Saini. 'A paralysing agent was administered in something that you ate or drank. Fortunately, all of us were at hand,' explained Saini.

'Poisoned? But how? I have been drinking only water— with the exception of the coffee that the waiter served us,' said Kurkude. 'You think that the restaurant staff wanted to kill me?'

'It's possible that our assassin has followed us. He could be lurking in the shadows and may have slipped the poison into your coffee so that he would be able to overpower you easily. It's difficult to tell, but it only strengthens my resolve that we need to get to Chandigarh fast, in double-quick time,' said Saini. 'Quite obviously we're dealing with a very cunning person—someone who seems to know our every move. Possibly this is someone who understands the spiritual and scientific explanations behind these seals.'

Taarak, who was within earshot, smiled to himself. Saini would be dumbfounded if he knew the extent of knowledge that Mataji possessed. 'Shall we get going, sir?' he asked deferentially.

'Yes,' replied Saini. 'If the professor feels strong enough.'

'I'm fine. Let's go,' said Kurkude as Taarak sat down in the driver's seat and turned the ignition key. As the journey resumed, Taarak's thoughts drifted back to his days of training under his mentor and teacher, Mataji.

'For generations, our land has been invaded by foreigners,' said Mataji to young Taarak after school one day. 'The Greeks, Huns, Mongols, Arabs, Portuguese, French and English plundered India of its wealth. It shall be your responsibility to right these historical wrongs.'

'But how, Mataji? I am just a young boy,' said Taarak.

'But one day you shall grow up. You shall realise that you have within you all the miraculous powers of the Kalki Avatar—the final incarnation of Vishnu. That's the moment I am waiting for,' she said.

'But what shall be my mission?' asked Taarak.

'To show the world that the cradle of civilisation was right here in India! To guide the misbelievers and to show them the errors of their ways!' exclaimed Mataji. 'The English rascals came to India and propagated the myth of an Aryan invasion. Significantly, there is no record of an invasion or migration in the *Vedas*, *Puranas* or *Itihasas*. The Western pseudo-scholars were simply unwilling to accept the fact that ours was an amazingly advanced civilisation that lay distinctly outside Europe, at a time far earlier than the one in which the patriarchs Abraham and Moses made their covenant with God!'

'But our history teacher in school tells us that there was an Aryan invasion in… in… 1500 BCE,' said Taarak, scratching his head to recall the date.

'That was based on Christian belief, not science! The Christians believed that the world was created at nine o'clock in the morning of 23 October, 4004 BCE. Working from that date, they established that the great Biblical flood—in the anticipation of which Noah built a massive ark to preserve living beings on earth—would have happened in 2448 BCE. They then postulated that the Aryan invasion would have happened around a thousand years later! *That* is the basis for what has been passed on to us as historical research for endless years,' scoffed Mataji.

'So the Western scholars were interested in propagating Christianity rather than serious historical research?' asked Taarak.

'Yes,' said Mataji. 'Western scholars who studied Hindu literature were initially convinced that the Krishna story had been borrowed from the life of Jesus Christ. In 1762, the Italian scholar P Georgi wrote that *Krishnu is a corruption of the name of the Saviour; the deeds correspond wonderfully with the name, though they have been impiously and cunningly polluted by most wicked imposters!* Another scholar, Albrecht Weber, painstakingly pointed out all the similarities between Krishna and Christ. Weber concluded that the Vedic concept of incarnations of God was also borrowed from the idea that Jesus Christ had been the Son of God. Yet another scholar, Dr F Lorinser, carried out a translation of the *Bhagavad Gita* but instead of admiring it for its original wisdom, he compared it to the *New Testament* and concluded that the *Gita* had mostly been inspired by the Bible!' exclaimed Mataji.

'So we were accused of having plagiarised the Bible?' asked Taarak.

'Yes. But luckily, the big break in favour of Krishna's antiquity came from a book called *Indica*—written around three hundred years before Jesus Christ by Megasthenes, the Greek ambassador to the Mauryan kingdom. Megasthenes described Mathura as a centre of Krishna-worship. The Western scholars who had been claiming that Krishna was simply a story inspired by the Christian Bible now had to eat their own words because it turned out that the Krishna story had existed much before Jesus Christ. For the first time ever, Indian literary sources were reviewed to see if they could substantiate what was written in the *Indica*. As it turns out, the grammarian Patanjali had written of Kansa's slaying by Krishna in the second century BCE; Kautilya's *Arthashastra* from the fourth century BCE mentioned Krishna several times; the greatest Sanskrit grammarian, Panini, talked of Vishnu-worship and Bhakti in the fifth century BCE. It was thus firmly established that Krishna—and Krishna-worship—predated Christianity by many centuries,' explained Mataji. 'Forced to eat humble pie, Western scholars now adopted the ingenious idea of suggesting that ancient Indian literature was not a product of local Indian populations but had been imported by conquering Aryans from Central Europe.'

Taarak nodded his head vigorously to show support for Mataji's declarations.

'We keep referring to Mesopotamia as the cradle of civilisation. That's nonsense. It was India! It was the drying-up of the Sarasvati that took our people and our culture there. The most sacred spot for Muslims from around the world is the *Kaaba* in Mecca. The world forgets the fact that the Kaaba was a pagan temple prior to the advent of Islam. The Kaaba contained 360 idols, representing each day of the year. The chief among these deities was the moon-god Hubal—remarkably similar to Shiv. Just like Shiv, Hubal was depicted as carrying the moon on his head. And just like Shiv, from whose holy abode the Ganga flowed down to us, Hubal had the sacred waters of Zamzam,' said Mataji. 'The Muslims retained many of the pagan rites associated with the Kaaba. They continued to circumambulate the Kaaba seven times—just like Hindus do around fire. They continued to wear white clothes during Hajj—just like the Jain munis of India do round the year. They even retained the symbol of Hubal—the crescent and star—and adopted it as an Islamic symbol!'

'How does that matter, Mataji? It only shows that we are all connected, doesn't it?' asked Taarak innocently.

'True, but what I'm telling you is that many of the traditions of Islam evolved from a set of pagan beliefs. It is possible that some of these pagan traditions had Vedic roots. Much later, Muslims came to believe that Hubal's three goddesses—*Al-Lat, Uzza* and *Manat*—had taken refuge in the Somnath temple of Gujarat, just a short distance from Dwarka. This was the main reason why waves of attacks by Muslim invaders took place on the Somnath temple!' said Mataji indignantly. 'That's why I need you to work diligently… so that you may set right historical wrongs.'

'I shall work hard, Mataji. I shall make you proud of me,' said Taarak allowing himself to be convinced of the righteousness of Mataji's cause. He silently vowed to do whatever was needed to make her happy.

43

*That brings me to the topic of Arjuna's wife, Subhadra.
I knew that my sister, Subhadra, was in love with
Arjuna. However, my elder brother Balarama had
arranged her marriage with Duryodhana. I advised
Arjuna to enter Dwarka in disguise and, rather
shrewdly, advised Subhadra to elope with him. She
needed very little encouragement, though! Balarama
was very angry with me. He planned to go after Arjuna
but when I convinced him that Subhadra had eloped with
Arjuna of her own free will, he grudgingly reconciled
himself to the situation. Subhadra would eventually
bear Arjuna a son. His name would go down in history
as Abhimanyu.*

Devendra Chhedi was surprised to receive a visit from
Inspector Radhika Singh and Sub-Inspector Rathore.
He almost wished he could ignore their presence, as he
scanned his printouts containing genetic markers. He
smiled contentedly as he took a puff from his cherry-
flavoured tobacco-laden pipe and then forced himself
to deal with the police officers who were looking at him
quizzically, wondering why he was smiling at them.

Chhedi was the world's leading authority in SCNT—
better known as Somatic Cell Nuclear Transfer. In SCNT,
reproductive cloning could be carried out by transferring

genetic material from the nucleus of a donor adult cell to an egg whose nucleus had been removed. The reconstructed egg, containing the DNA from the donor cell, would then be treated with chemicals and electric currents in order to stimulate cell division. Once the cloned embryo reached an appropriate age, it would be transferred to the uterus of a female host where it would continue to develop until birth.

Cloning had originally been discovered by Scottish scientists at the Roslin Institute who had created the famous sheep *Dolly*. Dolly had aroused global excitement and concern because of the scientific and ethical implications of cloning. The achievement, cited by *Science* magazine as the medical miracle of the decade, also generated uneasiness over cloning, soon to become an all-encompassing term used by researchers to describe different processes for duplicating biological material. Chhedi had worked his way up at the Roslin Institute before being offered a generous research grant by the Chandigarh-based Immuno Molecular Life Sciences Ltd to carry on his study with substantially elevated budgets and state-of-the-art facilities.

'Yes? What may I do for you?' asked Chhedi, holding out his hand to exchange greetings with the officers. As he got up from his chair, his long salt-and-pepper hair fell over his face. His crumpled lab coat partially hid a polka-dotted bowtie that was lopsided and covered with pipe ash.

'Sir, we need your assistance,' began Radhika Singh. 'You do remember the seal that was sent to you for safekeeping by your friend, Mr Anil Varshney?'

'I'm not at liberty to discuss this issue with you,' declared Chhedi pompously. He hadn't been sworn to secrecy by Varshney, but Chhedi was unable to pass up any opportunity to make people in authority squirm. It was this rebellious streak that had got him into trouble with the school principal when he had rigged his toilet to explode. Mercifully, the young Chhedi had been a better talker than detonations-expert and the principal had managed to get away with just a few tender spots on his rear. Chhedi had been rusticated, much to the chagrin of his father who had eventually cajoled the principal to think beyond his sore backside.

'Fair enough,' said Radhika quickly. 'The reason we're here is because Mr Varshney's murderer—someone known to you from your school days—Ravi Mohan Saini is on his way here to meet you. We believe that he has killed not only Anil Varshney but also Dr Nikhil Bhojaraj. In addition to that, he is a suspect in the death of Professor Rajaram Kurkude's secretary as well as in the kidnapping of Professor Kurkude himself.'

Chhedi's jaw dropped. What the hell was Saini up to? They had known each other in school. Saini had exhibited the same trace of rebelliousness as Chhedi but to a lesser degree. It was in stark contrast to the exemplary-schoolboy behaviour of Anil Varshney. The officers were right. He did need to give them a patient hearing. It was a question of risk to life. He cleared his throat. 'What exactly do you want from me?' he asked.

'Nothing complicated, sir. We would like to stay put, right here in your office until they show up. In the meantime, I shall be posting plainclothes officers all over your campus. It is our intention to recapture Mr Saini when he comes over to meet you. It shall also give us the opportunity to determine the where-abouts of Professor Kurkude,' explained Rathore.

'One more thing sir,' interrupted Radhika. 'It's possible that Saini may phone you in advance to tell you of his arrival. Please keep us informed so that we are better prepared for him. Please be informal and receptive to his requests. Say nothing that may tip him off that we're here.'

Chhedi nodded his head. 'I hear you loud and clear, Inspector. It shall be as you ask, but I also require your cooperation,' he said.

'What sort of cooperation do you need from us?' asked Radhika.

'The work that we're doing here is path-breaking research. We just cannot afford to have strangers roaming in and out of private work areas,' said Chhedi. 'You shall have to ensure that your men are restricted to non-access-controlled areas of this facility.'

44

Soon Yudhistira expressed his desire to perform the Rajasuya Yajna—a public coronation in which other kings would accept and acknowledge him as an equal sovereign. I suggested that the Pandavas first defeat Jarasandha—the mighty ruler of Magadha. Such a victory would make it impossible for any other sovereign to object to Yudhistira's sovereignty. I suggested that Bhima challenge Jarasandha to a duel. I told Bhima the secret to killing Jarasandha. Jarasandha's body had to be torn into two halves vertically in order to kill him. Bhima followed my advice and succeeded in splitting Jarasandha in two. This paved the way for Yudhistira's coronation. It also rid me of the biggest thorn in my side, Jarasandha.

Radhika looked around her. Rows upon rows of gleaming laboratory tables and equipment, cryo-freezers, specimen storage systems, electronic micro-scopes and DNA synthesisers stretched into the distance. Alongside were banks of computer servers where thousands of data sets from multiple research studies done on different platforms could be merged, and data from thousands of projects, finds, participants and sources could be analysed together, increasing the probability of gene discovery.

'If you don't mind my asking, what exactly do you do here?' asked Radhika, her interest piqued by Chhedi's statement.

'We're trying to use modern scientific techniques to uncover our past,' said Chhedi cryptically.

'Could you be a little less mysterious, sir?' asked Radhika, smiling as she located a few almonds in her pockets. Chhedi laughed. The woman was a livewire.

'My primary interest lies in our ability to rejuvenate ancient DNA,' said Chhedi, staring at Radhika as she popped an almond into her mouth.

'Ancient DNA? But isn't that pointless? There would hardly be any ancient DNA material for revival,' argued Radhika.

'You are mistaken, Inspector. Ancient civilisations knew more about stem cells than modern humans. Many Hindus would be intimately aware of a ritual that would be performed after childbirth for precisely this reason,' said Chhedi.

'Really? What ritual was that?' asked Radhika.

'After delivery, the midwife would take the umbilical cord of the new born child and place a small portion of it in an airtight copper capsule, and this capsule—known as a *Taviju Raksha*—would be tied below the waist of the child until he grew up,' explained Chhedi. 'The remainder of the umbilical cord would be placed in an earthen jar and buried underground. Doesn't it surprise you that modern civilisation has only just recently figured out that preserving stem cells from a child's umbilical cord using cryo-freezing is a prudent step?'

'So you think that the *Tavija Raksha* was not merely a religious ritual but a scientific one?' asked Radhika.

'The ancients knew far more about medicine than we're willing to believe,' replied Chhedi. 'Vedic surgeons wrote about plastic surgery, extraction of cataracts, dental surgery, caesarean sections and bone-setting. Surgery—known as *Shastrakarma* in the Vedas —was pioneered in the *Shushruta Samahita*. Shushruta's path-breaking treatise describes rhinoplasty in which a mutilated nose can be reconstructed through plastic surgery! The *Charaka Samhita* authored by Charaka discusses physiology, etiology, embryology, digestion, metabolism, immunity and even genetics. For example, Charaka knew the factors that determined the sex of a child. Why is it impossible to believe that the ancients knew of genetic cloning? Read between the lines, Inspector,' said Chhedi.

'Cloning? I don't recall any mention of it in our epics?' asked Radhika.

'Think carefully. When Lord Rama fought with Ravana, was he fighting one demon with ten heads or was he actually fighting ten people who had been genetically cloned from Ravana?' asked Chhedi.

Radhika digested the information slowly. She visualised Ravana battling Lord Rama, with the latter lopping off the former's head repeatedly, only to see it replaced by yet another. The geneticist wasn't entirely wrong. It could indeed have been possible that Ravana had succeeded in cloning himself so that any enemy would have to fight not just one but ten Ravanas.

'I assume that you're familiar with the stories of Durga slaying various demons?' asked Chhedi.

'Some of them,' said Radhika, chewing on an almond contentedly.

'According to the eighth chapter of *Devi Mahatmya* from the *Markandeya Puran*, there lived a demon by the name of *Raktabija*. You do understand what Raktabija means, don't you? It translates to *blood seed*. The story about Raktabija was that each time a drop of his blood fell to the earth, a new duplicate of himself would emerge. He was eventually killed by Durga. She succeeded in killing him by preventing his blood from reaching the ground. Isn't this yet another example of our ancient myths telling us about deeper scientific advances?' asked Chhedi.

Radhika was reeling from the onslaught of information.

'Our mythology tells us that Brahama took birth from the umbilicus of Vishnu. Was this just imagination or was it indicative of the fact that Vedic people knew of the presence and significance of stem cells in the umbilical cord?' asked Chhedi.

Greeted by silence, Chhedi asked, 'We know that Krishna's elder brother—Balarama—was transferred from Devaki's womb to that of Rohini. How would that have been possible without knowledge of in vitro fertilisation?'

Unknown to Radhika and non-academics, Chhedi had written a paper in which he had referenced the *Vishnu Purana*. It also said that Hari in the form of Brahama was the instrumental cause of creation. It was said that matter was imperceptible and invisible but had been infused with an intrinsic ability to trans-form, mutate, combine, recombine and permutate into visible substances. Chhedi had argued that there were pluripotential stem cells in the bone marrow and the blood in the umbilical cord, and that these stem cells were the ones that were capable of transforming themselves into any cell in the universe of the human body. When the *Vishnu Purana* spoke of *Akaasa*—it was simply referring to the universe's pluripotential stem substance.

45

Guests from all over the land attended the Rajasuya Yajna of Yudhistira. Included among the invitees were Duryodhana and Shishupala. Indraprastha had grown into the most magnificent city in the land and poets had begun comparing it to heaven. Duryodhana was extremely jealous. I'm told that while he was admiring the city, he slipped and fell into a pond. Draupadi, who happened to be in the vicinity, observed, 'A blind son of blind parents!' Duryodhana seethed with anger at the remark and took a personal vow that he would ensure Draupadi's humiliation exactly in the same way that she had enjoyed his. Indeed, it is true that careless remarks can come back to bite you!

'Do you realise that we have just crossed Karnal?' asked Saini from the front seat.

'Yes. Ten minutes ago. How is that important?' asked Priya.

'Well, somewhere between Karnal and Ambala, lies a very important location,' said Saini. Priya maintained her silence. She had grown weary of prodding answers from Saini. She believed he would blurt them out soon enough, anyway. He proved her right.

'Midway between Karnal and Ambala is the battlefield of Kurukshetra, where the Pandavas and Kauravas fought their epic war,' said Saini finally. 'If you both are in agreement, I would like to stop at *Jyotisaar*.'

'What is at Jyotisaar?' asked Kurkude.

'I'll explain later. Just let's get to Thanesar village and you'll understand everything,' said Saini.

Taarak asked for a few directions along the way and they reached the Kurukshetra-Pehowa road within ten minutes. Just five kilometres west of Thanesar stood the massive banyan tree that Saini wanted to visit. It was called Jyotisaar. The tree was encircled by a simple white fence and next to it stood a marble chariot depicting Krishna delivering his famous sermon to Arjuna. A signboard informed visitors of the significance of the location.

Saini got down from the car and began circling the tree slowly.

'What is so remarkable about this banyan?' asked Kurkude, impatiently.

'This, dear professor, is the Jyotisaar tree. "*Jyoti*" means "light" and "*sar*" translates to "core understanding". This tree is *the core understanding of light*, or ultimately *an in-depth understanding of God*. This tree is thousands of years old and is an offshoot of the holy tree under which Krishna delivered the *Bhagwad Gita* to Arjuna. It has withstood the test of time and has remained rooted here from time immemorial. It saw the battle being fought right here at Kurukshetra!' exclaimed Saini, reverentially touching the trunk of the tree. 'If only trees could talk, we would have all the answers by simply conversing with the Jyotisaar!'

'Some years ago, wasn't there talk of a resident having found bones belonging to the soldiers in the great war right here?' asked Kurkude.

'Yes, there is a man called Ram Prasad Birbal—a resident of this area—who claims that he has found bones dating from the Kurukshetra battle. But honestly speaking, his findings do not really matter. The thermo-luminescent dating of other relics in addition to carbon-dating at other Kurukshetra sites have yielded dates far older than the Indus Valley civilisation. Euan Mackie, an English archaeologist, has even discovered a clay tablet depicting Krishna's uprooting of the Yamala Arjuna trees. Guess where the clay tablet was discovered? In Mohenjodaro! Once again: proof that the Indus-Sarasvati was indeed the very civilisation that gave us the *Vedas*, the epics, the *Puranas* and the *Upanishads*.'

'Was there ever any doubt on that score?' asked Kurkude.

'The doubts were created by foreign historians,' replied Saini, as he knelt in front of the tree to offer prayers. 'Hundreds of sites of the Sarasvati civilisation were wrongly clubbed together and classified as the Indus Valley civilisation. It came to be regarded as a civilisation that apparently had no body of literature. On the other hand, the *Vedas*, which probably constitute the largest body of ancient literature anywhere in the world, were seen as sophisticated writing without a corresponding civilisation. The common-sense approach of linking the two together went contrary to the Aryan-invasion theory. This was in spite of the fact that the *Vedas* repeatedly allude to their sages performing their sacred rites on the banks of the Sarasvati. The discovery of the dried bed of the ancient Sarasvati is the strongest evidence to link the *Vedas* to Harappan culture. The *swastika*—a sacred symbol in the *Vedas*—has been found at innumerable places in Indus Valley sites. Archaeologists have also discovered fire altars, images of people in meditation, and sacred water tanks—all indications of the fact that the ones who built these magnificent cities were the same people who wrote the *Vedas*.'

'Wasn't there also a view that the *Vedas* were possibly written *after* the decline of the Indus Valley?' asked Priya, touching her head reverentially to the tree trunk.

'That theory has been disproved by the discovery of the ancient route of the Sarasvati,' retorted Saini. 'The *Rig Veda* in particular calls the Sarasvati the largest river of the region, *pure in its course from the mountains to the sea!* This means that the river was in full flow when the *Vedas* were written.'

'Did the Sarasvati continue to flow even during the time of the *Mahabharata*?' asked Kurkude.

'The *Mahabharata* describes the Sarasvati as a river that was no longer mighty—one that had begun to dry into isolated lakes in Rajasthan and Haryana,' said Saini. 'By simply reading ancient Vedic literature one can visualise the stages of the Sarasvati river. When the ice age ended, the massive glaciers of the Himalayas began to melt and this melting process made the Sarasvati exceptionally mighty. It remained in full flow until the glaciers had melted. But the end of the Sarasvati would have coincided with the end of Dwarka too, because the increasing sea levels would have inundated the city!'

Saini was about to stand up and walk towards the car when he noticed Kurkude in panic. The old man was feverishly searching his pockets. 'What's the matter, Professor?' asked Saini.

'The seal!' he cried. 'I can't bloody find it! Someone has stolen it!'

During the Rajasuya ceremony, the Brahmins asked Yudhistira to select a guest of honour. Yudhistira chose me because the Pandavas attributed their progress to my guidance. Shishupala could not bear to see the man who had stolen Rukmini away from him being given so much importance, and began insulting me in open court. Given that Shishupala was my cousin, I had granted his mother a boon that I would forgive a hundred insults by him, but not a single one more. I warned him after his hundred insults had been uttered but he kept going. As soon as Shishupala hurled his hundred and first insult, I released my Sudarshan Chakra and lopped off Shishupala's head. Some kings stormed out and attacked Dwarka to avenge Shishupala's death. I thus had to leave Indraprastha in a hurry in order to defend Dwarka.

The mood inside the car had turned sullen ever since the professor had discovered that the seal was missing. Taarak had helpfully suggested that they should consider going back to the restaurant where the professor had been poisoned. After all, it was possible that the missing item may have simply slipped out in the restroom or even when they had been carrying the professor out to the car. Saini knew that it was not an option that could be considered. The possibility of the police trailing them outweighed all other considerations.

Saini was feeling rather depressed himself. The first seal— given by Varshney to him—had been taken away by the police from his house. The seal that Varshney had planned to send Dr Nikhil Bhojaraj had obviously been taken by the killer given that it hadn't been found either at Varshney's home or in Bhojaraj's ship. The third seal—the one with Kurkude— was now missing. Even if they met Devendra Chhedi and saw the seal that Varshney was supposed to have sent him, it would be of little use in the absence of the other three.

'We'll just have to make the best of a bad situation,' said Saini to the others during a rest break when Taarak was away. 'We do have photographs of the missing seals. Unfortunately, the photographs only tell us what is on the face of the seals, not what is on the reverse. In any case, we'll make best use of the photographic evidence along with the actual seal that is in Chhedi's possession.'

'You're assuming that Chhedi will cooperate with us,' said Priya. 'We need to be careful. It's possible that the police may have already told him to hand us in.'

'You don't know Chhedi, Priya. The man hates authority of any sort. Schoolteachers, corporate honchos, government babus, politicians and policemen usually get his hackles up,' replied Saini. 'I doubt that he will turn us in. In fact, we were pretty good friends in school. He could never understand why I was best friends with Varshney instead of him!'

'Sir, we are on the outskirts of Chandigarh. I think that you had better find out the exact address so that I may seek directions,' said Taarak to Saini as he returned from his break. Saini nodded, turned to Kurkude and said, 'Could you possibly Google-search Devendra Chhedi on your Blackberry? I do recall that he was working for a company—the name was... what was it? Something like Immuno...'

'Immuno Molecular Life Sciences Limited,' replied Kurkude. 'I've found it. Want me to call?'

Kurkude called the number and handed over the phone to Saini. The call was made to the company's switchboard, which patched it through to Chhedi's secretary. 'Who should I say is calling?' she asked.

'Please tell him that it's Ravi Mohan Saini and that I'm seeking an urgent appointment with him,' replied Saini.

'Please hold for a minute, sir, while I transfer your call,' requested the secretary, subjecting Saini to some more elevator music. Chhedi came on the line within a minute. 'Roger, you old devil, how have you been?' he asked jovially, addressing Saini by his school nickname. Saini breathed a sigh of relief. There seemed to be no antagonism or distance in his demeanour.

'I have some stories to tell you, Dumpy, but can't do it over the phone. Can I come over? I'm in your neck of the woods already,' replied Saini, keeping up the friendly and informal tone.

'Sure. How does half an hour from now sound? I'm located at Chandigarh Corporate Plaza on the sixth floor,' said Chhedi.

'Perfect. Listen, did our common friend—Varshney—send you an artefact for safekeeping? He did? Good,' said Saini.

'Do you need directions to Chandigarh Corporate Plaza?' asked Chhedi, carrying on the conversation over the speakerphone at his desk while Radhika Singh and

Rathore sat opposite him, listening to every word exchanged between the two men. As the conversation ended, she nodded to Rathore who picked up his phone and began getting his men in place.

Sitting inside the car, Saini looked at the notepad in his hand. He jotted down a few sentences to remind himself of the status of the seals and those who had them:

Varshney: Had four seals—was supposed to send them to four friends—three were passed on but Bhojaraj's never reached him. Varshney was killed with a discus symbol imprinted on his forehead.

Bhojaraj: Was supposed to receive one seal, but didn't get it. Killed nonetheless, with a lotus symbol imprinted on his forehead.

Kurkude: Received one seal but it was lost or stolen during the car journey.

Saini: Received one of the seals directly from Varshney but it was taken away by the police when his residence was searched.

Chhedi: Received one of the seals and claims that it is still with him.

Saini looked at the bulleted points once again. Then his face drained of all colour. He looked at the names written down once again just to be sure that his mind was not playing tricks on him. It wasn't.

Varshney—Bhojaraj—Kurkude—Saini—Chhedi.

Krishna had been a Yadava, but the Yadavas had been composed of eighteen different clans, some of whom had fought on the Pandava's side and others on the Kaurava's. Some of the clans that had helped Krishna build the magnificent city of Dwarka were the Vrishnis, the Bhojas, the Kukuras, the Shainyas and the Chedis. Saini mentally struggled with the similarities as he made notes with a trembling hand:

Varshney—*Vrishni*
Bhojaraj—*Bhoja*
Kurkude—*Kukura*
Saini—*Shainya*
Chhedi—*Chedi*

Duryodhana, who was still seething with envy, returned to Hastinapur and decided that the time was ripe for revenge. Upon the advice of his maternal uncle Shakuni, he invited Yudhistira—who was addicted to gambling—to a game of dice. Unknown to Yudhistira, the dice were magical and Shakuni could make them fall any way that he wanted. As the game commenced and it looked like luck was not on his side, Yudhistira's kin pleaded with him to withdraw but he refused, believing that he would win back everything during successive wagers. I wish I had been there to take matters into control. Unfortunately, Yudhistira lost everything—first his chariots, then the jewels in his treasury, then the slave girls of his palace, his elephants, his horses, his cattle, his kingdom, his brothers, himself and finally, even his wife, Draupadi.

Priya had noticed the look of panic on Saini's face. 'What's the matter? Tell me,' she urged. They made Taarak stop the car once again and got out along with Kurkude, so as to be out of Taarak's earshot.

'Krishna was a descendant of Yadu. The all-encompassing term "Yadava" was used to describe Yadu's descendants,' began Saini. 'But the Yadavas were composed of several clans—eighteen in number. Amongst the Yadava clans mentioned in ancient Indian literature are the *Haihayas, Chedis, Vidarbhas, Satvatas, Andhakas, Kukuras, Bhojas, Vrishnis, Shainyas, Dasarhas, Madhus* and *Arbudas*. Now, when I see the names of the five people who have had the seals in their possession, I find it spooky that all five surnames have ancient Yadava connections!'

'Ancient Yadava connections? How so?' asked Priya.

'Krishna's grandfather was Shurasena, and some of his tribe came to be known as the *Shainyas*. Over several generations, the Shainyas eventually settled in the Punjab and came to be known as *Sainis*. That's my surname!' exclaimed Saini.

'Fine, but what about the others? How are they connected?' asked Priya.

'Another clan was established by a son of Satvata —also a descendant of Yadu,' said Saini. 'His name was *Vrishni* and that's the name by which his clan came to be known. They first settled in an area called Barsana in Uttar Pradesh and as they migrated to other parts of India they came to be known by various family names such as Varshnei, Varshnai, Varshnaya, Warshne, Varshni, Vrishni, Vrushni—or like my late friend Anil—*Varshney*.'

'Hmm. What about Nikhil Bhojaraj? That name sounds more Dravidian than north Indian,' said Priya.

'The word "*Bhoja*" literally means "bountiful". The name of this clan appears as the descendants of Mahabhoja,' answered Saini. 'The Bhojas went on to construct the Bhojeshvara Temple at Bhojpur—not far from Bhopal. They eventually assumed various family names, depending on the regions in which they settled—including Bhoj, Bhojwani, and Bhojaraj. A dialect of northern India—now famous for a rather risqué variety of Indian cinema—is known as Bhojpuri. It is from the Bhoja clan name that Dr Nikhil Bhojaraj derived his surname.'

'And my surname?' asked Professor Rajaram Kurkude curiously. 'In what way am I connected with Krishna's Yadava lineage?'

'Kautilya's *Arthashastra* describes the *Kukuras* as a Yadava clan. The *Bhagavata Purana* says that the Kukuras occupied the territory around Dwarka and that Kansa's father— Ugrasena—belonged to this group. Many surnames— including your own—such as Kukura, Kurkude, and Kurkure are derived from the clan's original name,' replied Saini.

'Does Devendra Chhedi fall into the Yadava lineage too?' asked Priya.

'Absolutely,' said Saini. 'The *Chedis* were definitely a Yadava clan. They were descendants of *Chidi*, the grandson of Vidarbha—a descendant of Yadu. They eventually carved out their kingdom in the region that is represented by modern-day Chhattisgarh and their descendants continue to be known by the same name—Chhedi. Can you blame me for finding this eerie?'

'What do you think is the reason that you five people were chosen?' asked Priya.

'Obviously, Varshney knew something that I don't,' said Saini. 'He specifically chose four other people who, like him, were Yadava descendants. Varshney was never one to do anything without a very specific reason.'

'Why don't you discuss it with Chhedi? He may have an alternative view. Geneticists also tend to be equally enthusiastic about issues of genealogy,' said Kurkude.

'You're absolutely right, Professor. This is a perfect issue for Chhedi to sink his teeth into,' said Saini as he thought about that fateful day when he had been visiting Kalibangan and Varshney had told him:

'You are not just my best friend Ravi, you are almost my brother. One day, you will realise that this statement was not made in a burst of sudden emotion but was based on logic. I know your genetic makeup, my friend!'

Draupadi said to me that it was the gatekeeper who informed her that her presence was being demanded by the Kauravas who had won her in a game of dice. 'Go and ask my husband whether he lost his own freedom first, or mine? If he had wagered himself first, he had no remaining rights over me, in which case he did not possess the authority to wager me!' said Draupadi. The open question in court was technically correct but it irritated Duryodhana who dispatched his brother Dusshasana to grab Draupadi by her hair and strip her naked in court. Draupadi had been sitting in a private room as she was menstruating. Barely covered, she prayed to me for protection. I ensured that the length of cloth covering her remained unending. As a result, Draupadi could not be disrobed. Draupadi took a vow that she would leave her hair untied until the day that she could wash it in Dusshasana's blood. Bhima took two terrible oaths. He vowed that he would drink Dusshasana's blood. He also vowed he would break Duryodhana's thigh on which he had lecherously invited Draupadi to sit!

'It's better that we split ourselves into two teams,' said Saini as they reached the parking area of the commercial building in which Immuno's laboratories and offices were located. 'If all of us walk in to Chhedi's office together and are greeted by a welcome committee of the cops, it will mean that there will be no one outside the police dragnet.'

'Good thought,' said Priya. 'I'm pretty certain that Radhika Singh believes that you've *kidnapped* Professor Kurkude. Why not let the professor stay in the car while the two of us go in first? If we do not emerge within an hour then Professor Kurkude can come looking for us. Is that acceptable, Professor?'

Kurkude nodded.

'Good. Now, the bigger concern is how to get inside without the police knowing. I can feel it in my gut that there is substantial police presence here, even though they're all in plainclothes,' said Saini.

In the distance was a small office inconspicuously labelled Radius Facilities Management. It was quite obviously the management company that had been assigned the task of managing the complex. Large corporate blocks such as this one always had a single entity providing housekeeping, janitorial services, gardening, security, pest control, waste management, mail room services and engineering support. The Radius office was located on the ground floor with two entrances—a front entrance overlooking the central atrium and a rear one overlooking the parking lot.

The rear exit of the facility management office was temporarily blocked by a truck, probably replenishing supplies. Saini smiled as an idea struck him. He turned to Taarak and said, 'You are intelligent enough to have figured out that I'm on the run. I can assure you that I'm no criminal. Would you be willing to help me by keeping the truck driver engaged?' asked Saini, keeping his fingers crossed.

'Sir, I may be young in age, but I have seen my fair share of crooks. You certainly do not fall into that category.

How long do I need to keep him occupied?' asked Taarak smiling.

'No more than ten minutes. That would give Priya and me enough time to pull out a couple of uniforms from the rear of the truck and slip away. Professor—you please stay in the car. Only come looking for us at the offices of Immuno if we're not back in an hour,' said Saini to Kurkude as he got out of the car. Priya followed him. They stopped some distance away as they waited for their chauffeur to walk up to the truck driver who was coordinating the unloading of the truck.

'You wouldn't have a cigarette that I could bum off you?' asked Taarak amiably when he reached the truck. The truck driver looked at him curiously. 'What do I look like? A *paan-bidi* stall? Get lost!' growled the truck driver.

Taarak knew that there were only two ways to engage— either by being friendly or by being a jerk. Since the former approach hadn't worked he had tried the latter. Taarak shuffled a little closer to the truck driver and whispered in his face, 'You don't look like a shopkeeper at all. More like a drug pusher!'

The driver used his right arm to aim a blow to Taarak's torso. Taarak swiftly sidestepped it and used his left hand to strike the outside of the truck driver's offending arm, thus leaving the right hand side of the trucker's body completely exposed. Taarak took advantage of it and delivered a single knee kick, which caused the truck driver to fall to the ground, clutching his leg in pain. By now a crowd had gathered around the two fighting men and it was the perfect opportunity for Saini and Priya to get into the truck.

Once inside, they quickly picked out janitorial uniforms with caps, besides window-cleaning sprays and dusters. They slipped out while the fight between Taarak and the truck driver was in full momentum, running towards the rear of the building where the garbage disposal area was located. They changed into their uniforms in double-quick time behind a dumpster and then walked over to the main entrance of the building. In front of them was the elevator bank.

'Immuno occupies the fourth, fifth and sixth floors of the building,' said Saini. 'We should go directly to the sixth floor—where Chhedi's office is located—and start cleaning. Our effort should be to blend in with the office routine and to make our way to Chhedi's office drawing virtually no attention to ourselves.'

On its way up the elevator stopped on the fourth floor. Two men got into the elevator and Saini gasped inwardly as he recognised one of them as Sub-Inspector Rathore. Saini immediately turned away towards the wall and began cleaning the U-shaped stainless steel handrail that ran on three sides of the elevator. He thanked his stars for not having shaved over several days. Priya took the cue, adjusted her cap downwards so as to partially block her face, got down on her knees and began cleaning the corners of the elevator floor. Saini was praying under his breath, trying his level best to remain calm.

Rathore was talking to Radhika Singh on his mobile phone. 'Yes, there are more than a dozen men at strategic points on the three floors. I have also stationed men downstairs in the main atrium so that no sudden exit is possible on Saini's part,' reported Rathore to his domineering boss. Saini exhaled in relief when Rathore and the other man got off on the fifth floor.

As they reached the sixth, both Saini and Priya gathered their cleaning supplies and walked into the office of Immuno Molecular Life Sciences Limited. The receptionist ignored them. They were simply janitorial staff, the lowest in the pecking order. Saini walked up to the receptionist's table, wished her politely, and did a quick spray and cleaning of the fascia of the reception desk. Priya noticed what looked like two plainclothesmen sitting in the visitors' area from the corner of her eye and was careful to avoid venturing near them. She busied herself cleaning the glossy walnut-finished laminate that lined the passage walls leading towards the executive offices.

King Dhritarashtra realised that before Draupadi uttered a curse, it was best that he intervene. He immediately ordered that everything that had been lost by Yudhistira be returned to the Pandavas, but Yudhistira was a glutton for punishment. Despite protestations and warnings from his family, Yudhistira was once again convinced by Duryodhana to play another round of dice in which Yudhistira lost yet again. As per the wager, the loser would be exiled to the forests for twelve years and would have to spend an additional thirteenth year incognito. In order to satisfy the conditions of the bet, the Pandavas, along with Draupadi, went into exile, leaving their mother Kunti to be cared for by Vidura. I was unaware of all these happenings because I had been busy repelling the kings who had attacked Dwarka.

Suspecting that the fight had gotten out of hand, a group of onlookers intervened and created some distance between the truck driver and Taarak. The truck driver was too busy nursing his knee to notice Taarak slipping away. The crowd mulled around the truck driver who was shouting obscenities, and Taarak used the opportunity to make his escape.

Taking purposeful and rapid strides, he reached his car in a remote corner of the parking lot. Professor Kurkude was sitting in the rear seat with the window down, reading a newspaper that he had bought from a vendor. Taarak opened the front door, got into the driver's seat and started up the engine.

'Hey! We can't leave yet,' protested Kurkude. 'I'm supposed to go looking for them in case they're not back with us within an hour.'

'I understand, sir. It's just that they had asked me to cause a distraction. I think I did it a tad too efficiently,' remarked Taarak. 'It's better that we get away from here for half an hour till the crowd clears up. We'll be back in time, I promise you.'

The car began rolling and within a short while they were on Sarovar Path heading towards Sukhna Lake, a massive manmade three-kilometre-long lake that had been created by building a dam on a seasonal stream. Chandigarh residents would visit the lake in the mornings or evenings for their walk or run. The lake also served as a popular picnic spot and a hub for pursuing water sports such as boating, yachting and water skiing.

Upon reaching the lake, Taarak steered the car towards the Lake Reserved Forest—a wide expanse of dense woods. He parked the car and got out. He opened the rear door for Kurkude and said, 'We'll need to spend fifteen minutes here. Luckily this area is secluded and it should be possible to get back to Chandigarh Corporate Plaza from here in another ten.'

The professor got out of the car and the two men strolled along the Jungle Trail that led to the Lake Reserved Forest. Kurkude did not notice that his driver was wearing a special belt pack around his waist.

Five minutes into the Jungle Trail, all human presence vanished and it became evident that the two men were alone. Taarak missed a step, allowing Kurkude to overtake him along the narrow pathway. The good professor was unaware that a chloroform-soaked handkerchief was about to be clamped around his nose and mouth. As Taarak's handkerchief made contact with Kurkude's face, the professor registered a look of terror as he struggled to avoid the fumes—but it was of no use. He was no match for Taarak's years of training.

No sooner had Kurkude passed out than Taarak picked up his comatose frame and placed him under a large peepal tree. Taking out his duct tape he quickly bound Kurkude's hands and gagged his mouth. He searched inside his waist pouch and found the self-inking rubber stamp that he had kept ready especially for this occasion. He carefully placed the rubber end on Kurkude's head. The symbol that emerged on Kurkude's forehead was that of a conch—yet another symbol of Vishnu.

Taking out a fresh scalpel, duly custom-engraved with the initials R.M., Taarak knelt down over Kurkude's outstretched foot and, with his usual precision, thrust the scalpel into Kurkude's left sole, leaving it embedded inside the flesh. Blood spurted from the foot as Taarak took out the paintbrush from his belt pack.

'You are special, Professor Kurkude,' he thought to himself as he dipped the paintbrush into Kurkude's blood. 'You get to die exactly as Lord Krishna did. Under a peepal tree.' Taarak began to write on the bark above Kurkude's head:

> *Mleccha-nivaha-nidhane kalayasi karavalam*
> *dhumaketum iva kim api karalam*
> *kesava dhrita-kalki-sarira jaya jagadisa hare.*

Having surveyed his handiwork, Taarak gathered up all the tools of his trade and walked over to the car that was parked a short distance away. In his head, he could hear echoes of the conversation that had taken place between him and Mataji many months previously.

'I shall do whatever you say, Mataji. But could you please explain to me why I must kill these men? They're simply scientists and researchers,' said Taarak.

'But they're doing the work of Satan,' spat Mataji. 'They're busy trying to dig up the eighth avatar of Vishnu while the tenth is far more important. Tell me, son, what happens when you place ten before eight? You get 108! The most powerful number in the world! Use the power, Taarak!'

'Your wish is my command, Mataji,' said Taarak respectfully. 'But could you tell me what these men have done that deserves death?'

'These men are busy searching for a secret that was left behind by Krishna,' said Mataji angrily. 'They cursorily read the *Mahabharata* and think to themselves, what could be this earth-shattering secret? Their little minds dwell on the Brahmastra—the divine weapon that could cause the destruction of a nuclear bomb. In so doing, they overlook the key secrets within the *Bhagwad Gita*—the sermon delivered by Krishna to Arjuna on the battlefield!'

'Specifically, which part of the *Bhagwad Gita* are you referring to, Mataji?' asked Taarak.

'Remember the part when Krishna tells Arjuna, *I am transcendental, beyond both the fallible and the infallible. And because I am the greatest, unborn and infallible, I am celebrated both in the world and in the* Vedas *as that Supreme Person. My transcendental body never deteriorates. I am without origin, middle or end. I am the generating seed of all existence,*' recited Mataji from her perfect memory.

'How does this provide a clue to finding the Krishna Key?' asked Taarak.

'The fools who read these passages think that Krishna is talking about his divine self. Alternatively, they think that he is alluding to the permanence of the soul. Indeed, Krishna does talk about this when he says, *that which pervades the entire body you should know to be indestructible. No one is able to destroy that imperishable soul.* But the fools do not understand that this passage about the indestructibility of the soul is not the same as the passage about Krishna's own infallibility, his permanence, or the fact that he is *the generating seed of all existence!*'

'So what does the earlier passage recited by you actually mean?' asked Taarak.

'It means that Krishna is alive! If Krishna is transcendental, infallible, unborn, and his body never deteriorates; if Krishna is without origin, middle or end and if he — Krishna — is the generating seed of all existence, then the only obvious conclusion is that he is alive!' thundered Mataji, as she continued counting her beads feverishly.

Emerging victorious from my battle to protect Dwarka, I rushed back to Hastinapur, but it was too late. I eventually found the Pandavas and Draupadi on the outskirts of the city. Bhima wanted to fight and take back their kingdom but I told him, 'You allowed your brother to wager everything. All of you are equally responsible. You must live thirteen years in exile as per the wager. It's your dharma.' Draupadi asked me, 'Was it my fault that I was wagered?' I cautiously replied, 'No, but it was you who insulted Karana as well as Duryodhana on previous occasions—this is the consequence. Don't worry, Draupadi, everyone who sat there watching you being humiliated will pay a heavy price. But first, all of you must get through these thirteen years! In the meantime, Subhadra, her son Abhimanyu, and Draupadi's children, shall move to Dwarka where I shall ensure that they are looked after.'

Saini and Priya mopped their way towards the executive office belonging to Chhedi. It was easy enough to find because it was located at the very end of the walnut-veneered wall that ran along the length of the passage. Unlike Kurkude's office, which had the secretary seated in an outer office room, Chhedi's office was independently accessed with the secretary seated in a separate cabin adjacent to that of her boss. An unmanned reception area outside Chhedi's office provided a few plush sofas and magazines for Chhedi's visitors.

Priya walked into the private reception area and began cleaning the sofas while Saini strolled towards Chhedi's office door and began polishing the handle. Within a minute, he had twisted the handle downwards, opened the door and walked in. Chhedi was alone, seated behind an enormous desk. He looked up as he saw his office door open. 'My office has already been cleaned in the morning,' he snapped absentmindedly at the janitorial duo.

'Dumpy, it's me,' whispered Saini as he closed the door behind Priya and him.

'Roger?' asked Chhedi curiously. 'Why are you in a cleaner's uniform?'

'Oh, so you spoke down to me from your high and mighty perch only because I was a lowly janitor?' joked Saini. 'On a serious note, though, it was the only way to reach you without being observed by the cops who are swarming all over.'

'And who is this fine lady with you?' asked Chhedi, his naughty eyes twinkling as he shook hands with Saini.

'This is Priya, my doctoral student. She has been on the run with me ever since Varshney's life was taken,' explained Saini as he realised that Chhedi had transferred a small piece of paper to his palm while shaking hands. Saini tried reading it but was unable to, because the writing was smudged from the sweat of his palms.

On a television screen in the secretary's room, Radhika Singh was sitting and watching Saini enter Chhedi's office. The camera microphone was also activated and every word of the conversation was being recorded. She watched Saini and Priya settle down in the visitors' chairs opposite

Chhedi's at the desk. Chhedi was saying, 'I have tried my best to keep the police out of my personal office. Please talk freely and tell me everything. I'll do whatever I can to help.' Radhika smiled. It had been a great idea to occupy the secretary's office because it was equipped with a camera and recording device. Chhedi often liked his meetings to be recorded so that his secretary could minute them later.

'Do you have the fourth seal?' asked Saini. Chhedi nodded and took out something from his desk drawer. He passed it to Saini who opened the envelope and carefully extracted the seal. He felt a tingle of excitement when he saw that the fourth seal was almost identical to the other three and definitely part of a set.

'Our school buddy—Varshney—had four such seals,' explained Saini. 'As of date, one is with the police, and two are missing. I have brought along with me photographs of the three others. Would you mind if we place them on your desk and try to make some sense of them?'

'Isn't this seal the equivalent of Krishna's passport system?' asked Chhedi.

'Yes,' said Saini. 'The *Harivamsa* says *Mudrayaasah gacchantu rajno ye gantumipsavah; Na chamudra praveshtavyo dwaar-paalasya pashyatah...* it's a directive that every citizen of Dwarka should carry a mudra—or seal—as a mark of identification and that it is the duty of the guards to see that every citizen carries the seal and that none without a seal are allowed to enter.'

'And what is the relevance of the three animals that are depicted on the seal?' asked Chhedi.

'These are motifs of a bull, unicorn and goat. They're considered to be representations of Vishnu. There are references to a very prominent unicorn in the *Mahabharata* called the "Ekashringa"—literally, the one-horned,' explained Saini.

'And, if you bring these seals together, what should they tell you?' asked Chhedi. 'In fact, what makes you believe that these four seals are not simply four isolated artefacts?'

'Because they're virtually identical—except for minor variations. The position of the three-headed animal appears slightly differently on each seal, but the faces are not even slightly at variance to one another, Dumpy. Varshney himself told me that they even had a base plate that was later lodged in a temple built by Raja Man Singh in the sixteenth century,' said Saini. 'Do you have a pair of scissors that I could borrow?'

Chhedi plucked scissors from the leather box on his desk and offered it to Saini.

'Now could I request you to access my web mail on your computer and take a printout of the photographs that Varshney had sent me of the four seals?' asked Saini. Chhedi obliged and soon Saini had all four photographs before him. He compared Chhedi's actual seal with the fourth photograph just to be sure that the photographs were indeed of the very same artefacts.

Saini then took the photographs that Chhedi had printed out and cut them into squares so that they resembled the actual seals. Taking the four photographs, he started shuffling them around on the table, almost as though he were solving a child's jigsaw puzzle. A few minutes later, a smile appeared on his face.

'Do you see what I see?' he asked Chhedi and Priya. Priya caught on immediately. It was impossible not to be stunned by the symbolism of the swastika that lay before them.

51

The Chandal Chaukdi—the devious foursome consisting of Duryodhana, Dusshasana, Shakuni and Karana—decided to attack the Pandavas in the forest and finish them off once and for all. Vidura pleaded before Dhritarashtra to stop them, but the blind king ended up scolding Vidura instead. Angry and hurt, Vidura decided to leave Hastinapur and go join the Pandavas in the forests. Soon thereafter, Dhritarashtra repented and sent messengers to bring Vidura back while disallowing any attack on the Pandavas. Since they could not attack the Pandavas, the Kauravas decided to humiliate them by setting out on a cattle census. They established their base camp near the Pandavas and cooked the very best gourmet delights in order to torment the Pandavas. Unfortunately for the Kauravas, they were attacked and captured by the forest Gandharvas, the divine messengers between the gods and humans. Not forgetting their duty, the Pandavas rescued the Kauravas from the Gandharvas, thus leaving the Chandal Chaukdi shamefaced.

'So we have a swastika—so what, Roger?' asked Chhedi. 'How has it added to your knowledge in any way?'

'Dumpy, the swastika is probably the oldest symbol of the Vedic civilisation. Unfortunately, it was adopted by Adolf

Hitler's genocidal Nazi party and acquired a negative connotation the world over,' said Saini. 'Among Hindus, however, it is extremely holy. The word "Swastika" itself is derived by combining two Sanskrit words "Su" and "Asti". Su means "good" and asti means "existence" or "life". The overall context of the symbol is thus of peace, good health, prosperity and happiness. The question that has always plagued me though, is this: is the swastika merely a symbol, or did it mean much more in ancient times? After all, an X in an algebraic equation does not mean the same thing as an X used to mark a spot on a map!'

'Are you trying to say that the swastika marks a specific physical location geographically?' asked Chhedi.

'I am not in any way discarding the symbolism of the swastika,' said Saini, hastily drawing a modern swastika on a notepad to illustrate his point before proceeding to elaborate.

'Just for a minute, though, let us forget the symbol we consider as the swastika today,' continued Saini. 'Today's swastika symbol is more geometric and defined. It also has sacred mathematical properties. It is *one* symbol that is composed of *eight* limbs. Notice the fact that 1 and 8 are at play here also? However, what was the original swastika? It was much curlier, somewhat like this.' Saini drew another symbol, but a gentler version, with curves.

'What's your point?' asked Priya, peremptorily.

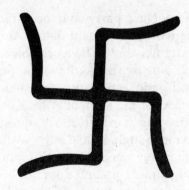

'Mathematicians Cundy and Rollett have defined the swastika curve mathematically,' continued Saini, ignoring Priya's curtness. 'It is a quartic plane curve representing the Cartesian equation $y^4 - x^4 = xy$. Want to see what their curve look like?' Without waiting for an answer, Saini drew an approximation of Cundy and Rollett's swastika curve on the notepad before him.

'When you see this curve, what does it remind you of?' asked Saini excitedly. His question was greeted by silence.

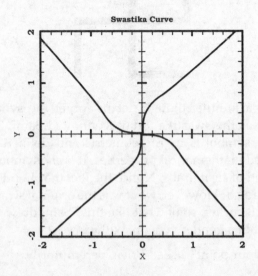

220

Realising that there were no volunteers, Saini spoke up once again. 'Don't you see the significance?' he asked, his voice rising. 'It's the very shape that represents the flow of four rivers from an elevated point!' he exclaimed. 'The swastika became a holy symbol much later. For the ancient Vedic sages, it represented a very holy destination. I've given both of you sufficient clues. Can you tell me of a hill or mountain that has four rivers?'

Priya was suddenly like the studious kid in the front row, eager to answer the teacher's question. 'I have it! It's the mountain from which four rivers—the Indus, the Sutlej, the Brahmaputra and the Karnali—flow down and outwards,' she rattled off.

'And what is the name of that mountain?' asked Saini, slipping into his academic role effortlessly.

'Mount Meru!' exclaimed Priya. 'Also known to millions of Hindu devotees as Mount Kailash!'

52

Some days later, when the Pandava brothers were elsewhere in the forest, Draupadi was surprised to find Jayadhrata, the husband of the Kauravas' only sister Dusshala, outside her cave. She could not understand the purpose of his visit but she offered him water, fruits and a place to sit. Little did she know that Jayadhrata had come to abduct her. It was his view that a woman could have a maximum of four husbands and that by having five, Draupadi was a prostitute by social norms. He grabbed hold of her and placed her in his chariot but Draupadi's screams were heard by the sages who immediately informed Arjuna and Bhima. Both brothers caught up with the chariot and Arjuna used his arrows to break the chariot's wheels. Bhima pounced on Jayadhrata and would have murdered him had Yudhistira not reminded him that killing Jayadhrata would leave their only female cousin widowed.

'I don't understand one thing, though,' said Chhedi.

'What's that?' asked Saini, once again attempting to read the note that Chhedi had passed him. Only a few words were clear. *Be... in... next... listening.* The missing words were badly blotted.

'Mount Kailash is viewed as the abode of Shiv. How does Krishna enter the picture?' asked Chhedi.

'*Shivaya Vishnu roopaya, Shiva roopaya Vishnuve; Shivasya hridayam Vishnu, Vishnoscha hridayam Shivaha!*' said Saini turning his attention away from the smudged note. 'The shloka means that Shiv is merely a form of Vish and that Vish is merely a form of Shiv. Shiv resides in the heart of Vish and Vish resides in that of Shiv. According to the Vedic sages, Mount Kailash was the centre of the world. It had four clear faces—thus resulting in its pyramid shape. As per mythology, the four faces were made of crystal, ruby, gold, and lapis lazuli. In Vedic times, it would have been considered the pillar of the world! Twenty-two thousand feet high, Mount Kailash lies at the heart of the world's *mandala* and is nestled within six mountain ranges that symbolise a lotus. The four rivers originating from Kailash supposedly flow down to the four quarters of the world and divide the world into four regions. The sacred character of this mountain goes way beyond Vishnu, Shiv, or Hinduism.'

'How?' asked Chhedi.

'The book of *Genesis*, in the Bible, describes the Garden of Eden, where Creation started. It says: *Now a river flowed out of Eden to water the garden; and from there it divided and became four rivers*. Kailash was the original Eden, my friend!' exclaimed Saini. 'Even today our own Mount Kailash is considered a sacred place in four religions—Bön, Buddhism, Hinduism and Jainism. Many of the world's greatest stories have their origin right here in India. Have you heard of the lost city of Atlantis?'

'It was the fabled city that was submerged by tidal waves,' said Priya, butting in excitedly. 'Plato first mentioned Atlantis in his dialogues *Timaeus* and *Critias*—written around 360 BCE, I think.'

'And do you remember the location of Atlantis as mentioned by Plato?' asked Saini.

'I think that Atlantis was described as lying *beyond the pillars of Heracles,'* answered Priya.

'Ah! And because the philosopher Plato was Greek, people simply assumed that he was talking about Heracles—a son of their supreme god Zeus. The same Heracles who was later adopted by the Romans as their own Hercules. Right?' asked Saini.

'True,' replied Priya.

'But we seem to have forgotten the fact that Megasthenes, the Greek ambassador in the court of Chandragupta Maurya, made the first written reference to Krishna and that in his account, he called Krishna by the very same name—Heracles. He went on to say that the Sourasenoi— the descendants of Shurasena, Krishna's grandfather— who lived in Methora—or Mathura—held Heracles in high esteem. Isn't it also curious that both Plato and Megasthenes lived around the same time? Isn't it possible that Plato was not referring to the Greek mythological figure of Heracles but to the Indian deity Krishna?' asked Saini.

'Are you trying to say that the story of Atlantis was actually the story of Dwarka?' asked Chhedi.

'Think about it,' said Saini. 'The term *pillars of Heracles* may not be a reference to the promontories that flank the entrance to the Strait of Gibraltar, but may instead refer to the sixty pillars of the original Dwarakadheesh Temple that had been built by Krishna's great-grandson Vajranabhji in Dwarka. Although the present temple is relatively modern—having been built during Emperor Akbar's rule—it is at the same spot at which Vajranabhji's original temple stood and it would have been right there during the visit of Megasthenes!'

'The hypothesis is sound,' said Chhedi. 'But where is the corroborating evidence?'

'If I recall, Plato had said that *in Atlantis there existed a confederation of kings, of great and marvellous power, which held sway over all the island, and over many other islands also and parts of the continent,'* recounted Saini. 'The Yadavas were a confederation of eighteen clans with several chiefs and a single governor—a structure very unique in those times. Isn't that another tantalising clue?'

'But did both cities get destroyed in the same way?' asked Priya.

'In the context of Atlantis, Plato says that *at a later time there occurred portentous earthquakes and floods, and one grievous day and night befell them, when the whole body of warriors was swallowed up by the earth, and the island of Atlantis in like manner was swallowed up by the sea and vanished.* On the other hand, the *Mahabharata* tells us that in Dwarka *the sea rushed into the city. It coursed through the streets of the beautiful city. The sea covered up everything in the city. The beautiful buildings were submerged one by one. In a matter of a few moments it was all over. The sea had now become as placid as a lake. There was no trace of the city. Dwarka was just a name—just a memory.* Incredibly similar stories, wouldn't you say?' asked Saini.

Sitting inside the secretary's office, Inspector Radhika Singh was listening to every word that was being exchanged with rapt attention. She continued counting her beads as she watched the meeting proceed inside Chhedi's office.

53

My cousin Arjuna wished to use his time in the forest wisely, and decided to pray for Shiv's divine weapon—the Pashupat. In a clearing he installed a smooth oval stone that represented a lingam, offered it flowers and then sat before it, his mind entirely concentrated on Shiv. Quite suddenly, a wild boar rushed towards him and Arjuna was forced to open his eyes and shoot a single arrow to stop the animal in the nick of time. When Arjuna walked up to examine the dead boar, he noticed that it had two arrows protruding from it. Next to the boar stood a hunter who claimed that he had shot the boar first. A duel followed in which the hunter defeated Arjuna. Dejected but determined, Arjuna went back to his prayers, only to wake up to the fact, barely a moment later, that the hunter had been none other than Shiv! Arjuna fell at the feet of the god, who now stood before him, and Shiv blessed him with the divine Pashupat.

'But myths around great floods have been around for aeons,' argued Chhedi. 'There are over five hundred legends centred on floods around the world. Ancient civilisations—including those of China, Babylonia, Wales, Russia, India, America, Hawaii, Scandinavia, Sumatra,

Peru, and Polynesia—all have their own versions of a giant flood. And that's not surprising, since most of these myths coincided with the end of the last ice age.'

'True. But the most famous story among them is that of Noah, who built the magnificent ark in order to save all living creatures from extinction,' said Saini. 'It's from the book of *Genesis* in the Bible. Almost all flood tales are frequently linked by common elements that parallel the Biblical account—the pre-event warning, the construction of a ship or barge, the saving of animals, and the releasing of birds to check if the flood had receded. The incredible pattern shared by flood myths from around the world is an indication that they were all referring to a historical event that had been passed down by word of mouth over several generations and over several lands.'

'You're not going to tell me that Noah's ark was built in India!' said Chhedi jokingly.

'Actually, yes,' said Saini. 'The story of Noah is almost identical to a Sumerian legend called *The Epic of Gilgamesh* and I've already told you that the Sumerians were simply Vedic inhabitants who had migrated westwards after the drying up of the Sarasvati.'

'So Noah was from India?' asked Chhedi in-credulously.

'Not Noah, but the historical event upon which the story of Noah's ark was based. Gilgamesh was the king of Uruk—modern-day Iraq—who fortified the walls of his kingdom,' explained Saini. 'In the epic we have Gilgamesh telling a ferryman that the walls of Uruk had actually been built by *seven sages*. The concept of the seven sages—or the *sapturishi*—is as old as Vedic civilisation itself! The Gilgamesh story was essentially a recounting of the flood that engulfed Dwarka that future waves of Vedic inhabitants carried with them into new lands such as Sumeria. Just take the name Noah and flip the two vowels in the middle. What do you get? *Naoh*—the Hindi word for boat! Even the very concept of man's creation is from India. The English word *man* is derived from the Sanskrit root *manus*—which is also the root of the Indian name *Manu*, the mythological progenitor of the Hindus.'

Chhedi and Priya were stumped. Saini seized the moment. 'For a moment, if we take the biblical Noah story literally, it's evident that the ark built by Noah would have had to be pretty large, right? In fact the Bible specifies the dimensions of the ark. It had a length of three hundred cubits, breadth of fifty cubits and height of thirty cubits. That's huge! It would have been taller than a three-storey building and would have had a deck area the size of thirty-six tennis courts. Which shipyard of that time would have been able to construct such a vessel?' asked Saini.

Priya caught on immediately. 'There was only one ancient port that could have dealt with that size—Lothal!' she said, warming rapidly to Saini's revelations.

'Precisely! Lothal's dockyard is the world's earliest known. It was the only shipyard that was capable of producing a ship of that magnitude in ancient times. In fact the word "navigation" is derived from the Sanskrit word "*navgati*"— the science of sailing,' said Saini. 'Lothal was the point from where massive ships would have plied the trade route into the Persian Gulf. The other possibility was Dholavira. Both Lothal and Dholavira were extremely close to Dwarka—in fact all three cities had close links.'

'In what way were they connected?' asked Chhedi.

'Dholavira was originally discovered in the 1960s by Jagat Pati Joshi and was excavated in the 1990s under the direction of R S Bisht,' said Saini. 'Bisht discovered that the city's length and width were precisely in a ratio of 5:4.

The main castle's proportions also followed the city's ratio of 5:4. Both ratios adding up to the sacred number nine.'

'But what does that have to do with Lothal?' asked Priya irritably.

'Here's where it gets really interesting,' said Saini, rubbing his hands in childlike excitement. 'Dholavira's unit of measurement is exactly equal to 108 Lothal angulas. See the Vedic mathematical connection once again?'

'Be that as it may,' said Priya, attempting to regain her cool, 'how does one explain the swastika—that you say is a representation of the abode of Shiv—being found on Krishna's seals?'

Chhedi, who had only been asking questions till then, spoke up. 'I have a theory,' he said.

Saini looked up at his school friend, slightly surprised. 'Yes?' he asked.

'If one were to view Krishna as being a historical personality rather than a mythological one, Krishna would have been like you or me—a bundle of bones, muscles, flesh, tissue and blood, right?' asked Chhedi.

Saini nodded.

'In this context, the *Bhagwad Gita* does not make sense,' said Chhedi. 'The sermon delivered by Krishna to Arjuna is one in which Krishna specifically tells Arjuna that he is eternal, permanent and indestructible.'

'What's the point that you are trying to make, Dumpy?' asked Saini.

'The point that I am making, Roger, is this: isn't it possible that when Krishna was killed by an arrow lodged in his left foot, what was witnessed was not a killing but a process of ancient DNA extraction?' asked Chhedi. 'And if this DNA had to be preserved, wouldn't the logical place to preserve it be under a sheet of ice that never thawed? Say a location like Mount Kailash?'

Inspector Radhika Singh looked at the monitor closely. She tightened her grip on her prayer beads. It was time to move in.

Having acquired the Pashupat from Shiv, Arjuna started climbing the Himalayas. Soon, he saw a gleaming chariot. The charioteer told Arjuna that Indra—Arjuna's father—had sent for him. Indra needed his help in fighting the Asuras. Arjuna fought along with Indra and they were victorious. Indra asked his son to enjoy the pleasures of paradise for some time, which Arjuna did. He was soon approached by one of the apsaras—Urvashi—who asked him to be her lover. Arjuna knew that Urvashi had been the wife of one of his ancestors and said, 'I look upon you as a mother figure. How can you expect me to make love to you?' Furious at the rejection, Urvashi cursed Arjuna that he would lose his manhood. Arjuna beseeched his father Indra for help. Indra was able to dilute the curse so that Arjuna would lose his manhood only for a year and that, too, at a time of his own choosing.

Saini looked at the note that Chhedi had passed him once again. Determined to decipher the blurred scrawl, Saini screwed up his eyes until he could discern the words: '*Be careful. Police in next room listening.*' Saini sat up in his chair with a start. They needed to get out immediately.

'Put your hands up,' shouted Radhika Singh as she flung open the door to Chhedi's office. Saini and Priya froze in their chairs. Chhedi, looking rather sheepish, mumbled softly, 'I'm so sorry, Roger. I had no bloody option but to cooperate with her. I did try to warn you, though.' Saini nodded grimly at his friend. If he had been put in a similar situation, he might also have done the very same thing.

Saini and Priya raised their hands as Rathore briskly walked over to them and cuffed their raised arms. 'Isn't this a wonderful reunion?' asked Radhika Singh sarcastically. 'I've so looked forward to the moment we would meet again.'

Her face suddenly lost its smirk when she felt the steely tip of a scalpel against her throat. Taarak had taken the elevator to the sixth floor and quietly walked over to Chhedi's office. He had softly tiptoed up behind Radhika while Rathore was busy handcuffing Saini and Priya. Once behind her, he had grabbed Radhika by her waist with one hand while holding a scalpel to her throat with the other.

'I shall cut this throat if you do not throw down your guns at this very instant,' he said decisively to Radhika and Rathore.

'Okay, easy does it,' urged Rathore as he took out his gun from his holster and gently dropped it to the floor. Radhika, who was still holding her gun, was paralysed with shock. She couldn't believe that the plan to recapture Saini and Priya was being foiled yet again.

'I said, drop it!' commanded Taarak in her ear. This time the order seemed to register and Radhika obeyed. No one in the room was more surprised than Saini. What the hell was his driver doing? Why was he getting himself involved like this?

'Now, uncuff her!' yelled Taarak at Rathore, pressing the scalpel a little harder against Radhika's neck so that a tiny droplet of blood emerged from the skin. Taarak was gesturing towards Priya.

Rathore walked over to Priya and unlocked the cuffs. Priya got up from her chair, walked over to Rathore's discarded gun that was lying on the floor and picked it up. Pointing it at Rathore, she said 'One move from you, and I'll fire this gun, you hear?'

Rathore nodded numbly. The policemen who were seated in the secretary's room watched the proceedings mutely through the open door as they acknowledged to themselves that there was very little they could do, given that weapons were directly aimed at both their bosses.

Keeping the gun pointed at Rathore, Priya shuffled over to the desk on which Chhedi's seal lay. She picked it up and placed it in her pocket.

'What are you doing, Priya?' whispered Saini in panic. 'We may be fugitives but we're not criminals. Don't do anything that may jeopardise your life.'

'Oh, shut up and spare me the lecture!' snarled Priya, her suddenly fiery eyes drilling into Saini's. 'I'm not your delicate doctoral student anymore, Professor Ravi Mohan Saini! I'm fed up of your persistent whining. It's better that you accompany the police to the lockup. That's the only place where you'll be safe!'

Saini was stupefied. The transformation in Priya was incredible. Gone were the gentle smile and delicate dimples. Instead, her face was flushed and there was a permanent scowl in place of the laidback smile. Having placed the seal in her pocket, she turned to Saini again. 'Now I have all four seals. Thank you for your location analysis, it will be most helpful, Professor,' she smirked. 'But I'm relieved that I don't have to listen to your boring lectures anymore.'

She walked over to Radhika Singh who was still frozen in a single spot with Taarak's scalpel at her throat.

'You can remove the steel from her throat, my child,' said Priya to Taarak. 'I shall now take care of her.'

'Yes, Mataji,' said Taarak respectfully, letting go of Radhika.

Priya pointed the gun directly at Radhika's head and said, 'You are my passport out of this office. Instruct your men, who are swarming all over the place, that I am to be given unhindered passage. One single suspicious move by anyone and your brains will lie splattered on the floor.' Radhika nodded mutely, too dazed to register this new turn of events.

'It's time for us to take your leave,' said Priya, mockingly, to the others in the room. 'Turn around,' she instructed Radhika. As Radhika did so, Priya put her left arm around Radhika's waist with her right hand pressing the gun to Radhika's ribs.

'You shall walk with me to the car. If I reach safely and leave, you have your life as a bonus. If I don't, you're dead meat,' she whispered as she nudged Radhika forward towards the open office door.

'Walk behind me,' she instructed Taarak. 'Keep a lookout that no one tries to assault me from the back.'

'Your wish is my command, Mataji,' said Taarak obediently, as they began walking towards the car with Radhika Singh as their captive. Vignettes of his life with Mataji coursed through Taarak's head as he walked behind her.

55

While Arjuna was with his father, the Pandavas decided to travel the length and breadth of the country. They bathed in holy rivers, visited ancient pilgrimage sites, meditated with rishis and discussed philosophy with sages. It was a time of learning and introspection. As their grand tour came to an end, Bhima summoned his son Ghatotkacha. His son arrived along with several Rakshasa friends and they helped the Pandavas scale the Himalayan heights where Arjuna awaited them. After a joyous reunion, Arjuna showed them the miraculous weapons that had been bestowed upon him. As soon as he uncovered them, the earth and the heavens began to shake. Arjuna realised that he was blessed with remarkably potent arms and that he could not afford to treat them casually.

'I don't mean to pry, Mataji, but I have always wondered, how did you become so strong?' asked Taarak after one of their training sessions had ended. They had been following the daily routine for over five years and Taarak had evolved into a fine specimen of strength, wisdom and humility. Priya smiled at the boy. Stretching out her arm, she tenderly touched his cheek and said, 'If it were anyone else asking, I would have killed him immediately for prying into my personal life, but I have grown fond of you, my child, so listen.'

'Many years ago when I was still a little girl, my mother died of cancer. My father was all I had left in this world. My father—Sanjay Ratnani—had yet to become India's highest-paid criminal lawyer. He had to work exceedingly hard and would often leave early in the mornings and return late at night, coping with hundreds of petty cases,' said Priya. 'We lived in a small one-bedroom apartment within a Mumbai chawl. We were not wealthy enough for me to be sent to boarding school and hence my father would leave me with our neighbour, a kind lady called Sarla Auntie.'

Priya paused. 'Sarla Auntie became a substitute for my mother. She would cook breakfast for me, walk me to school, help me with my homework and tuck me into bed at night. I would be fast asleep when my father returned from work and he would carry me into our apartment, thanking Sarla Auntie profusely for taking care of me.' Taarak was listening with rapt attention.

Priya continued, 'Sarla Auntie was a devout Krishna *bhakt* and she would, without fail, perform her daily prayers to Lord Krishna every morning. I loved her prayers, because they would end with sweets—the *prasadam*—that she would affectionately place in my mouth. I did not know that Sarla Auntie was unable to have children of her own. She had been married to an abusive drunkard of a husband via an alliance arranged by her poor parents. He had beaten her so viciously on the first night that her womb had been rendered incapable of bearing life. She had run to the local police station to lodge a complaint but the officer on duty, an obnoxious man called Garg, had told her that these things happened from time to time in all marriages, and refused to file an FIR! Even though her own life was wretched, Sarla would shower affection on me. I was probably the only thing that was still capable of inspiring love in her dark and morbid world.'

Priya took a gulp of water from a glass before proceeding. Obviously, remembering this part of her life was difficult. 'One day, when my father was still at work and Sarla Auntie was in the kitchen warming up my dinner, her husband staggered in, pissed out of his mind. He stared at me lecherously and lunged at me, trying to grab hold of my breasts. I fell down and he fell on top of me. He started unzipping his trousers so that he could rape me, when Sarla Auntie came running in and desperately struggled to pull him off me. He got up and swung his right arm viciously, catching her on her lower lip, which immediately began to bleed. He swung her around, and twisted her arm behind her back until I thought it would snap, while his other hand grabbed her hair and pulled her head back. I could see that Sarla Auntie was helpless and that the monster would kill her if he had his way. I ran into the kitchen and grabbed a knife that was lying on the counter—the one with which Sarla Auntie had been chopping onions for the evening meal. I held it tightly in my hand, ran behind Sarla Auntie's evil husband and plunged the knife as deep as I could in his back. He screamed in agony. Unknowingly, I had penetrated his lung and hemothorax. I watched as he fell to the ground, blood gurgling from his mouth.'

Priya wiped a tear from the corner of her eye as she resumed. 'Sarla Auntie was too shocked to move. She couldn't believe that I had just murdered her tormentor. She ran over to me and hugged me tightly. She then took the knife from my hands, cleaned the blood and fingerprints with her saree and grasped the knife firmly in her own hand so that her fingerprints would replace mine. She made me change out of my blood-stained dress into a clean one and made me wash my hands and face thoroughly. She then burnt the dress that I had been wearing in the steel dustbin in the kitchen. She told me to go to my own flat and wait there quietly for my father to return. She instructed me to maintain that I had not been with her that evening. I was reluctant to leave Sarla Auntie in the state that she was in, but she was unwilling to tolerate any argument from me. She asked me to keep Krishna in my heart permanently. She said that the world was an evil place and that her solace in life had been Krishna and I. She made me promise that I would worship Krishna each day. She then pushed me out of her flat, commanding me to run to my father's place.'

Taarak reached out his hand and held Priya's hand in his own. He was desperate to hug and comfort this vulnerable woman who had protected him like a mother when he most needed refuge. Priya continued, 'That night my father returned home a little after eleven at night. As was his usual custom, he first dropped in at Sarla Auntie's to pick me up. When he reached there he saw that Sarla Auntie and her husband were both lying dead on the floor, the husband due to a stab wound in his back and Sarla Auntie with a self-inflicted wound to her stomach—with the knife still in her hand. He immediately ran home—desperately worried for me—and found me hiding under the bed in the dark. He gently lifted me up, cuddled me in his arms and then picked up the phone to call the police.

The police arrived and inspected the premises. The investigating officer, Sub-Inspector Sunil Garg, harassed my father, asking hundreds of questions about my whereabouts that evening. It was almost as though he had pre-decided that I was the guilty party, even though the evidence clearly pointed elsewhere. When I poured out my heart to my father that night, he knew he had to do whatever it took to protect me. My confession would change our lives forever.'

56

One day, the breeze wafted some deliciously fragrant flowers into Draupadi's lap. She requested Bhima to fetch her some more of the same kind. Bhima set out, determined to find the flowers that Draupadi so wanted. He was like a man possessed with the desire to please her, and had no concern for the trees or animals he injured on his way. He finally reached a dense grove, but a sleeping monkey blocked his way. 'Get out of my way, old monkey,' said Bhima angrily. The monkey said that he was too old to move and that Bhima should move his tail to one side and proceed. Bhima, in spite of his superhuman strength, was unable to get the tail to budge. It was then that Bhima knew that the monkey was none other than the immortal Hanuman—his brother through their common father, the wind god, Vayu. Bhima eventually understood that I had asked Hanuman to teach a lesson in humility to Bhima. Bhima prostrated himself before Hanuman, begging his forgiveness. After being blessed lovingly by Hanuman, Bhima resumed his search for Draupadi's flowers.

'What happened when you told your father that you had killed Sarla Auntje's husband?' asked Taarak, now holding both of Priya's hands in his own.

'He began to cry. He held me in his arms and said that he would make sure that I was never put in such a situation ever again. He blamed himself and his work schedule for putting me in harm's way. The next day he went to meet Sir Khan and accepted a brief to fight a criminal case on his behalf,' said Priya.

'Who was Sir Khan?' asked Taarak.

'Sir Khan was the chief of a major Indian crime syndicate, no English knight,' replied Priya. 'He had earlier been a deputy of the notorious Dada Rahim and adopted the grand title of Sir Khan to denote his elevated status within Dada Rahim's organisation. Sir Khan had started his career as a minor pick-pocket and had graduated to smuggling, betting and counterfeiting. Eventually, there was a much-publicised split between Dada Rahim and Sir Khan, when Sir Khan broke away from the gang and started his own outfit. Sir Khan went on to become a multi-millionaire, setting up many legitimate businesses—including real estate development outfits, hotels, and movie production companies—in parallel with his flourishing illicit ones. The feud with Dada Rahim, however, continued, and both men sold each other out to corrupt policemen from time to time. Sir Khan had heard of my father's growing prowess in the courtroom and had sent word that he would like my father to represent him in all his pending criminal litigation, but my father had refused. He did not want to build his career by fighting on behalf of mafia bosses. That night, however, he decided that he needed to provide for my safety and security first. More importantly, he needed the help of someone who would get the police—including Garg—off our backs. He thus took the unprecedented step of representing Sir Khan.'

Priya looked at Taarak with affection and said, 'My father's career went into overdrive after he began representing Sir Khan. His income soared too. Within a few days of accepting

Sir Khan's brief, we moved into a wonderful apartment in the western suburbs, offered on instalments by Sir Khan to my father. We had domestic help and I was admitted into a new private girl's school. In school, our yoga teacher was someone who had trained under the Hindu Rashtra Sevika Samiti. She had spent most of her life attending *shakhas*, in which activities like physical fitness, yoga, and meditation would be given prime importance. She paid special attention to me and I soon began to look upon her as my spiritual guide. Under her personal supervision I became proficient in Sanskrit, Hindu scriptures, yoga, meditation and martial arts. I had not forgotten Sarla Auntie's dying words—to worship Krishna each day—and I continued the practice. The result was that I became strong, self-reliant and fervently devoted to preserving the dignity of Hinduism and the Vedic way of life.'

'So why did you become a history teacher, then?' asked Taarak.

'When I completed school, I decided that I wanted to study history so that I could gain a vital understanding of our heritage,' said Priya. 'My father was a little disappointed because he had been hoping that I would study law, but that didn't interest me as much as history did. I enrolled in St Xavier's College from where I obtained my BA and then proceeded to King's College, London, for an MA in history. While I was there, I came across documents that made my blood boil. It involved the efforts of European historians to prove that Krishna was a figment of Hindu imagination based upon the Jesus Christ story.'

'In what way did they do that?' asked Taarak.

'A discovery was made in Mora village—around seven miles west of Mathura—in 1882. On the terrace of a very old well, a large stone slab of inscriptions was discovered. Around twenty years later, a researcher—Dr J P Vogel—had the Mora Well slab taken away to the Mathura Museum.

He then tried to tamper with the slab and translations so that he would be able to show Hinduism in bad light. Reading about this incident brought home to me the fact that history is simply a version of events that can be easily influenced by the political, cultural and religious leanings of those who write it. I wanted to use my education to set this right. I wanted the historical authenticity of Krishna to be firmly established. Krishna should not be taught as mythology, but as history!'

'And that's why you became a teacher?' asked Taarak.

'Upon returning to India, I felt that I wanted to teach children history more than anything else in the world,' said Priya. 'This was a subject, which could mould their way of thinking and instil a sense of pride in their heritage. That's when I took up the job at your school. When your caning incident with Mr Kapoor happened, I could have been fired for inter-fering, but the school was worried that my father would prosecute them for allowing corporal punishment to happen within their portals. They had no alternative but to let me stay. And that's why you had me with you in school—and outside it!'

'Would you also like me to study history?' asked Taarak.

'No. I have arranged for you to get the best legal training. You shall be the lawyer that my father never had in me. But always remember your purpose in life. It is to establish the supremacy of Vishnu. Everything else in secondary,' she said.

'Is that why you have chosen to pursue a doctorate now?' asked Taarak.

Priya smiled. 'I'm not doing it for the degree, Taarak,' she replied. 'I have specially chosen to study under Professor Ravi Mohan Saini. He is someone who knows much more about the historical Krishna than I do. He will help me reach my destination quicker.'

57

The thirteenth year arrived. It was the year in which my cousins had to remain undetected. They disguised themselves and took up employment with King Virata of Matsya. Yudhistira became a Brahman—Kanka; Bhima became a cook—Ballava; Arjuna chose to lose his manhood and became a female dance teacher —Brihanalla; Nakula became a horse groomer—Damagranthi; Sahadeva became a veterinarian—Tantipala, and Draupadi became a beautician—Sairandhri. All six of them worked diligently and succeeded in pleasing their new master, King Virata and his wife Queen Sudeshna. The royal couple noticed that their new staff members were excellent workers but slightly different from the norm. They were much more confident and cultured than ordinary servants. Time flew by without incident, until the queen's brother, Kichaka, took a fancy to Draupadi.

Outside Chhedi's office, Priya held Radhika at gun-point, with Taarak protecting her from behind. They edged out of the office, walked down the walnut-veneered passage and reached the elevator bank As soon as one arrived, the three of them got in and descended to the lobby. Rathore took the stairs of the fire escape, clattering down in the vain hope of getting to the lobby before them. While running down, he continued to bark orders over his mobile phone. 'Keep the men on standby, but no one is to take a shot. I cannot afford to have these lunatics panic and kill our chief. Is that clear?' he shouted.

Once they reached the lobby, Priya pressed the gun harder into Radhika's ribs and nudged her towards the glass doors that overlooked the entrance foyer and car park. Within a few minutes, a military-green Jeep driven by a dark and unshaven thug rolled in. 'Pranam, Mataji!' he shouted out. Priya nodded. Sir Khan had sent his man dot on time for her.

'Get in the vehicle!' she barked at Radhika.

Radhika resisted and said, 'You've got a foolproof strategy for escaping. Why do you need me?'

She was rewarded with a swift knock on the head with the butt of the gun in Priya's hand. 'Do as I say and you stay alive! Argue, and you die,' hissed Priya as Radhika passed out from the blow. Priya, along with Taarak, lifted Radhika into the Jeep and gave instructions to the driver to step on the gas.

'Sir Khan has asked me to take you to Panchkula. A helicopter is waiting for you at Chandimandir Helipad,' shouted the driver over the sound of his screeching tyres. Rathore came running out and took a couple of shots at the Jeep's tyres but was unable to hit them, both bullets only ricocheting off the metal. Rathore swore under his breath. He knew that he had to keep the CBI Special Director Sunil Garg informed. He quickly dialled the number in Delhi and spoke into the phone.

'Yes, sir... I'm outside Chhedi's laboratory... Radhika Singh has been taken hostage by Priya Ratnani,' he explained.

'I'm sorry to hear that, Rathore. I'll put out a nationwide alert immediately. Don't try to follow her... instead, focus on getting all possible details from Saini so that we can figure out where they are headed,' said Sunil Garg, the Special Director of the CBI who happened to be having tea with a friend.

After the conversation ended, the CBI Special Director turned to Sir Khan and smiled. 'Everything is going as per plan. Now, what more do you want me to do?'

58

Kichaka was a lecherous fool, but he convinced his sister, Queen Sudeshna, to send Draupadi with some wine to his bedchamber. Worried about her own safety, Draupadi informed Bhima who quietly caught hold of Kichaka and beat him up. Kichaka died in the process, and Sudeshna suspected that Draupadi had played a role in his death. Sudeshna's other brothers decided that Draupadi would be placed on Kichaka's funeral pyre to be burnt alive. My strong cousin Bhima appeared like the wind, caught hold of Sudeshna's brothers and killed them all. No one saw Bhima, though. This allowed Draupadi to maintain the story that she was a Gandharva and that her kin could appear out of thin air to protect her. Worried about the implications of annoying the Gandharvas, King Virata allowed Draupadi to stay on inside the palace even though his wife wanted her to leave.

Saini was in shock. He sat stupefied inside Chhedi's office wondering how his kind and helpful doctoral student—Priya—had morphed into a raging inferno, spitting fire and venom. Mataji! He thought back and tried to make sense of what had just happened.

He recalled their halt for coffee and sandwiches at the restaurant on their drive from Jodhpur. *The waiter had* brought three cups of coffee. Priya had stretched out her arm and accepted the coffee that was on offer, passing on a cup each to Kurkude and Saini. Kurkude took a few sips of his coffee before getting out of the car to go to the restroom. He passed out in the bathroom due to chloral hydrate-poisoning. Taarak was the one who helped carry him to the car. The seal from Kurkude's pocket went missing subsequently. Priya and Taarak had colluded to steal Kurkude's seal.

His thoughts went back to Porbandar and their escape from the police van. *The van had swerved sharply to the right in order to avoid the crude IED that had been placed in their route. The van doors swung open and a black-masked commando carrying a small semi-automatic said 'Quick! Get out of the van! We have very little time — police reinforcements will be here soon!' He helped Priya off the van by extending his arm out to her for support and when she came down he quickly pressed an envelope containing cash into her hand. 'Take it,' he urged.* Saini cursed himself for not reading the signs of respect, concern and chivalry. The commando had been none other than Taarak helping his boss, Priya!

He struggled to remember their escape from Bhojaraj's boat into the sea. *'Is your mobile phone still in the pocket of your jeans?' Saini had asked Priya. 'Yes,' she had replied. 'If it's working, I want you to gift it to our host,' Saini had said. 'But it's our only means of communication...' Priya had protested. 'Buy another basic phone with a prepaid SIM card when we reach the city,' insisted Saini. Priya had nodded in agreement to what Saini was saying. She had quickly punched in a sequence of letters, numbers and characters into her phone. 'What are you doing?' asked Saini. 'Punching in the code for a factory reset. I don't want any of my messages to be accessible to others...'* Priya had been deleting all traces of her communication with Taarak!

His brain flashed back to his conversation with Priya in the Porbandar hotel room. *'I had no idea that you knew so much about chakras,'* Saini said in amazement. *Priya smiled. 'I spent several years learning meditation in school. It's a part of my life that I usually do not discuss,'* she said dismissively. *There was an uncomfortable silence for a few seconds.* Priya had been talking about her initiation into a religious order! Why hadn't he been smart enough to detect that?

He racked the deepest recesses of his memory to recall the day he had been arrested in his classroom by Rathore and Radhika. *Turning to Saini, Priya had said, 'Don't worry, Prof! As you know, my father—Sanjay Ratnani—is a leading criminal lawyer. I'll ask him to represent you. I'm sure he'll be able to clear up this mess. For the moment, though, I don't think you have any alternative but to go with them.'* She hadn't been helping him but setting him up so that he would take the fall for the murders!

Saini's head was spinning. He recalled fragments of the scene in the hospital infirmary. *'You spoke of four seals,'* said Priya. *'One was given to you—and was discovered by the police at your house. What did Varshney do with the other three?'* How had Priya known that there were four seals? He had never shared that information with her.

The conversation with Ratnani at the hospital bed came flooding back into his brain. *'My daughter respects you immensely, Professor,'* explained Ratnani. *'She's brought me into the picture to ensure that you don't spend the rest of your life in a lockup. Now, will you let me get on with the job of saving your ass?'* Saini looked at Ratnani and then at Priya. He saw her eyes pleading with him to accept her father's instructions. He sighed. *'Very well, I'll go along with whatever you say.'* Father and daughter had been ensuring that he moved on to Dwarka—where the next murder of Bhojaraj was scheduled to happen. They had been setting him up!

Saini saw Priya stirring from her nap as they neared Jodhpur. As she opened her eyes, she saw him smiling at her. 'Good morning,' he said to her, 'we're almost there. You want to get a bite to eat before we try meeting Kurkude?' She nodded. 'I'm starving. I also need to make a phone call.' 'To whom?' asked Saini. 'Dad. He must be worried sick about me by now,' she replied. Saini recalled the number of times that Priya would slink away to make private phone calls, particularly when they reached new destinations—it was to keep either Taarak or her father informed so that they could plan events in advance.

His mind wandered to the murder scene of Bhojaraj aboard the research vessel Radha. *'Do you know how to check a pulse?' asked Saini. Priya nodded. 'I don't know how to do it on the neck. You will need to cut the duct tape so that I can check his wrist,' she said. Noticing a pair of specimen scissors on one of the lab counters, Saini grabbed it and quickly cut through the duct tape layers, leaving yet more fingerprints on vital evidence for the police.* Priya had been making sure that his fingerprints were left on the scissors and duct tape. She had falsely claimed that she did not know how to take a pulse reading from the neck. Yet, she had done so in the case of Kurkude, when he was poisoned. *Saini had grabbed Kurkude's head by his hair and looked into his eyes. They looked like the lifeless eyes of a corpse. He rushed outside and called Priya in. She ran inside ignoring the sign that read 'Gentlemen'. 'Check his pulse!' yelled Saini. Priya bent down and placed two fingers under the angle of Kurkude's jaw to check the carotid pulse. 'He's alive,' she said.*

He cursed himself for leaving Kurkude in the car with Taarak. *'It's better that we split ourselves into two teams,' said Saini. 'Good thought,' said Priya. 'I'm pretty certain that Radhika Singh believes that you've kidnapped Professor Kurkude. Why not let the professor stay in the car while the two of us go in first? If we do not emerge within an hour, Professor Kurkude can come looking for us. Is that acceptable, Professor?'* She had been ensuring that Taarak could eliminate Kurkude when they were alone.

Saini's thoughts zeroed in on the immediate events of the past inside Chhedi's office. *Having placed the seal in her pocket, Priya turned to Saini again. 'Now I have all four seals. Thank you for your location analysis, it shall be most helpful, Professor,' she smirked. 'But I'm relieved that I don't have to listen to your boring lectures anymore.'* Saini realised that it was very possible that Sanjay Ratnani may already have organised for the seal in police evidence to be handed over to his daughter!

*News of the death of Kichaka and his siblings reached the
ears of Duryodhana. The killing had all the markings of
Bhima. Duryodhana now knew that my cousins—the
Pandavas—were hiding in Matsya. He also knew that
if he succeeded in catching them before the thirteenth
year was out, the Pandavas would have to go back to
the forest for another twelve years. It was a delicious
thought. He attacked Matsya when King Virata was
out on an expedition. The only one available to defend
the city was Uttara, Virata's son, and Brihanalla—
Arjuna in female disguise. Uttara was terrified of battle
but Arjuna was easily able to overcome the Kaurava
formations. Duryodhana was ecstatic. 'That is none
other than Arjuna,' he rejoiced. 'We have discovered
them before the thirteenth year,' he exulted. His uncle
Bhishma cautioned him, 'A year is calculated differently
between solar and lunar calendars. In my opinion,
Yudhistira could have revealed himself five months ago
without losing the wager!' Duryodhana vehemently
disagreed with Bhishma's view.*

While Saini was attempting to get his thoughts in order,
the Jeep carrying Radhika Singh and her captors was
screeching through the streets of Chandigarh, hurtling
towards Chandimandir Helipad in Panchkula. 'Where

are we going by chopper, Mataji?' asked Taarak, almost shouting to be heard over the din of the engine.

'Lucknow,' yelled Priya. 'From there we take a private charter to Nepalgunj on the Indo-Nepal border!'

'Why, Mataji?' asked Taarak.

'Because that is the place from which we can travel to Simikot along the Nepal-Tibet border. Simikot is the starting point for our trek to Mount Kailash!'

Both Priya and Taarak carried on their conver-sation inside the Jeep while Radhika's unconscious body lay stretched on the vehicle's floor between them. Priya should have reckoned that it was folly to be talking freely on the assumption that Radhika Singh was unconscious. Radhika Singh was always conscious of everything.

The Robinson R44 chopper stood silently at the helipad with a pilot and another man, awaiting Priya and Taarak. The R44 was a single-engine, four-seater light helicopter. The enclosed cabin had two rows of side-by-side seating for a pilot and three passengers.

They got out of the Jeep and Taarak lifted Radhika Singh's unconscious body to carry it into the helicopter, but the pilot stopped him. Turning to Priya he said, 'Mataji, this helicopter can take only four people. I am your pilot and this person here with me is your guide, who will assist you in getting to your destination at Mount Kailash. You and Mr Taarak Vakil can be the third and fourth passengers, but we don't have the engine capacity to carry a fifth.'

Taarak looked at Priya, waiting for her response. Instead, she turned to the Jeep driver. 'Since we can't take Radhika Singh with us, there's no point in trying to keep her hostage. Just dump her into Sukhna Lake. The place will soon be swarming with cops when Kurkude's body is discovered. Discovery of her body will be an added bonus for the police.'

King Virata thanked the Pandavas profusely for having protected his kingdom and gave his daughter Uttari's hand in marriage to Arjuna's son, Abhimanyu. A Brahmin was then sent by the Pandavas to meet Duryodhana in order to ask for their share of the kingdom. Duryodhana sent his father's charioteer Sanjay to inform my cousins that nothing was due to them because they had been discovered prior to completion of thirteen years as per the solar calendar, even though the required time period had elapsed as per the lunar calendar. Several sages and other learned men went to meet Dhritarashtra to warn him of the consequences of Duryodhana's refusal, but Dhritarashtra remained unmoved. It was then that I decided to intercede.

Rathore, Saini and Chhedi were sitting in the Immuno conference room. It was situated on the same floor as Chhedi's office and was fitted out with the very latest audio and video equipment. The notable absence was that of Radhika Singh.

Chhedi had asked his secretary to arrange for coffee and sandwiches but Rathore ignored the refreshments on offer. Rathore's mind kept wandering. He was worried about his boss who was missing in action.

'Priya consciously chose to wait until all four seals had been discovered before revealing her own identity,' said Saini. 'She then waited for me to figure out the fact that they represented the swastika—and consequently Mount Kailash. She now thinks that Krishna's secret lies there, but she does not have one important clue that I do.'

Rathore listened to Saini carefully. It had become evident that they had wasted a great deal of time by focusing police attention on Saini as the prime suspect. It was time to take advantage of his expertise in history instead.

'What clue do you have that Priya doesn't?' asked Chhedi.

Saini turned to Rathore. 'When your team searched my house, you found the seal that Varshney gave me, but on the day that you arrested me, I was carrying in my pocket a handwritten note from Varshney. The duty sergeant kept it with my personal effects when I was booked into prison. Do you have it with you?'

Rathore nodded. He pulled out the note from his file and passed it on to Saini.

Saini began reading the note that Varshney had handed over to him during their visit to Kalibangan. 'Varshney was a linguist and loved playing word games,' he explained as he read the note. 'I tried reading and rereading this note several times but was unable to make any sense of what my friend was trying to say. It's typical gobbledygook that Varshney adored.'

Saini passed on the note to Chhedi and said, 'Could you project an image of this note on the screen via the overhead projector? It will help if all of us jointly try to crack this.' With the note duly magnified on the white screen in front of them, everyone was soon absorbed in reading the strange paragraph penned by Varshney.

D'etale r'aknahs! Edise-Breta-Weulb DNA. Rats
anispiter. Axis Red Nerrus ajar! Sitih saliak roh salak.
XNI dialer, dial, devil. Pitta pott Felnox. Strap lamina
on stats. Peek slipup desserts. Tub trams. A kit saw
slarem. Un warder!

Could it be a code? Rathore tried examining every alternate letter, then every third letter, but was unable to discern a pattern. His mind kept wandering back to Radhika Singh. Every few minutes he would look at his phone expecting some information about Radhika but the phone remained silent.

Chhedi wondered whether the phrase was an anagram of some sort but even after using an online anagram resource he had come up empty-handed. Saini played with his pen as he attempted to coax meaning from the madness. His reverie was shattered by a booming voice.

'So, have we cracked this case yet?' asked Radhika Singh, walking into the conference room purposefully, oblivious of her dishevelled appearance. Rathore heaved a sigh of relief. It was good to see the chief alive!

'I have an entire contingent of men searching for you all over Chandigarh,' said Rathore to Radhika. 'Sorry we were unable to prevent your abduction.'

'Relax, Rathore.' The fact that it was a four-seater helicopter became my deliverance,' joked Radhika.

'But I sent a team to the helipad. You were not to be found anywhere,' said Rathore.

'The Jeep's driver had been given instructions by Mataji to drive towards Sukhna Lake and to dump me into the lake so that I would drown,' explained Radhika. 'Upon reaching there, he lifted me off the floor of the vehicle and placed me on the ground thinking that I was unconscious. He then returned to the Jeep to get rope with which to tie my hands and feet before dropping me into the lake.'

'But another team is already at Sukhna Lake. Why didn't those fools find you?' interrupted Rathore.

'They did but a little later. It wasn't their fault that it was a secluded area,' said Radhika. 'As it turns out, just as the driver picked up the rope to tie me down I scared the living daylights out of him. I crept up behind him and cursed into his ears at full volume. He spun around to find my face inches away from his own, snarling. Before he could react, my sledge-hammer fist had smashed into his jaw and he went crashing to the ground.'

Rathore laughed. He could visualise the scene as it must have played out.

'While he was on the ground, a heavy spanner fell down from his Jeep,' continued Radhika. 'The driver was a glutton for punishment. He picked up the spanner and came towards me, swinging it menacingly at me. I calmly took aim. The kick to his privates was swift and strategic. He passed out. I hope he isn't planning to father any children any time soon!'

Radhika had used the rope to tie up the driver. She had then used the driver's cell phone to try and call Rathore but before she could get through to him she had been spotted by the police team that had discovered Kurkude's body. They had wanted to inform Rathore immediately but she had ordered them not to. She wanted to examine Kurkude's body for herself first.

After an hour of crime scene investigation, Radhika had been forcibly bundled into a police car by Rathore's deputy and dropped off at the Immuno office. She now had to face the far more difficult job of wording an appropriate explanation to Saini. She turned towards him. 'First of all, you have my sincerest apologies, Mr Saini,' said Sniffer Singh, magnanimously admitting her mistake. 'It has now become evident that you could not have been responsible for the serial killings that have happened. I was following the wrong scent.'

Saini smiled at her but there was sadness in his eyes. 'You were doing your job, Inspector. I just wish that we could have been saved the running around. There was no way that I would ever have imagined that Priya was the enemy. She was the sweetest, most caring individual that I ever knew,' said Saini. He did not say that he had found himself falling in love with Priya during the past few days. He silently admonished himself for having let his feelings get the better of him.

'Do you have any thoughts about what our next step should be, ma'am?' asked Rathore, looking at Radhika.

'We can't let them get away,' said Radhika. 'We've had Varshney brutally killed in his house. We then saw Bhojaraj murdered on his ship. We've also had to deal with the slaying of Kurkude's secretary—Miss Gonsalves. We've now discovered the body of Kurkude himself on the shores of Sukhna Lake. Both Priya—or Mataji or whatever her real name is—and Taarak Vakil must be brought to justice.'

'We have another equally serious problem,' said Saini. Radhika, Rathore and Chhedi looked at him questioningly.

'We do not know what the Krishna Key actually holds in store. It could very well be a DNA sample, but it could equally be a nuclear device or ancient weapon. Irrespective of what it is, we cannot allow Priya and Taarak to get their hands on it,' said Saini.

'I know that they are headed to Mount Kailash,' said Radhika. 'They thought that I had been knocked unconscious but I was simply pretending to be that way. I figured that it would give me a chance to listen in on their conversation. We have to go after them!'

Saini stared at Radhika blankly. She soon realized that he wasn't staring at her but at the screen behind her on which Varshney's note had been projected. 'Fool!' muttered Saini.

Radhika Singh was not amused. 'I beg your pardon?' she said.

'I have been such a fool!' clarified Saini. 'The answer has been hovering right before my eyes and I chose to ignore the obvious!'

'You've cracked the code?' asked Chhedi excitedly.

'It's utterly simple. One merely has to read the passage in reverse order, letter by letter, ignoring the punctuation marks and spaces,' answered Saini. He began rewriting the letters from the last letter of the bottom sentence and worked his way upwards, right to left, on each sentence. He soon had a readable paragraph before him:

> *Redraw numeral swastika, smart but stressed pupils!*
> *Keep stats, no animal parts. X on left-top at tip. Lived,*
> *laid, relaid in X. Kalash or Kailash it is? Raja surrender.*
> *Six are tips in a star. And blue water beside. Shankar*
> *elated.*

'Fine, you now have a more readable paragraph but it still means absolutely nothing to us,' said Radhika to Saini.

'Ah, but it makes perfect sense to me,' said Saini, grinning from ear to ear.

I reached Hastinapur and decided to stay with Vidura. The next day, I met with the blind Dhritarashtra and his sons. Duryodhana said, 'I have administered Indraprastha well. We don't need the Pandavas to return.' I replied that it was inconsequential whether Duryodhana's rule was competent or not. A word once given was to be honoured. Indraprastha was to be returned to the Pandavas after thirteen years. The Pandavas had kept their word and it was now the duty of the Kauravas to keep theirs, but Duryodhana refused. I bargained. I said, 'Give them five villages instead and I will convince them to accept the offer in order to maintain peace and harmony.' Duryodhana, however, was adamant. 'I shall not part with a single needlepoint of land,' he thundered. I countered, 'Then there shall be war at Kurukshetra. By refusing to honour your commitment you have compromised dharma.' The dimwit—Duryodhana —got angry and tried to have me arrested! I assumed my omnipotent form and that was sufficient to scare the living daylights out of all of them. War was now inevitable.

'The answer lies in Vedic mathematics,' explained Saini to Radhika.

She looked up from the glass of milk and a handful of almonds that she had requested Chhedi to arrange for her. 'These policewomen!' thought Chhedi. 'Most of them are nuts!'

'Ancient Indian mathematicians had invented what they called the magic square. It's a 3 x 3 arrange-ment of the first nine digits excluding the zero. The unique property of the magic square is that any row, column or diagonal of the square always adds up to the same number—fifteen,' said Saini, drawing the square for Radhika, Rathore and Chhedi.

				15	
	8	1	6	15	
	3	5	7	15	
	4	9	2	15	
	15	15	15	15	

'In the centre is a single digit surrounded by eight digits. Notice the one-eight pattern? *One* digit surrounded by *eight* digits. The eight surrounding digits represent the four cardinal directions as well as the four ordinal directions. In short, they represent the universe—infinity. If one adds up the eight surrounding digits, one gets forty. Notice that the ratio of the centre digit—five—to the sum of the eight digits that surround it—forty—is a repetition of the *one-eight* pattern,' Saini demonstrated. 'According to the sages, zero is nothing. One is the beginning. Eight is everything. 18, 108, 1008, 10008—and other numbers like these—represent the very beginning to the very end!' he said. 'Eight is supreme. That's why Krishna was the *eighth* child; he was the *eighth* avatar of Vishnu; and was born on the *eighth* day of Rohini!'

Guessing that the others were too dumbfounded to speak, Saini continued. 'Another key property of the magic square is that one can obtain the swastika by seeking out the squares that add up to twenty-five.'

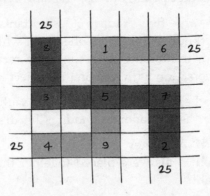

'As you can see, at the very heart of the magic square is the number five. What is a five-sided polygon with equal sides called? A regular pentagon. But here's the real magic… each interior angle of a regular pentagon is 108 degrees! See the magic of *one*, *zero* and *eight*, yet again?' asked Saini.

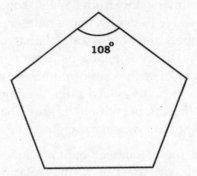

'Five at the centre of the magic square; five sides of a pentagon; five Pandavas were at the centre of the

Mahabharata war, Draupadi had five children, Yayati had five sons, the chariot flag of Bhishma bore five stars, Krishna asked Duryodhana for five villages, and *Panchamrut* is a mixture of five elements that is used in Hindu worship. Is it therefore surprising that the Americans decided that their most important war headquarters should be in the shape of a regular pentagon?' asked Saini slyly.

'And there are five Yadava descendants—Varshney, Bhojaraj, Kurkude, Saini, and Chhedi—of which three are already dead,' muttered Chhedi morosely, recalling Saini's private conversation with him on the subject.

'How does the magic square help us with Varshney's decoded note?' asked Radhika, ignoring Chhedi's interjection.

Saini smiled. 'Varshney is pointing us to a number. When the four seals were placed together they created a swastika, right?'

'Right,' said Chhedi.

Saini continued. 'Let's examine Varshney's deciphered note. *Redraw numeral swastika, smart but stressed pupils!* Varshney first admonishes us for being smart but stressed out and says that we should look at a swastika—not the symbolic one but the numeric one, from a magic square. *Keep stats, no animal parts.* He then says that a redrawing by keeping only the numbers and not the animal images may help. In short, what Varshney is telling us to do is to replace the symbolic swastika with a set of numbers while ignoring the animal motifs. *X on top-left at tip.* Varshney then points us to the specific number within the grid. The value of X on the top-left tip of the swastika is eight.'

Saini paused for a moment before taking the analysis further. '*Lived, laid, relaid in X.* By replacing X with the number eight, the sentence now reads as *Lived, laid, relaid in eight.* Any guesses for what Varshney is alluding to?'

'The avatars of Vishnu?' asked Chhedi. 'Krishna *was* the eighth avatar of Vishnu.'

'True, but the avatars of Vishnu are ten, with the tenth one yet to appear. No, Varshney isreferring to a specific place, and the only one that I can think of is the Somnath temple—so very close to Dwarka,' said Saini.

Before I left Hastinapur, I decided to have a word with Karana. 'You are supporting a man who has not kept his word. I know you to be a righteous person, Karana. Why not end your support to Duryodhana? It would force him to rethink and we would all be saved a terrible war,' I said to him. Karana respectfully told me that Duryodhana had stood by him when the rest of the world had forsaken him. He could not and would not abandon Duryodhana in his hour of need. I then told Karana the secret of his birth and that he was actually a Pandava—that, too, the eldest. He was entitled to the Pandava throne, as well as Draupadi as his wife. Karana knew that I was telling him the truth and I could sense the struggle within him, but he remained firm. 'A word once given is not to be broken. I have promised my permanent loyalty to Duryodhana,' he said. 'If it means fighting my own brothers, so be it!'

'I thought that the swastika denoted Mount Kailash. Where does Somnath come in?' asked Radhika.

'The Somnath temple was created and destroyed eight times,' explained Saini. 'There's a fascinating legend that surrounds the origins of Somnath—known as Prabhas Patan during Krishna's times. It's the very place where

Krishna breathed his last. It's believed that the first temple was constructed by *Soma*—the moon god—in gold, and hence the name *Somnath*. The next one was built by Ravana in silver, and the third one was built by Krishna, in sandalwood. If we were to set aside the legends, we'd have to acknowledge the well-established historical fact that King Bhimdev of Anhilwad built the first temple at the present site—in stone—and this one is said to have existed before the beginning of the common era.'

'So the one built by Bhimdev is officially counted as the first?' asked Chhedi.

'Yes,' replied Saini. 'The second temple was built by the Vallabhi chieftains who were Yadavas. This temple was probably constructed in the seventh century.'

'What happened to it?' asked Rathore.

'In the year 725 CE, Junayad—who was the Arab governor of Sindh—sent his armies to destroy the temple. Thereafter, the Pratihara king Nagabhata II reconstructed the temple in the ninth century. This third temple was a substantial structure built from red sandstone,' said Saini.

'Ah. So this was the one that was destroyed by Ghazni?' asked Chhedi.

'Precisely. In 1024 CE, Mahmud of Ghazni, in what would be central-east Afghanistan today, attacked Somnath, after crossing the Thar Desert. After looting all the riches of the temple, he destroyed most of it—including the main Shiv lingam,' said Saini. 'The fourth temple was then constructed by the Paramara king, Bhoj of Malwa and the Solanki king, Bhima of Anhilwara, sometime in the eleventh century.'

'Who destroyed that one?' joked Chhedi.

'Actually, no one,' replied Saini. 'The wooden structure had to be replaced due to wear and tear. King Kumarpal of Pali replaced the wooden structure with a stone one—so that would have been the fifth temple.'

'I'm assuming that someone razed the fifth temple,' said Radhika blandly.

Saini smiled. 'Unfortunately, yes. In the year 1296, the temple was once again desecrated and eventually destroyed by the Turkic Afghan, Sultan Allauddin Khilji's army. According to some accounts, Raja Karan of Gujarat was defeated and was forced to flee, while fifty thousand "infidels" were put to the sword. The Delhi Sultanate captured over twenty thousand slaves. Mahipala Deva—the Chudasama king of Saurashtra—rebuilt the temple in the early part of the fourteenth century and his son Khengar installed the Shiv lingam around fifteen years later. This was the sixth Somnath temple.'

'What happened to it?' asked Rathore.

'Well, in 1375, the temple was attacked by Muzaffar Shah I, the Sultan of Gujarat. Somnath was plundered again by Mahmud Begda—another Sultan of Gujarat —in 1451. The final blow fell in 1701, when the temple was destroyed by Mughal Emperor Aurangzeb. He built a mosque on the site of the temple. Around eighty years later, another temple was built at a site adjacent to the mosque, jointly by the Peshwa of Pune, Raja Bhonsle of Nagpur, Chhatrapati Bhonsle of Kolhapur, Queen Ahilyabai Holkar of Indore and Patilbuwa Shinde of Gwalior. This was the seventh temple.'

'And the eighth?' asked a wondering Radhika.

'More than a hundred and sixty years passed before Sardar Vallabhbhai Patel—India's first home minister—took upon himself the responsibility of reconstructing the temple at the original site,' explained Saini. 'The mosque was shifted to a nearby site and the *praanpratishthha*—the ceremony invoking God—was performed in the temple by the first President of India, Dr Rajendra Prasad, on 11 May 1951. This was the eighth—and current—temple. Varshney knew that we would find the number eight at the top-left tip of the swastika and this was his clue signifying that our search needed to be at the Somnath temple—a structure that had been built, destroyed and rebuilt eight times.'

'Er, I'd like to say something,' said Chhedi hesitantly.

'Yes?' asked Saini.

'Mount Kailash is located above Lake Mansarovar,' began Chhedi. 'I was there last year. At one time there were eight monasteries that were built as strategic points surrounding the lake. Chinese forces destroyed most of them when they overran Tibet, but now the monasteries are being rebuilt. Couldn't Varshney have been referring to the eight monasteries of Mount Kailash?'

'You may be absolutely right, Dumpy. Based upon what you've just said, it could be either Somnath or Mount Kailash,' Saini granted. 'In fact, Varshney alluded to the fact that it could be either, with his line, *Kalash or Kailash it is?*'

'Kailash refers to Mount Kailash but what does he mean by Kalash?' asked Chhedi, reasonably.

'Simple,' explained Saini. 'The Somnath temple—like any other Shiv temple—has a *kalash*—a metal pot with a large base and small mouth that is large enough to hold a coconut on top. You can see this kalash atop the present Somnath temple too. When Varshney says "Kalash or Kailash", he is simply reaffirming our own doubt that the location of the secret could be either Somnath or Mount Kailash.'

'But what does the remaining part of Varshney's note, *Raja surrender*, mean?' asked Radhika. 'How is that part of the note connected with Somnath?'

'Varshney is probably referring to the worst attack that Somnath witnessed—the one by Mahmud of Ghazni,' said Saini.

63

The fact of the matter was that even though Karana had been loyal to Duryodhana, he continued to be treated terribly in the Kaurava camp on account of his supposed low birth. When Karana declared that he would ensure victory for Duryodhana, the elder Bhishma mocked him. 'You couldn't save Duryodhana from the Gandharvas when the four of you went after the Pandavas! It was the Pandavas that saved you from the Gandharvas! Remember also that it was Arjuna who prevented you from defeating King Virata!' A furious Karana roared at Bhishma, 'You have achieved nothing in life. You didn't even have the courage to get married. I refuse to fight under you!' Bhishma retorted that he was relieved that he would not have to tolerate Karana in his ranks. I heard about this later and consoled myself that such infighting would play to the advantage of the Pandavas.

'Can you run a search for *Zakariya bin Muhammad bin Mahmud* on the internet for me?' asked Saini, turning to Chhedi.

'How does one spell the name?' asked Chhedi, beginning to type the search request into his tablet.

Saini spelt out the name for Chhedi and, turning to Radhika, said, 'Zakariya was a Persian traveller and wrote a book titled *Asaru-l Bilad wa Akhbaru-l' Ibad*, in the thirteenth century,' said Saini. 'Translated, the title means *Monuments of Countries and Memoirs of Men*. He has provided a vivid description of the Somnath temple and the destruction of it by Ghazni.'

'Ah! Here it is,' said Chhedi, searching the relevant extract on his tablet. 'Zakariya says that *Somnath is the celebrated city of India, situated on the shore of the sea, and washed by its waves. Among the wonders of that place was the temple in which was placed the idol called Somnat. This idol was in the middle of the temple without anything to support it from below, or to suspend it from above. It was held in the highest honour among the Hindus, and whoever beheld it floating in the air was struck with amazement, whether he was a Musulman or an infidel. The Hindus used to go on pilgrimage to it whenever there was an eclipse of the moon, and would then assemble there to the number of more than a hundred thousand.'*

'Continue reading the extract,' said Saini. 'He will go on to describe how rich Somnath was.'

Chhedi continued. 'Zakariya says that *everything of the most precious was brought there as offerings, and the temple was endowed with more than ten thousand villages. There is a river—the Ganges, which is held sacred between which and Somnut the distance is two hundred parasangs. They used to bring the water of this river to Somnat every day, and wash the temple with it. A thousand Brahmins were employed in worshipping the idol and attending on the visitors, and five hundred damsels sung and danced at the door. All these were maintained upon the endowments of the temple. The edifice was built upon fifty-six pillars of teak, covered with lead. The shrine of the idol was dark but was lighted by jewelled chandeliers of great value. Near it was a chain of gold bells weighing two hundred maans. When a portion of the night watch closed, this chain used to be shaken to rouse a fresh lot of Brahmins to perform worship.'*

Saini nodded. 'Just imagine—ten thousand villages, one thousand Brahmins, five hundred dancing girls, massive bells and chains of solid gold... incredible,' he muttered. 'If you go further into the extract, you will read Zakariya's description of the attack by Ghazni—referred to as *Yamin-ud Daula Mahmud.*'

Chhedi continued reading from where he had left off. *'When the Sultan Yamin-ud Daula Mahmud went to wage religious war against India, he made great efforts to capture and destroy Somnat, in the hope that the Hindus would then become Muhammadans. He arrived there in the middle of December in the year 1025. The king looked upon the idol with wonder, and gave orders for the seizing of the spoil, and the appropriation of the treasures. There were many idols of gold and silver and vessels set with jewels, all of which had been sent there by the greatest personages in India. The value of the things found in the temples of the idols exceeded twenty thousand dinars. When the king asked his companions what they had to say about the marvel of the idol, and of its staying in the air without pedestal or support, several maintained that it was upheld by some hidden support. The king directed a person to go and feel all around and above and below it with a spear, which he did, but met with no obstacle. One of the attendants then stated his opinion that the canopy was made of lodestone, and the idol of iron, and that the ingenious builder had skilfully contrived that the magnet should not exercise a greater force on any one side—hence, the idol was suspended in the middle. Some coincided, others differed. Permission was obtained from the Sultan to remove some stones from the top of the canopy to settle the point. When two stones were removed from the summit, the idol swerved to one side, when more were taken away, it inclined still further, until at last it rested on the ground.'*

Chhedi reached the end of the extract. Saini declared, 'Ghazni went down in history as the most hated looter to reach Somnath. He was fanatical about destroying the Shiv lingam. Mahmud personally took on the task of smashing the temple's lingam to smithereens. The stone fragments from the lingam were transported back by him to Ghazni. These fragments were scattered upon the steps leading to the city's Jamiah Masjid—a new mosque that was under construction. The idea was to ensure that the feet of worshippers at the mosque would tread all over the lingam's fragments as they entered the mosque. The defenders of the Somnath temple had been several Rajput clans—including one led by the ninety-year-old Raja Brahmadeva. But they were unsuccessful in repelling Ghazni's attack. Eventually, fifty thousand people lost their lives and Raja Brahmadeva had to concede defeat. Many of the Hindus fighting at Somnath escaped by boat in the middle of the night and, soon, the temple was left defenceless. Hence, Varshney's clue—*Raja surrender*—the king gives up.'

'Er, I hate to spoil the party but that sentence could just as well pertain to Mount Kailash,' said Chhedi.

64

With the declaration of war, kings from all over the land, along with their armies, horses, chariots and elephants, began to arrive at one of the two camps— the Kauravas' or the Pandavas'. Some of them found themselves unwittingly sucked into the wrong side. The king of Madra—Shalya—was related to the Pandavas, and arrived with every intention of fighting alongside them. On the way to Kurukshetra he was happy to find that arrangements for feeding his men and animals had been made by the Pandavas. It was only later that he realised that his hosts had been the Kauravas. Having enjoyed their hospitality, he could not fight for their enemies. He came running to me and told me of the predicament he found himself in. 'Be at peace with yourself,' I said. 'At some point of time they will ask you to drive Karana's chariot. Whenever that happens, please remember to praise Arjuna repeatedly. You will be helping us by making Karana insecure.'

'How could this clue have any bearing on Mount Kailash?' asked Saini.

'We know that Mount Kailash is located in modern-day Tibet. When the Chinese forces occupied Tibet, the ruler of Tibet—the Dalai Lama—was forced to flee to India, where he established a Tibetan government-in-exile. Thus, the sentence, *Raja surrender*, could very well be alluding to Mount Kailash.'

Saini nodded, finding new respect for Chhedi's reasoning. *Who would have ever thought that the schoolboy Dumpy would one day grow up to be a life sciences researcher, one who could also decipher mythological riddles*, thought Saini, smiling inwardly.

'Let's consider the next sentence of Varshney—*Six are tips in a star*,' suddenly interjected Rathore, finally warming to the exercise.

'The original doors of the Somnath temple had six-pointed stars for decoration,' replied Saini. 'The doors were taken away by Ghazni and they were installed in his tomb upon his death. There's a lithograph of Ghazni's tomb in the book *Afghaunistan*, a travelogue written by Lieutenant James Rattray. In that lithograph you can see the Somnath doors with their six-pointed stars in the carving.'

Chhedi had run a search on the internet and had located an image of the lithograph in question. 'See the stars on the doors?' he said, passing the tablet out to the others.

'But what exactly is the significance of the six-pointed stars on the doors?' asked Rathore, humbly.

'Six-pointed stars represent the ultimate union of Shiv and Shakti,' explained Saini. 'The upright triangle represents the erect phallus and the inverted triangle represents the female genitalia—or *yoni*. The intersection of the two triangles represents fertility—the union of male and female. This sacred symbol was later carried by Vedic immigrants to Sumeria, where Abraham was born. The religion that Abraham founded—Judaism—would later adopt a version of this very symbol. They called it the Star of David.'

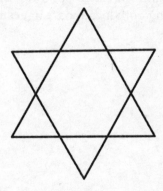

'Doesn't it mean that the secret is in Somnath, then?' asked Radhika. 'Isn't this the clinching piece of evidence in favour of Somnath?'

'No,' said Saini, judiciously. 'The six-pointed star is part of the natural symbolism of Mount Kailash, too. Mount Kailash is surrounded by six mountain ranges. These are depicted as the petals of a lotus—the symbol of Parvati's fertility—or the yoni. In that reasoning, Mount Kailash is the phallic symbol embedded in a yoni of six mountains. Mount Kailash is in itself symbolic of the six-pointed star.'

'But we've still not discussed the final two lines of Varshney's note,' said Radhika. '*And blue water beside*. He then talks of *Shankar elated*. Could one of these sentences help us decide between the two locations?'

'No,' replied Saini. 'The Somnath temple is located on the seashore so it has water right next to it. Similarly, Mount Kailash has two lakes—Mansarovar and Rakshastal—located at its base. Shankar is simply another name for Shiv, and both sites are famous for Shiv worship. Hence the phrase *Shankar elated* does not help us in choosing one or the other.'

'So where should we head?' asked Radhika.

'Maybe we should consider splitting up into separate teams and visiting both locations,' suggested Saini.

I advised Yudhistira that he should issue an open invitation for alliance to anyone who felt that Duryodhana's actions were anti-dharma. Two brothers of Duryodhana—Vikarna and Yuyutsu —did not concur with him. Both had been deeply ashamed when Draupadi had been dragged into court. But while Yuyutsu decided to join the Pandavas, Vikarna stayed faithful to the Kauravas, even though his personal views were opposed to those of Duryodhana. Vikarna was among the hundred Kauravas that Bhima eventually slayed, although his killing proved to be the most difficult. Within my own tribe of Yadavas, there were fissures too. The ones under Kritavarma went over to the Kaurava side, while the ones under Satyaki decided to side with the Pandavas. The only Yadava whose position was unclear was mine. Would I side with the Pandavas or with the Kauravas? Both sides wanted me, but for different reasons.

Priya and Taarak arrived in Nepalgunj, which lay along the south-west border of Nepal, by private charter, along with their guide. The immigration authorities of Nepal cleared them on priority because Sir Khan had contacts at the highest levels to facilitate his smuggling operations.

They directly transferred to a fixed-wing aircraft, which took them from Nepalgunj to Simikot. Their guide asked whether they wished to take a break before proceeding by chopper to Hilsa—on the Sino-Nepalese border—but they refused. A military escort joined them in Hilsa and accompanied them across the Friendship Bridge to the border checkpost from where their Land Cruiser crossed into Burang—along the southern border of Tibet.

'Keep these with you,' said the guide, handing over some pills to Priya and Taarak.

'What are these?' asked Taarak suspiciously.

'Diamox 125 mg,' replied the guide.

'Great,' replied Taarak sarcastically. 'What the hell is it, and why am I supposed to be taking it?'

'It will help reduce mountain sickness. You need to start taking it before you reach higher altitudes,' said the guide. 'Would you like to break your journey here in Burang? There is a guesthouse here—it's rather basic, but you can get a clean bed to sleep in, hot water for a bath and a meal before we proceed to Lake Mansarovar.' Both Priya and Taarak realised that they were indeed very tired, and chose to take up the offer.

The next morning they drove along a smooth Chinese highway from Burang to Darchen. Emerging from their Land Cruiser, the guide negotiated for three horses at a discounted price of nine hundred yuan per animal. He then quickly arranged oxygen tanks and ColdGear outfits that would help maintain their core body temperature.

'Make sure you keep drinking this hot soup,' said the guide, handing them flasks before mounting his own horse. 'Please also increase your Diamox to four pills for the day. Trust me, you'll need it by the time we get to Dharmala Pass.'

Before they could even commence their trek, however, the guide was informed of excessive snowfall near the Dharmala Pass. Reluctantly, the group returned to Darchen, awaiting clearer weather. Priya's thoughts slipped back to her father as she waited for Mount Kailash to allow them up.

'You need to come with me to Pali Hill today,' said Sanjay Ratnani. Pali Hill was a posh locality in the western Mumbai suburb of Bandra where all the Bollywood personalities had their homes.

'Why?' asked Priya, taking another bite of her apple at the breakfast table.

'It's important, Priya. Sir Khan wishes to meet you,' said her father hesitantly.

Priya raised her eyebrows. 'He wants to meet me? You have always consciously chosen to keep me as far away from your work as possible and now you suddenly want me to go and meet him?' she asked in surprise.

'Yes, Priya. He needs to discuss something important and he wants you to be part of the discussion,' said Ratnani.

A few minutes later, they were driving through the gates of Sir Khan's lavish mansion. The house was outlandish. It was famous in gossip circles because it boasted a swimming pool that was sixty feet in length and was equipped with an underwater music system. The other most-talked about feature of the house was a billiards table on a gold-plated trestle.

Sir Khan came outside to the driveway to receive them. 'My lucky day that I get to see my lawyer on a matter that does not involve keeping me out of prison,' joked Sir Khan as he shook hands with father and daughter. He was dressed in casual jeans and a white linen shirt. On his balding head was a straw hat that gave him the appearance of a mafia don—very appropriate to his stature.

On his left wrist he wore a platinum Patek Philippe Sky Moon Tourbillon watch that cost over a million dollars. His feet were encased in soft-leather Stefano Bemere moccasins. In his shirt pocket was a thick Aurora Diamante jewel-encrusted pen, and in his mouth was an even thicker Cohiba cigar.

Sir Khan had started out as a petty thief, had graduated to feared mafia don, and through years of reading, self-learning and social interaction, had acquired the veneer of business respectability and intellectual curiosity. He ushered Ratnani and Priya into his expansive private study that had a single glass wall overlooking the massive swimming pool, and allowed them to settle themselves on the plush oversized sofa, before offering them iced tea. His butler served the drinks discreetly, and withdrew, leaving them alone. Turning to Priya, Sir Khan said, 'I specifically asked your father to bring you along, Priya. Thank you for coming.'

Priya blandly replied, 'I'm curious to know why.'

'As your father knows, I am very active in the antiquities market. I love acquiring artefacts—the older the better,' said Sir Khan. 'Recently, I bought this piece of lead plating encrusted with precious stones. It is said to have adorned one of the pillars of the Somnath temple before it was destroyed by Mahmud Ghazni.' He held it out to her.

'Lead pillars? Why did Somnath have lead pillars?' asked Priya, running her fingers over the very old and rather battered lead plating.

'That's the question that I asked myself too,' smiled Sir Khan. 'We know that it was an extravagant temple in which the lingam lay suspended mid-air through the ingenious use of a lodestone roof, which created just enough magnetic pull to keep the structure suspended. We know that the pillars were of teak-wood and encased in lead plating—like this one—and were embedded with precious stones. But why have golden chains, golden bells, embedded rubies—and lead pillars? Why not gold?'

Priya and Ratnani maintained their silence. Sir Khan was not a man used to being interrupted.

'The original accounts tell us that there were fifty-six gold pillars that were each encrusted with gems by different Shivdharmi kings. These pillars were studded with fabulous stones such as diamonds, emeralds and rubies. But when we read later accounts of the attack by Ghazni, we are told that there were fifty-six lead pillars. What happened to the gold pillars?' asked Sir Khan.

'Possibly they were replaced somewhere between the ninth century, when the Pratihara king Nagabhata II reconstructed the temple in pink sandstone, and the year 1024, when Mahmud Ghazni attacked?' said Priya tentatively, recalling her history notes.

'That's not possible,' said Sir Khan. 'Somnath was at the peak of its prosperity prior to Ghazni's attack—in fact it was precisely this prosperity that attracted Ghazni in the first place.'

'So what other explanation could there be?' wondered aloud Priya.

'Have you heard of nuclear transmutation?' asked Sir Khan.

*Both Duryodhana and Arjuna came to Dwarka to win
me over to their side. I was sleeping when Duryodhana
walked in. He chose to sit at a spot by my head. Arjuna
came in later and chose a spot by my feet. When I woke up,
I saw Arjuna and asked, 'What do you want, Arjuna?'
Duryodhana was angry and protested, 'I came first, so
I should be asked first!' I was in no mood to indulge his
pettiness. 'I saw Arjuna first and hence shall ask him
before I ask you,' I said. Turning to Arjuna, I said, 'You
can have either me or my army? Which do you want?'
Arjuna did not hesitate for even a moment. He knew
that he wanted my strategic skills and not my men. 'I
want you, Krishna. Only you,' he said. Duryodhana,
too, was happy. As a result of Arjuna's choice, he ended
up with my army, thus taking his tally to eleven armies
against the seven Pandava ones.*

'Nuclear what?' asked Priya.

'Nuclear transmutation. It is the conversion of one chemical
element into another. Here, read this summary that I was
able to obtain from the director of the Bhabha Atomic
Research Centre,' said Sir Khan, passing over a single page
of laser-printed material to Priya. Priya quickly read it
aloud for the benefit of her father.

'Nuclear transmutation is the conversion of one chemical element—or isotope—into another,' read Priya. 'In effect, the atoms of one element can be changed into atoms of other element.'

'Transmutation can happen either through radio active decay or nuclear reactions. In the former, certain radio-active elements decay naturally over time, resulting in completely new elements. For example, Potassium 40 naturally decays into Argon-40, which is free argon found in the atmosphere. In the latter, transmutation can be caused by particle accelerators and nuclear power reactors by exposing elements to neutrons produced via an artificially-created nuclear chain reaction,' said Priya, reading from the paper.

'It has been proved scientifically that it is possible to turn lead into gold via neutron bombardment. This was the quest of medieval alchemists through the ages. It has also been proved that it is much easier to turn gold into lead through neutron capture or beta decay than the reverse. In either case, results would be achieved by leaving the material in a nuclear reactor for a long period of time.' Priya reached the end of the page and looked up at Sir Khan in amazement.

'Are you trying to tell me that the Somnath pillars were originally gold that turned into lead because of a nuclear reaction?' she asked.

'I'm not the one saying it. It's what every piece of history seems to be telling us,' said Sir Khan. 'Do you know that Somnath is built exactly at a point such that there is no land along the longitude that leads from it right down to Antarctica? There's only miles of ocean—not even a tiny island lies along that single longitude. An inscription to this effect in Sanskrit can be seen on the *Baan Stambh*—or Arrow Pillar—erected on the sea-protection wall at Somnath

Temple. Why is this geographical curiosity relevant? It is only relevant if one believes that the water emerging from Shiv lingam was irradiated.'

Priya sat listening to Sir Khan with her mouth agape. The don smiled a smile of satisfaction as he noticed her response. 'It is a well-known fact that power plants or nuclear plants create their own magnetic fields. When Ghazni's men saw the suspended Shiv lingam they thought it was held up by lodestone in the roof. They did not comprehend that the lodestone had been installed to keep the lingam *down*—by creating an opposing magnetic field to the one created by the lingam—rather than to pull it *up*!'

'But how did the ancients know how to create nuclear power?' asked Ratnani.

'It's not so remarkable when one considers the fact that ancient yogis of India knew even how to levitate,' said Sir Khan, puffing out yet another cloud of Havana fumes.

'That's true,' said Priya. 'I read about this in *Autobiography of a Yogi* by Paramahansa Yogananda. The ancient spiritual masters definitely had the ability to lift their bodies into thin air at will. It came from advanced spiritual practices in which they could actually alter the flow of electric currents through their body so that a magnetic field would lift them off the ground.'

'And it was this very technology that was used to build the pyramids in Egypt—a combination of acoustics and electromagnetism that allowed massive stone blocks to be shifted easily,' explained Sir Khan. 'A couple of years ago, a team of scientists at the University of St Andrews recreated levitation of objects in the laboratory by reengineering the *Casimir Force*—a force of nature which usually causes objects to stick together. Once reengineered, the Casimir Force could be used to repel instead of attract. Professor Ulf Leonhardt and Dr Thomas Philbin showed that the same effect could be used to levitate bigger objects too, even a person!'

'In effect, modern science is now telling us that levitation—which was disregarded as science fiction of Indian mythology—is indeed possible and that ancients could have had the ability to achieve those miracles,' said Priya.

'*The Philosopher's Stone* was the legendary alchemical substance that was believed to have had the power of turning base metals into gold or silver,' said Sir Khan. 'Indeed, for many centuries it was the object of most chemical experiments in Europe. The Philosopher's Stone was also believed to be an elixir of life—because it had the power to bestow immortality. Isn't it possible that Ghazni may have been inadvertently destroying the world's true Philosopher's Stone when he smashed the Shiv lingam of Somnath?'

'So why did you want to meet me and tell me all this?' asked Priya, breaking her resistance to ask the all-important question.

'Because I believe that you could help me uncover an incredible secret. It is monumental but it needs some-one with your knowledge of history to find it,' said Sir Khan simply.

Duryodhana then visited my elder brother—
Balarama—who had always had a soft corner
for him. In fact, Balarama had planned for our
sister Subhadra to marry Duryodhana, but I had
upset his plans by getting Subhadra to elope with
Arjuna. 'Join us, Balarama,' said Duryodhana. 'Even
though I was unable to marry your sister, there is no
reason why we should not be allies in war.' Bhima
reached Balarama at the same time. 'You are the one
who taught me to wield the mace, sire. You know that
your brother Krishna is always right. Please stand
by us and against those who are not righteous,' said
Bhima to Balarama. Balarama considered the situation
carefully and then spoke to both Duryodhana and
Bhima. 'Why such anger and bitterness? Over land?
Embrace each other and enjoy the rest of your lives
as friends, not enemies.' Neither side took his advice,
though. Balarama decided that he would proceed on
a pilgrimage along the Sarasvati and would fight for
neither. Before leaving, he advised both sides to follow
the rules of war meticulously.

The decision was taken. They would split into two teams—
Radhika and Saini as one, and Chhedi and Rathore the
other. The first team would travel to Mount Kailash on the

trail of Priya and Taarak. The second team would travel to Somnath to determine whether the four ancient seals were actually pointing them there, as suggested by Saini.

'Why would the Krishna Key point us to either Mount Kailash or Somnath?' asked Radhika. 'After all, both sites are consecrated to Shiv, not Vishnu.'

'Ah, but Vish and Shiv are two sides of the same coin,' said Saini smiling. '*Hara Hara Mahadev* is Shiv but *Hari* is Krishna. You can always find *Hara* and *Hari* in the same place!'

'So whether it was Shiv or Vish, their worship was prevalent in Vedic times?' asked Radhika.

'Fire altars have been discovered at many Indus Valley sites. Also bathing places like the Great Bath of Mohenjodaro used for ritual cleansing—a religious activity that you can still see on the banks of the Ganges every day. Most importantly, virtually all construction along the Indus-Sarasvati has been done using bricks of uniform dimension. The ratio of height to width to length is a consistent 1:2:3,' informed Saini.

'How does this ratio tell us that this was a Vedic civilisation?' asked Radhika.

'We know the tremendous mystical importance that the Vedic seers attached to the number 108 right? But 108 is derived from the multiplication of an ancient sequence. The sequence is 1^1, 2^2, 3^3 and 108 is simply the result of 1^1 x 2^2 x 3^3. Why were the Indus Valley residents using bricks in the ratio 1:2:3 if they were not Vedic?' asked Saini as they trekked their way to the Cave of the Thirteen Gold Stupas on Kailash's southern face.

Radhika and Saini's journey had started with a flight from Lucknow to Kathmandu. From Kathmandu, they had flown fly by a group-charter airplane towards the fabled hidden land of Dropoling—renowned for its rare medicinal herbs. They had continued on foot through incredibly beautiful wilderness towards the Tibetan border, crossing over a high pass to reach the ancient trading post of Burang where an amiable guide who went by the name of Sherpa Dorji joined them.

Their visit coincided with the full moon day of *Sagadawa*—a day when Tibetans traditionally celebrated the Buddha's birth, death, and enlightenment—and hundreds of Tibetan pilgrims had already begun their three-day ritual circumambulation of Mount Kailash, huddled together at night in tents hastily erected next to fifteenth-century Buddhist temples. Crossing the eighteen-thousand-foot-high Dolma-La pass, Radhika and Saini were reminded by Sherpa Dorji that the circumambulation of Mount Kailash signified a passage into a new life, completely cleansed of all past karma.

They managed the outer circumambulation of Mount Kailash on the first day, looking out for Priya and Taarak as they walked, but neither Mataji nor her fanatically devoted pupil were anywhere to be seen. 'Damn, we've missed them,' muttered Saini under his breath, cursing the delays that they had experienced along the way to Kailash. 'Maybe we should consider doing the *Nandi Parikrama* tomorrow to see if we can find them.' The Nandi Parikrama was also a circumambulation of Mount Kailash but along a much tougher circuit. This particular trek was only meant for seasoned mountaineers because it involved steep sections as well as rock falls.

As they trudged along, they met an ascetic. He wore very few clothes, in spite of the sub-zero temperatures and still seemed very comfortable. His hair was long and fell in thick braided dreadlocks around his shoulders. On his face and upper body he had smeared holy ash and on his forehead was a painted third eye. 'Hara Hara Mahadev!'

he shouted. Saini and Radhika folded their hands in obeisance before the holy man. 'I know what you seek,' said the sadhu cryptically. 'Remember one thing though... the philosopher is more important than the stone.' Before Saini or Radhika could ask him what he meant, he took a puff from a chillum of charas and danced into the wilderness, oblivious to the startled expressions of Radhika and Saini.

The next day, Radhika, Saini and Dorji walked in single file along a extremely narrow path. The rarefied air and pressure of walking uphill constantly soon had both Radhika and Saini out of breath. Their walk from Silung Gompa to Astapad Mountain had taken about an hour. They did not stop there but carried on to the confluence of two rivers—Silung and Kailash Ganga. A short descent brought them to Ling-Singjen—a horse's hoofprint considered very holy by the Tibetans.

As Radhika and Saini neared the base of Southern Kailash it started snowing heavily. Stopping was not an option so they continued along a rocky pathway down to a valley. On one side was Nandi Hill and on the other was Ravana Linga Mountain. In front of them stood the majestic Mount Kailash. They had been trekking for over eight hours before reaching the base of the vertical south wall face of Kailash. They were now ready for the worst part of the trek—the final half-kilometre climb to the Saptarishi Cave along an almost vertical wall using mountain climbing ropes provided by Dorji.

68

As the battle was about to begin, both armies saw Yudhistira take off his armour and put down his weapons. He stepped off his chariot and walked towards the Kaurava forces. A confused Arjuna ran forward and asked his brother why he was heading towards the enemy unarmed but Yudhistira was deep in thought and did not bother to reply. I gently explained to Arjuna that Yudhistira was simply seeking the blessings of the elders—Bhishma, Drona and Kripa. I could discern a malevolent glee emanating from the Kaurava forces. Most of the men seemed to think Yudhistira had decided to surrender even before the battle had commenced. Yudhistira walked up to Bhishma. Bending down, he touched the elder's feet reverentially and said, 'Grandsire, give us your permission to commence battle. We have dared to battle you—our unconquerable grandsire— and we seek your benediction.' Bhishma's eyes glistened with tears as he blessed Yudhistira and said, 'May you emerge victorious.' Yudhistira sought blessings from his gurus—Drona and Kripa—as well as from as his uncle Shalya, and then returned to the Pandava forces to start battle.

Radhika and Saini pulled themselves over a final ledge. They had reached the Saptarishi cave—almost a balcony on the south face of Kailash at a height of eighty metres from the base. The Tibetans had constructed chortens—or miniature stupas—along the balcony. Radhika and Saini were unaware of the fact that two of the stupas were not inanimate.

Radhika and Saini unstrapped their backpacks and sat down on the narrow ledge of the cave. Sherpa Dorji clambered down the rope once again in order to bring up additional supplies that had been left behind at the base of Kailash's south wall. They looked around the cave. It was filled with Tibetan chortens as well as deities and offerings placed by Hindu, Buddhist, Jain and Bön pilgrims. On the walls pilgrims had written a variety of prayers and shlokas. Radhika noticed one in particular. It said, '*Ilah sarasvati mahi tisro devirmayobhuvaha varhiha sidantasridhaha.*'

'What does this mean?' asked Radhika, pointing to the shloka on the wall.

'It's a verse from the *Rig Veda*, said Saini. 'It literally translates to: *O Ilah, Sarasvati and Mahi, the three goddesses who bring delight, please be seated, peacefully, on the grass.*'

'I haven't heard of Ilah or Mahi. In modern Hinduism we have Lakshmi and Durga, but no Ilah or Mahi,' said Radhika.

'That's because Ilah was another name for Durga,' explained Saini.

'Doesn't it sound a lot like Allah?' asked Radhika, her curiosity piqued.

'You are spot-on,' remarked Saini. 'Prior to the advent of Islam, the word Allah had already existed. It was derived from two Arabic words, *al*—meaning "the", and *ilah*—meaning "deity". Over a period of time, the combined phrase *al-ilah* came to be pronounced as Allah.'

'What evidence is there that it was a pre-existing name?' asked Radhika.

'The existence of the word Allah prior to Islam is evident from the fact that the prophet Mohammad's own father had the name *Abd-Allah*—what is today commonly pronounced *Abdullah*. Translated, it meant servant of Allah,' replied Saini. 'This is the best evidence of the fact that the name Allah was in use prior to the advent of Islam.'

Radhika shook her head in amazement. Listening to Saini was almost enchanting. He always had delicious morsels of historical, mythological and theological information to share. The acrimony between police-woman and murder suspect was gradually transforming itself into mutual respect and friendship.

'It's interesting to note that Semitic languages, including Hebrew and Aramaic, that evolved from the Persia-Syria region, also had an equivalent word prior to Arabic,' continued Saini. 'The Aramaic form is *Elaha* while Hebrew uses the plural form of *Elohim*. The question that we must then ask ourselves is this: from where did Al-Ilah, Allah, Elaha or Elohim emerge? If one simply considers the date of the *Rig Veda* and the evidence of westward migrations of Vedic people, it is possible that these words had a common root in Ilah—a goddess worshipped in Vedic times.'

'So, monotheistic religions such as Judaism, Christianity and Islam may have inadvertently borrowed from a polytheistic one such as Hinduism?' asked Radhika incredulously.

'Well, in the *Rig Veda*, one comes across a verse that says *"ekkam satya vipra bahuda vidhaante"*. It means, *Truth is one, God is one, although sages may call him by a variety of names.* This is the essence of Vedic philosophy. It is a misconception that the Vedic faith is polytheistic,' said Saini taking a gulp of hot water from his flask.

At that very moment, the silence and stillness of Mount Kailash was shattered by a resounding gunshot. While Radhika and Saini were completely preoccupied in their philosophical discussions, two of the Tibetan chortens had morphed into the human figures of Priya and Taarak. They had quietly moved over to the edge of the balcony and clambered down the rope that had been used by Radhika and Saini to climb up.

Sherpa Dorji was heading back towards the base of the cave when he saw the two strangers running away from the base of the south face. They were carrying away the rope that was needed to access the cave. 'Hey!' shouted Dorji. 'What do you think you're doing? Where are you taking my rope?'

Instead of replying to his question, Taarak had simply turned around, taken out his gun and fired a round into the air. The purpose was not only to warn Sherpa Dorji that there was no point in attempting to fight but also to set in motion a natural chain of events that would finish off the two pesky intruders—Radhika and Saini—once and for all.

As the gun went off, there was an ominous loud rumble and the earth began to tremble. Seated in the cave of the south face of Mount Kailash, Radhika and Saini felt the ground shake as massive quantities of boulders, snow and debris began rolling down from Shiv's abode. Within a few seconds the avalanche was in full motion. Radhika and Saini clung to one another under the ledge of the Saptarishi Cave as they watched the only entrance to the cave fill up with boulders and ice.

'Are you hurt?' asked Saini urgently, as he held Radhika tightly. There was no reply. He repeated the question. In panic, he shook Radhika a little, but soon realised that he was shaking a corpse. He frantically placed his hand in front of her face to discern if she was breathing, but he could not feel her breath.

Saini's eyes moistened as the reality that Radhika was dead hit him. He continued to cradle her body in his arms as he felt his tears well up. He felt her head and discovered a mild bump underneath her wet hair. Obviously, some falling debris had hit her. He cursed himself for slipping into his academic role and taking his eye off the ball. It had got Radhika killed while he himself was well and truly stuck.

Saini remembered the tutorial that Priya had given him about checking for a pulse. He placed two fingers under the angle of Radhika's jaw to check her carotid. He prayed fervently that he would detect even the faintest beat of life, but there was none. 'No!' shouted Saini. 'Why don't you open your eyes, Radhika?' he asked, almost wishing to trick himself into believing that she was alive. But there was no reply. Soon there was only darkness—and the sub-zero chill of a morgue.

69

Warriors on both sides took an oath to honour the traditions and rules of battle. By the time that the battle ended, all rules would have been forgotten. In front of the Pandavas, stood the mighty army of the Kauravas. Different flags symbolising key warriors fluttered in the air—flags of Bhishma, Drona, Duryodhana, Kripa, Jayadhrata and Aswatthama. Seeing the scale of the Kaurava forces, Yudhistira said to Arjuna, 'The opposing army is incredibly large. Our strategy should be to concentrate our forces into a needlepoint. It is the only way that we will be able to fight them.' But Arjuna was in no condition to respond. He was overwhelmed with the scene and seemed terrified.

Radhika Singh had just started teaching history, geography and civics at the Mayo College in Ajmer. Her husband, Commandant Hari Singh of the Border Security Force, had recently been promoted from Deputy Commandant and the increased pay had allowed them to get married. Their respective fathers had been buddies in the Indian Army and had decided to introduce the children to one another, in the hope that love would blossom and that they would get married. The strategy had worked.

Commandant Hari Singh had been sent off to Jammu & Kashmir as part of a BSF battalion handling counterinsurgency and counter-terrorism operations. Hari Singh's team established an intelli-gence network and created ground-level relationships with informants. The result was that they were able to kill Rafique Baba—a key operative of the *Jaish-e-Mohammed*. Hari Singh's team raided Rafique Baba's secret camp in Srinagar and killed him in the gun battle that followed. As reward for his efforts, Hari Singh was granted leave along with a generous bonus, and he proceeded to Ajmer to spend some quality time with his wife. Little did he know that his victory had not gone unnoticed within the leadership of the Jaish-e-Mohammed. Two sharpshooters were instructed to track down Hari Singh and eliminate him.

That evening, Hari Singh had taken his pretty wife to a movie and they had eaten a hybrid Indo-Chinese meal from a small restaurant near the cinema. They had walked back to their house hand-in-hand, enjoying the intimacy of the moment. As they reached the garden gate to their government-allotted quarters, Hari had been hit by a barrage of bullets. The two masked gunmen who had been hiding behind the bushes had continued firing until Hari's body was riddled with holes.

At first, Radhika's reaction had been that of intense despair as she fell to her husband's side, pleading with God to keep him alive. It was followed almost instantaneously by intense rage directed at the men who were running towards the gate. The gardener had been trimming the hedges that day and his shears happened to be lying on the ground. She picked up the heavy hedge-trimmer and charged towards the attackers who were fleeing the scene. Her shears plunged into the leg of one of the assailants who fell to the ground. His comrade did not stop to help his mate and ran even faster from the scene of the crime. Hearing the gunshots, neighbours had also rushed out and surrounded and captured the injured terrorist who was lying face down on the grass.

Radhika retreated into a cocoon that she did not want to ever emerge from. The flames of her husband's pyre died down, but Radhika's despair and anger didn't. She would wake up in the mornings hoping to feel him by her side in bed. She would stand by the window expecting to see him walking in—upright and brisk as usual. She was unaware that she was in severe clinical depression and needed professional help. Even after several weeks of remaining holed up in her house, Radhika continued to wait by the window.

One day, there was a crowd in the garden that ran along the front of the BSF staff quarters. An exponent of the *Bhagwad Gita* had arrived in Ajmer from Rishikesh and was delivering a lecture. Radhika did not attend it but stood by the window listening to his words.

The man was saying, 'For the soul there is neither birth nor death at any time. He has not come into being, does not come into being, and will not come into being. He is unborn, eternal, ever-existing and primeval. He is not slain when the body is slain. The soul can never be cut to pieces by any weapon, nor burned by fire, nor moistened by water, nor withered by the wind. This individual soul is unbreakable and insoluble, and can be neither burned nor dried. He is everlasting, present everywhere, unchangeable, immovable and eternally the same.' At that moment, it occurred to Radhika that she had found the answer to a very big question.

She ran out of her house in her dishevelled state and fell at the feet of the guru from Rishikesh. He smiled at her and handed over a rosary of 108 beads to her. 'Whenever you are in despair, just recite your husband's name as many times as there are beads,' he said. 'You will be infused with strength.'

And so it was that Radhika Singh took to chanting her husband's name while counting her prayer beads. She didn't know it then but the spiritual master from Rishikesh had suggested her husband's name merely because Hari was another name for Krishna. Inside the Saptarishi cave, Radhika began her final journey to join her husband Hari Singh wherever he was.

'You shall not die,' said Saini as he continued to hold Radhika's lifeless form in his arms. What Saini hoped was that Radhika was in *forced hibernation*—more commonly known as *suspended animation*. It involved the sudden halting of chemical reactions in the body due to lack of oxygen combined with freezing temperatures.

Research had shown that ninety-nine per cent of garden worms died within twenty-four hours of exposure to temperatures just above freezing point. But, when first deprived of oxygen, the garden worms survived ninety-seven per cent of the time. Upon rewarming and reintroduction of oxygen, the worms reanimated and showed normal life spans. Saini recalled from discussions with his colleagues at the University of Memphis that there were many examples of humans who had appeared frozen to death. They had no heartbeat and were clinically dead. There were significant documented cases of humans who had been successfully revived after spending hours without a pulse in extremely cold conditions.

In the fervent hope that Radhika was alive, Saini felt around him for his backpack. It contained a towel with which he could dry Radhika's hair. His main worry was that any moisture or residual snow on her would aggravate her hypothermia. Staying dry and adequately layered was the key to preventing it. He quickly unzipped the bag, took out the towel and began rubbing her hair dry. Also inside his bag was a torch but he knew that it would only provide light for an hour or so before the batteries ran out. It was better to preserve it for later.

He checked his flask and saw that it was only half full. He fumbled around for Radhika's backpack and was relieved to find that her flask also contained water. Staying hydrated was extremely critical in fighting hypothermia. He also noticed that her backpack con-tained cigarettes, a lighter as well as a pack of almonds in addition to her prayer beads. A non-smoker himself, Saini ironically found himself grateful to Radhika for being a smoker. The lighter would be of immense use in starting up a small fire. The idea was to stay dry, hydrated and warm till such time as help arrived.

He got up from where he was seated and lifted Radhika in his arms. He made his way deeper into the Saptarishi Cave and found a dry spot that was free of snow. Using Radhika's backpack and towel he fashioned a pillow for her and laid her down gently on the floor. Then, switching on the flashlight, he began searching for wood and rags that would help him light a fire.

Fool, he thought to himself midway through the task. Lighting a fire inside a cave with limited ventilation would use up all the remaining oxygen inside. Instead of being cold they would simply asphyxiate to death! He looked at Radhika. He prayed like he had never prayed before, willing every power and god to rescue Radhika from the jaws of death. He briefly closed his eyes and opened them again as soon as he heard a sound.

She was shivering and was incoherently mumbling something. She was alive! Saini sat down next to her and poured some hot water from his flask into the cup. He lifted her head and brought the cup to her lips. He was relieved when he saw her drink. He tightened the cap of the thermos and returned it to the backpack. He then pulled Radhika towards him and held her tightly, hoping that his embrace would provide her with much needed warmth.

70

Arjuna looked at the massive Kaurava army, which had been organised in vyuha formation by Bhishma. Arjuna asked me to drive the chariot to a midway point between the two armies so that he could have a better view of both sides. Once I had done so, Arjuna carefully observed his grand-fathers, uncles, teachers, brothers, sons, friends and relatives. He was overwhelmed. The Gandiva fell from his hands and Arjuna sat down. 'Of what use will be a kingdom or wealth when it is to be obtained by spilling my own family's blood?' he asked me. 'I would rather be killed by my cousins than wage war against them. I do not want to fight!'

'Hari-Hari, Hari-Hari, Hari-Hari,' the Rishikesh guru was saying to Radhika. 'Keep chanting Hari-Hari, Hari -Hari, Hari-Hari.' With each repetition of the word, his voice seemed to get louder. It was almost as though he were reciting the name to the background rhythm of a percussion band. In her delirious state, Radhika did not realise that what she was hearing was actually the sound of helicopter rotor blades. She had been tied to a rope that had been brought up to the Saptarishi Cave by a rescue team led by Sherpa Dorji who had gone trekking several miles to seek emergency help after his standoff with Taarak.

Radhika had then been lowered down to the base of the mountain from where she had been carried by sherpas and Saini to a small helicopter. Saini and Radhika were now headed to Darchen where a small but functional first-aid centre funded by the Swiss Ngari Korsum Foundation would provide emergency medical help. As they flew towards Darchen, Saini had a breath-taking view of Mount Kailash in the distance, nestled within six mountain ranges and the all-embracing Mansarovar lake. Saini was able to see in reality that the six-pointed star symbolism of Mount Kailash was very much true. As he gazed at the mountain, he thought of the Sri Yantra, a symbol of energy used by Hindus around the world in their homes.

The more he looked at Mount Kailash, an upright pyramid—almost phallic—resting in the yoni of the surrounding valleys, the greater was his realisation that whether it was the six-pointed star, or the Sri Yantra, both were representations of creation—the intersection of Shiv and Shakti. Ironic indeed, thought Saini to himself, that Shiv—a force of destruction—was mostly depicted via a symbol of creation. *Shiv and Vish were indeed two sides of the same coin.*

'Is this really about duty or is this your fear speaking?'
I asked Arjuna. He looked up at me. Ignoring my
rebuke he asked, 'How can I be expected to shoot arrows
at Bhishma or Drona? They are the elders that I have
looked up to all my life. Why should I be responsible for
such a heinous crime?' I smiled at Arjuna and placed
my hand on his shoulder. 'Arjuna, the truly wise do not
grieve—either for the living or the dead. As clothes are
changed, similarly the soul adopts and discards bodies.
The soul cannot be pierced by your arrows nor can it
be burnt by fire. It cannot be wet by water nor can it be
dried by air. It is permanent and universal. Knowing
that the soul cannot be destroyed—it is never born and
never dies—how can you possibly kill?' I asked the
troubled warrior.

Sanjay Ratnani and Sir Khan sat inside the don's Rolls-Royce. It was a Silver Phantom that had been specially customised for Sir Khan. The vehicle had been provided with armour reinforcement, which allowed the car to withstand rifle attacks, automatic gunfire, sniper assaults, and even explosions from hand grenades.

Sir Khan loved bling, and his car took the concept of bling to an entirely different planet. Many of the trimmings that would usually feature walnut or cherry wood panels had been replaced by eighteen-carat gold plating. The process of customising the car had taken over a year.

Sir Khan's phone began ringing. It was his lieu-tenant who had been given the assignment of providing the getaway vehicle for Priya. He had also been given the added task of killing Radhika Singh. As Sir Khan heard the voice at the other end, his face turned red in anger. He let loose a stream of the filthiest expletives at the man, describing in detail the manner in which he would deprive the man of vital body parts on account of his failure to eliminate Radhika.

'Has Priya contacted you?' he asked, turning to Sanjay Ratnani as he hung up.

'Just once, when she was on her way to Mount Kailash. After that there has been no communication,' replied the lawyer. 'If she had found what interests you, she would have called.'

Sir Khan reluctantly nodded. 'You're probably right, but I still cannot shake off the feeling that Mount Kailash is indeed the place where we should be looking.'

'Why?' asked Ratnani.

'Mount Kailash is often called the *Axis Mundi*—the centre of the universe,' replied Sir Khan. 'In different religions and cultures it is called by various alternative names such as the Navel of the World, the World Pillar, Kang Tisé, Kang Rinpoche, the Precious Jewel of Snow, Meru, Sumeru, Swastika Mountain, Nine-Storeyed Mountain, Mount Astapada, and Mount Kangrinboge. The importance attached to Mount Kailash can be discerned from simply the number of names that people have attached to it!'

'But what makes Mount Kailash so important? So sacred?' persisted Ratnani.

'Various factors—including geography and myth —have contributed to the spiritual importance of Mount Kailash,' said Sir Khan. 'The mountain only reaches 6,714 metres. There are several peaks within the Himalayan range that are significantly higher. The beauty and majesty of Kailash, however, do not lie in its height but in its unique shape. Kailash has four flat faces—and each face corresponds with the cardinal points of the compass. This is one of the reasons that many believe that Kailash is a manmade pyramid instead of a mountain.'

'Manmade pyramid?' asked Ratnani incredulously as he looked at the picture handed him by Sir Khan.

'Possibly,' replied Sir Khan. 'Although Mount Kailash has been bestowed with nature's bounty, it sits in isolated splendour—which ensures that Kailash is not dominated by a neighbouring mountain. It is Sumeru—the spiritual core of the world. The land surrounding Mount Kailash is the origin of four life-giving rivers, the Indus, Brahmaputra, Sutlej and Karnali—a tributary of the revered Ganges. Two lakes lie at the foothills of the mountain. Mansarovar Lake, probably one of the highest freshwater lakes in the world, is round in shape, like the sun. The lower lake, Rakshastal, is a saltwater lake and is shaped like a crescent moon. The two lakes thus symbolise solar and lunar energy. It is perfectly plausible that humans may have fashioned a pyramid at this sacred spot.'

'If it were manmade, who built it? Buddhist lamas? Vedic sages? Or powerful druids like the ones who built Stonehenge?' asked Ratnani.

'Kailash is seen differently by various world religions,' explained Sir Khan. 'To Tibetans and Buddhists, the mountain is the home of Demchog. For Hindus, Kailash is the abode of Shiv. The Jain tradition reveres Kailash as the site where Sage Rishabhadeva attained enlightenment. Even prior to the advent of Buddhism, the Bön religion of Tibet worshipped the nine-storeyed mountain. It could have been any of them that built it.'

'What is it about Kailash that fascinates you?' asked Ratnani, baffled by the extent of knowledge that the don had accumulated about the subject.

'Not just me, my friend,' smiled Sir Khan. 'Mount Kailash has fascinated everyone. Sometimes, due to the contrast between snow and rock and the play of light and shadow, one can discern a swastika symbol on the south face of Kailash. It is truly a magical place. The mountain and the paradise-like land that surround it have been even called Shambhala and Shangri-La by the Russians!'

'The Russians? What did they have to do with Mount Kailash?' asked Ratnani.

'Tsar Nikolai Romanov of Russia had significant ties with the tutor of the thirteenth Dalai Lama,' replied Sir Khan. 'It was this rather close friendship that facilitated the opening of St Petersburg's very first Buddhist temple. Nicholas Roerich was one of the artists who provided artwork for this Buddhist temple. He spent several years in Tibet. His painting *The Path to Kailas* can be appreciated even today. Why were the Russians so interested in Mount Kailash? I began to ask myself whether their interest was in the mysticism of a lost paradise or whether it was the quest for a hidden power.'

'Hidden power? Like a weapon?' asked Ratnani.

'Possibly,' replied Sir Khan. 'Just before World War II started, the Buddhist lamas had new visitors. This time not from Russia, but from Nazi Germany. Leaders like Heinrich Himmler seemed to believe that this region was the home to the original Aryan race and that wonderfully potent powers could be acquired from here that would help the Nazis rule the world.'

'Was Himmler able to gain anything from Tibet?' asked Ratnani.

'The fact of the matter is that this continued fascination for Kailash resulted in a study,' said Sir Khan. 'It was one of the most dramatic and profound propositions ever made. The Russians declared that they believed that Kailash was a massive, manmade pyramid. Their study also revealed that it was the nucleus of a much larger network of smaller pyramids. This is a photo of the layout of Kailash as sketched by the Russians.'

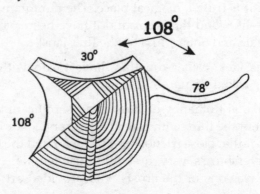

Ratnani looked at the photo held out by Sir Khan but couldn't understand the significance. Sir Khan sighed. It was so painful to educate the uninitiated.

'The shape and layout of Kailash is far too scientific to be considered an absolutely natural creation. If you see the curvature of the west face, it measures 108 degrees—exactly the divine Vedic number. The north face is much less concave—just 30 degrees, but when we add this to the curve of the ridge that adjoins Mount Kailash, we once again get 108 degrees—another instance of the Vedic sacred number. This could not be an entirely natural occurrence!'

Ratnani screwed his eyes to view the picture more carefully.

'Mount Kailash is almost the equivalent of a massive human-built pyramid,' continued Sir Khan. 'The four faces are perfectly aligned with the cardinal points of the compass. The curvatures of the faces add up to 108 degrees. The sides are almost perpendi-cular to the ground and the drop is breath-taking. One can observe horizontal strata of stone layers with clear divisions between the strata. I don't know what lies at Mount Kailash but I know that whatever lies there had to be of supreme importance for Kailash to exist!'

Arjuna was still looking dazed. I tried a slightly different approach. 'Even if you are unable to comprehend the eternal nature of the soul, the fact is that you are a Kshatriya and it is your dharma to fight,' I said. 'War is the greatest opportunity for a Kshatriya. If you win, you shall enjoy the pleasures of a kingdom. If you die, you shall attain heaven because you died while performing your duty. If you turn your back on this war, generations will label you a coward. You must learn to treat victory and defeat equally. When you do your work with a sense of duty, without worrying about the possibility of reward, your actions become selfless and you become a true yogi!' I paused, hoping that my words would have some effect on the shattered warrior who stood in the chariot that I was steering.

Priya looked across the table at Taarak. They were back at base camp in Darchen. In front of them were two cups of hot tea and buttered toast.

'There is no way that the Chinese authorities will let us climb to the summit, Mataji,' said Taarak, biting into his toast. 'Mount Kailash is revered as a sacred entity, hence one cannot climb it. Mountain-climbing expeditions are strictly forbidden. One can only climb up to the Saptarishi Cave—where we've succeeded in trapping Saini and that pesky policewoman—but no further. The only person who ever climbed to the very top was an eleventh-century Buddhist monk—*Milarepa*.'

'There was absolutely nothing of significance inside the Saptarishi Cave,' said Priya, sipping her tea. 'I examined all the stupas inside the cave carefully before Saini and the policewoman arrived. Absolutely nothing! If there is anything at all, it will lie at the summit. What if we attempted the climb surreptitiously?'

'We would need sherpas and supplies. The risk of being discovered by the Chinese authorities would be tremendous,' said Taarak. 'Moreover, if we go by the Russian study on Kailash that you were given—the one that seems to suggest that Kailash could be a human-engineered marvel—then the secret could very well lie at the core of the pyramid instead of the peak,' argued Taarak. Priya nodded silently in agreement. Her thoughts wandered back to the initial meeting with Sir Khan initiated by her father.

'I am given to understand that a recent diving expedition off the Dwarka coast has revealed an ancient city. It could very well be the fabled Dwarka of Krishna,' Sir Khan had said to her.

'Isn't that good news?' she asked.

'Not necessarily. I have been personally investing my own resources into finding the secrets of Krishna,' replied Sir Khan. 'I spent hard cash to acquire this lead plating from the Somnath temple. I even sent my own expedition to Mount Kailash, but alas, I could not find anything. Only an abundance of theories, no practical evidence.'

'But the discovery off the Dwarka coast may offer some tantalising clues, couldn't it? I'm told that they've discovered hundreds of ancient ship anchors, showing that the city would have had a flourishing maritime trade. They've even discovered a statue of Vishnu under the sea,' said Priya, recalling the report that she had read in a newspaper.

'I need you to get inside Krishna's mind,' said Sir Khan. 'If he were to leave something momentous and significant here on earth, what would it be? And where would he leave it?'

'How can I get into the mind of a god?' asked Priya. 'That, too, an avatar that lived five thousand years ago?'

'The most knowledgeable person in the field of Krishna research is a fellow called Ravi Mohan Saini. He's a professor at St Stephen's College in New Delhi. If you became his student, you would have the inside scoop on cutting-edge finds,' explained Sir Khan.

'Why not befriend the explorers who are diving in Dwarka instead?' asked Priya.

'Because they are *specialists*,' said Sir Khan, using the word with scorn. 'They only look at one set of finds in isolation. They do not have the ability to connect the dots across multiple finds. Moreover, I have done some digging into Saini's background. He has deep friendships with virtually all the scientists and archaeologists who are involved in related research areas. With your masters' degree in history, you could easily gain access to Saini by convincing him to enrol you as a doctoral student.'

Priya thought about it for a moment. 'I returned from Kings College hoping that I would be able to teach history to children,' she said at length.

'And so you shall,' replied Sir Khan smiling. 'There's one child in particular that I specifically want you to teach.'

'Who is he?' asked Priya.

'His name is Sampat Sharma. He's the son of a wealthy horse breeder—Mr V Y Sharma. I have already arranged a part-time teaching job for you at the school that he attends,' said Sir Khan. 'You shall keep the teaching assignment until Saini accepts you as his doctoral student.'

'But why this particular school and this specific boy?' asked Priya, a little hesitantly.

Sir Khan looked at Ratnani and laughed. 'I knew there was a reason that your daughter would be perfect for this assignment, Sanjay. She has spunk! I like that.'

Turning to Priya he said, 'I have commissioned a research study to discover the next Kalki avatar!'

'Kalki avatar?' asked Priya. 'You mean the tenth incarnation of Vishnu who is prophesised to appear towards the end of Kaliyug?'

'Yes. I've decided that I shall not wait for the real Kalki avatar to appear. I shall create my own,' chuckled Sir Khan. 'For that I need someone who has all the right markers. This boy fits the role perfectly.'

'What purpose will he serve?' asked Priya.

'He shall be your student, Mataji,' said Sir Khan solemnly. 'He shall help us clear obstacles that stand in the way of reaching Krishna's secret. Are you ready to serve?'

'To become a true yogi, a person must cast off all his desires. He should treat pleasure and pain as equals. He should be free of attachment—as also from anger, fear, desire, jealousy or craving. This state is not easy to attain because the mind is like a wild animal. If you concentrate and meditate upon me, you too can attain this state,' I explained to Arjuna. The confused warrior asked me, 'If the purpose of one's life is to attain this state of bliss, then why make me fight this war?' I then had to explain to him the fact that there were two independent paths available to the state of bliss. The first path was through knowledge and the other was through action. Arjuna's salvation lay in his actions and in performing his duty.

Chhedi and Rathore were at the steps of the Somnath temple. They had arrived the previous day and had scheduled to spend the following day with Mrs Desai, a professor of architecture from Gujarat Vidyapith. Mrs Desai's husband was a friend of Rathore's and Mr Desai had suggested that his wife would be able to give them an in-depth tour of Somnath like no one else could.

'Call me Amita,' she said pleasantly as she met them outside the gates of the temple. 'So, shall we start the grand tour?'

The men nodded. 'Lead on,' said Chhedi grandly.

'I figure that both of you are already familiar with the number of times that this temple was built and destroyed so I shall not go into details of that,' began Amita. 'Let me just say that after the 1706 destruction, the present *mandir* was not reconstructed until 1951. After Indian Independence in 1947, a committee was constituted with the objective of rebuilding the temple at the very spot along the seashore where the original temple had stood. Sardar Vallabhbhai Patel played a critical role in spearheading the project and that's why you see his statue right here at the entrance.'

'Is this temple similar to the one which was destroyed in 1706?' asked Chhedi.

'Good question,' replied Amita. 'The present temple was completed in 1951 and, for the most part, duplicates the original structure. The stone façade appears golden at sunset, which is very much in keeping with the Somnath legend. As you can see, the present mandir is built in traditional design, and is a symmetrical but sinuous structure. It has a fifty-metre-high tower that rises in clusters and can be observed from great distances. Vedic architects from all over India contributed to the reconstruction. Here's a picture of the ruins of Somnath as sketched in 1869.'

Rathore and Chhedi gasped. Looking at the ruins, one could picture the extent of the onslaught that Somnath had faced from attackers down the ages. 'Here's a picture of the present structure that you are now looking at,' said Amita, handing over her album to the men.

'What about the Shiv lingam inside? Is that new or is it the original?' asked Rathore.

'The Somnath lingam has always been considered the most important of the twelve Jyotir lingams in India,' replied Amita. 'The ancient lingam was believed to be *Swayambhu*— or self-born. Unfortunately, it was smashed to pieces in the year 1026. All the lingas that were installed thereafter ended up getting destroyed by a succession of attackers. The present lingam is the largest of the twelve in India. It's a greyish granite block about a metre high and around sixty centimetres in diameter. During an archaeological excavation in 1940 by the Archaeological Survey of India, the original slab on which the lingam rests was discovered and the new lingam was fixed on this.'

'There was something I recently read about the doors having been taken away by Mahmud Ghazni and being returned to the temple later,' remarked Chhedi.

'Ah. Yes, in 1842, Edward Law, the First Earl of Ellenborough, issued the Proclamation of the Gates. In this proclamation he ordered the British troops in Afghanistan to bring back the sandalwood gates that had been taken away by Ghazni from Somnath.'

'I had heard about how Krishna was shot in his foot by a hunter near Somnath. Does the Somnath temple commemorate the spot where he died?' asked Rathore.

'No,' replied Amita. 'The Somnath temple existed many hundreds of years prior to Krishna. In fact we know that Krishna reconstructed the temple during his own lifetime also. Hence, the Somnath temple does not commemorate the spot where Krishna was killed. Just north of Somnath— on the way to Veraval —is another temple called *Bhalka Tirtha*. It is this particular temple that is located on the site where Krishna was shot. Very close to the temple is a cave known as *Baldev Gufa*. According to legend this is the cave where Krishna's elder brother Balarama gave up his body and went back to his Sheshnag form.'

As the trio walked along the temple pathway, a priest with a gentle face appeared. He appeared to be headed towards the Dwarakadheesh temple. Around his shoulders was a saffron shawl bearing innumerable impressions of a single chant, *Hare Krishna*. He was bald, except for the Brahmin's lock at the back of his head. From his shoulder ran a sacred thread diagonally across his chest. On his forehead was a simple tilak and around his neck were sacred beads. 'Hare Krishna,' he chanted. The trio folded their hands and the holy man smiled and conveyed his blessings. 'I know what you seek,' said the pujari cryptically. 'Remember one thing though... the philosopher is more important than the stone.'

It was then that I decided to tell Arjuna the truth about myself—about my divinity. 'I take on a human manifestation and the fools do not recognise me as the supreme one. I am the creator of your universe. I am the objective of meditation, ritual and prayer. I am the stuff that makes the soul of all beings. I am the beginning, middle, and end,' I said as I took on my universal omnipotent form. Arjuna was now able to see me as divinity and said, 'I am now convinced of the truth that you speak. I shall no longer doubt you. Instead, I shall fight, because that is my duty!'

Radhika awoke to find Saini sleeping on the chair next to her bed. She felt vaguely that she was in some sort of hospital or infirmary, but her mind was hazy. The hypothermia had taken its toll. She stretched out her arm and tapped Saini's shoulder. He awoke with a start but was pleasantly relieved to see Radhika smiling at him.

'You scared the living daylights out of me,' he said to her. 'Inside the cave, I really thought that you were a goner.'

'It's not that easy to kill Radhika Singh. I'm like the proverbial bad penny—I keep returning,' she joked. 'Let's get out of here. This place will make me sicker than I already am.'

Saini nodded. Getting Radhika there had been stressful, and waiting for her to recover had been even more so. He was fed up of the hospital and was keen to return to the search as soon as possible. Chhedi had spoken to him on the phone earlier in the morning and had told him that Somnath had thrown up a few clues but no major discovery. 'Any idea where Priya Ratnani and Taarak Vakil are?' he had asked.

'No idea,' replied Saini, describing to Chhedi the encounter that Sherpa Dorji had with Taarak and the avalanche that followed, leading to them being trapped inside the Saptarishi Cave.

Chhedi was dumbfounded. 'Listen, Roger, you had better get back to base. We've had too much death around us, we don't need any more,' he tried to reason.

Saini laughed it off. 'Listen, Dumpy, you mentioned something right now about the doors of Ghazni's tomb. Where are they?'

'You mean the sandalwood ones brought back from Afghanistan by the British?' asked Chhedi.

'Yes—the ones that turned out to be replicas of the original ones. Where are they presently located? Those doors may hold the key,' said Saini into the phone.

'Well, the gates were removed from Mahmud's tomb and brought back to India. They were then kept in one of the storage rooms of the Agra Fort where they continue to sit till today,' said Chhedi.

'Do you recall seeing an illustration of those doors?' asked Saini.

'Indeed I do. The six-pointed stars were rather prominent,' replied Chhedi.

'Not a six-pointed star, my friend. It's a symbol of the union between Shiv and Shakti,' corrected Saini.

'So, what do you want me to do now?' asked Chhedi. 'I have Rathore with me and we're ready to move from here.'

'Go to Agra. We'll meet you there. I think it's important for us to see those doors,' said Saini. 'Given that we are in Tibet, it may take us a little longer to get there than you.'

'What do you want us to do till you arrive?' asked Chhedi.

'Well, besides checking out the doors in the Agra Fort, maybe you and Rathore ought to visit the Taj Mahal—rather romantic by moonlight, I'm told.'

75

*On the eve of the war, sage Vyasa visited the palace
of Dhritarashtra. The sage told him, 'Terrible days
lie ahead. I have seen terrible omens in the skies—a
conjunction of Saturn with Aldebaran, retrograde Mars
before reaching Antares and also a lunar eclipse near
Pleiades. All your sons and the kings supporting them
shall soon be dead. It is ordained, so there is no need for
you to feel sorry. If you wish, I shall grant you eyesight
so that you can observe the battle.' Dhritarashtra was
shocked by the candid words of Vyasa, and requested
that he be left blind so he wouldn't have to see the
carnage that was about to follow. The sage bestowed
Dhritarashtra's charioteer Sanjaya with perceptive
vision so that he would be able to keep the blind king
informed of all the events that were happening on and
off the battlefield.*

'Why are we going to Agra?' asked Radhika sitting inside
the guesthouse in Nepalgunj on the Indo-Nepal border.
They were now on the final leg of their return journey from
Mount Kailash to India.

'There must have been a very good reason for Mahmud
Ghazni to carry doors bearing the symbol of Shiv-Shakti
back to Afghanistan. We must have a look at them,' replied
Saini as he stretched back on the sofa.

'But why aren't we considering other locations? Mathura, Gokul and Vrindavan are places associated with Krishna's early life. Isn't it possible that one of these places may hold the clue?' asked Radhika.

'Honestly speaking, I believe that a great deal that is written about Krishna's early life is fabrication,' replied Saini. 'Krishna was a great statesman and strategist. He probably led a rather serious life—with much of his early life devoted to studying under Sage Sandipani. The tales about his being a playful and naughty cowherd were added on much later. Mathura, Gokul and Vrindavan have much more tourist value than historical.'

'You can't simply write off these locations as parts of myth,' exclaimed Radhika.

'There isn't a clear answer in such matters,' said Saini. 'I visited Mathura a couple of years ago. My tourist guide took me to the *Krishna Janmasthan* temple —supposedly located at the very spot where Krishna was born. There is a narrow passage that leads to a tiny room, which is possibly the prison cell where Krishna was born. The funny thing is that, just a short distance away from the temple, is a fort that lies in ruins. It is called *Kansa Quila* and it is possibly the place from where Kansa ruled Mathura. Raja Man Singh of Jaipur had the fort rebuilt in the sixteenth century to duplicate the original Kansa Quila. It was always my understanding that Vasudeva and Devaki were imprisoned within the dungeons of Kansa Quila, and hence the existence of a separate temple to mark the birth location of Krishna struck me as odd. To add to the confusion, there is a second Krishna Janmasthan temple that claims to be the real one. You see my point?'

Radhika nodded. 'Is it a similar situation at Gokul?'

'Actually, the situation is even more complicated in Gokul,' said Saini. 'Gokul lies around fifteen kilometres south-east of Mathura. Driving from Mathura to Gokul, one has to cross the Yamuna, and one can see the exact spot where Vasudeva would have supposedly crossed the river, holding Krishna above his head in a basket. The problem is that there are two towns located two kilometres apart. One is called *Mahavan* and the other is called Gokul. Both Mahavan and Gokul claim to be the original Gokul—the village where Krishna was left as a baby with Nanda and Yashoda. Each town has a *Putana Mandir* to mark the spot where the demon Putana was killed by Krishna. Both towns have a *Nanda-Yashoda Bhavan* to indicate the house where Krishna's adoptive parents lived.'

'I imagine that Vrindavan also holds no clues?' asked Radhika.

'The reality is that Krishna-devotion is so deeply entrenched in most of the region that it's virtually impossible to distinguish history from myth,' replied Saini. 'Most of the Krishna story, in art and music, revolves around the Krishna and Radha romance. But Radha is not mentioned even once in *Srimad Bhagavatam*. One can't find her name anywhere in it! The earliest text to mention Radha by name is the poem *Geet Govind* by the poet Jayadeva in the twelfth century—more than four thousand years after the life of Krishna!'

'What do you suggest we should do?' asked Radhika.

'Well, if we can't find the Radha and Krishna love story in Vrindavan, we will definitely find the Mumtaz Mahal and Shah Jahan love story in Agra. Let's get there and see those Somnath doors,' said Saini conclusively, as Radhika's phone began to ring.

76

On the first day of battle, the odds favoured the Kauravas. On the second day, they favoured the Pandavas. By the third day, Bhishma had decided that it was necessary to incapacitate Arjuna so that the Kaurava forces could move towards a decisive victory. Bhima, Arjuna, Abhimanyu, and Ghatotkacha—the finest Pandava warriors—proved to be helpless before Bhishma. The problem, as I saw it, was Arjuna's soft corner for Bhishma. He was doing everything possible not to hurt the old man. It was then that I decided to step in. I told Arjuna that since he was incapable of destroying Bhishma, I would do it myself. I assumed the form of Narayana—the destroyer—and stepped off the chariot, running towards Bhishma. Seeing me in all my glory, Bhishma put down his weapons and bowed before me. 'What greater glory can I hope for? To be killed by your Sudarshan Chakra guarantees my liberation!' he said. I had no intention of stepping into combat, but my desire was to motivate Arjuna to take the war seriously. Arjuna came rushing after me and begged me to preserve my vow of not bearing arms and promised that he would fight with new determination.

'Is it possible to speak with Mr Ravi Mohan Saini?' asked the voice.

'Yes, he's here,' replied Radhika, handing over her phone to Saini, wondering where she had heard the voice before. She struggled for a moment before giving up. *I must be mistaken*, she thought to herself.

'Hello? Is that Mr Saini?' asked the voice as Saini took the phone.

'It's me,' replied Saini.

'Mr Saini, I have been trying to track you down for the last several days,' continued the voice at the other end. 'My name is Rajendra Raval and I am the manager of South Delhi Safety Vaults Ltd, here in New Delhi.'

'What can I do for you, Mr Raval?' asked Saini, a little disoriented.

'One of the safe deposit boxes here belongs to a company— VSKBC Heritage Ltd. The authorised signatory for operating the box is Mr Anil Varshney. A few days ago I received word that Mr Varshney had died,' replied Mr Raval. Varshney's words from the Kalibangan visit came flooding back into Saini's head:

These four seals also have a base plate—a ceramic plate that can hold them together. The plate came up for auction in Sotheby's recently and I was able to convince my employers—VSKBC Heritage Ltd—to bid for it. We succeeded in buying it for a rather large sum of money. It's now in a safe deposit box. The instructions to the vault management are that if anything should happen to me, they are to contact you and apprise you of the contents.

'Yes, I do recall Varshney mentioning the safe deposit box,' said Saini after a moment's pause. 'When may I come in?'

'This particular branch of South Delhi Safety Vaults Ltd is located at New Friends Colony. We are open seven days a week from ten in the morning till eight at night,' replied Mr Raval.

Saini made a note of the name, address and operating hours of the establishment.

'You will need identity proof so that we know that you are who you say you are,' elaborated Mr Raval.

'Sure, I'll bring along my passport,' said Saini. He tried remembering what Varshney had told him about the contents of the box.

The base plate was handed down through generations even though the seals were lost in antiquity. The base plate eventually reached the hands of Raja Man Singh who was a great Krishna devotee in the sixteenth century. Raja Man Singh had a Sanskrit inscription engraved into the plate and installed it in a Krishna temple that he built in Vrindavan.

'See you tomorrow in Delhi,' said Saini.

'Yes, see you tomorrow,' said CBI Special Director Sunil Garg, staring at the trembling manager, Mr Rajendra Raval, who had remained frozen in his seat throughout the conversation.

77

By the ninth day, I knew that as long as Bhishma remained alive and active on the battlefield, the Pandavas would not be able to win. I decided to use Shikhandi to neutralise Bhishma. Shikhandi had been born a girl—Amba—in a previous birth. Bhishma had refused to marry Amba and, in turn, Amba had sworn revenge. After practising severe austerities, she had received a divine boon that she would be able to kill Bhishma in her next life. Amba then committed suicide to hasten her reincarnation—as the daughter of King Drupada. Fearing an attack by Bhishma, Drupada had exiled his daughter to the forest. During her exile, the girl met a Gandharva who offered to exchange his male form for her female one. Having assumed a male form, Shikhandi had returned and enlisted in the army of Drupada, rising to the rank of commander. I knew that if Bhishma were attacked by Shikhandi, he would not fight back owing to the fact that he viewed Shikhandi as a woman, not man. Just as I had predicted, on the tenth day Bhishma threw down his weapons before Shikhandi while a volley of arrows from Arjuna incapacitated him.-

Chhedi and Rathore had taken a flight out of Jamnagar into New Delhi. Having checked into the Qutab Hotel, they showered and headed out for an evening meal to Mehrauli. It was a little past nine at night and they settled down in the lounge of a famous watering-hole a short distance from the Qutub Minar. They had pre-booked a taxi that would pick them up from their hotel and drive them to Agra the next morning.

'History is a fascinating game of connect-the-dots and this location is where the Somnath saga ends,' said Chhedi, taking a sip of his whiskey. 'The Qutub Minar and its surrounding buildings—the *Quwwat ul-Islam Mosque*, the *Alai Gate*, and the *Alai Minar*—were constructed by the Turk Qutb-ud-din Aibak, the first Sultan of Delhi in the thirteenth century. But Qutb-ud-din Aibak was himself merely a slave of Muhammad Ghori. Ghori was a descendant of the Ghorid tribes who had defeated the Ghaznavid empire of Mahmud Ghazni—the looter of Somnath. See how the journey from Somnath ends here in Delhi?'

Rathore looked away from Chhedi uninterestedly. He needed more whiskey but couldn't tolerate Chhedi for another hour. He was fed up of the man's pompous and self-opinionated behaviour. It seemed that there was absolutely no subject that Chhedi could not lecture on.

'I don't know about you, but I need a stroll and some fresh air,' lied Rathore as he got up from their table.

'We haven't ordered our dinner yet,' complained Chhedi.

'You go ahead and order. I'm taking a walk and will meet you tomorrow morning in the lobby at seven o'clock for our drive to Agra. Have a good night,' said Rathore, quickly turning around so that Chhedi could not argue.

He walked out of the restaurant and headed towards the Quwwat-ul-Islam mosque bordering the south perimeter of the Qutub Minar. According to a Persian inscription still visible on the eastern gateway, the mosque had been built using parts recovered from the demolition of twenty-seven Hindu and Jain temples.

Further ahead lay the Qutub Minar itself, soaring two hundred and thirty-eight feet into the sky. It had been built as a victory tower to commemorate the defeat of Prithviraj Chauhan, the last Hindu king of Delhi, at the hands of Muhammad Ghori in 1192 CE. Rathore stopped at a kebab joint near the mosque and ordered a kathi roll so that he would be able to eat while walking. He needed to clear his head. The events of the past few days had left him rather disturbed.

He pulled out of his pocket the fax that had been transmitted to him from Jodhpur. It had been sent by Kurkude's research centre. Rathore had completely forgotten about Radhika's instruction to check whether any information had been accessed from Professor Kurkude's secretary's terminal. He had remembered it that very morning and had picked up a phone to dial the research lab in Jodhpur. 'Yes, sir, data was indeed downloaded via the terminal's USB port,' said the information technology head. 'It pertained to radioactivity level readings taken across India by our research teams.'

'Could you tell me, in brief, what those readings were?' Rathore had asked.

'Better still, I can send you a map of the locations where we found that the readings were elevated,' said the IT chief. True to his word, he had faxed to Rathore the map derived from the radioactivity readings—the very same readings stolen by Taarak. Rathore looked at the fax as he ate his kathi roll.

Analysis had never been his strong point and Rathore folded the map and put it back in his pocket as soon as his kathi roll was consumed. He looked at his watch. It was past eleven. Time to head back towards the hotel for much needed sleep. He decided to take a quick round of the Qutub complex before heading back.

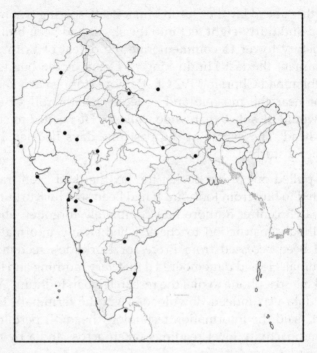

In the distance he could see the famous Iron Pillar of Delhi. The pillar that weighed more than six tons had been fashioned sixteen hundred years previously by Emperor Chandragupta Vikramaditya of the Gupta dynasty. The pillar had initially stood in the centre of a complex comprising twenty-seven temples that had eventually been demolished to build the mosque and the tower. The pillar had always been a source of fascination to metallurgists who had been unable to comprehend how ancient Indian blacksmiths had succeeding in creating an iron pillar that had stood corrosion-free for hundreds of years.

As Rathore approached the pillar he noticed that a beggar seemed to have fallen asleep within the steel fence that surrounded the pillar. He ignored him and headed over to the Alai Minar—an incomplete tower that Alauddin Khilji, the most powerful of his Turkic-Afghan dynasty, had started to build to rival the Qutub Minar. Rathore turned and took a walk along the perimeter of the Qutub complex, looking appreciatively at the tombs of Muslim rulers of Delhi that dotted the boundary. He was soon back near the Iron Pillar.

Out of curiosity he looked at the base of the pillar where the beggar had fallen asleep. What he saw made his hair stand on end. Lying on the circular wooden platform at the base of the Delhi's most famous pillar was no sleeping beggar but the lifeless body of Devendra Chhedi. 'Damn!' cursed Rathore to himself as he ran forward. 'I should never have left him alone.'

At this time of night the area was deserted and Rathore called up the number of his counterpart in Delhi to seek assistance. Reaching the pillar, he climbed the steel fence that barricaded it from unruly tourists and knelt down beside Chhedi. He quickly placed two fingers in the hollow between Chhedi's windpipe and neck muscle. He pressed lightly, praying that there would be a faint pulse but was out of luck. Had he not taken the leisurely stroll along the perimeter circuit he might have been in time to save Chhedi.

He stepped back from the body and surveyed the scene of the crime. Chhedi was seated with his back to the pillar and with his legs stretched out before him on the circular wooden platform that surrounded the pillar. Stuck in his left foot was a surgical scalpel from which blood had poured out in copious quantities to form a massive puddle within which Chhedi sat. On his forehead was the impression left by a rubber stamp. It was a mace, the fourth symbol of Vishnu.

Around halfway up the pillar was a Sanskrit inscription in Brahmi script. It indicated that the pillar had been erected as a standard in honour of Lord Vishnu by a valorous king—Chandragupta Vikram-aditya. Below the engraved inscription of sixteen hundred years was another Sanskrit one written sixteen minutes previously in Chhedi's blood— also in honour of Vishnu.

> *Mleccha-nivaha-nidhane kalayasi karavalam*
> *dhumaketum iva kim api karalam*
> *kesava dhrita-kalki-sarira jaya jagadisa hare.*

Rathore continued talking on his mobile phone as he coordinated with the Delhi police to reach the spot. From the distance, Taarak Vakil watched the scene unfold as he dialled Priya's number on his iPhone.

As Bhishma fell, Arjuna created a bed of arrows on the ground so that Bhishma could rest on them and decide when he would give up his mortal frame. Arjuna shot a couple of more arrows into the ground from which fresh water sprang up to quench the old warrior's thirst. Karana would now join the war and Drona would take over the command of the Kaurava forces. Unlike Bhishma, who simply wanted to push the Pandavas back without necessarily harming them, Drona wanted at least one of the key Pandavas to fall. The battle strategies became much fiercer in response to this change.

Priya saw her phone screen flash. It did not make a sound as it was on silent mode. She was in Mumbai, seated in the luxurious study of Sir Khan along with her father. She picked up the phone, heard Taarak's information and put the phone down. Looking up at Sir Khan she said, 'Chhedi is dead. All four have been eliminated as per your instructions.'

'This makes it easier to take our quest to finality,' said Sir Khan.

'I have done whatever you wanted me to because I thought it would help me find Krishna. I have travelled the length and breadth of this country, including braving the snowy slopes of Mount Kailash, but still have no idea what I'm looking for,' said Priya. 'Is it a nuclear Brahmastra or is it ancient DNA left behind by Krishna?'

'Should I put an end to your confusion? Should I tell you once and for all what it is that I hope to find?' asked Sir Khan.

'Please,' begged Priya. Her face was flushed and her heart was beating rapidly. It was the moment that she had been waiting for.

'I am searching for a stone,' replied Sir Khan. 'It's not just any stone. In Western literature it has been called the Philosopher's Stone, but in Hindu mythology, this stone had a very specific name.'

'What is that?' asked Priya, breathing heavily in anticipation.

'It is known by the name *Syamantaka*,' declared Sir Khan, releasing a puff of Cuban cigar smoke from his mouth to add dramatic effect to his words.

'The Syamantaka? But surely that's just myth,' began Priya.

'You are mistaken,' interrupted Sir Khan. 'The Syamantaka was not a jewel as claimed in mythological texts. It was a stone that had almost magical properties. It is said in the *Vishnu Purana* that the Syamantaka originally belonged to Surya—the sun god. The stone had specific alchemic properties and was capable of producing eight *bharas* of gold daily. The modern equivalent would be around a hundred and seventy pounds of gold each day!'

'What happened to the Syamantaka?' asked Sanjay Ratnani.

'The story about the Syamantaka stone goes like this,' began Sir Khan. 'Satrajit, a Yadava chief, prayed to Surya devotedly. When Surya appeared before him and granted him a wish, Satrajit asked for the Syamantaka, which Surya generously bestowed upon him. Satrajit presented the stone to his brother Prasenajit.'

'So the stone became the possession of Prasenajit?' asked Ratnani.

'Only for a short while,' replied Sir Khan. 'Prasenajit was attacked by a lion. Having killed Prasenajit, the lion made off with the stone but was himself attacked by Jambavan— the king of bears. Krishna was known to have had his eye on the stone and thus he was suspected of having killed Prasenajit. Krishna was able to track down the bear's cave and retrieve the stone.'

'Krishna kept the stone thereafter?' asked Ratnani.

'No. Krishna returned the stone to Satrajit who felt terrible for having wrongly accused Krishna. As recompense he offered his daughter Satyabhama's hand in marriage to Krishna along with the Syamantaka. Krishna accepted the hand of Satyabhama but refused to accept the stone.'

'What happened next?' asked Ratnani.

'Some time later, Krishna was on a journey away from Dwarka when a plot was hatched to kill Satrajit,' said Sir Khan. 'Another Yadava by the name of Satadhanwa killed Satrajit, took the Syamantaka and left it with Akroora—the one who had helped Krishna by warning him of Kansa's intentions. When Krishna heard of it, he tracked down Satrajit's murderer and killed him. Then Krishna called Akroora and forced him to confess. Akroora told Krishna the truth about the conspiracy. Krishna allowed Akroora to remain the custodian of the stone on one condition: the stone was to always remain in Dwarka.'

'*Did* the stone remain in Dwarka?' asked the old lawyer.

'Neither the *Puranas* nor the *Mahabharata* talk about what happened to the Syamantaka after Krishna's death and the inundation of Dwarka, but we do know that Krishna and his Yadava clans were in Prabhas Patan—modern Somnath—when Dwarka was inundated,' said Sir Khan. 'Krishna was killed accidentally by the hunter Jara in Prabhas Patan. Just think about it, isn't it possible that the Syamantaka was kept in Somnath after Krishna's death? More specifically, isn't it rather likely that it was kept *inside* the temple for safekeeping?'

'Let's assume that you are right, how can we be sure that the Syamantaka was an alchemist's stone?' asked Priya.

'When Mahmud Ghazni attacked Somnath, he took away virtually everything that he possibly could,' said Sir Khan. 'There were several solid gold and silver idols inlaid with precious gems. It is said that the estimated value of the loot was twenty million dinars. It's impossible to calculate the equivalent in modern exchange rates. What we do know is that Mahmud Ghazni and his army carted off around six and a half tons of gold. Based upon the historical chart of gold prices maintained by the Bank of England, the modern-day value of Ghazni's gold would have been around two hundred and sixty billion dollars! Before returning to Ghazni, Mahmud demolished the temple and set fire to whatever remained. If we open up our minds to the possibility of alchemy, isn't it a reasonable hypothesis that much of Somnath's gold may have come from an alchemical process?'

Priya was stunned into silence.

Sir Khan spoke once again. 'Isn't it also possible that the Syamantaka was not really a stone but an ancient alchemical isotope that was capable of nuclear transmutation? Isn't it conceivable that the Syamantaka was stored within the lingam and that it was this Syamantaka that created the magnetic field that allowed the lingam to hover off the ground?'

'But a lingam cannot be hollow,' argued Priya.

'I'm not so sure of that,' said Sir Khan. 'There are some very interesting accounts of Mahmud Ghazni's attack on Somnath. According to Firishta, a Persian historian who lived in the sixteenth century, Mahmud approached the Shiv lingam with his mace, ready to destroy it. Firishta says that the temple priests offered to put together a huge ransom if Ghazni would spare the sacred symbol of Shiv. Ghazni apparently declared that he wished to be remembered as a breaker of idols rather than as a seller of idols. Having said that, he swung his mace down on the lingam. It is here that Firishta's account gets really interesting. Firishta says that some stones came pouring out from the lingam when it was shattered.'

'And it's your view that Firishta's account is accurate?' asked Priya.

'Most modern historians have dismissed Firishta's account of this incident because lingams are usually solid stone blocks,' replied Sir Khan. 'But what if Somnath was different? After all, there is no Shiv temple anywhere in the world that has a magnetically suspended lingam even today. If Somnath could have one several hundred years ago wouldn't it have been even more likely that the lingam would have been kept hollow to reduce its weight? Then why is it impossible that the lingam may have yielded the Syamantaka stone that lay inside it?'

'For one thing, if the Syamantaka was nuclear, then it would have ended up killing its worshippers,' argued Priya.

'It wasn't a nuclear bomb,' exclaimed Sir Khan. 'It had nuclear properties, though. And it is precisely because of the radiation produced that the Somnath lingam was always kept covered in the leaves of the *bel* tree.'

On the twelfth day, Drona noticed that I was making a determined effort to keep Arjuna away from Karana. There was a reason for this. On the morning before entering the battlefield, an old beggar had sought alms from Karana. The generous Karana had said, 'Ask for anything and it's yours.' The beggar had asked for Karana's armour that used to be part and parcel of his body, like an impenetrable sheath. Karana was unaware that the old beggar was Indra—the father of Arjuna. Karana immediately took a knife and surgically removed his armour. Seeing this magnanimity, Indra was moved and gave him a spear in return—a spear that could only be used once and would never miss its mark. I was simply protecting Arjuna from Karana's spear—a spear presented to Karana by Arjuna's own father, Indra.

'Bel leaves? But offering bel leaves to Shiv is an old Hindu tradition. It has nothing to do with science,' said Priya.

'Ah, you are wrong,' said Sir Khan softly. 'Yes, the Bel tree is considered sacred by Hindus and the usual offering to the Shiv lingam is its leaves. But the choice of this offering is lost in antiquity.'

'I'm lost myself,' said Sanjay Ratnani helplessly.

Sir Khan laughed. 'The botanical name for Bel is *Aegle marmelos*. Some years ago, an article appeared in the *Oxford Journal*. Three scientists had discovered that Aegle marmelos had a radio protective effect. Their study demonstrated that it protected human peripheral blood lymphocytes against radiation, DNA damage and genomic instability. They concluded that it achieved this through "scavenging of radiation". Isn't it possible that the Syamantaka was indeed a radioactive substance and that the Somnath lingam needed to be kept covered with bel leaves in order to inhibit and absorb the radiation that it emitted, so that it would be safe for others to visit?'

'You think that the lingam was a floating one due to a magnetic field created by the nuclear isotope—the Syamantaka?' asked Priya.

'Sure I do,' replied Sir Khan. 'Isn't it surprising that Ghazni invaded India seventeen times and survived, but died within a few years of attacking Somnath? Ghazni lay dead due to a lethal strain of tuberculosis at the age of fifty-nine. It is a well-known fact that Ghazni took pieces of the lingam to be installed as foot scrapers on the steps of the public mosque and his palace. Isn't it possible that Ghazni had unwittingly signed his own death warrant by carrying off irradiated material that affected his lungs?'

'He could also have died of battle wounds or fatigue. Ghazni was attacked by Indian warriors on his way back to Afghanistan,' said Priya.

'True. On his way back to Ghazni, Mahmud *was* attacked,' said Sir Khan. But who do you think attacked him? The *Jats*. I find that very interesting indeed, and I'll tell you why in just a minute. First, let me tell you a little about the Jats.'

'What is so interesting about the Jats?' asked Priya.

'Patience, Priya,' admonished Sir Khan, taking a break and pouring himself some water. He took a sip of it and settled down in his usual armchair.

'When Krishna departed for Dwarka after the eighteenth battle with Jarasandha, it is said that Krishna founded a federation of his Yadava clans. It was known as the *Gyati-sangh*. Each member of the sangh was called a *Gyat*. Over hundreds of years, the word *Gyat* morphed into the word *Jat*. The Sanskrit grammarian Panini uses the sutra, *Jat jhat sanghate*, indicating that by Panini's time, the word Gyat had indeed evolved into Jat. Doesn't it make sense that when Ghazni was carting off treasures from Krishna's Somnath—possibly including the Syamantaka stone —he was attacked by Jat warriors who could trace their lineage thousands of years earlier to Krishna himself?'

'Are you saying that the Jats attacked Ghazni because they wished to recover the Syamantaka?' asked a wide-eyed Priya.

'Yes. What they did not realise was that Ghazni was doing precisely the same thing!' exclaimed Sir Khan.

'What?' asked Priya incredulously. 'You mean to say that Ghazni was not after riches? That he did not attack because of his hatred for idol worship? That his objective was only to take away the Syamantaka?'

'Well, he certainly wanted those other things too. But he specifically wanted the stone. After all, Ghazni himself was a descendant of Krishna,' said Sir Khan, smiling.

*On the thirteenth day of battle Drona organised his
men into the dreaded Chakravyuha formation.
Yudhistira was caught inside along with Abhimanyu —
Arjuna's sixteen-year old son. Abhimanyu had heard
Arjuna describe the formation while he was still in his
mother's womb. As a result, he knew how to breach the
formation and get others out but did not know how to
escape himself. 'I can breach it, but you'll have to come
back and get me,' said Abhimanyu to Yudhistira, who
agreed. Abhimanyu's efforts paid off and all the Pandava
warriors were able to exit except Abhimanyu. Inside
the Chakravyuha, Abhimanyu was surrounded and
attacked simultaneously by Duryodhana, Dusshasana,
Kripa, Drona and Aswatthama. 'Isn't it against the
rules of conduct for so many to attack just one?' asked
someone. 'They broke the rules by getting a woman to
attack Bhishma. There are no rules now,' said Drona.
Arjuna was overcome by grief when he heard the news
at sunset. It suited me perfectly. Arjuna now had
the required rage and desire for revenge within him,
something that had been sorely lacking till then.*

'This is madness,' said Priya angrily. 'If you weren't
my father's saviour I would have killed you on the spot
for uttering such obscenities. To call that warmonger

and looter, Ghazni, a descendant of Krishna is to insult the Lord!'

'Relax, Priya,' urged Sir Khan. 'I shall explain everything. Don't worry, just be patient for a little longer.'

Once Priya had calmed down, Sir Khan resumed. 'Have you read a book on the Rajputs by a historian called A. H. Bingley? It was published in 1899.'

'No. I've heard of it though. We had it listed as reference material at Kings College. I think it was called the *Handbook on Rajputs.*'

'Very good,' said Sir Khan. 'This is what Bingley says in his book about the Yadavas: *It would appear that Yadava settlements were at Indraprastha and Dwarka. After the death of Krishna, many of the Yadavas were driven out of India, founded Ghazni in Afghanistan and ruled over the whole of that country and portions of Central Asia as far north as Samarkand.'*

'Ghazni? As in the capital of Mahmud Ghazni's empire?'

'Yes. Mahmud Ghazni's capital is the very same place that the Yadavas migrated to five thousand years ago. Thus the later Muslim rulers of this region were themselves of Yadava lineage!'

'Incredible,' whispered Priya, almost dumbfounded.

'The point that I'm making is this: it was Krishna's own genetic descendants who were battling for the Syamantaka stone after the Somnath attack. One group consisted of Muslims under Ghazni—descendants of Yadavas having migrated to Ghazni many thousands of years previously. The other group consisted of rulers of north-west India who called themselves Jats and were also Yadava descendants!'

'Do you think that fighting over the Syamantaka may have caused the ancient nuclear blast in Rajasthan that was being investigated by Professor Kurkude?' asked Priya suddenly.

'Unlikely. There exists an alternative explanation for the Rajasthan radioactivity, though. In the Fifties, Dr Paul Kuroda—a scientist from the University of Arkansas— brought to the world's attention the possibility of naturally-occurring nuclear reactors within the earth.'

'Naturally-occurring nuclear reactors?' repeated Priya in disbelief.

'Yes. The key ingredient for such a reactor is a specific isotope of uranium known as U-235. This particular isotope is found naturally in small quantities. Dr Kuroda hypothesised that if sufficient quantities of U-235 were aggregated under suitable conditions, the pooled U-235 would result in self-sustaining fission. Such a reactor would not be possible in nature today because most of the earth's natural U-235 has decayed. But thousands of years ago, this would indeed have been possible. It is very possible that the Rajasthan radiation levels noted by Kurkude may have been the result of this.'

'Where is the Syamantaka today,' asked Priya wearily, now exhausted by the spate of revelations.

'We know that Ghazni died a few years after the Somnath attack,' replied Sir Khan. 'Thereafter, his own empire was attacked and taken over by the Ghorids—the ancestors of Muhammad Ghori. It is possible that the Syamantaka thus passed from Ghazni to Ghori. Ghori was defeated by Prithviraj Chauhan in 1191 but the next year Ghori returned to India and not only defeated Prithviraj Chauhan but also captured him and took him back to Ghazni, where he was later blinded.'

'What happened to Prithviraj Chauhan?' asked Ratnani.

'It's common knowledge that Prithviraj Chauhan's child-hood friend, Chand Bardai, followed Ghori in disguise and befriended Ghori, gaining his trust. What is not commonly known is that fact that a whole team of Rajputs had gone along with Chand Bardai. Their ostensible purpose was to recover the Syamantaka, to save Prithviraj Chauhan and to kill Ghori,' said Sir Khan.

'Did they succeed?' asked the senior Ratnani.

'Chand Bardai and Prithviraj Chauhan cooked up a plan,' replied Sir Khan. 'Bardai told Ghori that Chauhan was capable of shooting an arrow at a target with sound as the only clue. Ghori was very curious and wanted to see this feat. Bardai told him that since Prithviraj was a king, he would only take orders from another king. Ghori called for Prithviraj and ordered him to aim for a ringing bell but Prithviraj Chauhan aimed for the source of Ghori's command instead. Ghori was instantly killed by Prithviraj Chauhan's arrow.'

'Was Prithviraj Chauhan able to escape?' asked Ratnani.

'No,' replied Sir Khan. 'Both Prithviraj Chauhan and Chand Bardai had come prepared with daggers and they killed one another after Ghori died. This was to prevent giving Ghori's men the satisfaction of killing them. That too is common knowledge.'

'What is the not-so-common knowledge?' asked Priya suspiciously. Sir Khan laughed vigorously at the question.

'The not-so-common knowledge is that the group of Rajputs that had accompanied Chand Bardai managed to secure possession of the Syamantaka and return to India. It was the key objective of the trip,' said Sir Khan.

'What evidence do we have of this?' asked Priya.

'On the outskirts of modern-day Ghazni is the domed tomb of Muhammad Ghori,' replied Sir Khan. 'Just a couple of metres away is another tomb which is a lot smaller, but this second tomb has a muddy earth pit in the centre—

coinciding with the grave. Hanging above this spot is a thick rope. Visitors who come to pay their respects to the departed Muhammad Ghori first visit the smaller tomb, which is said to contain the remains of Prithviraj Chauhan. They catch hold of the rope for support and vigorously stamp upon the grave of Chauhan whom they view as the killer of Ghori.'

'And the retriever of the Syamantaka,' said Priya wryly.

The reason that no one had been able to help Abhimanyu could be traced to Jayadhrata—the brother-in-law of the Kauravas. He had gathered reinforcements and had blocked the entry of Yudhistira and others into the Chakravyuha. Arjuna took a terrible oath: 'I swear that if I do not eliminate Jayadhrata before sundown, I will immolate myself!' Drona was delighted to hear of this. 'All we need to do is to protect Jayadhrata and Arjuna will have to set himself alight by tomorrow night!' he said. The fourteenth day dawned and battle commenced. The entire Kaurava army positioned itself between Arjuna and Jayadhrata and throughout the day Arjuna was frustrated as all his attempts to reach Jayadhrata were foiled. The sun disappeared and the Kauravas rejoiced. Arjuna prepared to immolate himself, but I told him that I had covered the sun with my own hand to create the illusion of sunset. With the Kauravas having let down their guard, Jayadhrata would be undefended. 'Just listen carefully for his laughter and shoot your arrow accordingly,' I instructed. As soon as Arjuna's arrow met its mark, I released my hand and the sun shone mightily once again.

'What happened to the Syamantaka after the Rajputs returned to India from Ghazni?' asked Priya.

'The stone moved from one secret location to another within the various Rajput kingdoms,' said Sir Khan. 'The usual choice for hiding it was always in the temple dedicated to the *Kuldevi* or *Kuldevta*—the family deity—of the royal clan in whose kingdom the stone happened to be. The problem was that hundreds of temples were being demolished by successive Muslim rulers in the early days of Islam and hence the stone had to be shifted very regularly.'

'And this strategy was successful?' asked Priya.

'For the most part,' answered Sir Khan. 'The last Rajput ruler who had possession of the stone was Raja Man Singh who was the king of *Amer*—later known as Jaipur. Man Singh ruled from 1550 to 1614 and had made peace with the Mughals. He was one of the *navaratnas*—the nine jewels—of Akbar's court. Man Singh's aunt, Jodhabai, was married to Emperor Akbar.'

'Man Singh brokered a deal with the enemy,' spat Priya. 'It could very well be that he handed over the Syamantaka to Akbar. After all, he was Akbar's vassal.'

'That could be one possibility, indeed,' said Sir Khan. 'But bear in mind that Raja Man Singh was one of the most ardent and committed Krishna devotees ever. He financed the construction of a grand seven-storeyed temple dedicated to Krishna in Vrindavan. It is said that the cost of construction was ten million rupees. By today's standards that would be hundreds of millions! It seems unlikely that such an ardent Krishna devotee would let go of something as precious as the Syamantaka.'

'So where could it have gone?' asked Priya.

'The answer is to be found in the Krishna Key—the four seals that were found in Dwarka, Kalibangan, Kurukshetra and Mathura,' said Sir Khan. 'The four seals could also be placed like the pieces of a jigsaw puzzle on a ceramic baseplate. The baseplate had continued to be handed down from generation to generation even though the seals had remained hidden under the sands of time until archaeologists discovered them recently. The baseplate was also in the custody of Raja Man Singh and it is said that he had a Sanskrit inscription engraved on it and installed it in the Krishna temple that he built in Vrindavan. His intention was that only devoted Krishna bhakts would ever be able to discover the Syamantak.'

'I have the four seals,' said Priya. 'Where is the baseplate that you speak of?'

'Before I answer that, look at the four seals closely. You will find that all of them have a square peg at the back,' said Sir Khan.

Priya took out the four seals from her handbag and placed them on the coffee-table in front of the sofa. Indeed, each seal seemed to bear a square peg on the reverse.

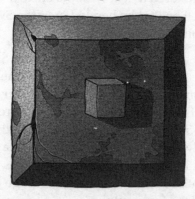

'Such a peg used to be provided on ancient seals so that one could run a ring or string through them. But with these four seals, there is no hole for a ring or thread. What this means is that the pegs are simply meant to secure the four seals firmly to the baseplate. The baseplate had four squarish holes that corresponded to the four square pegs on the seals. Something like this,' said Sir Khan, quickly sketching what the baseplate had looked like for Priya.

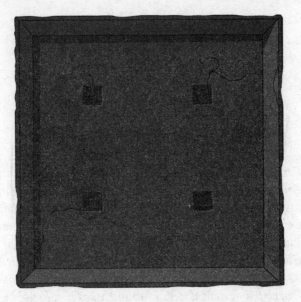

'That still doesn't answer my question. Who was the last owner of the baseplate?' asked Priya.

'I was,' said Sir Khan simply.

For the first time, battle continued through the night. An angry Drona said, 'If Krishna can make day into night, we are free to treat the night as day!' I decided that we needed Ghatotkacha—the rakshasa son of Bhima. Rakshasas were ideally suited to fighting at night. Ghatotkacha came immediately upon being summoned by his father and killed Kauravas by the thousands. Duryodhana rushed to Karana and asked him to use his spear—the one gifted by Indra. Karana was reluctant because he wanted to use it on Arjuna but he was compelled by Duryodhana to do as he said. Ghatotkacha let out a bloodcurdling scream as the spear plunged into his chest. 'Don't fall on the Pandava forces,' I shouted. 'Increase your size to the maximum extent possible and then fall on the Kaurava formations. Even in death, you shall be serving your father!' Ghatotkacha followed my instructions perfectly, and thousands of Kaurava warriors died as he fell on them. Bhima was wild with grief, but I was relieved. Indra's spear was no longer available to Karana.

Sir Khan took another puff of his cigar and looked at the old black and white photograph of his father that adorned his side table. His thoughts wandered to his childhood and the happy moments that he had spent with his father in simpler times. For a few moments he forgot about the interesting discussion that he was engaged in with Priya.

Sir Khan had not been born with that particular name. His mother had named him *Kanha*—a name favoured by Krishna-bhakts. She had passed away within a year of his birth. Kanha's father had been the local tinsmith in the village of *Besnagar*, located in the heart of Madhya Pradesh.

His father, Jagatsingh, would tell him wonderful stories about their ancestors, who had been artisans and craftsmen in Mughal times. 'Seven generations ago, your ancestors were great builders who constructed the finest temples,' he would tell his son.

The children would often play near a clearing that had a pillar at its centre. To the locals it was known as *Khamb Baba* and they would kneel down before the pillar and apply vermillion paste to its base. Besnagar was not a very busy place even though one could easily drive to it from the Buddhist site of Sanchi. Jagatsingh would make the children sit near the pillar and explain its history to them.

'This pillar has been here at this spot for two thousand years. The local inhabitants of Besnagar knew that this pillar was holy but we did not know why. In 1877, an English archaeologist came here and saw the pillar. His name was General Alexander Cunningham. He saw the column but did not notice the inscription at the bottom because it had been smeared over the years with successive layers of vermillion that we villagers would regularly apply to it,' he said as the children listened with rapt attention.

'Did the Englishman try to steal it?' asked Kanha.

'Oh no, he was fascinated by it but was unable to make any sense of it,' replied Jagatsingh. 'Around twenty years later another English visitor—one Mr Lake—visited Besnagar.

He undertook the task of removing the layers of vermillion that had entirely covered the base over hundreds of years.'

'And what did he find?' asked the curious children.

'He uncovered an ancient inscription. He succeeded in deciphering it because it was written in *Brahmi*—the ancient Indian script that was used during Mauryan times,' said Jagatsingh.

'Did the Brahmi inscription tell him who built it?' asked Kanha excitedly.

'It turned out to be what would later come to be known as the *Heliodorus column*,' replied Jagatsingh. 'It had been built and installed by Heliodorus—the Greek ambassador to this region in 113 BCE. King Antialkidas—the Greek king of Taxila, had sent Heliodorus as ambassador to the court of King Bhagabhadra, who ruled Besnagar. Apparently, Heliodorus had been one of the earliest Greek converts to Vaishnavism.'

'And what did the inscription say?' asked the children.

'The inscription on the column said that *this Garuda column of Vasudeva, the God of gods, was erected here by Heliodorus, a worshiper of Vishnu, the son of Dion, and an inhabitant of Taxila, who came as Greek ambassador from the Great King Antialkidas to King Kasiputra Bhagabhadra, the Savior, then reigning prosperously in the fourteenth year of his kingship. Three important precepts when practiced lead to heaven: self-restraint, charity, and conscientiousness,*' intoned Jagatsingh. 'You do realise what this means, don't you?'

The children remained silent, confused by the information given to them by their mentor. Jagatsingh took a deep breath before resuming.

'What this inscription tells us is that Heliodorus—a Greek ambassador—had become a devotee of Vishnu and was fully conversant with ancient texts as well as religious observances,' said Jagatsingh. 'It is thus evident that several other Greeks would also have adopted Krishna-worship under the influence of their ambassador. Till then, British historians had held the view that Krishna was simply a corruption of Christ and that legends of Krishna had been absorbed from the Bible. The Heliodorus column proved all of them wrong. It proved that Krishna-worship and the Vaishnava tradition predated Christianity by many hundreds—if not thousands—of years.'

83

I knew that we needed to get rid of Drona if the Pandava forces were to gain the upper hand. I asked Bhima to kill an elephant named Aswatthama, which was also the name of Drona's son. The next day, I asked all the Pandava warriors to loudly proclaim that Aswatthama had died. Drona refused to believe the other warriors, so he turned to Yudhistira, who had the stellar reputation of never telling a lie. 'Is it true, Yudhistira? Is Aswatthama really dead?' asked Drona. A guilty Yudhistira nodded and said, 'Yes. Aswatthama is dead... maybe it was an elephant, or possibly it was a man...' but Drona never heard the second part of the sentence. He put down his weapons, got off his chariot and sat down in meditation. 'Kill him,' I shouted, but the Pandavas were worried. 'He's a Brahmin — how can we kill him?' they asked. 'He was the son of a Brahmin but lived the life of a Kshatriya. Let him die as a Kshatriya on the battlefield!' I shouted. Finally, Dhrishtadyumna — the son of Drupada — pulled out his sword and beheaded Drona.

One day, Jagatsingh called Kanha and told him, 'Son, today I wish to share an important piece of information with you.'

'Yes, Father, what is it?' asked Kanha.

'Seven generations before me, our ancestors were master builders. They had worked on building several important temples and palaces. Through all these years, this small square ceramic plate has been handed down from generation to generation in our family,' said Jagatsingh to his son. 'Today, I am handing it over to you.'

Jagatsingh handed over to Kanha a small earthen plate— around four centimetres long and an equal four centimetres wide. On the face of the plate was written a Sanskrit shloka. On the reverse side were four squarish holes.

'What is the significance of this plate, father?' asked Kanha.

'It is taken from a temple. In that temple lies an ancient secret. This plate indicates the location,' replied the teacher.

'Why are you giving it to me?' asked Kanha.

'Because I am worried about the future. Hindu-Muslim tensions are running high in Besnagar and they could escalate into full-scale riots any day. I have lived my life but you still have yours ahead of you. Promise me that you will guard this with your life, my son,' said Jagatsingh as he hugged his son.

'I promise, Father. You have my assurance that I shall not let you down,' said Kanha, proudly examining the ceramic plate.

The next day Besnagar had erupted in flames accompanied by an orgy of violence. Kanha had run through the village streets looking for his father but had been unable to find him. Violent gangs of Hindus rounded up Muslim clerics and teachers and set them alight while Muslim gangs targeted Hindu tradesmen and shopkeepers. At the end of the day, Jagatsingh's body had been found floating in a well. He had been beaten over the head by a brick.

There was no time to shed tears and Kanha found himself running towards Vidisha junction, the closest railway station to Besnagar. He had clambered aboard the first train that he saw leaving and was just in time. All the remaining trains were eventually set alight. He had no clothes, no money, and no food. All that he had was the small ancient ceramic plate that his father had given him.

The railway guard took pity on the boy and allowed him to remain on board until the train reached Bombay Central. Kanha had stepped onto the platform only to find himself adrift on a sea of humanity. He spent the entire day at the railway station, begging passers-by for food, but the city seemed to have residents that were deaf, dumb and blind. By the time night fell, he dropped down in a corner of Bombay Central—hungry, exhausted and dehydrated.

When he awoke the next morning, he was surprised to find a kind face staring at him. In his hands the stranger held a small glass of hot jaggery-tea and in his other hand was a newspaper packet that held a few luscious samosas. 'Eat,' he commanded Kanha, who gratefully gulped down the tea in between mouthfuls of the spicy samosas.

'What's your name?' asked the young man who had fed him.

'Kanha,' he answered.

'That name will never work in this city—it's not powerful enough to inspire fear. I'm giving you another one—Khan. My name is Rahim. I shall teach you everything there is to know. You may call me Dada, because I'm the big dada in these parts. Got it?'

'You're Muslim?' asked Kanha nervously, having just witnessed Hindu-Muslim riots in his hometown.

'No, I'm an English Protestant. What kind of stupid question is that?' asked Rahim indignantly.

'But my new name—Khan. How can I use that? That's a Muslim name and I'm Hindu,' said Kanha.

'There's hardly any difference between the sound of Kanha and Khan! In any case, you won't be Muslim simply by adopting a Muslim-sounding name!'

Kanha nodded and smiled shyly. Thus began his life as Khan instead of Kanha.

Tormented by the fear of losing her children, Kunti went to the riverbank where Karana was in meditation. Kunti stood behind him silently and waited. When he finished and turned around, he noticed Kunti and bowed down before her. 'The son of the chariot-driver Adhiratha bows to you. What can I do for you, O Queen?' he asked. Kunti told Karana of the true circumstances of his birth. She also requested him to join his brothers, the Pandavas, instead of fighting for Duryodhana. Karana was sad but firm. 'What you are asking me to do, respected Mother, is against my dharma. You deprived me of a mother's love and threw me—a helpless baby—into the river, and you now talk of my duty? You kept quiet all these years but have chosen to meet me today, when you are worried about your five acknowledged sons, the Pandavas. No, I cannot forsake Duryodhana—the one who stood by me. But since you have come to me with a request, I promise you that I shall not kill Yudhistira, Bhima, Nakula or Sahadeva. The fight shall be between Arjuna and me, and irrespective of which one of us dies, you shall be left with five sons alive.'

'Today I'm going to teach you the two-finger snag,' said Rahim. 'You will need to stand behind the person, make a "V" with your index and middle finger, and insert them ever so slightly into the rear pocket. While you are behind the mark, I shall be in front causing a distraction. During this distraction, your mark will not sense you snagging the wallet and jerking it out. Here's a wallet that I stole yesterday. I'm placing it in my own back pocket. Now, try the technique on me.'

Khan clumsily tried to snag the wallet but Rahim swung around and gave him a terrific slap on his face. 'That's too slow!' he snapped. 'These methods must be executed quickly and with zero hesitation. You are less likely to be caught jerking the wallet out than trying to handle it gently. Remember, the only time that a slow and deliberate strategy will work is if the pockets are very loose. C'mon, try it again!'

The procedure was repeated several times and Khan's cheeks were burning red with the number of successive slaps that they received. On the tenth attempt, Khan succeeded in snagging the wallet and Rahim swung around to congratulate him. Rahim ended up on the receiving end of a tight slap from Khan.

Rahim started laughing. 'Congratulations. You have taken the first steps towards surviving in this city,' he said grandly.

The next day, Rahim taught him about jacket pockets. 'A jacket will usually have four pockets: two main outer pockets, an inner pocket and the breast pocket. It's relatively simple to pick outer pockets because they hang loose from the body and are hence quite safe to pick without detection. All one needs is a little distraction to get the victim to turn his head and you're done.'

Khan listened, absorbed and practised. Practice makes perfect, he would keep reminding himself each day. On the second day he tasted victory when he succeeded in snagging a wallet that contained four hundred rupees.

He had never seen so much money at once. Rahim coolly counted the money, tossed the wallet aside and gave him two hundred rupees. 'All your takings shall be split fifty-fifty down the middle,' he said as he pocketed his own share of the loot. I am much more experienced than you and hence shall share twenty-five per cent of my own takings with you.'

Khan nodded in agreement. Dada Rahim was being fair.

'What is that piece of pottery that you seem to carry with you everywhere you go?' asked Rahim, pointing to the ceramic plate Khan had brought from Besnagar.

'It bears an ancient inscription. It belonged to my father. He gave it to me just before he died,' explained Khan, tears welling up in his eyes. Rahim took his new-found friend into a bear hug and said, 'Ssh. You may not have a father anymore but you do have a new brother.'

The next day turned out to be a momentous one for Khan and Rahim. A gentleman carrying a briefcase was about to board a local train. Rahim bumped into him, grabbed the briefcase and ran away. As had been planned in advance, Khan ran after Rahim, delivered a couple of choreographed blows and retrieved the briefcase for the eternally grateful man. It was the oldest con trick in the world but its efficacy was unparalleled. The relieved man turned out to be a cashier who had been carrying a few hundred thousands of rupees in cash in his bag, to be deposited in the bank. Hugely happy with the return of his briefcase, he gratefully rewarded Khan with ten thousand rupees.

'You have brought me luck,' said Rahim to Khan as they split the earnings between them. 'This is our opportunity to become big. Are you ready to transition to the big time?'

'Sure. What do you have in mind?'

'Well, we now have capital, so we can try this on shop-keepers. Have you heard of the short count?'

'No. What is that?'

'Let's role-play. You are the shopkeeper and I'm the customer. I've just bought something worth ten rupees from you. I now pay you using a hundred-rupee note,' said Rahim handing over one to Khan.

'Here's your change, sir,' said Khan, taking out nine soiled ten-rupee notes from his pocket and handing them over to Rahim.

Rahim said, 'I have another tenner of my own to add to the nine notes that you've just given me. Could I request you to give me a hundred in exchange for my tens?'

Khan took out a hundred and handed it over to Rahim. Rahim took the hundred and acted confused. He added the hundred-rupee note that he had just received to the nine tenners and gave it to Khan.

'You've made a mistake, sir. You've just given me a hundred and ninety rupees instead of a hundred,' said Khan.

'Oh, have I? Here's another ten, to make it an even two hundred. Could I request you for two one-hundreds please?' asked Rahim smoothly, as Khan nodded in agreement.

'Did you understand the con?' asked Rahim.

'What con?' asked Khan.

'You just gave me two hundred for a hundred that be-longed to you, not to me! When I gave you a hundred and ninety, it included a hundred rupees taken from you. It was *your* money, not mine!' said Rahim chuckling. 'Now we need to make a list of all the shops where we can execute this con over and over again for larger amounts.'

Time flew as the partnership of Khan and Dada Rahim flourished. One day, the cashier that Khan and Rahim had conned walked up to the two of them. Both boys nervously gulped, fearing that their game was up. Instead of handing them over to the cops, the cashier smiled and said, 'You two are bloody ingenious. I have a proposition for you.'

Rahim eyed the man suspiciously and reluctantly said, 'Go on, I'm listening.'

'I receive payments from my customers but very often a few currency notes turn out to be fake. There's not much that I can do about it. If I pass these on to you, can you get rid of them for me? Fifty per cent is yours if you do,' offered the cashier. They shook hands. It was Rahim and Khan's first exposure to circulating counterfeit notes. Over the years, it would lead them to set up counterfeiting operations of their own.

85

With Karana at the helm of operations, the Kaurava army once again went back to fighting according to the rules of war. On the sixteenth day, Nakula fought Karana. Karana effortlessly destroyed Nakula's chariot and cut Nakula's bow. Nakula was at Karana's mercy but Karana did not kill him. Instead, Karana told him, 'One day you shall be proud of this fight.' Nakula related his humiliation to Yudhistira but did not observe the smile hovering on my face. Meanwhile, in the Kaurava camp it had been decided that Shalya would be Karan's charioteer. Shalya had already been given instructions by me to continually praise Arjuna so as to increase Karana's feelings of insecurity. In spite of this negativity, Karana was able to humble Yudhistira, breaking his bow, his chariot and finally his armour. When Yudhistira was standing helplessly, awaiting the final blow of death, Karana told him, 'You can never defeat me. You may be a Kshatriya by birth but are more a Brahmin at heart. Now go!'

'Do you still have that ceramic plate that you had brought with you from Besnagar?' asked Rahim over breakfast. The two young men were seated in Khan's apartment in Lokhandwala—a newly-developed tony suburb of

Mumbai. They had acquired two apartments side-by-side, as their illegal operations had grown.

'Yes,' replied Khan, taking a bite of his masala omelette while completing exercises in written English in the book that lay open next to his breakfast plate. *Father, you were unable to teach me much, but I shall continue to learn even in the absence of a formal education*, thought Khan.

'There's an international auction house that wants to see it. They say that they could get upwards of a million rupees if they could get to authenticate its age,' said Rahim cautiously.

'Tell them not to waste their time,' said Khan between mouthfuls. 'It's a family heirloom and I'm not going to sell it.'

Rahim did not push the point further. Changing the topic he asked, 'Are we all set for our trip to Dubai?'

'Yes, tickets and visas are done. I'm still not clear why you want to make this trip,' replied Khan.

'Dubai has recently imported over two hundred tons of gold,' replied Rahim.

'What does that have to do with us?' asked Khan.

'Every Indian family is estimated to hold over five grams of gold. Even the poorest Indian may scrounge in every other aspect of his life but will, without fail, put aside some gold as savings. Add this to the gold ornaments of the Indian rich and the total Indian stock should be well over ten thousand tons! The German Federal bank only has about four thousand tons in its vaults,' replied Rahim.

'How does that concern us?' asked Khan. 'We're counter-feiters, not jewellers!'

'My estimate is that over two hundred million dollars' worth of gold will be smuggled into India each year, most of it from Dubai. It's time we got a piece of the action,' said Rahim.

'Who are we meeting in Dubai?' asked Khan.

'There's this chap who has perfected the art of melting gold into matchbox-size ingots and sewing them into canvas jackets—apparently, each jacket accommodates a hundred bars. They're perfect for wearing on fishing boats!' said Rahim, laughing. 'Here, try this one on.'

Khan got up and tried on the jacket that had been filled with matchboxes instead of gold. 'You have now worn the coronation robes, so I now dub thee Sir Khan!' joked Rahim, as he grandly tapped a fork on Khan's shoulders.

The joke was eventually shared with all the team members and from that day on, the name stuck—Sir Khan.

86

Seeing the bravery and chivalry of Karana, Shalya stopped praising Arjuna and began extolling Karana's virtues. This brought tears of joy to Karana's eyes. As Arjuna's chariot approached that of Karana, Dusshasana stepped forward to protect the Kauravas' star warrior. Bhima engaged him in a duel as he angrily remembered how Dusshasana's vile hands had pulled Draupadi by her hair. Bhima was able to smash Dusshasana's chariot and break his bow. As soon as he fell to the ground, Bhima pinned him down and ripped open his chest with his bare hands. As Dusshasana's blood spurted from his heart, Bhima put his lips to the fountain, thus obeying the terrible oath that he had taken to avenge Draupadi's insult. He then cupped Dusshasana's blood in his hands and took it to Draupadi so that she could bathe her hair in it, and fulfil her own promise.

Some months later, their new office had been freshly painted in pale gold distemper. It was reflective of the newly-acquired status of the two men who controlled an empire from it. Dada Rahim and Sir Khan sat back in their leather-backed swivel chairs and toasted one another. The decision to start smuggling gold from Dubai into Mumbai had made them rich beyond their wildest dreams. They now had well over a hundred handpicked men working for them. Between Dada Rahim and Sir Khan, they controlled counterfeiting, betting, and smuggling operations in Mumbai.

On Khan's birthday, Dada Rahim bought a gold chain with a pendant bearing the name 'Sir Khan' in gothic letters. Khan had laughed, thanked Dada Rahim for the touching gesture and had immediately worn it around his neck. It was a simple pendant in eighteen-karat gold.

Khan looked at the black and white photograph of his father on his desk. He knew that it was not what his father would have wanted for his son. He would have disowned him if he had been alive to witness the dramatic rise of the infamous Sir Khan. 'What option did I have, Father?' Khan would softly whisper to his father's spirit when he was alone and contemplative. He took out the key from his pocket and unlocked his desk drawer to locate the ceramic base plate. Running his hands over the plate his father had given him brought him comfort. It was the equivalent of the effect that a pacifying stuffed toy had on a crying child—instant tactile succor.

The drawer was empty. He opened the second drawer, thinking that he may have mistakenly placed it there, but that, too, was empty. He turned to Dada Rahim and asked, 'Does anyone else have access to our private office? I can't find my father's ceramic plate.'

'You are going to thank me, my friend,' said Dada Rahim, lighting up a Marlboro.

'Thank you for what?' asked Khan suspiciously.

'You've been hanging on to that thing for ever so many years,' said Dada Rahim. 'I decided that you needed to move on. I took a photo of it and sent it to Sotheby's. They did a quick valuation and decided that it was worth over five million rupees in auction. They set a reserve price of four million and auctioned it. It went for six! The money has been deposited in your bank account, not that a trifling sum like that is of any real consequence to you.'

Khan leapt out of his chair, landed in front of Dada Rahim and began raining blows on him. 'You sold off the last remaining relic of my father! May you burn in hell, you filthy scoundrel!' he shouted as he caught hold of Dada Rahim's throat and began to throttle him. Dada Rahim struggled for breath but was eventually able to free his neck from Khan's grasp. He managed to land an uppercut on Khan's chin that felled him to the floor. Khan recovered smartly and attacked yet again, head-butting Dada Rahim with a fury he'd never experienced before.

Both men were evenly matched and the scuffle carried on for several minutes before they both lay sweating and bloody on the office floor. It was at that moment that they realised they had not just lost a ceramic plate but also a valuable friendship. It was also the end of a lucrative partnership that would be written and spoken about for many years after their divorce.

Finally, the two greatest warriors on the battlefield —Arjuna and Karana—faced each other. They progressively used more potent weapons—divine astras of Agni, Varuna, and Indra. Karana used his guru Parashurama's Bhargavastra, which inflicted heavy casualties on the Pandavas. In return, Arjuna used his Brahmastra on the Kauravas. Karana fired his Magastra, the deadliest weapon in his arsenal, at Arjuna, but I pressed our chariot into the ground and this saved Arjuna. Now fate began to work against Karana. Karana's chariot wheels got stuck in the ground. He got down to try and free the wheels and pleaded with Arjuna that, by the rules of war, he ought to be given time to do so. I started laughing, mostly to prevent Arjuna from becoming chivalrous. I said to Karana, 'You talk of righteousness? You sided with Duryodhana in his evil schemes. You never protested the humiliation of Draupadi. You remained a mute spectator to the killing of Abhimanyu. What righteousness do you talk of?' I urged Arjuna to kill Karana quickly, while we had the advantage. Arjuna sent an arrow which sliced Karana's head off his body and soon the great warrior was no more.

'I need you to find out who bought that ceramic plate from Sotheby's in auction,' said Sir Khan to ACP Sunil Garg. Just below the rank of Joint Commissioner of Police, Garg had just the right level of ambition to allow himself to be led around on a leash by Sir Khan.

Ever since his much-publicised split with Dada Rahim, Sir Khan had gone on to open a slew of businesses. It had started with acquiring properties that were the subjects of litigation. Sir Khan would buy out the interest held by one or more of the parties to the dispute. Knowing that Sir Khan was involved, the other litigants would immediately offer to settle out of court, fearful of the consequences of picking a fight with him. Upon acquiring several properties, Sir Khan had decided to float a real estate development company of his own. One of his deputies had innocently asked him, 'Boss, we know nothing about construction. Why are we getting into this line of work?' Sir Khan had laughed and said, 'In the real estate business, it doesn't matter *what* you know. It only matters *whom* you know.'

And indeed the business had flourished. Every corporator, municipal official, and relevant secretary in the state government was soon eating out of his hands. They were happy to pass Sir Khan's files, no matter the number of fire, safety, environmental or zoning violations, because they knew that Sir Khan was not someone to be messed with.

After leaping into real estate, Sir Khan leapt into the bed of the hottest Bollywood leading lady—Kaavya. Kaavya had sizzled on screen in the role of a sleazy bar dancer in her debut movie, and Sir Khan was smitten. He had sent her a hundred long-stemmed roses each morning until she agreed to have lunch with him. 'Lunch? Next time, it shall be dinner,' he thought to himself as his valet helped him slip his feet into his soft-leather Stefano Bemere moccasins. By the time lunch ended, Sir Khan had decided to finance Kaavya's next film. It was a rather long lunch that extended well beyond dinner, the most delicate negotiations being conducted in Kaavya's bed.

Having financed a couple of movies, Sir Khan realised that most producers were strapped for cash. He decided that he would make movie-financing into a regular business. He would not only finance movies but also buy up their foreign distribution rights in advance. The desperate producers had no option but to sign over lucrative territories to Sir Khan, if they wanted his money.

Sir Khan was a regular at the finest hotels around the world. In Mumbai, a suite of the Taj Heritage Wing remained reserved for his private dinner parties. In Delhi, the grandest suite of The Imperial would be made available whenever he visited the capital. In London, Sir Khan would check in at The Savoy; in Dubai he used a private chopper to land at the Burj al Arab; in New York his preferred hotel was the Pierre on Fifth Avenue and in Paris, the George V.

Wining and dining his way through umpteen tours and meals, Sir Khan soon found that he preferred to stay in hotels where he owned a substantial equity stake. This led him to create his own hotel chain, which had the added advantage of having access to some of the finest properties of his real estate arm. Sir Khan's flourishing real estate, film and hotel businesses provided him with ample opportunity to launder the money that he received from his illicit businesses in counterfeiting, betting and smuggling. Legitimate businesses now provided an outward veneer of respectability to Sir Khan.

ACP Sunil Garg—Assistant Commissioner of Police—sat in Sir Khan's private study and opened his file. He cleared his throat and began. 'Sotheby's auctions are usually open to the public and attendees have no obligation to bid. The reserve price on the ceramic plate had been set at fifty thousand pounds. The lot was knocked down at seventy-five thousand pounds, which was the ultimate price. Sotheby's then organised the delivery of the lot in private with the buyer.'

'Thank you for educating me in the Sotheby's auction processes,' said an irritated Sir Khan. 'I simply want to know who bought it.'

'Ah, yes. Please bear with me for a moment,' said Garg gently. 'If an item is up for auction, potential bidders must register beforehand in addition to supplying some valid proof of assets. Unfortunately, this data remains private with Sotheby's. Serious bidders—such as collectors or trusts—often do not attend the physical event and prefer to bid anonymously by phone. These are the rules of a Sotheby's auction and they must be followed. This is precisely what happened with the ceramic plate.'

'I like rules that are made for others and exceptions that are made for me,' said Sir Khan. 'Are you trying to tell me that you do not know who bought it?'

'No. Interested buyers register to bid either in person at Sotheby's auction centres or online on the Sotheby's website,' replied Garg. 'The auctioneer requires buyers to provide proof of identity and a bank reference. What my contact at Sotheby's has revealed to me is that it was bought by VSKBC Heritage Ltd. The bank reference supplied was that of BNP Paribas.'

'And who owns VSKBC Heritage Ltd?' asked Sir Khan.

'I don't know yet,' said ACP Garg. 'But I'm trying to find out.'

'Well, Garg, you know that plum posting up for grabs in the CBI? The one that could ensure your elevation to the post of CBI Special Director? That's on my to-do list but I'll only start working on it once you tell me who bought that ceramic plate,' said Sir Khan, puffing on his Havana contentedly as he watched the policeman squirm.

After ninety-nine Kaurava sons and Karana had been killed, Duryodhana went before his mother Gandhari for her blessings. Gandhari told Duryodhana to take a bath at dawn and meet her completely naked. She said, 'My eyes have remained shut for so many years that they are radiating my power of piety. Once I cast my gaze on your body, you will become immune to any weapon. The next day, Duryodhana had his bath as instructed and was on his way to his mother when I stopped him on the way. 'At least cover your privates,' I mocked on purpose. The fool Duryodhana took a banana leaf and tied it around his waist before reaching his mother. When she took off her blindfold, she exclaimed, 'What have you done, O Duryodhana? Now you will not be invincible below the waist because my eyes have been unable to see your body entirely.' I now knew that Duryodhana would have to be attacked below his waist for him to die.

Sir Khan forced his mind back to the present.

'That still doesn't answer my question. Who was the last owner of the baseplate?' Priya was asking.

'I was,' Sir Khan had replied.

'You? How?' asked Priya, stupefied.

'My father belonged to a line of Rajput craftsmen and builders,' explained Sir Khan. 'My ancestors had worked not only for Raja Man Singh but also for the Mughal emperors. It is very possible that one or more of my ancestors may have been responsible for building the Vrindavan temple of Raja Man Singh. Unfortunately, the policies followed by Akbar in treating Hindus on par with Muslim subjects came to an abrupt end with Aurangzeb. He attacked Man Singh's Vrindavan temple and demolished three of the seven floors. If you visit Vrindavan today, you can see the floors that remain. It is possible that the Syamantaka and the base plate, too, had to be moved to yet another location.'

'How did the baseplate become yours?' asked Priya.

'My father gave it to me before he was killed,' said Sir Khan, recalling the words of his father on that fateful day in Besnagar.

Son, today I wish to share an important piece of information with you. Six generations before me, our ancestors were master builders. They had worked on building several important temples and palaces. Through all these years, this small square ceramic plate has been handed down from generation to generation in our family. Today I am handing it over to you. It is taken from a temple. Inside that temple lies an ancient secret. This plate indicates the location. Promise me that you will guard this with your life, my son.

Sir Khan sighed and took another long puff of his Cohiba cigar. He told Priya and Ratnani of how he had been unable to keep his promise to his father. How he had carelessly allowed the family heirloom to be stolen by Dada Rahim and auctioned for a few lousy bucks and how he had fallen out with Dada Rahim thereafter. In the process he had ended up becoming obsessed not only with getting back the baseplate but also with finding the secret that lay behind it.

'Do you still recall what was written on the baseplate?' asked Priya.

'There was a Sanskrit inscription that my father had tried to make me memorise but I never succeeded in learning it. I do not remember it even vaguely,' replied Sir Khan ruefully.

'Any idea who bought it from Sotheby's?' asked Priya.

'What we were able to find out was that it was purchased by a company called VSKBC Heritage Ltd. Unfortunately, we did not know who was behind the company because of a very complicated holding structure,' replied Sir Khan.

'So we're stuck?' asked Priya.

'No. Sunil Garg—for whom I pulled many strings in New Delhi in order that he may be made a Special Director in the CBI—finally came through,' replied Sir Khan, smiling in a self-congratulatory way. 'Garg conducted a nationwide search of safe deposit vaults to find out whether any safe deposit locker had been rented by a company called VSKBC Heritage Ltd. It turned out that a safe deposit box in the New Friends Colony branch of South Delhi Safety Vaults had indeed been rented by such a company.'

'And?' asked Priya—but her mind lingered on the name of Sunil Garg. It sounded eerily familiar. She forced the thought out of her mind.

'And the signatory who could operate the box was Anil Varshney—our Kalibangan linguist,' replied Sir Khan.

'We would need a court order to access a vault rented by a man who subsequently died,' said Ratnani, speaking from a legal perspective.

'But no court would give us that right since we are not his immediate blood relatives or executors,' explained Sir Khan. 'So I asked Garg to find a solution. Garg found that

Varshney had left instructions that the contents of the box were to be handed over to Ravi Mohan Saini in the event of Varshney's death. Garg got one of his men to rent a locker in the same establishment and ensured that it was used to store unlicensed firearms. Using this as a pretext, the CBI raided the establishment and threatened the manager with dire consequences if he did not cooperate. Saini will be visiting South Delhi Safety Vaults tomorrow in order to access the safe deposit box.'

'What do you want done?' asked Priya.

'I want you to go to Delhi tonight and I want you to be there at the safe deposit box tomorrow when he reaches there. I want you to retrieve the baseplate and finish off Saini once and for all,' replied Sir Khan quietly.

Duryodhana, who had been inconsolable when he heard the news of Karana's death, went weeping to his grandfather, Bhishma, who lay on a bed of arrows. Bhishma now revealed to him the secret of Karana's birth. Duryodhana was shattered. He could not believe the immense sacrifice that his friend had made for him by fighting his own blood brothers and dying in the process. The next day, Drona's son, Aswatthama, suggested that Shalya be given command of the Kaurava army. Duryodhana accepted the suggestion. I understood that, given Shalya's righteousness, the only one who would be in a position to defeat him was Yudhistira. A duel between Shalya and Yudhistira ensued in which Yudhistira's javelin brought Shalya down. Kripa, Ashvatthama, Shakuni, Kritavarma and Duryodhana were now the only Kaurava warriors left. Duryodhana took direct command over the forces and fought valiantly. Shakuni, the evil uncle who had prompted the gambling match, was soon killed by Sahadeva. Duryodhana's kin rushed to help their eldest, but Bhima killed them all. The eighteen days of war had virtually decimated all eighteen divisions of the two armies.

'The original brief was to decimate the four people who stood in our way. The ones who came between us and the Syamantaka—the four researchers,' replied Priya. 'That's why Taarak left the four symbols of Vishnu at each murder.'

'Ah, Vishnu may hold four symbols in his hands but his fifth symbol—the snake—touches his feet. The serpent Sheshnag—the one who took birth as Balarama, the brother of Krishna—lies at Vishnu's feet,' proclaimed Sir Khan. 'Five at the centre of a magic square; five sides of a pentagon; five Pandavas at the core of the Mahabharata war; five children of Draupadi; five sons of Yayati and five obstacles to be eliminated. Saini is the last one, Priya.'

'Saini is probably the only one who would be able to decipher the Sanskrit inscription on the baseplate and use it to pinpoint a location,' said Priya, still immersed in deep thought. 'If we kill him, the Syamantaka may remain lost for ever.'

'If we don't, Saini finds the Syamantaka and we lose the opportunity to get it for ourselves,' countered Sir Khan. 'My tussle with the members that constitute VSKBC is an age-old one—one that has never abated.'

'How?' asked Priya.

'I have since learned that VSKBC is simply an acronym for Vrishni—Shainya—Kukura—Bhoja—Chhedi,' replied Sir Khan. 'These were the Yadava tribes that helped Krishna build his fabled city of Dwarka, using ways of reclaiming land from the sea. Varshney was a direct descendant of the Vrishni line—to which Krishna himself had belonged. He took it upon himself to seek out other like-minded Yadavas who would help him acquire the Syamantaka. He thus created VSKBC Heritage Ltd to find and acquire the Syamantaka. He had a sufficient number of investors who knew the value of the antiquities that were likely to be recovered from the research effort.'

'You mentioned that it's an age-old tussle between Varshney's outfit and yours. What did you mean by that?' asked Priya.

'My father was of Rajput stock. The VSKBC members were Jats,' explained Sir Khan.

'What's the difference?' asked Ratnani.

'Krishna's Yadava tribes were either concentrated around Indraprastha or Dwarka,' began Sir Khan. 'When Dwarka sank, the Yadavas living there had to find a new home. Some of them moved to the region that we now call Iran-Iraq. The maritime links between Dwarka and the Persian Gulf were flourishing even during Krishna's times, so this was not a problem. When they got there, they noticed the four rivers there, which reminded them of the four rivers of Mount Kailash. They called their new home Sumeru—or holy mountain.'

'What about the Yadavas who were living in and around Indraprastha—modern-day Delhi?' asked Priya.

'They continued to go forth and multiply all over the north-west of India. They were known as the Jats—the word having been derived from Krishna's Gyati-Sangh,' answered Sir Khan.

'What happened to the Yadavas who moved to the Persian Gulf region?' asked Priya.

'The Yadavas who had moved towards the Persian Gulf eventually occupied areas in eastern Iran and southern Afghanistan. They came to be known as the Indo-Scythians because of genetic intermingling. When they arrived back in India in later years, they were called the *Sakas*—because the area that they occupied in Iran and Afghanistan was known as Sakestan. It was the Sakas that evolved into the Rajputs.'

'So the Jats and Rajputs were essentially the same people—descendants of Krishna's Yadava clans?' asked Priya.

'Absolutely. But the sands of time obliterate historical truths. We find that the Rajputs and Jats continued to engage with each other in battle down the ages of modern Indian history,' replied Sir Khan. 'One could say that I represent the Rajput faction and Saini represents the Jat faction. Hence the battle over Krishna's Syamantaka continues even today.'

'But how can you be a Rajput with a name like Sir Khan?' asked Priya.

Sir Khan laughed. 'That was just a title given to me by Rahim when I landed in Mumbai. My real name was Kanha—another name for Krishna,' he explained. 'Do you see this pendant that I wear around my neck?' Sir Khan took off the gold pendant that Dada Rahim had presented him with many years ago and handed it over to Priya. Priya examined it curiously.

It was an ordinary gold pendant on which the words 'Sir Khan' were engraved in gothic font. 'I know you are called Sir Khan and that you wear a pendant which bears that name. So what?' asked Priya blandly.

'Just rotate the pendant you have in your hand a hundred and eighty degrees so that the letters are upside down,' instructed Sir Khan. Priya did as she was asked—and gasped at the result.

Sir Khan smiled at her. 'The honorific bestowed upon me by Dada Rahim was—ironically—also an anagram of Krishna. Now, tell me, should I ask Sunil Garg to meet you at the safety vault so that you can take care of Saini?'

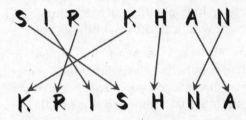

Priya's face suddenly went fiery-red with rage. In the deepest recesses of her brain she had finally managed to make the connection. Sunil Garg! It was the name of the policeman who had troubled her father to the point that he had been left with no alternative but to accept briefs on behalf of Sir Khan! It was the very same Garg who had also refused to write up an FIR for Sarla Auntie and had allowed her to be repeatedly abused by her drunkard husband. Her father had not realised that he had been set up by Garg and Sir Khan! His hand had been forced so as to propel him into the arms of Sir Khan.

'Garg will ensure that you are present when Saini comes to check the contents of the safe deposit box,' continued Sir Khan. It was the last sentence that he would ever utter. The Ninja spike that left Priya's hand twirled in the air momentarily before it pierced Sir Khan's throat. His eyes continued to vacantly stare at Priya in frozen horror, as blood spurted out from the centre of his neck. The cigar fell to the floor and the glass of water on the side table crashed to tiny fragments as it hit the Italian marble of the floor.

Ratnani got up from his chair in panic when he saw what his daughter had done. By the time that he reached Sir Khan's bleeding body, it was all over. It had all happened within a couple of seconds. Sir Khan's body slumped forward in his armchair as the blood from his throat dripped on the floor, forming a puddle much like the ones created by Taarak the previous four times.

Priya stood up calmly and walked over to her father, quietly urging him not to touch anything. 'What now?' asked Ratnani with a slight waver in his voice.

'Everything else goes as per plan,' replied Priya. 'Lord Krishna shall ensure that the Syamantaka comes to us, and us alone. Sir Khan tricked you into his camp by using Garg! It was about time that I removed this hurdle in my path.'

'How are we going to get out of here?' whispered Ratnani. 'Sir Khan's men are outside. They'll kill us the moment we open the door.'

'I have an idea,' said Priya, grabbing hold of the don's mobile phone that lay on the side table. She began typing a text message.

'To whom are you sending a message to from Sir Khan's phone?' asked Ratnani.

'To the chief of Sir Khan's security detail. He's sitting a few feet away from the door to this room. It says that he should ask all hands to rush to the swimming pool annexe because a tip-off has been received regarding a bomb having been planted there,' said Priya laughing maniacally.

'And what happens after we leave here?' asked Ratnani.

'I bring this saga to a final conclusion,' Priya said flatly to her father, her eyes glinting as if they had turned to ice.

Duryodhana saw the deserted battlefield in which no Kaurava soldiers remained. He wearily rode his horse towards Lake Dwaipayana and submerged his body in the comforting water in order to regain his strength. He was soon joined by Sanjaya, Dhritarashtra, Aswatthama, Kripa and Kritavarma. They tried boosting his morale and were somewhat successful. Duryodhana now appointed Aswatthama as commander of his non-existent army. In the meantime, puzzled by the sudden disappearance of Duryodhana, we sent out spies to find out where he was. When we got the news that he was at Lake Dwaipayana, we went there ourselves.

Saini and Radhika walked down a flight of stairs to a well-lit basement. Rathore had been unable to join them, because he was completing local police formalities related to Chhedi's murder. The news of Chhedi's death had left Saini shattered. 'We should never have split up,' he said to Radhika. 'It's my fault. If we had remained together, the chances of Taarak getting away with yet another murder would have been very slim.'

Radhika had allowed Saini to mourn and vent but she also realised the importance of visiting the vault. She convinced Saini to move forward with inspecting the safe deposit box immediately. Like most such establishments, this one, too, was located below street level for reasons of security. Rajendra Raval, the manager of South Delhi Safety Vaults Ltd, was waiting for them at the reception desk and brightened a little too enthusiastically when Saini introduced himself.

'Ah, Mr Saini, how nice to meet you!' he exclaimed. 'Yes, I was waiting for you. If you'll bear with me for a moment, I'll just have you sign a few documents that absolve us from any legal liability once you have operated Mr Varshney's safe. After that you may open the safe deposit box. May I offer you a cup of coffee in the meantime?' Both Saini and Radhika declined. Complimentary beverages seemed to stir up memories of poisoned cups of coffee being handed out by Priya. Radhika delved into her pockets for some almonds and popped a few into her mouth before offering some to Saini. 'Have some,' she said. 'Almonds contain brain-boosting elements and you need all your intellect to be supercharged!' Saini declined grumpily.

'May I have your passport, please?' asked Mr Raval. Saini took it out from his jacket's inner pocket and handed it over. Mr Raval gave it a quick look and then said, 'I'll be back with the original and a copy. Please give me a minute.'

As he went into the administrative office behind the reception, CBI Special Director Sunil Garg—who was viewing the developments on a surveillance video monitor—tapped Raval on the shoulder and curtly said, 'He has come to check the contents of a safe deposit box, not to ask for the hand of your daughter in marriage! Be more businesslike or he will smell a rat. Now, take him to the vault and let's see what's inside!' Raval nodded his head vigorously and left after making a copy of Saini's passport on the duplicating machine. He had to do everything himself this day because the office staff had been given the day off—on Garg's specific instructions.

Mr Raval led Saini and Radhika through the massive grille doors into a dazzlingly bright room. The rectangular room had safe deposit boxes lined up on all four walls except for the portion where the grille doors were located. The safe deposit boxes were packed together in a gleaming matrix that stretched from floor to ceiling, the higher boxes accessible via a movable ladder. Extra rows of boxes were also laid out like supermarket shelves in the centre of the room.

'Now let me see, what was the number of the box?' Mr Raval asked himself absentmindedly. He paused, looked down at the clipboard in his hand and said to Saini, 'Got it! Number 894! It's at the far end of this aisle. Please follow me.'

Saini and Radhika walked silently behind Mr Raval. Number 894 turned out to be one of the smaller safety deposit boxes on the premises. Mr Raval placed his key into the slot and turned it clockwise. He then took out the key and placed it into the second slot that would, in ordinary course, have been used for plugging in Varshney's key. Turning the key clockwise in the second slot produced a light clicking sound and the safe door swung open. Mr Raval pulled out a metallic rectangular box, no more than a foot long and six inches wide. He placed the box on a moveable steel table and courteously retreated. He did not draw attention to the fact that the table had been strategically placed at a point where the viewing angle of the ceiling-mounted surveillance camera was perfect.

Saini held his breath. His hands trembled as he unsnapped the catch on the side of the metallic box. Radhika stopped him. She took his trembling hand in her own and gave it a gentle squeeze, smiling. Saini was grateful for her presence and reassurance. He took a deep breath and opened the lid.

At Lake Dwaipayana, Bhima challenged Duryo-dhana to a duel with maces. My brother, Balarama, had just returned from his pilgrimage along the Sarasvati and was present to witness the duel between his two students. Bhima found it difficult to bring down Duryodhana, who was far better at wielding the weapon of choice. I kept patting my own thighs to signal to Bhima that the only way he would be able to incapacitate Duryodhana would be by breaking his thighs. Finally taking the hint, Bhima lashed out with his mace at Duryodhana's thighs — contrary to Balarama's rules that disallowed hitting below the waist. Duryodhana crumpled to the ground with his legs broken. An enraged Balarama lifted his plough to kill Bhima and it was with great difficulty that I convinced my brother that Duryodhana was the one who had lecherously asked Draupadi to sit on his lap and that Bhima was simply fulfilling a noble oath.

Saini observed the contents of the metallic box carefully. A piece of foam had been placed inside the box to prevent the artefact inside from shifting. Within the foam was a groove that had been cut perfectly to accommodate the item. It was a small earthen plate—around four centimetres long and an equal four centimetres wide. The face of the plate was blank except for four squarish holes that would accommodate the pegs of the four seals. A raised edge ran around the perimeter of the base plate so as to keep the seals snug.

Saini lifted the ceramic plate off the foam and turned it around. It was inscribed with a Sanskrit shloka. It was quite evident that the shloka had been engraved much later, probably during Raja Man Singh's times, whereas the plate itself was of far older provenance, dating back to the days of a prosperous Sarasvati civilisation.

'What does it say?' asked Radhika.

Saini began to translate slowly. He carefully noted down each sentence on paper and read out each word carefully as he translated the Sanskrit shlokas:

> *Seek Shiv at the highest point, Seek Vish by the sea;*
> *Give up your quest, for they are one, only your heart*
> *can see.*

> *When creation and destruction are unified, And 894*
> *reigns supreme; Where coconuts and lotuses adorn my*
> *crown, by the river I shall be.*

Cast aside hatred and learn to love, Man Singh says to you. Search my temple of seven floors, and you will find me too.

You seek the stone that turns lead to gold, but verily do not find; search instead for the faithful stone that can truly transform your mind.

'Any ideas what it could mean?' asked Radhika.

Saini kept staring at the Sanskrit inscription. 'Did you notice that the inscription talks of the number 894. Isn't it ironical that Varshney specifically chose safe deposit box number 894 to hold this artefact?' he whispered in awe.

Radhika looked at the open door of the safe deposit box. Indeed, it was 894. 'What is the significance of 894?' she asked.

'I honestly don't know,' replied Saini. 'The first part of the inscription seems to be telling us that seeking Shiv at Mount Kailash—*Shiv at the highest point*—would be of no use. Similarly, seeking Krishna at Somnath—*Vish by the sea*—would also be futile. We have indeed tried at both places and failed.'

'So in what direction could it be pointing us?' asked Radhika.

'There is only one place that I can think of,' said Saini, recalling Varshney's words to him during their fateful tour to Kalibangan:

The base plate was handed down through generations even though the seals were lost in antiquity. The base plate eventually reached the hands of Raja Man Singh who was a great Krishna devotee in the sixteenth century. Raja Man Singh had a Sanskrit inscription engraved into the plate and installed it in a Krishna temple that he built in Vrindavan.

'What place is that?' asked Radhika.

'The Radha Govinda temple of Raja Man Singh in Vrindavan,' said Saini. 'It was seven floors high and it was only during Aurangzeb's time that the seven floors got whittled down to three.'

'Hold it right there!' shouted the voice. Saini and Radhika who had been completely absorbed in examining the ceramic plate had not noticed a figure holding a revolver creeping up towards them. Saini and Radhika put their hands up in the air and slowly turned around from the table to face Taarak Vakil.

92

*When the Pandavas returned to camp, I asked Arjuna
to get down from the chariot first, even though it was
contrary to norm: usually, the charioteer got down and
the warrior then followed. Arjuna was a little irritated
by this breach of protocol but nonetheless alighted.
After he had gotten off, I too alighted and the chariot
burst into a fireball. A shocked Arjuna asked me what
had happened and I explained to him that many divine
weapons of Drona and Karana had hit his chariot,
which should have been destroyed much earlier. I had
used my divine powers to absorb the shock. Arjuna
felt embarrassed because he knew now that one of the
main reasons he had been able to survive near-death
situations was because of his divine charioteer.*

In the administration office sat CBI Special Director Garg,
watching and hearing the events unfold on his video
monitor. Next to him sat Mr Rajendra Raval, the manager
of the safe deposit box rentals company. Both of them sat
without the slightest movement, because their hands were
bound behind their backs and their lips were sealed shut
with duct tape. Behind both of them stood Priya holding a
.44 Magnum revolver taken from Garg's own holster.

Taarak, dressed in expensive casuals, was a change from
his persona as a driver. Saini softly said, 'There's nothing

here that's worth losing life over. Tell us what you want. We don't need to fight for it.'

Saini's voice seemed to have a calming effect on Taarak. 'The ceramic baseplate is all I want. Hand it over and no one will be harmed,' he said equally softly. Saini picked up the ceramic plate and slowly extended it towards Taarak, who took it from Saini gently. It was almost as though the scene was being played out, frame by frame, in slow motion.

Taarak placed the ceramic plate in his belt pack while keeping his eyes trained on Radhika and Saini. Within a minute, another figure appeared at the door to the vault room. It was Priya. 'How nice to see both of you once again,' she commented caustically, pointing her Magnum at Radhika while Taarak kept his gun trained on Saini.

'If both of you would be so kind, please stand facing the wall,' Priya requested with mock courtesy. Saini and Radhika were in no condition to argue and did as they were told. Taarak quickly walked up to them and patted them down. Since neither was carrying any weapons, he proceeded to the next step—binding their hands behind their backs with duct tape. He then gagged them by wrapping duct tape around their mouths.

'You may now turn around,' instructed Priya. 'Thank you for cooperating. While I would have loved to stay and chat, it's critical that I find the Syamantaka. Professor Ravi Mohan Saini, you have always occupied a special place in my heart. That's why I could not allow my dear boy Taarak to do this on his own. Heaven forbid, we cannot treat you on par with the rest!'

Turning to Radhika, she said, 'You have my heart-felt apologies, Inspector. I am aware of the story about your husband's sad demise and the fact that you had to see him die. I daresay you may have developed some protective feelings towards Professor Saini over the past few days, especially after the intimate moments that you spent together in the Saptarishi Cave. It is therefore with immense sadness that I must make you sit here and watch him die!'

There was a flash of terror in Radhika's eyes as she saw the gleaming scalpel emerge from Taarak's belt bag.

93

Soon, Aswatthama, Kripa and Kritavarma reached Duryodhana who was lying on the ground writhing in pain from his fractured legs. When Aswatthama got to know of the manner in which rules had been broken, he was overwhelmed with rage. He took an oath to kill all the Pandavas and their remaining allies. Even though Kripa and Kritavarma were not in agreement with his evil plans, Aswatthama crept into the Pandava camp at night and searched for the Pandava brothers. He saw the five sons of Draupadi asleep and mistakenly thought that they were the Pandava brothers and ruthlessly slayed them. After killing several others in the Pandava camp, he set it on fire. He rushed back to Duryodhana and gave him the good news regarding the supposed death of the Pandavas. Duryodhana took a look at what was supposed to be the head of Bhima and recognised it as that of one of Draupadi's sons. 'Oh, what have you done, Aswatthama?' cried an anguished Duryodhana as he breathed his last.

The room was deathly quiet except for the muffled sounds of Radhika struggling to get her hands free. In front of her sat Saini with his back to a wall of safe deposit boxes, with his arms bound behind his back and his mouth sealed shut with duct tape. On his forehead was a rubber stamp impression of a serpent—Sheshnag, the fifth permanent fixture of Vishnu.

Saini was unconscious, having been mercifully sedated by Taarak before he plunged the Swann-Morton scalpel into his left foot. Just above Saini's head was one of the large safe deposit boxes on which Taarak had written the usual Sanskrit shloka in Saini's own blood.

Mleccha-nivaha-nidhane kalayasi karavalam
dhumaketum iva kim api karalam
kesava dhrita-kalki-sarira jaya jagadisa hare.

The puddle of blood around Saini's comatose body was getting bigger by the second. Radhika struggled frantically with the duct tape around her wrists. She laboured to breathe through the gag across her lower face. She knew that it was just a matter of time before Saini died.

The bright white fluorescent lights inside the vault room had been deliberately left switched on by Priya so that Radhika would be able to see him die. It would also allow the cameras inside the vault room to transmit the scene to the video monitor in the administrative office that continued to be watched by Garg and Raval, duly bound and gagged.

Taarak and Priya had removed the security tape that had recorded their initial entry. Placing the rewritable CD along with the ceramic baseplate in their bag, they had locked the vault grille and the door to the administrative back office, leaving all the lights switched on at full intensity. As they had reached the outer entrance, Priya had smiled sweetly at the armed guard. 'Oh my, what a big gun you have,' she had purred into his ears seductively while Taarak had used the distraction to sedate him. The keys to the establishment had been pulled out of the guard's pocket and his unconscious form had been unceremoniously shoved down the stairs. Emerging into the bright sunlight, the duo had locked the main entrance to the premises of South Delhi Safety Vaults Ltd and had made off swiftly.

Pick up the phone, thought Rathore, as he desperately waited for Radhika to answer. He was sitting in a taxi on his way to South Delhi Safety Vaults Ltd. Rathore was eager to update Radhika that a data dump of whatever had been stolen by Taarak had been mapped and faxed to him. His boss, however, had her phone mysteriously switched off— alternatively her phone had gone out of range. Something was terribly wrong. 'Driver, if you can get me there in three minutes, there's another two hundred rupees as tip,' he said as he tapped the taxi driver's shoulder.

Inside the vault room was an analogue clock. Each time that the second hand moved forward it made a clicking sound. It was the only sound inside the vault room besides the laboured breathing of Radhika. After a few minutes she gave up the struggle—it was no use. The duct tape had been wound too tight. She suddenly felt a warm sensation along her thighs. Looking down she saw that Saini's pool of blood had spread towards her and had begun to drench her own clothes.

Draupadi wailed when she was told she had lost all her children. Long before her tears had dried, all she wanted was revenge. I stepped in. 'This endless cycle of an eye-for-an-eye cannot be allowed to continue. Let's send the scouts to look for Aswatthama and find a way to neutralise his Brahmastra. He is the son of Drona but has neither the qualities of a Kshatriya nor of a Brahmin.' When Aswatthama was finally cornered, he hurled his Brahmastra towards Abhimanyu's widow—Uttari, hoping that it would eliminate all the unborn descendants of the Pandavas. I stepped in front of her in order to absorb the impact. By now, I was furious. I uttered a deadly curse, the only curse that I had ever uttered. 'O, Aswatthama, you shall be unable to die for three thousand years. Your wounds will fester with pus, and boils shall torment every part of your body!' I declared, leaving him to wander the earth for three thousand years in misery.

Throwing the promised additional two hundred rupees at the cabbie, Rathore leapt out of the taxi. The entrance gate of South Delhi Safety Vaults was locked. Something is bloody wrong, thought Rathore to himself. All safety vault companies retained the services of armed guards outside the premises even on days when they were shut. Today was neither a weekend nor a public holiday, yet the gate was shut and there was no armed guard outside.

He hastily dialled the Delhi Police control room and asked for backup. He then lifted a rock from the landscaped garden near the entrance and began smashing it at the lock of the gate. Rathore knew that any tampering would set off a security alarm and sure enough, within a few seconds the air was pierced by a deafening noise as the alarm screamed disapproval. It was a matter of minutes before the security chief of the company would arrive. He silently prayed that they would get there fast enough.

About two minutes later, he heard the wailing of a siren as a security van screeched to a halt outside the premises. Rathore hastily pulled out his identification and introduced himself. 'I'm Sub-Inspector Rathore, and I believe that my colleagues are trapped inside. Please have this gate opened immediately,' he instructed. Within fifteen seconds, the security chief had opened the gate with his own master key. Rathore whipped out his gun and stealthily made his way down the stairs, backed up by the security chief.

They saw the security guard lying near the base of the steps. He had been knocked out cold by the chloroform combined with the hasty dispatch down the stairs. 'Open the gates to the vault,' ordered Rathore. The security chief looked at him. 'I can't do that by myself,' he explained. 'I need authorisation from the branch manager. Let's check for his key.'

The security chief headed to the administration office and tried the door. It was locked. He punched in a sequence of digits and the door swung open. Within a minute, Mr Raval had been freed, along with the CBI Special Director. Both men maintained a cautious silence about the role of the CBI Director. For the moment at least, Garg was as much of a victim as anyone else on the scene.

'Hurry,' said Rathore as Raval and the security chief got the vault door opened. Rathore rushed inside and had to steady himself to prevent slipping. Looking down, he found himself standing in a large puddle of blood. It seemed to flow from Saini, and from Radhika, who lay bound and gagged opposite him.

Rathore turned very quickly to Radhika. Her terrified eyes registered relief as soon as she saw Rathore. He ripped off the duct tape that covered her mouth and began searching for the source of blood. 'Don't waste your time, Rathore, it's not from me. They've killed Saini,' she said, pointing in the direction of the prone body and the shloka written above his head.

'Damn!' muttered Rathore. He crawled over to where Saini lay, and placed two fingers under the angle of Saini's jaw to check the carotid pulse. 'It's faint, but we still have a pulse,' yelled Rathore exultantly. The security chief nudged Rathore aside. The police control room had sent armed officers and an ambulance.

'Elevate the bleeding foot!' shouted the medical officer. 'We need him to be lying down so that we reduce the blood flow.' His assistants jumped to action and pulled Saini from a sitting position down to a flat one on the floor, while raising the leg from which the scalpel was protruding. Snapping on a pair of gloves, the medical officer eased the scalpel out of Saini's foot and handed it over to his assistant. 'There's no way that we will be able to halt blood flow from the foot until it is operated on,' he said. 'Just apply pressure behind his knee and groin. The main arteries that supply blood to the leg are located there,' he commanded as one of the assistants prepared to move Saini to a stretcher and into the waiting ambulance.

As they transferred Saini into the ambulance, Radhika saw Sunil Garg. He smiled at her and introduced himself.

'I came here because I had been tipped off that this crime was likely to happen, but I was overpowered by the assailant,' he said, brushing dust off his shoulders.

So, this is the familiar voice that I heard on the phone, Radhika thought. *It wasn't Raval calling for Saini. It was Garg!*

95

Gandhari and the blind Dhritarashtra, assisted by their hundred daughters-in-law, searched the now silent battlefield for the corpses of the Kaurava princes. The Pandavas saw their mother, Kunti, also wandering there. 'Who do you seek, Mother?' they asked. 'Karana,' she replied. 'Why seek the charioteer's son, Mother?' asked Arjuna. 'Because he was your eldest brother,' she said softly. Arjuna's anguish had no limits. He had not only killed Bhishma and Drona, but also his brother, Karana. Kunti told them the story about how she had tried out the boon while unmarried, and how Surya had given her Karana. She told them about how he had lately discovered that he was a Pandava, and how he had nevertheless chosen to stay loyal to Duryodhana, while ensuring that five brothers continued to live. The Pandavas recalled how he had spared their lives on each occasion when he had the chance to finish them off. 'Why didn't you tell us?' asked Arjuna. I replied on behalf of his mother. 'If she had told you, would you have been able to fight him?'

The old Radha Govinda temple in the centre of Vrindavan, along the Mathura-Vrindavan road, had seen the best and worst of times. Constructed by Raja Man Singh in 1590, the temple had received cartloads of pink sandstone for its construction, the entire money for the raw material having been personally donated by Emperor Akbar himself. Less than eighty years later it had been attacked by Aurangzeb and the seven-storeyed structure had been reduced to just three after the ferocity of the assault. The temple had remained empty ever since. A replica idol had been installed in a newer although smaller temple located behind the original one.

Priya and Taarak entered the cathedral-like structure, which was in a state of decay and disrepair. A Sanskrit inscription on the temple confirmed that Raja Man Singh had built it. Just below the inscription was a square inset that had four protruding square pegs within. 'Give me the ceramic plate,' said Priya hurriedly. Taarak took it out of his belt bag and handed it over to her. She gently placed the plate into the inset. She had to slightly nudge it into place but it was a perfect fit. Raja Man Singh had indeed installed this baseplate in his own temple.

'This was obviously a rather important construc-tion of its time,' said Priya as she pulled out the baseplate from the groove and held it in her hands. 'The benevolent Akbar is said to have made a pilgrimage here and this was one of four temples that were constructed in honour of his visit. Many thousands of labourers and craftsmen toiled for over five years to complete it.'

Priya and Taarak quickly began to comb the ruins. The plan of the temple was in the shape of a cross with both length and breadth of the nave equal to around a hundred feet each. Every square inch of the walls bore intricate decorations and fine carvings. Seeing the decaying state of the temple made Priya's blood boil.

'How can we be sure that it's this particular temple, Mataji?' asked Taarak.

'Didn't you hear the translation that Saini provided?' asked Priya. *Cast aside hatred and learn to love, Man Singh says to*

you. Search my temple of seven floors, and you will find me too.
This was a temple of seven floors and was constructed by
Raja Man Singh. We're exactly where we ought to be!'

'But what about the sentence that says: *When creation
and destruction are unified, And 894 reigns supreme; Where
coconuts and lotuses adorn my crown, by the river I shall be,*'
asked Taarak.

'This was a temple that was created and destroyed within
the very same century. This wonderful structure was
created by the generosity and religious tolerance of one
Muslim ruler and was destroyed by the iconoclasm of
another. It very much signifies creation and destruction at
one place,' said Priya.

*'Where coconuts and lotuses adorn my crown, by the river I shall
be.* What about the lotus, Mataji?' asked Taarak.

'Look at the ceiling,' said Priya, pointing upwards. 'It has a
sculpted lotus weighing several tons.' Taarak followed her
gaze and saw the magnificent flower.

'And the coconuts?' asked Taarak.

'See the carvings? You will see the lotus motif and
coconut symbol in several places. Before you ask, we are
in Vrindavan—along the banks of the River Yamuna—so
the condition that talks about the temple being by a river
is met.'

'Yes, but what does the number 894 signify, Mataji?' asked
Taarak.

'I have no idea, but it's hardly relevant, given that most
of the other conditions are perfectly satisfactory,' replied
Priya. 'This is the place that we need to search.'

'But it's an ancient temple and it's rather large. Where
should we start?' asked Taarak.

'I would say that the most likely place would be the *garbhagriha*,' said Priya.

'What's a garbhagriha?' asked Taarak curiously.

'The garbhagriha is the *sanctum sanctorum*—the innermost sanctum of a Hindu temple where the idol is placed,' answered Priya. 'In Sanskrit, *garbha* means womb and *griha* means chamber or house. So garbha-griha means *the womb chamber*. It is the most sacred spot in the temple. Only the temple priests were allowed inside and hence it would also have been the most secure spot to store anything precious.'

'Where is the garbhagriha of this particular temple?' asked Taarak.

'That's the problem,' said Priya. 'What is now the inner sanctum of this temple was not the original inner sanctum.'

'But I thought that all temples were constructed according to the principles of *Vaastushastra*. How could a critical location like the inner sanctum change?' asked Taarak.

'The temple had to be slightly remodelled by the British when they began repairs. During Aurangzeb's attack, his demolition men had begun from the roof and worked their way downwards. According to historical accounts, when only three floors remained it seems that the ground began to tremble violently and Aurangzeb's squad had to run for their lives because they were worried that the temple would come crashing down on them.'

'Do we have any records that show where the original inner sanctum was?' asked Taarak.

'None,' replied Priya. 'The first one was constructed by disciples of Chaitanya Mahaprabhu, the ardent Vaishnavite from Bengal. These disciples became the very first priests of this temple. Sadly, no trace of that garbhagriha remains.

We know that this layout is in the shape of a cross so the best guess should be the centre of the cross.'

They walked briskly through the dark interiors towards the core of the temple. Taarak switched on his flashlight because light from outside was non-existent towards the centre. Priya gasped as they reached the geographic centre of the temple. Right at the spot where the idol would have once stood, was a three-foot-wide crater—a pit large enough for two people to descend into.

'Someone had the same idea as us,' muttered Priya angrily as they stood at the edge of the pit and peered down. Whoever had dug the pit had done a professional job of it. It went down more than twenty feet, and rough edges along the circumference had been smoothened out to prevent injury. Mounds of dug-up earth lay piled along the edges. From the ceiling hung a thick rope that went deep into the hole. 'Whatever was there has probably gone,' cursed Priya. 'Let's have a look anyway.'

Both Mataji and her pupil made their way down the knotted rope, Taarak holding the flashlight in his mouth as he spiralled downwards, with Priya following. As their feet touched terra firma, Priya got down on her hands and knees and began frantically running her hands over the muddy earth floor.

At that moment there was a flash of light from above. Priya and Taarak looked up in alarm. It was difficult to discern the face but the voice was unmistakeable. It was the raspy voice of CBI Special Director Sunil Garg. Before Priya and Taarak could reach for it, he cut the rope that hung down into the pit. They now had no way of getting out. 'It is always a pleasure to see old friends,' said Garg amiably. 'I figured that both of you have had far too much activity and stress recently. A nice, cool and dark place like this one will help you relax and unwind.'

Suddenly, there was a shower of earth and pebbles that hit Priya and Taarak from above.

'*Om Shri Prithvi Rakshasaaya Namah,*' chanted Garg as he shovelled the first scoop of earth down below.

'Hey!' shouted Priya angrily. 'We can make a deal. I think I know where the stone is. Just listen to…'

'The time for deals is over, Mataji,' he yelled. 'You should have thought about it when you left me in the vault to be picked up under suspicious circumstances by the local police! *Om Shri Maangalya Daayakaaya Namah,*' recited Garg, as he shovelled another mound of earth from above.

Priya spat out earth that had fallen into her mouth. 'I may have left you captive but I didn't kill you,' she argued.

'So we're even,' yelled Garg. 'When you were a little girl, I could have arrested you and sent you to a remand home for the murder of your Sarla Auntie's husband, but I didn't. *Om Shri Maangalya Daayakaaya Namah,*' he chanted as he shovelled even more earth into the pit.

Deep within the recesses of the hellhole, Mataji and Taarak sat down on the floor and began to recite the names of the Lord. They knew their time had come.

96

I sent the Pandavas to seek the blessings of Dhritarastra and Gandhari. Gandhari and Draupadi hugged each other and cried—both were mothers who had lost all their children. Vidura had advised Gandhari, 'Please be careful not to curse the Pandavas, or else this land will have no ruling dynasty left.' Accordingly, Gandhari kept her anger in check. But once she reached the battlefield where the bodies of her sons lay strewn, her anger returned. Having sat there in dejection for several hours, she eventually felt hungry, and smelt the fragrance of mangoes overhead. Desperate for food, she made a pile of stones to climb on and pluck the fruit from the tree. Having eaten the fruit, she realised in horror that she had not used stones, but the bodies of her dead sons, to get to the fruit. She then recognised that it was I, teaching her about the power of illusion. At that instant, she cursed me. 'You too shall lose your loved ones, Krishna! You shall watch helplessly as your clan self-destructs by turning on one another, and you shall die like an animal at the hands of a hunter!'

The hospital room in which Saini awoke was bright and airy. He had been unconscious for over two days. Outside his room stood Rathore, intent on ensuring that the likes of Priya and Taarak could not enter. Inside the room, Radhika sat by his bed, praying for his recovery. When he stirred, she was absolutely ecstatic. Leaving aside all her reserve, she kissed him on his forehead. It seemed the most natural thing to do. 'They said that had they reached you five minutes later, you would have bled to death,' she said with tearful eyes while running her fingers through his hair tenderly. Saini smiled weakly. He shifted his body slightly and came alive to the fact that his left foot was tightly bandaged.

'They've put stitches in your foot,' clarified Radhika. 'Apparently, the gash had cut through your artery.'

Saini laughed weakly. 'Following the clues of the Krishna Key has placed me in a hospital bed twice and you once. By the time the secret is finally discovered, we shall both have medical qualifications!'

'I don't care about the Krishna Key or what it leads to, anymore,' said Radhika softly. 'I was pretty certain that I had lost you forever, Ravi. Please, can't we just give up this quest? They had to pump more than seventy units of blood into you!'

Saini changed the topic. 'How did I get here after the scalpel was used on me?' he asked. Radhika told him about how Rathore had been trying to call her phone and how this had led him to the premises of South Delhi Safety Vaults. 'I shudder to think what would have happened if Rathore had not done what he did,' explained Radhika.

'Where is he?' asked Saini softly. Radhika stepped out of the room and motioned Rathore to join them inside. Rathore was relieved to see that he had been able to save at least one of the intended five victims. He joked about it with Saini.

'Why were you trying to get in touch with Radhika?' asked Saini, struggling to pull himself up. Radhika restrained him. Instead, she pressed the electronic button on the side of the hospital bed to raise him a little.

'When Kurkude's secretary was killed, some data was stolen from her terminal. We managed to find out what it was,' explained Rathore.

'And what was it?' asked Saini.

'It was the data recorded by Geiger counters across the country, regarding the level of radioactivity,' replied Rathore. 'The research team converted the data dump into a map and plotted the points for me. This was faxed to me the day that Chhedi and I reached Delhi. I wanted to share this information with my boss but her phone was obviously out of range in the basement of the vault.'

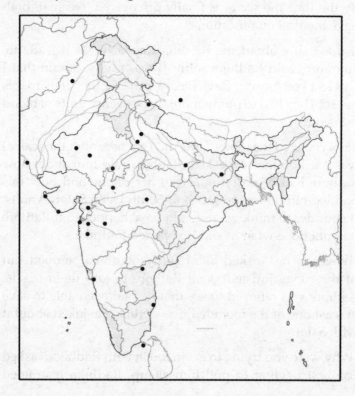

'Could I see the map, please,' asked Saini, weakly stretching out his hand. Radhika sighed. He had stood before the very gates of death and had barely returned alive, yet he was incapable of pulling himself away from the search.

Rathore saw Radhika's reaction and attempted to dodge the request. 'It is Latin and Greek to us non-technical types. Very little that can help us,' he began. Saini smiled at him. 'Humour me. Let me give it a shot,' he requested.

Rathore shrugged his shoulders helplessly for Radhika's benefit. He pulled out the folded fax message from his pocket and handed it to Saini who immediately got absorbed in studying it.

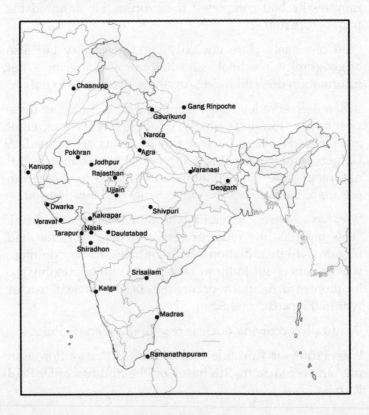

'There's a pattern here,' said Saini to Rathore. 'Could I borrow your pen, please?' Rathore obliged by pulling out his and handing it over.

'Could you pull that table over here?' he asked Radhika, pointing to the wheeled dining trolley. Radhika pulled it closer to Saini quite reluctantly. 'I still don't understand why we are wasting time on this issue. Can't you give it up, Ravi?' she pleaded.

Saini smiled at her. 'I promise that after I look at this map you shall not hear about the issue anymore. Deal?'

Saini placed the fax containing the map on the table before him and began labelling the locations. Within about ten minutes he had completed the process. He admired the map before him.

'You obviously were not only good at history but also at geography in school,' said Rathore with a grin. 'What information does this add? Anything that can help us?'

'It's rather simple, really,' replied Saini. 'Look at these twenty-four locations closely. Of these twenty-four, eight are locations where nuclear power plants are located. A Geiger counter recording a high level of radiation is but natural in these eight locations. So let me cancel these from our map.' Saini struck the eight names and locations off.

'We have sixteen remaining locations,' continued Saini. 'This includes the Jodhpur region, where Kurkude had observed high radiation levels initially. In my opinion, we can cancel out Jodhpur because it is quite possibly the location of a naturally-occurring ancient nuclear reactor within the earth,' said Saini.

'Naturally-occurring nuclear reactors?' asked Radhika.

'Yes. Professor Kurkude had discussed that option with me,' answered Saini. 'It's based on the findings of Dr Paul Kuroda.'

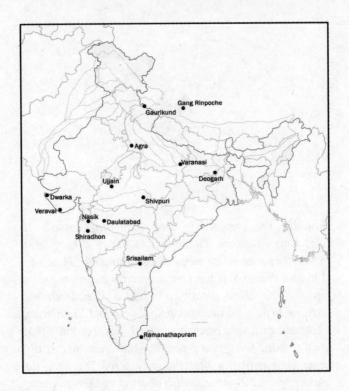

'Then what?' asked Rathore.

'We can also eliminate Pokhran which was the test site used by the Indian government to carry out a controlled explosion,' said Saini. 'Radiation levels are bound to be high there, too. Now, we are left with just fourteen locations.' Saini looked at the remaining locations once again.

'See anything strange?' asked Saini, showing the map to Radhika and Rathore. Both of them looked, and relooked, but they could not see anything of consequence.

'What is of consequence,' pointed out Saini, 'is that with the exception of Agra and Mount Kailash, all remaining twelve locations are the sites of sacred Shiv lingams—in fact the twelve most sacred ones in India!'

97

Finally, the cremations and mourning ended. It was time to crown Yudhistira as the new king. But Yudhistira was in no mood to be coronated. 'How can I wear a crown that has been won after killing my own family?' he asked in anguish. Just as I had advised Arjuna to fight on the battlefield, I now told Yudhistira, 'You can certainly become a hermit, but wouldn't that mean abandoning your people—the ones that really need your empathy after this massacre? You have the power to once again establish dharma in this kingdom; do not run away from your duty,' I said. Yudhistira internalised the truth of what I was telling him and agreed to sit on the ancient Kuru throne of Hastinapur. As Brahmins recited prayers, the people of Hastinapur bowed before their new king and showered flower petals on him.

Radhika stared at the map before her once again. Saini had knocked out the city names and had replaced them with the names of the Shiv lingams... he was absolutely right! Excluding Agra and Mount Kailash, the remaining twelve locations were indeed the dwellings of the most sacred lingams of India.

'Somnath has always been considered to be *the* most sacred among the twelve,' said Saini.

'What I cannot understand is why we have Agra and Mount Kailash also on the map,' commented Radhika. Saini did not reply. He seemed to be momentarily lost in his own thoughts. He was racking his brains trying to remember exactly what Priya had said when she had held them at gunpoint inside the vault:

Thank you for cooperating. While I would have loved to stay and chat, it's critical that I find the Syamantaka. Professor Ravi Mohan Saini, you have always occupied a special place in my heart. That's why I could not allow my dear boy Taarak to do this on his own. Heaven forbid, we cannot treat you on par with the rest!

The Syamantaka! She believed that the Krishna Key was actually pointing them towards the Philo-sopher's Stone!

'We need to talk to Priya,' said Saini.

'What? She tried to kill you!' exclaimed Radhika.

'Be that as it may. She seems to have information that we don't,' replied Saini.

'I doubt that you will ever be able to meet her again,' said Radhika.

'Why? Because she will have found the secret and run?' asked Saini.

'No, because by now she will be in the hands of Sunil Garg,' said Radhika, a cat-like smile hovering on her lips.

'What does he have to do with this?' asked Rathore.

'After the medical team had stabilised you, I told Garg that I was on to him. I told him that I knew that he had been sitting inside the vault all the time. I informed him that I had caught on to the fact that he had made the telephone call to you—not Mr Raval. I suggested to him that if he didn't want his own murky role in the whole business to emerge, and ruin his illustrious career, it would be better that he took care of Priya and Taarak,' said Radhika, measuring her words carefully. Rathore laughed while Saini was too dazed to speak. Radhika Singh had proved yet again why she had such a formidable reputation in the police department.

'If we can't ask Priya, we must reason this out for ourselves. The reason that Mount Kailash is on the map is precisely the same reason why Somnath is there,' said Saini enigmatically.

'Don't talk in riddles, Ravi,' said Radhika with a hint of irritation.

'The Syamantaka is a transformative isotope,' said Saini. 'An element that can transform a given element into another. It has been proved by modern science that transmutation happens best through nuclear processes. To that extent, it is evident that the Syamantaka could have been a nuclear isotope.'

'How does that tell you anything about Mount Kailash being on the map? We went there ourselves! There was nothing besides a great big white sheet of ice,' said Radhika.

'I wouldn't expect anything to be there. My hypo-thesis is that Mount Kailash is not a mountain but an alchemist's pyramid!' said Saini confidently.

'What in heaven's name is an alchemist's pyramid?' asked Rathore, longing to sink his teeth into good old- fashioned cases of theft, kidnapping and extortion, instead of esoteric ones like these.

98

After the coronation ceremony was over, I asked Yudhistira, along with his brothers, to go seek the blessings of Bhishma, who was still alive on his bed of arrows. Yudhistira sat by Bhishma's side and learned the duties of kingship from the old man. The conversation between Yudhistira and Bhishma lasted for several days, in which Bhishma tried to answer all the questions that Yudhistira had. Eight days after the full moon that had followed the Mahabharata war, Bhishma gave up his breath and passed on. The man who had renounced the throne and had taken the powerful oath of remaining celibate all his life so that his father could marry another woman, was an example that the Pandavas would need to live up to.

'The goal of alchemy is transformation from lower forms to higher forms,' began Saini. 'While the most common way of thinking about alchemy is turning lead into gold or vice versa, alchemy is much more relevant in the spiritual sense—the final aim being to produce life from death. The pyramid is the ultimate symbol of alchemy. The Egyptian pharaohs were buried in pyramids precisely because they believed that the pyramid had the power to transform death into life.'

'How exactly would a pyramid breathe life into death?' asked Radhika.

'For that we must understand the concept of *Orgone*,' replied Saini.

'Orgone? What is that?' asked Radhika.

'Alchemy is based on the theory that what we call *God* is merely a life force,' said Saini. 'Orgone is that life force. It has been called by various names in different cultures— *aura, ether, chi, ki, mana, akaasa* or *praana*—but they all mean exactly the same thing. The theory of Orgone was originally proposed by Wilhem Reich in the 1930s, but the concept of praana has existed in India from ancient Vedic times. Orgone was believed to be a massless substance very similar to luminiferous ether but correlated with living energy rather than inert matter. Reich believed that deficits in bodily Orgone were the cause of many diseases— including cancer. Putting aside fancy terminology, Orgone was merely the life or spirit that God puts into all creation. It is to be found in fresh food, fresh water, and fresh air— hence the ayurvedic insistence on eating fresh food.'

'Why have we never heard of Orgone before? Why do doctors and medical professionals not talk about Orgone?' asked Radhika, intrigued by Saini's revelations.

'Reich established the Orgone Institute to carry out research into the concept of life force,' responded Saini. 'Unfortunately, his research discovered that Orgone tended to be deficient near telecom towers and chemical plants—among other things. Vested interests from these industries lobbied hard and soon the US Food & Drug Administration obtained a federal court order barring the institute's work. Reich was jailed and all Orgone-related information was systematically destroyed. Orgone soon became a discredited, fringe science theory. Funnily enough, the National Centre for Complementary and

Alter-native Medicine in the US still treats Orgone as a model for some clinical procedures!'

'How does the pyramid fit into this Orgone theory?' asked Radhika.

'The pyramid played the role of what was called the *Orgone Accumulator*—a giant machine that would suck life energy from air, water and earth and concentrate it at a single point,' replied Saini.

'So, the Egyptians were actually placing their pharaohs into an energy accumulator so that they would not only be preserved but also reborn with fresh energy?' asked Radhika.

'Precisely,' answered Saini. 'A pyramid has four faces that are exposed to the air, but it has a fifthside—the one it rests on. The ancients believed that the five sides could garner praana—or life energy—at the core of the pyramid. This was in conformity with the Vedic idea that the number five was at the centre of the world. A pyramid was thus a vital tool for the ancient alchemist.'

'Is Orgone real?' asked Rathore incredulously. 'Is there any scientific proof that it exists?'

'Most Orgone research has been driven under-ground because of the stigma attached to it by the scientific research establishment. Much of the con-tinuing experimentation is in the domain of work by enthusiasts and amateurs,' said Saini. 'For example, one amateur Canadian researcher from Vancouver built a full-sized copper pyramid in Abbotsford. He distributed several cuts of meat throughout the inside of his pyramid. According to his observations, the meat near the walls of the pyramid rotted, while a cut of meat in the centre of the pyramid remained entirely preserved even after months.'

'Do you believe that?' asked Radhika.

'The question is not whether *I* believe,' replied Saini. 'The important deduction to be drawn from this conversation is that the ancients *did* believe it. Mount Kailash was possibly a giant life energy-absorption device and it was quite probably the very source of the material that came to be known as the Syamantaka stone in Krishna's times. This material may possibly have had nuclear properties, thus allowing for a transmutative effect when it was placed inside the Somnath lingam.'

'So you think that Mount Kailash was a giant man-made pyramid?' asked Radhika.

'It may not have been man-made,' said Saini. 'It could have been a mountain that was chiselled down to the perfection required by alchemists of that age. It is astonishing to find that the four faces of Mount Kailash are perfectly aligned with the four cardinal points of the compass. It is even more surprising that, to the west, it has a 108-degree concave face and that the two north faces also add up to 108 degrees. This cannot be pure coincidence.'

'And the purpose of this pyramid was to collect praana—or Orgone—that could eventually be used as a transformative substance?' asked Radhika.

'Yes. Even the *Bhagvatam Purana* talks of how the world is made up of five elements that it calls the *Panchabhuta*. These are earth or *prithvi*, water or *jal*, fire or *agni*, air or *vaayu*, and ether or *akasha*. The Mount Kailash pyramid—which has five sides including the base—was a giant accumulator meant to trap life energy from each of these five elements,' replied Saini.

'So the radioactivity that has been recorded at Kailash and at Somnath is one and the same, because the origin is from the Syamantaka stone?' asked Radhika.

'In fact, the radioactivity at all the locations is due to the same reason,' replied Saini. 'It is very possible that after

Ghazni's invasion, the Jats and the Rajputs might have felt that it was wiser to keep moving the stone from one location to another. Temples would have been a natural choice. The problem, of course, was that those were iconoclastic times, and most temples would have been under threat of extinction.'

'So where would one find the stone today?' asked Rathore.

'The only location that stands out as being the odd one out is Agra—it has no reason to be on the list,' said Saini. 'Yet, Agra is the very location that the British chose to deposit the doors of Ghazni's tomb. I'm told that they still lie inside one of the storage rooms of the Agra Fort. I would say that my best hunch would be to go look in Agra.'

99

Shortly after Bhishma's passing away, Abhimanyu's widow—Uttari—went into labour. Everyone was excited—this was to be the last surviving member of the next generation. As the women looked on, Uttari's waters broke and she delivered a baby boy. But soon there was panic because the child refused to cry. Hearing the women wail, I rushed to Uttari's quarters and took the newborn in my arms. I gently whispered into the baby's ears, 'Don't be afraid. This earth is not as evil as you think it is. There's also goodness and happiness. Come, little one, come.' Encouraged by my words, the infant opened his eyes and smiled. 'Welcome to the world, Parikshit,' I said, smiling.

Rathore had been despatched to Agra to visit the fort, and Saini had been allowed to leave the hospital two days later on the express condition that he would not overly exert himself and that he would use a crutch so as to avoid placing too much pressure on his left foot. Radhika had been by his side throughout his hospital stay, almost nursing him back to health.

That evening, Radhika and Saini went out for dinner to an Italian restaurant in Mehrauli. Ignoring the menu, they ordered a bottle of Chianti and followed it up with another bottle of Barolo. By the time those several glasses of wine had been poured and consumed, the two had also succeeded in pouring out their hearts to one another. When they contemplated ordering a Barbaresco, the establishment politely pointed out that it was way past closing time.

'After two days in hospital, I took a turn for the nurse,' quipped Saini. There was a smile on his face but his eyes were absolutely serious. Saini settled the tab and got up from the table. Radhika helped Saini with his crutch as they walked back towards the parking lot where Saini's car lay parked. They held hands like teenagers and took comfort in the knowledge that they had each found a soulmate.

'Your place or mine?' asked Radhika lightly, as she settled into the driver's seat. She was staying at the same hotel where Rathore had booked himself in, whereas Saini's house was fifteen minutes away. 'Mine,' said Saini absolutely seriously, staring into her eyes.

'And this time I promise that I will not search the premises or take away anything as evidence,' she said with a straight face.

As they entered Saini's home, they fell together on the couch, and Saini kissed Radhika on her lips for the first time. She held on to him tightly almost as though she wanted to consume him and, in turn, be consumed by him. Their lovemaking was gentle but passionate, almost like the graceful and unhurried movements of a slow waltz. After they had made love on the couch, they went upstairs to Saini's bedroom and lay on the bed side by side, with Radhika's head nestled against his chest. Saini felt a sensation of wetness on his chest and looked down to see Radhika crying. 'Don't worry,' she said softly, 'it's just that it's the first time that I've been with anyone since Hari died'.

In the morning, they went down to the kitchen only to find that the refrigerator was mostly empty. Fresh milk had been left by the milkman at the entrance though and they made tea. A packet of oat-meal biscuits came to the rescue and breakfast consisted of those dunked in tea. Radhika, who rarely drank tea, given her propensity for whole milk and almonds, kept losing her biscuits in her tea. She finally gave up. 'Women do not know how much and for how long to put it in,' teased Saini. 'That's why God assigned the job to men.'

'Careful, you'll be having dry biscuits for the rest of your life if there's no tea to dunk it in,' admonished Radhika. Within minutes they were back on the couch, but this time their passion did not manifest itself as a waltz so much as a delicious tango.

As they showered together later, Saini asked, 'What say we take a romantic trip—just you and me?'

Her eyes lit up. 'Oh yes! That would be wonderful. Which destination was on your mind?' she asked eagerly.

'I'm told that the Taj Mahal is very romantic at this time of the year,' he said smiling.

100

The birth of Parikshit brought back joy to Yudhistira because he now knew that the Pandava lineage was secure. He decided that it was time to perform the Ashwamedha Yajna. A royal horse would be set loose and would be allowed to roam freely for a year. Kingdoms that allowed the horse to pass through would automatically accept Yudhistira's suzerainty. Those kingdoms that did not would have to battle Yudhistira. The horse wandered through many lands, including those of Shakuni and Jayadhrata, and was not stopped. Even though they had been enemies of the Pandavas, they were now allies. In Manipura, Arjuna was welcomed by its ruler — Babruvahana — who was actually Arjuna's son from Princess Chitrangada. Arjuna chided the young man. 'This is not warrior-like, my son! Fight me. Don't make it so easy for me to overrun your kingdom!' Babruvahana not only fought but also succeeded in piercing Arjuna's heart with his arrow. Arjuna was revived by the power of a magical gem provided by Babruvahana's stepmother, a Naga princess, Uloopi. Arjuna eventually returned to Hastinapur, along with the sacrificial horse, bringing even greater power and glory to the Pandavas.

Arriving at the entrance of the tomb complex and the imposing thirty-metre-high gatehouse, Saini and Radhika walked hand-in-hand through the ornamental *Charbagh* gardens of the Taj Mahal. The first sight of the Taj Mahal was breath-taking in every detail—the glorious central dome, the forty-metre-high minarets at each of the four corners, the River Yamuna flowing behind the Taj, the colourful floral inlays, and the exquisite marble latticework.

Saini and Radhika were content. They had each other and they were strolling through the gardens of the Taj Mahal— the eternal symbol of undying love. The romantic mood was temporarily shattered by the buzzing of Radhika's telephone.

'It's Rathore for you,' said Radhika, handing over the phone to Saini.

'The gates which are on display at the Agra Fort are replicas, not originals,' said Rathore to Saini dispensing with customary pleasantries.

'How can we be sure?' asked Saini.

'They're made of local deodar wood from the province of Ghazni, not sandalwood—the material used in the original Somnath doors,' replied Rathore.

'Was carbon-dating carried out on them?' asked Saini.

'Not as far as I know,' replied Rathore. 'The Islamic calligraphy was evident on the doors, hence carbon-dating was redundant. The doors were not from Somnath. But I did find out something rather interesting from the tour guide.'

'What?' asked Saini.

'In 1842, Edward Law, who was the First Earl of Ellenborough, issued the Proclamation of the Gates,' said Rathore. 'In this proclamation he ordered the British troops in Afghanistan to bring back the sandalwood gates that had been taken away by Ghazni from Somnath. The regiment that was responsible for bringing back the gates was the Jat Regiment.'

'Okay, so the Jats wanted the doors back and they got them back. What happened to the doors after that?' asked Saini.

'Well, the gates had apparently been reinstalled in Ghazni's tomb. After lengthy debates in the British House of Commons, the gates were removed from Mahmud's tomb and brought back to India, but they turned out to be replicas instead of the originals. They were kept in the Agra Fort where they continue to sit till today,' said Rathore.

'Thanks for the update. We're just about getting started on our tour of the Taj Mahal. If you like you can come here and join us,' said Saini, hanging up. He and Radhika continued walking towards the Taj Mahal.

As they neared the monument, Saini stopped for a moment. He looked up at the central dome of the Taj Mahal and continued to stare. Radhika nudged him and said, 'I thought that you only had eyes for me.' Saini continued to stare at the dome. Realising that something had caught Saini's attention, Radhika asked, 'What is it, Ravi? What have you suddenly seen?'

'Do you see the pinnacle?' asked Saini.

Priya nodded. 'Sure. It has the familiar Islamic crescent on the top. What's bothering you?' she asked.

'Look at it closely,' said Saini. 'It's not merely a crescent with stars, as is the usual Islamic symbolism. Yes, the crescent is indeed present, but above it is a water pot containing bent mango leaves with the leaves supporting a coconut. Do you see what I am saying?'

Radhika gasped as she peered at the pinnacle with greater focus. For years, she had assumed that the symbol was entirely Islamic but had never paused to study it carefully. 'What exactly are you trying to say?' she asked.

'Look at the building itself. Does anything strike you about its shape and design?' he asked, continuing to stare at the monument.

'Well, it has four towers at the corners and a bulging dome in the centre,' said Radhika, keeping her voice light.

'No, no, forget the towers—or the dome—for the moment,' said Saini, impatiently. 'Just look at the shape of the structure! We all think that the Taj Mahal has a square layout but that's merely an illusion created by its square base and four corner minarets. When you observe the structure carefully you will see that it has eight facets—it's an octagon. Look at it again!'

'Why is the fact that it is octagonal so important?' asked Radhika, slightly confused by Saini's new obsession.

'The number eight is sacred to Hindus because it represents the four cardinal and four ordinal directions. But why should eight sides be of any relevance to a Muslim tomb? Look up again, Radhika.'

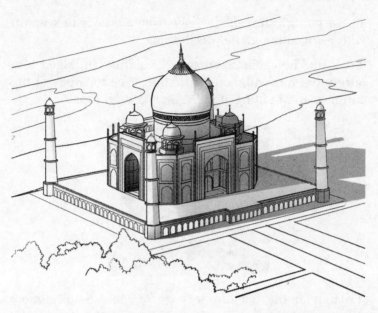

Radhika obeyed his instructions for fear of hurting his feelings, but she wasn't sure what exactly he wanted her to see. 'See the main dome?' he asked, pointing to it in the distance. 'That is not a naked dome. On top you have an inverted lotus flower—again a Hindu symbol!'

Saini suddenly caught Radhika by her hand and pulled her towards the main entrance arch of the monument. 'Where are we going?' she asked, as she trotted briskly to keep up with Saini, although he was limping.

'Look up,' he again commanded. Radhika indulged him once more but with some irritation. 'See the apex of the entrance arch? Sitting atop the arch is a red lotus!'

'Enough of the outside, let's go in,' said Saini, almost dragging Radhika along. They walked up the steps of the marble plinth on which the Taj Mahal stood and headed towards Mumtaz Mahal's cenotaph. As they approached it, Saini urgently whispered, 'Look at that. Do you see what I see?'

'What?' asked Radhika, now thoroughly disoriented by the rapid-fire questions and answers.

'Look at the enclosure that holds the cenotaphs of Mumtaz Mahal and Shah Jahan,' urged Saini. 'Notice the shape. It's an octagon—eight sides yet again! This preponderance of Hindu features in a Muslim shrine is incredible!'

'Why are the tombs off-centre?' asked Radhika.

'Because the central one is that of Mumtaz Mahal,' replied Saini. 'The Taj Mahal was never planned with a view to accommodating Shah Jahan too. So, when Shah Jahan's cenotaph was eventually placed side-by-side with that of Mumtaz Mahal, the graves began to look off-centre. The more important fact to note, though, is that these aren't the real tombs.'

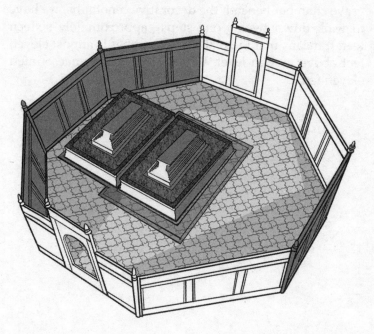

'What do you mean? Who lies buried there if not Shah Jahan and Mumtaz Mahal?' asked Radhika with some of her old asperity.

'What I meant was that the tombs one sees here on this level are merely decorative. The real graves lie one level below, and that is the next greatest mystery of this structure,' said Saini, pulling up a small sketch of the vertical layout of the Taj Mahal on his phone.

'To get from the garden level to the main terrace of the Taj Mahal we walk up steps that take us four feet higher,' explained Saini. 'We then climb the steps of the marble plinth. These steps ascend almost nineteen feet. We then ascend four more steps outside the cenotaph and two more steps in the doorway. This takes us up a further four feet. In all, we ascend twenty-seven feet from the garden to the level of the cenotaph. But to go down to the real grave chamber beneath the decorative cenotaphs, we have to walk down twenty-one steps—approximately sixteen feet. It means that the real grave chamber is almost eleven feet above garden level. What lies in those unaccounted eleven feet?'

101

Yudhistira ruled his kingdom according to the precepts laid down by dharma. Parikshit grew up to be a handsome young man. Dhritarastra and Gandhari continued to live in Hastinapur and Yudhistira did everything possible for their wellbeing. Eventually, the old blind king thought that it was time to give up the comforts of the palace and retire into the forests. 'Let's go, Gandhari,' he said to her. His half-brother, Vidura, decided to follow, and so did the Pandavas' mother, Kunti. Yudhistira tried to stop them but they were determined. One day, when they were resting in the forest, a fire broke out. 'Run!' shouted Dhritarastra as soon as he discovered that a forest fire had started. 'Why?' asked his wife. The old king considered the fact that they were at the end of their lives anyway. The elders thus continued to calmly sit in the forest, allowing the flames to consume them.

'What could be within those eleven feet?' asked Radhika, now visibly excited.

'Before we explore what could be there, let's just step back for a moment and understand the history of this structure a little better, shall we?' asked Saini, adopting his professorial demeanour.

Radhika smiled. 'Sure, Professor, why don't you enlighten me?' she said teasingly.

'In the Government of India's National Archives lies a document. It is called the *Badshahnama*—the official history of Shah Jahan written by the emperor's chronicler, Mullah Abdul Hamid Lahori.'

'And what does it say?' asked Radhika.

Saini smiled and said, 'It says that upon the death of Mumtaz Mahal, Raja Man Singh's palace in Agra —at that time owned by Raja Jaisingh, his grandson—was selected for burial of Arjumand Banu Begum alias Mumtaz-ul-Zamani—Mumtaz Mahal's real name. The *Badshahnama* says that although Raja Man Singh's family valued the property greatly as an ancestral heritage, they were agreeable to part with it gratis for the Emperor Shah Jahan. However, out of scruples that were so very essential in matters of bereavement and religious sanctity, Jaisingh was granted a piece of government land in return.'

'Are you telling me that this was a Hindu raja's palace at one time?' asked Radhika.

'Well, some of it,' responded Saini. 'We can't tell which parts are original and which were added on later. What we do know is that it belonged to the family of Raja Man Singh and that it was given to Shah Jahan so that he could create a final resting place for his queen.'

Radhika was quiet. Her head was reeling with all the information Saini had thrown at it. 'Come with me to the river bank,' said Saini. They quickly left the Taj complex and went to the riverbank.

'Ravi,' complained Radhika. 'You're dragging me around all over the place!'

Saini pulled out the notebook and read aloud from it.

Seek Shiv at the highest point, Seek Vish by the sea; Give up your quest, for they are one, only your heart can see. When

creation and destruction are unified, And 894 reigns supreme;
Where coconuts and lotuses adorn my crown, by the river I shall
be. Cast aside hatred and learn to love, Man Singh says to you.
Search my temple of seven floors, and you will find me too. You
seek the stone that turns lead to gold, but verily do not find;
search instead for the faithful stone that can truly transform
your mind.

'*Where coconuts and lotuses adorn my crown, by the river I shall*
be! You just saw the dome of the Taj—it has an inverted
lotus. The Islamic pinnacle on top also has a coconut and
kalash. Here, we are standing right *by the river*—along the
banks of the Yamuna. The inscription was not pointing us
towards Vrindavan, but towards the Taj Mahal!' said Saini,
by now thoroughly electrified.

'But the Taj Mahal is not a seven-floor structure,' argued
Radhika.

'Radhika, you are making the same mistake that all casual
observers make. See, from here you now have a riverside
view of the Taj Mahal,' said Saini pointing to its dome.

'The marble structure that we call the Taj Mahal is apparently three-storeyed—to the casual observer. But if we add the grave level below the ornamental cenotaph, as well as the large hall in the dome, we can recalculate that the structure is actually five-storeyed. Below the plinth are two more storeys that reach down here to the river level. Behind this row of arches are twenty-two sealed rooms. They were sealed during Shah Jahan's times and have been never opened since. The point I am making is that the Taj Mahal is actually a seven-storeyed structure! *Cast aside hatred and learn to love, Man Singh says to you. Search my temple of seven floors, and you will find me too!'*

102

In the meantime, in Dwarka, my foolish son, Sambha, had decided to play a prank on a group of visiting sages — Vishvamitra, Kanva and Narada. His friends disguised him as a pregnant woman and asked the sages whether the child to be born would be male or female. The sages, angered because they had seen through the deception, cursed all the Yadava clans. 'Neither male, nor female. You shall deliver an iron bar, one that will spell the final destruction of the entire Yadava tribe!' they thundered. Gandhari's curse on me was playing itself out through the sages. Soon, an iron rod emerged from Sambha's thigh. Balarama, who was nearby, panicked, ground it into powder and threw it into the seas along with a small piece that refused to be ground. The powder was washed ashore to Prabhas Patan, where it mutated into reeds that were strong as iron bars, awaiting the final theatre of destruction.

'But the Taj Mahal is not a Hindu temple, it's an Islamic mausoleum,' countered Radhika.

'Yes, but it was a palace *before* it became a tomb. And every palace would have had a temple. Most importantly, this was a property that belonged to Raja Man Singh. The evidence is all there!' insisted Saini, excitedly.

'But why does Man Singh talk about creation and destruction being unified?' asked Radhika.

'Did you notice the tiling pattern as we approached the monument?' asked Saini, hardly apropos of what Radhika had just said.

'How could I have?' asked Radhika caustically. 'You were constantly prodding me to look up at the dome!'

'Let's go back,' said Saini, and they returned to the Taj Mahal's gardens. Radhika was quick to spot, this time round, what Saini had been alluding to. The tiling work had six-pointed stars embedded as a pattern within!

'As I told you earlier, the six-pointed star represents the union of Shiv and Shakti,' said Saini. 'The coming-together of male and female is the starting point of creation. The symbolism of the Sanskrit inscription is to be found in its entirety at the Taj Mahal. The mausoleum not only represents death—because it is a memorial containing the bodies of Shah Jahan and Mumtaz Mahal—but also represents the rising of beauty from the muddy riverbank of the Yamuna. Creation and destruction in one place! *When creation and destruction are unified...*'

'And 894 reigns supreme...' interrupted Radhika. 'You cannot ignore the line that talks about the number 894. How does that fit in with the location?' asked Radhika.

'You obviously do not know much about mystical numbers,' said Saini, with a superior air. 'I've had a chance to think about it and this is what struck me. Among Hindus, 108 is considered the holiest of numbers. You will find that 18, 108, 1008, 10008—and further similar variations—are all considered sacred. The *Mahabharata* has 18 chapters; there were 18 Yadava clans of Krishna; Jarasandha attacked Mathura 18 times; the Mahabharata war lasted 18 days; 18 armies fought the great battle; there are 18 chapters in each of our *Vedas*; there are 18 *Puranas*; there were 18 *Maharathi*—or exalted—warriors in the Mahabharata war; there are 18 chapters in the *Bhagwad Gita*...'

'Yes, yes, I know. But how does 108 relate to 894?' asked Radhika.

'Have some patience, Radhika,' admonished Saini gently, but with the same patronising air. 'All shall be revealed soon. 108 is holy for the Hindus but in the Islam of the Indian subcontinent, the number 786 is considered very holy, almost the equivalent of Allah.'

'Why?' asked Radhika, befuddled by the mysterious numerical theories being presented to her.

'In Arabic, there is a method known as the *Abjad*—or ordinal—method. Each letter has an arithmetic value assigned to it from one to one thousand. The very first verse of the Qur'an is *Bismillah al-Rahman al-Rahim*, and if you take the numeric values of all the letters of this first verse in accordance with the Abjad order, the total is 786,' explained Saini.

103

In the thirty-sixth year after the Mahabharata war, Balarama and I went along with the entire Yadava clan to Prabhas Patan to honour those who had died at Kurukshetra. After the religious ceremonies were over, our fellow Yadavas became drunk on wine, and an argument ensued between the various clans—Vrishnis, Bhojas, Kukuras, Chedis, and Shainyas—regarding the rights and wrongs committed by the parties to the Mahabharata war. Intoxicated and angry, the men turned the argument into a violent brawl in which they plucked out the reeds that had mutated from the iron powder and struck each other. Balarama and I could not bear the sight of our near and dear ones killing each other, and ran into the forests. No one survived. The first part of Gandhari's curse—that I would lose all my loved ones and would watch helplessly as my clan self-destructed—had come true.

'So 786 is sacred in Islam because of the Abjad value of the first Qur'anic verse?' asked Radhika.

'There is another explanation offered by Vedic scholars about the Islamic 786,' answered Saini. 'As you know, the modern numerals that we use in the Western world are commonly called *Arabic numerals*. What is often forgotten is the fact that Arabic numerals originally started out as

Hindu numerals. What the world uses today—including the zero —was the numeral system developed by Indian mathematicians in which a sequence of digits could be read as a number. Persian mathematicians in India adopted the Hindu numeral system and passed it on to the Arabs further west. The Arabs shared the system with Europe during the Middle Ages, and hence, the system came to be known as Arabic.'

'So the numerals that we commonly use today across the world—zero through nine—are actually Hindu numbers?' asked Radhika.

'Yes, absolutely. Now if I take the three digits—7, 8 and 6—and write them in Hindu numerals, what do they look like?' asked Saini, as he took out a pocketbook and pen and noted down the three digits.

'Now, see what happens when I bring these three numerals together,' said Saini. Radhika looked on in amazement as he combined the three digits together in a formation that looked very familiar.

'You will notice that the three digits—7, 8 and 6—when brought together resemble the Hindu Om. Actually, they represent the mirror image of an Om,' amended Saini as he continued drawing. 'Finally, flip around the mirror-image

Om and you get the Hindu Om that we are all familiar with,' he said, proudly displaying his artistic skills.

'So what's the connection between 786 and Om?' asked Radhika, puzzled even more by this further demonstration.

'It's impossible to say. Theories abound. Purist Islamic scholars denounce 786 completely. Their view is that the Prophet Mohammad was completely against astrology and numerology. The practice continues to be popular in most of south Asia, though, with many Muslims choosing to make 786 part of their vehicle's licence plates or phone numbers. Many of them write the number 786 on the top of important agreements and letters, almost in the manner that Hindus draw the Om symbol on top of documents— with a view to invoking God's blessings,' said Saini.

'You still haven't told me how the three digits 894 mentioned in the Sanskrit inscription relate to all of this,' said Radhika, who was by now quite weary of numbers.

'It's simple. The Taj Mahal represents the age of Akbar, Jehangir and Shah Jahan, when Hindus and Muslims had begun to learn to live with one another,' replied Saini. 'The fact that prominent Hindus such as Raja Man Singh, Tansen, Birbal and Todar Mal were among the *navaratnas* of Akbar's court is testament to that fact. Akbar contributed to building Man Singh's Vrindavan temple. Man Singh's family contributed their property in Agra to Shah Jahan to build Mumtaz Mahal's tomb. The number 894 is simply the addition of 108 and 786! The Taj Mahal represents Hindu-Muslim creative energies at their very best!'

104

Balarama knew it was time to return to the heavens. He sat under a tree and meditated and gradually allowed his life to slip out with his breath. Some moments later, I saw a serpent emerging from the inert body of Balarama. My brother had returned to his original form of Lord Sheshnag. I knew that it was time for my departure from earth, too. I sat under a banyan tree, crossed my left foot over my right one and absentmindedly shook my foot, as I revisited vignettes from my life. Seeing my shaking foot through the bushes, a hunter called Jara mistook it for the ear of a deer and shot an arrow in its direction. The arrowhead was made from the only iron piece that Balarama had been unable to grind down. Thrown into the sea, it had been swallowed by a fish and Jara had found the piece in its belly. The poor nervous hunter, upon realising what he had done, could not believe the heinous act that he had committed, but I blessed him and told him not to grieve—he had simply been an instrument in fulfilling my destiny. The second part of Gandhari's curse—that I would die like an animal at the hands of a hunter—had also come true. I allowed the poison to wash through my body, permitted my praana to slip out, and returned to Vaikuntha. My sojourn as Krishna—Vishnu's eighth incarnation on earth—was over.

'This particular Sanskrit inscription on the base plate by Raja Man Singh was already available with your friend Varshney. Why did he send us off on a wild-goose-chase to Mount Kailash and Somnath if he knew that the secret was to be found right here in the Taj Mahal?' asked Radhika.

'But was Varshney really pointing us towards either of those places?' asked Saini. 'I'm not so sure. Let's review Varshney's note again, shall we?' He flipped back to the page where he had rewritten Varshney's gobbledegook in reverse order. Varshney's cryptic message said:

Redraw numeral swastika, smart but stressed pupils! Keep stats, no animal parts. X on left-top at tip. Lived, laid, relaid in X. Kalash or Kailash it is? Raja surrender. Six are tips in a star. And blue water beside. Shankar elated.

'The first step was to redraw the swastika as a mathematical magic square and eliminate the images while keeping the numbers. He then asked us to look at the left-top tip. That gave us the number eight. Because we were so obsessed with Somnath and Mount Kailash, we imagined that Varshney was either referring to the number of times that Somnath had been rebuilt or to the number of monasteries built around Lake Mansarovar. But in the sentence *Lived, laid, relaid in X*, Varshney was referring to the tombs of Shah Jahan and Mumtaz Mahal that had been buried within eight walls—eight walls of the cenotaph and eight walls of the octagonal Taj Mahal itself! I was a fool to not see it sooner! Similarly, with the line *Kalash or Kailash it is?* Varshney was pointing us in the direction of the pinnacle that could pass off either as a kalash or as a pinnacle. We ended up thinking that he was referring either to the kalash of Somnath or to Mount Kailash.'

'But what about the line where he says *Raja surrender?*' asked Radhika. 'There was no battle over the Taj Mahal, as in the instance of Somnath or Tibet. What surrender is Varshney speaking of?'

'Varshney is alluding to the fact that Raja Man Singh's family had to surrender the property—the land and structures on the banks of the Yamuna—to the Mughal emperor Shah Jahan,' explained Saini. 'The rest of Varshney's message fits in perfectly with what I've just shown you. *Six are tips in a star*—you just observed the six-pointed star in the floor tiles of the Taj. *And blue water beside*—the Taj is built on the banks of the Yamuna.'

'But the final line, *Shankar elated,* does not fit in. The Taj Mahal has nothing to do with Shankar—or Shiv.'

Saini smiled. 'Don't you want to know what Raja Man Singh's palace in Agra was called?'

'What?' asked Radhika, completely perplexed.

'It was called *Tejo Mahalay*,' replied Saini.

'Tejo Mahalay? What does it mean?' asked Radhika.

'It literally translates to the *Great Abode of Tej*. The Rajput and Jat kings of the time used to call Shiv by the name *Tejaji*,' explained Saini. 'Hence the name of the palace meant *Great Abode of Shiv*. Calling a palace the residence of a deity was fashionable among Hindu royalty. Even today you can visit Udaipur and drop in at the *Shiv Niwas* Palace—again literally meaning the very same thing—the *Abode of Shiv*.'

'Are you trying to tell me that the name Taj Mahal is derived from Tejo Mahalay and not from Mumtaz Mahal's name?' asked Radhika.

'Oh, absolutely,' replied Saini. 'Read the *Badshah-nama*. Her real name was Arjumand Banu Begum also known as Mumtaz-ul-Zamani. The term Mumtaz Mahal was not used even by the court chronicle. Do you know how the city of Agra got its name?'

'How?' asked Radhika.

'The temple on the palace grounds of Raja Man Singh was dedicated to *Agreshwar Mahadev Nagnatheshwar*. The city derived its name from *Agreshwar*—yet another name for Shiv,' replied Saini.

'And if the name of this place was indeed Tejo Mahalay, then it follows that Varshney's clue about Shiv was absolutely accurate,' murmured Radhika softly, almost to herself. 'But why would Man Singh's family give up a palace property—possibly bearing a temple dedicated to Shiv—to the Mughals for a tomb?'

'I can assure you that they gave it up willingly and enthusiastically,' said Saini, smiling slyly.

105

My father, Vasudeva, heard of the terrible events at Prabhas Patan and died of grief and shock. Dwarka was now a scene of thousands of funeral pyres and wailing Yadava women. Arjuna rushed to Dwarka to look after the women and children that remained, but he was too late. The rains came lashing down and the seas rose. Waves pounded the walls and fortifications of my beloved Dwarka until the foundations melted. Within a short time, the sea was calm again, but there was no sign of my fabulous city, which lay submerged beneath the now calm waters.

'Willingly and enthusiastically? Why?' asked Radhika. 'And if an ancient secret lies buried here at the Taj Mahal, where do we dig for it?'

'That's precisely it, Radhika. We can't dig,' said Saini. 'This is now a sacred spot built to honour the dead. One can't desecrate it. And that's exactly what Raja Man Singh's family knew. This was the very reason that they gave up the palace so easily to the Mughal emperor. In an environment where temples could be destroyed on a whim, they concluded that the best way to preserve the secret of the Syamantaka was to have a Muslim mausoleum over it. It was the ultimate insurance policy!'

'If we can't dig for direct evidence, is there any corroborating pointer that the Syamantaka lies here?' asked Radhika.

'Do you know that the gardens around the Taj Mahal were planted with very specific shrubs?' asked Saini. 'Mentioned in the records are *ketaki, jai, juhi, champa, maulashree, harshringar* and *bel*. Bel has a radioprotective quality. Harshringar is used for treating respiratory ailments. Ketaki is used for treating blood disorders—these were all medicinal herbs! They were planted at the Taj because the the Syamantaka would have released radiation and these herbs would have neutralised the effects of it.'

For once, Radhika had nothing to say.

'Another interesting nugget to consider is this,' continued Saini. 'In the *Badshahnamah* we are told that in 1632, a fence of solid gold was placed around Mumtaz Mahal's sarcophagus. It contained over forty thousand *tolas* of pure gold. Some years later the fence was no longer seen at the site. Why? Isn't it possible that the railing had not started out as gold but only transmuted to gold later on and hence needed to be removed for security reasons? Alternatively, isn't it also possible that the railing was originally gold but transmuted to an alternative metal and was thus removed because it was no longer in keeping with the richness of the surroundings?'

'Is there any way to be sure that the transmutation happened?' asked Radhika.

'There is one further piece of evidence that points the way—the white marble of the Taj Mahal,' said Saini.

'How does the marble tell us anything about the Syamantaka?' asked Radhika.

'Marble is the end-product of a process of meta-morphosis of limestone under terrific heat and pressure. The purer the original limestone, the purer the whiteness of the marble.

Over the last two decades there has been a vociferous debate over the yellowing of the Taj Mahal on account of pollution in Agra as well as acid rain,' explained Saini.

'Yes, I heard that many industries were shifted away from the precincts of the Taj Mahal because of this,' said Radhika.

'But ask B B Lal, a scientist with the Archaeological Survey of India, and you will get a different opinion. He has stated in writing that chemical and petrographic studies have shown that the marble of the Taj Mahal has not undergone mineralogical alteration, nor is there any evidence of chemical weathering. No impact of acidic gases in the air has been detected, as there is hardly any perceptible sulphation of the marble!'

'If it isn't particulate matter, it could be acid rain,' countered Radhika.

'The National Environmental Engineering Research Institute—or NEERI—published a report on the basis of which polluting industries were ordered to move out of the vicinity,' replied Saini. 'Funnily enough NEERI's claims regarding acid rain were contradicted by its own data. For example, data on rainwater quality showed pH values between 6.1 and 7.7—a perfectly neutral range, indicating that there was no acid rain.'

'So if it isn't the pollution or acid rain, what exactly *is* causing the Taj Mahal to turn yellow?' asked Radhika. Saini smiled once more.

'A research study carried out some years ago showed that when marble statues in Europe were cleaned using laser irradiation, the surface colour of the marble underwent a change,' said Saini.

'You're not saying what I think you're saying, are you?' asked Radhika.

Saini laughed outright this time. 'I'm saying precisely what you think I'm saying. The higher Gieger counter readings in Agra on Rathore's map were due to radiation. Stones such as granite and marble have natural radiation properties but no one had bothered to check whether the radiation from the marble was within ordinary limits. It is this slightly elevated radiation that is causing the colour change—radiation from a source that lies somewhere within this marble edifice! Let's call Rathore and tell him to come over quickly,' said Saini as he dialled Rathore's number.

At that moment Saini felt the cold steel of a snub-nosed revolver against his back. 'Do not move,' hissed the voice, pressing the gun harder into Saini's back. From the corner of his eye, Saini saw that there was another figure standing behind Radhika too. Mataji and Taarak were back from their muddy grave in Vrindavan! Saini quickly slipped his phone into his trouser pocket.

'You thought that you could get rid of us by leaving that CBI dog—Sunil Garg—to kill us. It's now our chance to get even,' spat Priya as she held Radhika at gunpoint.

'Where is Sunil Garg? What have you done with him?' Radhika demanded to know.

'I have found that corrupt men are the easiest people to do business with,' said Mataji with a demonic smile on her face. 'While he was vigorously shovelling earth down the temple pit to bury us alive, I persuasively explained the magical powers of the Syamantaka stone to him. He soon realised it was worth his while to partner us. He was given the job of following you both to see your ultimate destination.'

'It has been a pleasure getting to know you both,' said Taarak, 'but now it's time for us to bid adieu to both of you. Please start walking towards the riverbank. Do not even think of raising an alarm because Mataji and I shall not hesitate to pull the trigger on either one of you.'

With a sharp nudge, Taarak indicated to Saini that he should move. Cautiously, Saini and Radhika began to walk back towards the banks of the Yamuna with Taarak and Priya following at close quarters so as to prevent the general public from knowing that they were holding guns. Within a few minutes they were back at the lowest point of the Taj Mahal edifice—the red sandstone rooms overlooking the Yamuna. Tourists never ventured to this part of the monument and the stretch along the river was isolated except for a solitary figure who stood in front of one of the massive arches that had been sealed during Shah Jahan's reign.

Taarak waved at the figure from the distance and the figure waved back. Sunil Garg was awaiting the arrival of high dividend prisoners.

106

The survivors clung to boats to reach the mainland, from where Arjuna took them to Hastinapur. On the way, they were attacked by wandering thugs. Arjuna raised his Gandiva to annihilate them but was unable to use it. It was only then that the knowledge burst upon him that all his power had emanated from me. He fell to his knees, sobbing like a child. When the tears stopped, he saw a vision of me as a toddler, gurgling for milk. I was reminding him that life continues and that there is always hope for a new day and a fresh start. Arjuna gathered the surviving women and children and took them to Mathura—the city from where I had brought the Yadavas to Dwarka. Many years later, my great-grandson, Vajranabhi, would become chief of Mathura.

'Welcome to the newest prison facility of Agra,' mocked Sunil Garg as Saini and Radhika approached the archway where he stood.

'You shall soon be history, Garg,' admonished Radhika. 'The world shall soon know that you were working against the interests of the CBI and were part of Sir Khan's team.'

'Hmm. History—such a fascinating word,' replied Garg, ominously. 'I think that the English dictionary calls it a record of past events and times, especially in connection with the human race. The question in my mind—Radhikaji—is this. Who will write *your* history? Who will tell the world that besides Mumtaz Mahal and Shah Jahan there are two other people buried inside the Taj Mahal? Who will inform tourists that these two other people are Radhika Singh and Ravi Mohan Saini? Visitors will know of the love between Shah Jahan and Mumtaz Mahal but will never know of the love between Radhika and Ravi. What a terrible shame… all that passion entirely wasted!'

Ravi gulped. Garg, Priya and Taarak planned to lock them alive in one of the forgotten rooms of the Taj!

'Enough small talk,' said Priya to Garg gruffly. 'Let's get this over with.'

Garg pushed the old arched door and it creaked open. The room was one among a network of twenty-two that had remained shut since Mughal times. It was musty, humid and stank of animal excrement. Saini suddenly felt a flutter of wings against his face. Bats! These rooms were infested with bats!

'Welcome to the Hotel California,' said Garg with deliberate cruelty. 'You can check out any time you like but you can never leave.'

'Why would you want to kill us?' asked Radhika. 'Professor Saini has already discovered the location of Krishna's most prized possession. Why eliminate the very people who could lead you to it?'

'I cannot afford to have both of you alive,' said Garg to Radhika. 'You threatened to expose me if I didn't do what you wanted. It's my turn to make sure that you can never open your mouths ever again. As for the stone, forget it. A legacy of Krishna—who was a manifestation of Vishnu—would never be left in a palace named after Shiv. Quit wasting everyone's time.'

'Shiv is merely a form of Vish and Vish is merely a form of Shiv. Shiv resides in the heart of Vish and Vish resides in that of Shiv. At least do your homework before you jump to conclusions!' retorted Saini.

'So Vish and Shiv are the same?' asked Radhika purposely, hoping that any extended discussion would buy them time.

'To understand what Shiv and Vish are, we need to go back to the creation of the universe,' replied Saini. 'Modern science says that at the beginning of time there was a great explosion—the *Big Bang*. Around 13.7 billion years ago, all energy was concentrated at a single point—physicists call this point a *singularity*—and this single point has been in a state of expansion ever since. It is from this single event that all the energy of the universe—and consequently all matter—came into existence.'

'Why are we wasting time?' asked Taarak impatiently. 'Let's get this over with and not lose more time in pointless conversation!' But Saini and Radhika's strategy had succeeded in getting Mataji hooked. She gestured Taarak to keep his impatience in check.

'Now, consider the Big Bang in conjunction with Albert Einstein's theory that $E=mc^2$,' continued Saini, ignoring Taarak's outburst. 'Simply put, energy and matter are interchangeable. In fact, subsequent exploration into atomic structure has taught scientists that matter is actually an illusion and that atoms are composed of *nothingness*—energy fields that merely create the illusion of matter. In simple terms, all matter that makes up the universe is actually energy. Einstein's equation also tells us that energy cannot be created or destroyed. It can merely be converted from one form to another, or transferred from one place to another.'

'Then how can we credit the Big Bang for having *created* all the energy of the universe—if energy cannot be created or destroyed? There seems to be an apparent contradiction between the Big Bang and Einstein's theories,' said Radhika.

'Precisely,' said Saini. 'But by observing distant stars, astronomers have found that their light patterns stay constant, but move further down the light spectrum over time. This means that the stars under observation are moving further and further away over time, thus clearly proving that our universe is continuously expanding outwards, and consequently the Big Bang theory.'

'So the fact that the universe expanded and is continuing to expand is proven?' asked Radhika.

'Yes,' said Saini. 'But the question that no physicist has been able to answer is this: from what source did we derive the energy that was within the singularity that exploded? The problem with the Big Bang model is that it explains the expansion of a single point into the universe as we know it, but doesn't explain where the energy required for the Big Bang originally came from. This is where the *Upanishads* provide a wonderful framework.'

'What do the *Upanishads* say?' asked Radhika.

The answer came from Priya who had been listening to the conversation between Radhika and Saini. 'According to Hindu scriptures, the universe never came into existence at any given point of time. It always existed, but remained in a state of perpetual flux,' said Priya. 'What we call *the universe* is simply *the present universe*. Each universe starts with a Big Bang, and expands to a point, before it starts shrinking. The universe eventually collapses back into the singularity from which it had emerged and a new expanding universe begins once again. This is the reason that 108 is considered sacred. *One*—represents the singularity from which the universe emerges, *zero*—the egg or *anda* of the present universe, and *eight*—infinity or the maximum extent of expansion in the eight directions from which contraction must happen.'

Saini nodded, agreeing with his former student. 'This theoretical framework within the *Upanishads* conforms perfectly with Einstein's theory that energy cannot be created or destroyed. Most importantly, it solves the perennial question: what was there before the singularity?'

Garg and Taarak looked at each other helplessly. The devious Saini and resourceful Radhika had succeeded in pulling Priya into this useless conversation.

'How does this relate to Vish and Shiv?' asked Radhika.

'What is the Sanskrit word for universe?' countered Saini. 'In ancient Hindu texts, the universe is called *Brahamanda*. The word Brahamanda is derived from two words— *Brahama* and *Anda*. Brahama means *expanding* and anda means *egg*. It's a fitting description of the expanding egg-shaped universe as described by the Big Bang theory. Vish simply represents *expansion* of energy into matter and Shiv represents *contraction* of matter back to energy—the energy of the universe remaining constant and unchanged.'

'So the ancient seers of India explained the Big Bang ages before the theory was proposed to the modern world by Edwin Hubble?' asked Radhika.

'Yes,' replied Saini. 'With a few modifications, Hindu scriptures are in perfect conformity with the Big Bang and Einstein's equation.'

'I hate to interrupt this fascinating conversation,' said Garg caustically, 'but I have back-to-back appointments on my day-planner today. I must get going.' He waved his gun in the direction of Radhika and Saini. 'Sit down on the floor,' he instructed. Overcoming her aversion to the excrement-covered floor, Radhika sat down cautiously. Saini followed.

'Tie them up and then gag them,' instructed Garg. Taarak stepped forward and deftly bound their hands and legs with duct tape. He proceeded to gag them with more tape.

'Excellent!' commented Garg. 'You have trained him well,' said Garg to Priya as he noticed the ease with which Taarak carried out his task. 'C'mon let's get out of here and leave these two sweethearts to do whatever it is that they want to do,' he said, walking towards the arched door, followed by Taarak and Priya. Saini and Radhika struggled against their restraints in panic. Rising Yamuna levels often flooded these rooms during certain hours and there was very little possibility of them being found alive if they were locked up in these long-forgotten chambers.

'Isn't this a touching sight?' asked Garg, with a parting leer. 'The monument of love now has a new pair of lovebirds. Till death do us part...'

The arched doorway opened and for a brief moment the room was bathed in sunlight. Garg, Priya and Taarak stepped out. The massive teak door was slowly pulled shut and Saini and Radhika heard a rusty padlock being cajoled into position. In a moment the squeaking stopped and then there was complete darkness. A few minutes later, Saini felt his trousers drenched. He looked down and strained his eyes against the darkness. It was the waters of the Yamuna. The river was in spate that fateful day.

107

Parikshit was soon old enough to handle the administration of the kingdom. The Pandava brothers, along with Draupadi renounced their kingdom and headed for the mountains. They started climbing Mount Mandara with a mongrel tailing them. The first to stumble and fall was Draupadi. Even though she was duty-bound to love all five husbands equally, she had preferred Arjuna, manipulated Bhima and lusted after Karana. Next, Sahadeva fell. His intellect had made him arrogant. A short while later, Nakula fell. His good looks had made him uncaring towards the feelings of others. A few steps later, Arjuna fell. Even though he had been a great archer, he had remained envious of other archers, including Karana. Finally, Bhima fell. He had been a glutton all his life and had eaten without feeding others. Yudhistira and the dog were the only ones who reached the gates of heaven. The gods welcomed Yudhistira but on the condition that he leave the dog outside. Yudhistira declared that he would renounce heaven rather than give up the dog who had earned as much right to be there. The gods smiled and told Yudhistira that the threatened exclusion of the dog had been yet another test. They welcomed him in, and showered him with petals.

'We've left them to die inside but we still don't know the location of the Syamantaka stone,' said Priya as they walked away from the riverbank. 'We could spend years searching the Taj Mahal and never discover it. Do you think that we should go back and take Saini's help?'

'He's bluffing,' said Garg. 'He knows only as much as we do. He knows that the Syamantaka is some-where here within the Taj complex but has no clue of the exact location.' The trio hurried towards the steps leading from the riverbank up to the Taj Mahal.

'Stay where you are, put your weapons down and your hands up in the air,' shouted Rathore through a megaphone as he ran down the steps from the opposite direction. On his right and left were over a dozen khaki-clad policemen holding rifles. Garg raised his handgun to take a shot at Rathore but before he could squeeze the trigger he screamed in agony as his right hand was shattered by a bullet. He fell to the ground sobbing in pain. Priya and Taarak knew that the game was up. They put down their weapons slowly and raised their hands in surrender. Within minutes, all three were in a police van headed to the District Jail of Agra.

Rathore ran towards the sealed rooms along the banks of the Yamuna. 'Check all the doors to see which one has been recently opened,' he yelled to the men who were now wading knee-deep in river water to reach the sealed doors of the sandstone structure that constituted the foundation of the marble Taj.

'Sir, this door has been opened and locked again. The lock is brand-new,' shouted one of the men.

'Break the lock open!' commanded Rathore.

The lock was broken and the heavy door was pushed open. Given the fact that there was over three feet of water held back by the door, it went rushing into the room as soon as the door was ajar. As light flooded into the room, Rathore saw the figures of Saini and Radhika standing in a corner, huddled together. He had reached them well in time. The water would have drowned them if they had remained locked in for a few hours more.

'Thank heavens you decided to phone me and leave the call connected,' said Rathore to Saini as he breathlessly cut open the restraints that bound and gagged Saini and Radhika.

'This is the second time that you've saved my life,' said Saini gratefully to Rathore.

'Let's hope that I never have to do it again... I hope that the duty sergeant locks up those three and forgets the key,' said Rathore with feeling, as he led Saini and Radhika out of the waterlogged room and into sunshine.

The police team quickly arranged blankets and tea for them and they gratefully sat down on the steps leading to the Taj, sipping the comforting tea.

'We still don't have the Syamantaka,' said Rathore dejectedly.

'I know the answer,' said Saini simply.

Radhika and Rathore stared wide-eyed at Saini in disbelief. 'You *know* where it lies? Then why are we wasting time here? Let's get to it!' said Rathore.

Saini smiled at them. 'Much has been written about the ornamental cenotaph and the real grave chamber several feet below it,' said Saini. 'There has also been much speculation about the twenty-two rooms that can be accessed from the banks of the Yamuna. The fact, though, is that all of these places can be accessed via passages or doors—as we have just seen. The Syamantaka was far too valuable to have been left in spaces that could eventually be accessed. No, if the Syamantaka was kept anywhere, it would have to be at a location that would remain sealed to future generations.'

'And where would that be?' asked Rathore.

'Give me your phone,' said Saini to Rathore. Saini went to the internet browser of the smartphone and pulled up a vertical plan of the Taj Mahal.

'See this?' he asked, pointing to the image of the Taj Mahal on the screen. 'Everyone admires the Taj Mahal for its beautiful dome—the most outstanding feature of this monument. What is not known to most people is the fact that the Taj Mahal boasts a double-dome, a false ceiling inside a large, outer skin. So while the outer dome retains its imposing volume, the inside has comfortable proportions which would otherwise be cavernous.'

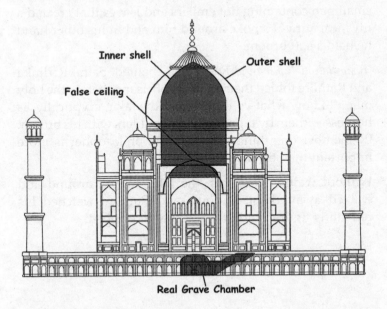

'Are you saying that the Syamantaka is located in the room below the dome?' asked Radhika.

'No, that can be accessed. I'm talking about the space between the inner shell and outer shell. That space is entirely sealed and there is no way to access it without damaging the dome itself,' said Saini.

'So we've travelled the length and breadth of India searching for the Syamantaka and now that we're at the location where it lies, we can't reach it?' asked Radhika, feeling let down.

At that moment, the discussion between Saini, Radhika and Rathore was interrupted by a Muslim fakir. On his head was a green skullcap that had the first line from the Qu'ran embroidered in gold. A long white beard flowed from his chin to his chest. He wore a white kurta that had seen better days and around his neck hung several chains with an assortment of *taweez* lockets. In one hand he held a small pan containing hot embers and leaves that created a mystical aura of smoke around him and in his other hand he held a soft broom.

'*Bismillah al-Rahman al-Rahim!*' he chanted. Saini, Radhika and Rathore folded their hands in obeisance before the holy man. 'I know what you seek,' said the fakir, cryptically, as he blessed them by tapping their shoulders with his broom. 'Remember one thing though… the philosopher is more important than the stone.'

Without waiting for alms, the fakir turned around and walked away. Saini, Radhika and Rathore watched his retreating figure. And then the penny dropped!

Having reached heaven, Yudhistira was shocked to find that his one hundred Kaurava cousins were present, while his wife and brothers—including Karana—had been consigned to hell. He asked to be taken to where they were. He was very angry that Duryodhana and his ninety-nine brothers were enjoying the pleasures of heaven while his brothers and wife were disallowed that privilege. I appeared before Yudhistira and said, 'You ruled their lands for thirty-six years and still did not give up your anger. You call yourself a son of Dharma and still cannot be dispassionate— how can you hope to attain heaven?' Yudhistira understood, then, that everything in the world is made from me. Understanding that everyone and everything is divine, was the mark of a true yogi—one who had understood that the philosopher and the stone were made of the very same stuff! He had passed his final test. Thereupon Yudhistira, his brothers and Draupadi moved in to heaven.

'Did you have the same sense of déjà vu that I just did?' asked Saini of Radhika and Rathore. 'Why did I get the feeling that this had happened before?'

'Because it had,' replied Radhika. 'At Mount Kailash we met a half-naked sadhu who said the exact words to us—*the philosopher is more important than the stone*. Before we could ask him what it meant he had danced away—somewhat high on charas!'

'That's bloody strange,' said Rathore. 'When Chhedi and I were in Somnath, we were met by a pujari who mouthed the identical words. It's spooky!'

Saini thought about it for a moment and then started laughing. Both Radhika and Rathore watched him, bemused. Had Saini finally lost it? Had all the stress of the past few days made him utterly insane? Saini eventually calmed down and explained himself.

'We came here thinking that we would find the Syamantaka—the philosopher's stone that was used by alchemists to turn base metals into gold, right?' he asked.

'That's right,' said Radhika. 'But you now say that there is no way to reach it. The Taj Mahal is a sacred tomb and cannot be desecrated. Moreover, the Syamantaka is located in the secret panel between the inner and outer shells of the dome and that place is impossible to reach.'

'We know that the goal of alchemy is transformation from lower forms to higher forms,' began Saini. 'But it is the uninitiated who think that this means transforming lead to gold. On the contrary, alchemy is about transforming yourself—making yourself a better person. The stone is irrelevant, it's the transformation that it brings in the person who meditates upon it that is much more relevant. *The philosopher is more important than the stone!*'

'So, the Syamantaka has no magical properties?' asked Radhika.

'The point I'm making is that every stone is a Syamantaka,' said Saini. 'When we stand before an image inside a temple and pray fervently, we end up transforming ourselves through our own positive vibrations. The stone miraculously turns magical. The real alchemy happens inside us. That's where the magic is!'

'But there are many temples where people flock to worship precisely because the idol is said to have special powers. Many people have been the beneficiaries of such divine intervention,' said Rathore.

'It's not because of the stone but because of the philosopher who uses it,' said Saini. 'When thousands of people stand before a stone idol and pray to it, they end up harmonising their energy. Energy and matter are the very same thing according to Einstein and the *Upanishads*—but thoughts, mind, and spirit are also energy. Victor Hugo once said, "Where the telescope ends, the microscope begins, and who can say which has the wider vision?" What he meant was that both the telescope and the microscope help us peer into exactly the same phenomena—bundles of energy in constant motion. Our collective energies make miracles happen, not the stone idol.'

'So the Syamantaka is not a nuclear isotope that changed the Somnath pillars from lead to gold or magically transformed the handrail around Mumtaz Mahal's tomb?' asked Radhika, the disappointment evident in her voice.

'It may very well have been,' said Saini. 'But that was not the reason for its power. The power came from the millions of devotees who believed that it indeed had the power to transform their lives. By simply believing that their lives could be transformed, they succeeded in converting their thoughts into reality.'

It was a quiet moment of reflection for the three people who stood near the Taj Mahal.

The monument began to change colour from white to a golden hue as the sun began to set. Saini reached out and held Radhika's hand. Rathore noticed and smiled.

He was happy that his boss had finally found happiness in her otherwise empty life. If there was a miraculous transformation to be observed, then it was the one that he was seeing right before his very eyes. Rathore quietly got up from the spot where he had been seated on the steps. He slowly walked away, leaving Radhika and Saini to admire the world's finest monument devoted to love.

It was alchemy in progress.

References & Acknowledgements

In my quest to produce a work of fiction that was based upon sound research, I depended on several sources. Some of these ran contrary to the fictional premise that I wrote about but they were still invaluable in developing the construct. Listed below are the books, papers, journals, websites, blogs, and audio/video resources that I used to write my novel. Material was not necessarily used from all of these sources but many of them opened the doors to further research and hence I have attempted to keep this list as complete as possible.

Books

1. *Ancient Atomic Bombs*; Jason Colavito; eBook, 2011. Download link: http://www.jasoncolavito.com/uploads/3/7/5/9/3759274/colavito_-_ancient_atom_bombs.pdf

2. *Archaeology of Bet Dwarka Island*; A. S. Gaur Sundaresh & K. H. Vora; Aryan Books International, 2005

3. *Arise Arjuna: Hinduism and the Modern World*; David Frawley; Voice of India Publishing, 2010

4. *Arms and Armour: Traditional Weapons of India*; E. Jaiwant Paul; Roli Books, 2005

5. *Autobiography of a Yogi*; Paramahansa Yogananda; Yogoda Satsang Society of India, 2010

6. *Bhagvad-Gita, As It Is* (Second Edition); A.C. Bhaktivedanta Swami Prabhupada; Bhaktivedanta Book Trust, 1986

7. *Dawn & Devolution of the Indus Civilization*; R. Rao; Aditya Prakashan, 1991

8. *Dwarka—Krishna's Dhaam by the Sea*; Subhadra Sen Gupta; Rupa & Co, 2002

9. *Encyclopaedia of Vedic Mathematics*; Shukla; Cyber Tech Publications, 2011

10. *Ethnography of Ancient India*; Robert Shafkr; Otto Harris Sowitz, 1954

11. *From the River of Heaven: Vedic Knowledge for the Modern Age*; David Frawley; Motilal Bansarsidas, 2002.

12. *Hand Book on Rajputs*; A. H. Bingley; Asian Educational Services, 2006

13. *Hindu Manners, Customs and Ceremonies*; Chitralekha Singh & Prem Nath; Crest Publishing House, 2002

14. *Hinduism: The Eternal Tradition (Sanatana Dharma), 2nd revised edition*; Voice of India Publishing, 2008

15. *How I Became a Hindu: My Discovery of Vedic Dharma*; David Frawley; Voice of India Publishing, 2000

16. *Indian Theism from the Vedic to the Muhammadan Period*; Nicol Macnicol; Hardpress Publishing, 2012

17. *Indus Script Cipher: Hieroglyphs of Indian Linguistic Area*; S. Kalyanaraman; Sarasvati Research Center, 2010

18. *Jaya—An Illustrated Retelling of the Mahabharata*; Devdutt Pattanaik; Penguin Books, 2010

19. *Kalki Purana*; B. K. Chaturvedi; Diamond Pocket Books, 2010

20. *Krishna—A Joyous Celebration of the Divine*; Chandrika; Vakils, Feffer & Simons, 2011

21. *Krishna—A Sourcebook*; Edwin F. Bryant; Oxford University Press, 2007

22. *Krishna—The God who Lived as Man*; Bhawana Somaaya; Pustak Mahal, 2009

23. *Krishna—The Man & His Philosophy*; Osho; Jaico Publishing House, 1991

24. *Krishna: A Journey Through The Lands & Legends of Krishna*; Dev Prasad; Jaico Books, 2010

25. *Krsna Dvaipayana Vyasadeva—Srimad Bhagavatam (Bhagavata Purana)*; translated by Anand Aadhar; Third Revised Edition, 2010

26. *Lord Krishna—His Lilas & Teachings*; Sri Swami Sivananda; Divine Life Society Publications, 1996

27. *Myth of the Aryan Invasion of India (Third Edition)*; David Frawley; Voice of India Publishing, 2002

28. *Myth=Mithya: A Handbook of Hindu Mythology*; Dr Devduttt Pattanaik; Penguin Books, 2006

29. *On the Shri Jantra & Khat Kon Chakra (Six-Angled Wheel) or Double Equilateral Triangle*; E.C. Ravenshaw; The Journal of the Royal Asiatic Society of Great Britain & Ireland, Volume XIII, 1849

30. *Sacred Sacrifice: Ritual Paradigms in Vedic Religion and Early Christianity*; Rick Franklin; WIPF, 2005

31. *Science and Spirituality from a Hindu Perspective*; V. V. Raman; Zygon, March 2002.

32. *Science of the Sacred: Ancient Perspectives for Modern Science*; Compiled by David Osborn; Lulu Press, 2009

33. *Search for the Historical Krishna*; Rajaram N S; Prism Publications, 2006

34. *Sri Krishna—The Darling of Humanity*; A.S.P. Ayyar; Bharatiya Vidya Bhavan, 2001

35. *Taj Mahal, The True Story*; P. N. Oak; A. Ghosh, 1989

36. *Taj Mahal: Analysis of a Great Deception;* Dr V. S. Godbole; Itihas Patrika Prakashan, 2007

37. *The Atlantis Dialogue: Plato's Original Story of the Lost City and Continent by Plato*; edited by Aaron Shepard, translated by B. Jowett; Shepard Publications, 2001

38. *The Cycle of Time*; Simone Boger; eBook. Download link: http://www.cycleoftime.com/thebook.php

39. *The Gates of Somnat Temple;* The Asiatic Journal & Monthly Miscellany, Vol I, Third Series, May-Oct, 1843

40. *The Indus Valley Civilization—A Contemporary Perspective*; Gregory L. Possehl; Vistaar Publications, 2009

41. *The Lost City of Dvarka*; S R Rao; Aditya Prakashan, 1999

42. *The Lost River: On The Trail of the Sarasvati*; Michel Danino; Penguin Books, 2010

43. *The Mahabharata Retold*; C. Rajagopalachari; Bharatiya Vidya Bhavan, 2005

44. *The Quest for the Origins of Vedic Culture: The Indo-Aryan Migration Debate;* Edwin Bryant; Oxford University Press, 2004

45. *The Wonder that was India*; Thomas R. Trautmann; Picador, 2004

46. *Underwater Archaeology of Dwarka and Somnath*; A. S. Gaur Sundaresh & K. H. Vora; Aryan Books International, 2008

47. *Unsealing the Indus Script—Anatomy of its Decipherment*; Malati j. Shendge; Atlantic Publishers, 2010

48. *Vedic Civilization*; R. K. Pruthi; Discovery Publishing House, 2004

49. *Vedic River Saraswati & Hindu Civilization*; S. Kalyanaraman, Aryan Books International, 2008

50. *Vishnu—An Introduction*; Devdutt Pattanaik; Vakils, Feffer & Simons, 2007

Papers & Articles

1. *108: Significance of the Number;* Stephen Knapp; Download link: http://www.stephen-knapp.com/articles_to_read.htm

2. *A Search for the Historical Krishna*; N. S. Rajaram. Download link: http://www.mirroroftomorrow.org/blog/_archives/2009/4/1/4139571. html

3. *An Ecological View of Ancient India*; David Frawley. Download link: http://www.vedanet.com/our-online-articles-topmenu-2/20-ancient-india-and-historical-issues/44-an-ecological-view-of-ancient-india

4. *Aryan Invasion—History or Politics*; N. S. Rajaram; November 2006. Download link: http://www.archaeologyonline.net/artifacts/aryan-invasion-history. html

5. *Asaru-l Bilad of Zakari'ya Al Kazwini in the History of India as Told by its Own Historians*; The Posthumous Papers of the Late Sir H. M. Elliot; John Dowson, Calcutta: Susil Gupta, 1956, vol. 10. Download link: http://www.infinityfoundation.com/mandala/h_es/h_es_asaru_ frameset.htm

6. *Axis Mundi: Questions, Enigma, Mysteries*; Evelina Rioukina, UNECE. Download link: http://www.unspecial.org/UNS640/t47.html

7. *Closing the Chapter on the Aryan Problem*; Navaratna Rajaram. Download link: http://www.archaeologyonline.net/artifacts/decline-of-ai.html

8. *Discoloration of Marble during Laser Cleaning by Nd:YAG Laser Wavelengths*; S. Kleina, F. Fekrsanatia, J. Hildenhagena, K. Dickmanna, H. Uphoffb, Y. Marakisc, V. Zafiropulos. Download link: http://144.206.159.178/ft/68/31995/556305.pdf

9. *Evaluation of the Radioprotective Effect of Aegle Marmelos*; Ganesh Chandra Jagetia, Ponemone Venkatesh and Manjeshwar Shrinath Baliga. Download link: http://mutage.oxfordjournals.org/ content/18/4/387.short

10. *Hidden Horizons: Unearthing 10,000 Years of Indian Culture*; David Frawley and N.S. Rajaram. Download link: http://www.vedanet. com/our-online-articles-topmenu-2/20-ancient-india-and-historical-issues/131-hidden-horizons-unearthing-10000-years-of-indian-culture-preface

11. *Hinduism Predates Christianity*; Stephen Knapp; Download link: http://www.stephen-knapp.com/articles_to_read.htm

12. *History of Indian Science*; Subhash Kak; July 2002. Download link: http://www.ece.lsu.edu/kak/grolier.pdf

13. *Indic Language Families and Indo-European;* Subhash Kak. Download link: http://www.archaeologyonline.net/artifacts/Indic%20 Language%20families.pdf

14. *Kalki—The Next Avatar of God & the End of Kaliyuga;* Stephen Knapp; Download link: http://www.stephen-knapp.com/articles_to_read. htm

15. *Knowledge of Planets in the Third Millenium BC;* Subhash Kak; January 1996. Download link: http://www.cs.okstate.edu/~subhashk/ QJRAS96.pdf

16. *Krishna and the Unicorn of the Indus Seals;* Dr David Frawley. Download link: http://jayasreesaranathan.blogspot.in/2008/12/ unicorn-of-indus-seals.html

17. *Legend of Dwaraka;* T. R. Gopaalakrushnan. Download link: http:// www.mahabharataonline.com/articles/mahabharata_article. php?id=32

18. *Linguistics and Civilization;* David Frawley. Download link: http:// www.vedanet.com/our-online-articles-topmenu-2/20-ancient-india-and-historical-issues/110-linguistics-and-civilization

19. *Mathematics of the Swastika Curve;* Wolfram Mathworld; Download link: http://mathworld.wolfram.com/SwastikaCurve.html

20. *Measurement of Radioactivity and Radon Exhalation Rate in Different Kinds of Marbles and Granites;* N. Walley El-Dinea, A. El-Shershabya, F. Ahmedb, A.S. Abdel-Haleemc. Download link: http://www. sciencedirect.com/science/article/pii/S0969804301001075

21. *On the Chronological Framework for Indian Culture;* Subhash Kak. Download link: http://www.ece.lsu.edu/kak/chro.pdf

22. *Reclaiming the Chronology of Bharatam;* Narahari Achar; July 2006. Download link: http://sites.google.com/site/sarasvati96/ reclaimingthechronologyofbharatam: narahariachar%28july2006%29

23. *Sanskritization: A New Model of Language Development;* David Frawley. Download link: http://www.vedanet.com/our-online-articles-topmenu-2/20-ancient-india-and-historical-issues/161-sanskritization-a-new-model-of-language-development

24. *Science in Ancient India;* Subhash C. Kak. Download link: http:// www.ece.lsu.edu/kak/a3.pdf

25. *Scientific Verification of Vedic Knowledge;* Swami Visnu. Download link: http://www.archaeologyonline.net/artifacts/scientific-verif-vedas.html

26. *Sea Level Rise and Inundation of Coastal India;* Dr Nachiketa Das; November 2008. Download link: http://blogs. ivarta.com/Global-warming-Sea-level-rise-inundation-coastal-India/ blog-206.htm

27. *Six Destructions of Somnath by Islam;* Voice of India Features; Download link: http://voi.org/index2.php?option=com_content&do_ pdf=1&id=547

28. *Swastika: Its Real Meaning;* Stephen Knapp; Download link: http:// www.stephen-knapp.com/articles_to_read.htm

29. *The Astronomy of the Age of Geometric Altars;* Subhash Kak; May 1995. Download link: http://www.cs.okstate.edu/~subhashk/QJRAS95.pdf

30. *The Europeanization of the Vedas and its Distortions;* David Frawley. Download link: http://www.vedanet.com/our-online-articles-topmenu-2/20-ancient-india-and-historical-issues/53-the-europeanization-of-the-vedas-and-its-distortions

31. *The Incurable Hindu Fondness for P.N. Oak;* Koenraad Elst. Download link: http://koenraadelst.blogspot.in/2010/06/incurable-hindu-fondness-for-pn-oak.html

32. *The Mahabharata and the Sindhu-Sarasvati Tradition;* Subhash Kak; Download link: http://www.ece.lsu.edu/kak/MahabharataII.pdf

33. *The Questionable Historicity of the Mahabharata;* SSN Murthy; JNU. Download link: http://www.ejvs. laurasianacademy.com/ejvs1005/ejvs1005article.pdf

34. *The Sign for Zero;* Subhash C. Kak; Download link: http://www.ece. lsu.edu/kak/SignZero.pdf

35. *The Trouble with the Trapezium;* N. Raghuraman. Download link: http://dev.tehelka.com/content/trouble-trapezmium

36. *The Vedic Literature of Ancient India and its Many Secrets;* David Frawley. Download link: http://www.grahamhancock.com/forum/ FrawleyD1.php

37. *The Vedic Religion in Ancient Iran and Zarathushtra;* Subhash Kak; 2003. Download link: http://www.archaeologyonline.net/artifacts/ Vedic%20Religion%20in%20Ancient%20Iran.pdf

38. *Unravelling Dholavira's Geometry;* Michel Danino. Download link: http://www.iisc.ernet.in/prasthu/pages/PP_data/paper1.pdf

39. *Vedic Archaeology;* Swami B.G. Narasingha. Download link: http:// gosai.com/writings/vedic-archeology

40. *Vedic Origins of the Europeans: the Children of Danu;* David Frawley. Download link: http://www.vedanet.com/our-online-articles-

topmenu-2/20-ancient-india-and-historical-issues/162-vedic-origins-of-the-europeans-the-children-of-danu

41. *Was Allah the Moon God of Ancient Arab Pagans?* Syed Kamran Mirza; Download link: http://www.faithfreedom.org/Articles/skm30804.htm

42. *Was the Taj Mahal a Vedic Temple? The Photographic Evidence*; Stephen Knapp; Download link: http://www.stephen-knapp.com/articles_to_read.htm

43. *Why 108?*; Dr Koenraad ELST, Ph.D. Dowanload link: http://koenraadelst.bharatvani.org/articles/misc/why108.html

Blogs & Websites

1. *108 Names of Shri Kalki.* http://www.scribd.com/doc/34624127/108-Names-of-Shri-Kalki

2. *About the Lineage of the Yadavas.* http://en.wikipedia.org/wiki/Yadava

3. *Aggregation of Information on Dwarka and Mahabharata.* http://www.hinduwisdom.info/Dwaraka.htm

4. *Ancient Voice: Rig-Veda.* http://ancientvoice.wikidot.com/article:rig-veda#toc6

5. *Ancient Voice: The Vrishnis.* http://ancientvoice.wikidot.com/mbh:vrishnis

6. *Best Evidence for Ancient Nuclear War?* By Philip Coppens. http://www.philipcoppens.com/bestevidence.html

7. *Date of Rigveda—Controversies in History.* http://controversialhistory.blogspot.com/2008/01/date-of-rig-veda.html#.TshzLmDrar8

8. *Dvarka and the Tsunami* by Soumya Aravind Sitaraman. http://www.hindumoon.com/articlesdvaraka.html

9. *Dwarka and the Mahabharata* by Amlan Roychowdhury. http://ezinearticles.com/?Dwarka-And-The-Mahabharata&id=1768511

10. *Encyclopedia for Epics of India (on Krishna).* http://mythfolklore.net/india/encyclopedia/krishna.htm

11. *Human Genome Project Information: Cloning Fact Sheet.* http://www.ornl.gov/sci/techresources/Human_Genome/elsi/cloning.shtml

12. *Interview of Manish Pandit by Rediff in 2009 entitled "Krishna Existed. School Texts Are Wrong."* http://news.rediff.com/slide-show/2009/aug/29/slide-show-1-lord-krishna-existed.htm

13. *Kailash Mansarovar Yatra.* http://kailash.ramaswami.com/home

14. *Kailash Yatra with Kailai Bala.* http://kailaibala.blogspot.in/

15. *Kalki's Symbols, Hand Signs and Sword.* http://naziat.org/hand.htm

16. *Krishna's Seal for the City of Dwarka.* http://www.indoeurohome.com/Krishna-Vishnu.html

17. *Mausala Parva, English Translation Online.* http://www.philosophy.ru/library/asiatica/indica/itihasa/mahabharata/eng/gbmb16xt.html

18. *National Institute of Oceanography: Dwarka Project.* http://www.niobioinformatics.in/otherProject2_gujarat.php

19. *Nuclear Transmutation.* http://cn.wikipedia.org/wiki/Nuclear_transmutation

20. *Omkar, Swastika, the Saffron Colour and Purna-kumbha by Sudheer Birodkar.* http://www.hindubooks.org/sudheer_birodkar/hindu_history/omkar.html

21. *Online Sanskrit & English Translation of Harivamsa.* http://mahabharata-resources.org/harivamsa/vishnuparva/hv_2_058.html

22. *Out of Africa or Out of Eden: Does Science Contradict the Bible? Rich Deem.* http://www.godandscience.org/apologetics/humans_out_of_africa.html

23. *Physicists Have 'Solved' Mystery of Levitation (Telegraph).* http://www.telegraph.co.uk/news/1559579/Physicists-have-solved-mystery-of-levitation.html

24. *Ritualistic Animal Sacrifice in Ancient India.* http://arachnid.wordpress.com/2009/07/31/ritualistic-animal-sacrifice-in-ancient-india/

25. *Saroj Bala's blog about Ancient India: online resource for the drying up of the Sarasvati.* http://sarojbala.blogspot.in/p/mystery-of-sarasvati-river.html

26. *Science & Technology in Ancient India (Ancient Symbolism and Hidden meaning of Shiv-Ling)* by Kanchan Raste, May 2011. http://www.theinduslink.com/3364/science-and-technology-in-ancient-india

27. *The Last Days of Dwarka (from the Scriptures).* http://www.philosophy.ru/library/asiatica/indica/itihasa/mahabharata/eng/gbmb16xt.html

28. *The Meaning of Shiv Ling.* http://www.visionabove.com/spirituality/the-meaning-of-shiv-ling/

29. *Umbilical Cord in Hinduism* by Dr Peyyeti Murali Mohana Rao. http://ramrali19.blog.co.uk/2009/04/03/hinduism-5881584/

30. *Vedic Knowledge Online: Dwaraka.* http://veda.wikidot.com/dwaraka

31. *Year of Mahabharata—Full Article Text.* http://www.salagram.net/mahabharata-year.html

32. *Yoga at the Speed of Light and the Meaning of 108* by Linda Johnsen. http://www.lovearth.net/108.htm

Video & Audio

1. *Aliens in the ancient city of Dwarka? History Channel 7.5 min. documentary.* http://www.youtube.com/watch?v=JIN-qiXgTzg

2. *Dwaraka Giant Underwater City found in India.* http://www.youtube.com/watch?v=GM4h887ilY8

3. *How the melting of the ice age would have submerged Dwarka. 40 minute documentary.* http://www.youtube.com/watch?v=tPiQrkkIKMk

4. *Islamic rituals with Hindu or Pagan connections.* http://www.youtube.com/watch?v=GRx3Fe3wzyY&feature=player_embedded#

5. *Krishna: History or Myth? Brilliant astronomical dating of Mahabharata.* http://www.youtube.com/watch?v=NmXHQzAtP4w and http://www.youtube.com/watch?v=Pb9kU4z-1A8&feature=related and http://www.youtube.com/watch?v=-2_DuCpE808&feature=related

6. *Scientific Verification of Vedic Knowledge by Stephen Knapp (30 minutes)* http://www.youtube.com/watch?v=Ud1oEFfOrbQ

7. *Speech of SR Rao in Gujarat.* http://deshgujarat.com/2007/02/21/dwarka-of-krishnaarcheologist-sr-raos-speech-english-mp3/

8. *The legendary city of Dwarka. 8.5 mins. video.* http://www.youtube.com/watch?v=2CbTyxy1MWo

9. *Underwater pictures of submerged city of Dwarka along with relevant quotes from Mahabharata and Puranas.* http://www.youtube.com/watch?v=P51hvsruKjY&feature=related

10. *Vedic Science: The Big Bang and the Theory of Relativity From the Ancient World* http://www.youtube.com/watch?v=oOJG9rNIcdI